I0639355

My Sweet

Alyssa

Book 1 From the Brothers In All Series

By

Gina Rose

Editors: Sybrina Durant and Brian Cross

Copyrighted 2014

Paperback
ISBN-13: 978-0-9960940-6-1, ISBN-10: 099609406
Ebook ISBN-13: 978-0-9960940-7-8,
ISBN-10: 0996094075
Paperback ISBN-13: 978-1500350864,
ISBN-10: 1500350869

BISAC Codes:

FIC027000   FICTION / Romance / General

FIC027070   FICTION / Romance / Historical / Regency

Contact Sybrina@sybrina.com.

Prologue

1806
Northumberland, England

"Alyssa, you have visitors awaiting you in the drawing room," Mrs. Hopkins, her governess said as she entered the room.

She looked up in surprise. "Who would be visiting me?"

She was a bit annoyed that her free time had been interrupted. She was reading her new Gothic horror novel and had just reached a very scary part.

"Your Uncle Morley and his daughter Diana have come to call, all the way from London. They said it was a matter of utmost importance. They ask that you attend them right away as they are pressed for time," she told her rather sternly.

Alyssa didn't like the sound of that. She hadn't seen her uncle in eight years since she was five years old. What could he want with her? She simply couldn't imagine what he would have to discuss with her, important or otherwise.

"I shall see them right now, Mrs. Hopkins. Thank you," she said, putting aside her novel.

She hurried downstairs to the drawing room. Upon entry she saw her uncle, along with her cousin, sitting impatiently on the sofa. She couldn't help but observe her cousin must be nearing marriageable age. That was somewhat surprising. She expected the young girl from her memory. Her uncle still looked like the same grumpy person he always was. He scowled at the door while awaiting her.

"Hello, Uncle Morley, Diana. It's so good to see you both," she greeted them, sweeping into the room.

"Sit down child. We have much to discuss," her uncle said, ignoring her greeting and sparing none for her in return.

She did as she was instructed, quickly sitting on the sofa opposite them. She folded her hands in her lap and sat primly as she had been taught to do by Mrs. Hopkins, then nodded for him to begin.

She noticed that her Uncle Morley Habersham, Earl of Glenmont, looked particularly sour this day. This caused a real sense of foreboding to rest in her belly. She stiffened her spine in an attempt to control the shivers and waited for him to commence.

"I'm afraid we are not here for a social visit, child. We have come to collect you to bring you back to London. It was your father's will that you should be entrusted into my keeping upon his death. His ship was lost at sea during a violent gale, you see. There were no survivors. Therefore, I am now your legal guardian until you reach the age of five and twenty," he said, without even a hint of sympathy.

She sat in stunned silence, trying to absorb his unbelievable words. She couldn't make them mesh with the scene in front of her. She looked upon the faces of her relatives, noting her uncle appeared to be irritated … as if he were being put upon. Her cousin appeared to be rather smug, as if she were privately laughing about some joke that only she were privy to.

She blinked her eyes and shook her head, trying to make sense of what she was seeing and hearing. How could they be sitting here in front of her, acting as though it were an everyday occurrence to deliver such horrific news without so much as a hint of remorse? Father dead? What was this madness? She sat disbelieving, continuing to note the absurdity of their demeanor. Truly alarmed now, her throat began to constrict as her pulse thundered through her head making her feel dizzy, as though she would swoon.

"This simply can't be true," she croaked out, as the room started to spin. She tried to stand to escape their presence but when she did, she toppled over, falling into the void of darkness.

"Look Papa. The silly chit fainted," Diana pealed as she gawked at her cousin, who lay heaped on the floor.

"Go tell the butler to have her things packed and ready within the hour," the earl instructed, with annoyance at his daughter's calloused comment.

Chapter One

1811
Mayfair, London

Alyssa turned eight and ten today. Though you would never know it, as nary a word was mentioned by anyone. As usual, there were no celebrations or gifts in observance of the day. It was just a day like any other, except she was no longer seven and ten. She had been instructed to prepare a room for the arrival of Alistair Sinclair, the Earl of Keith, who was the stepson of her Uncle Morley.

It was made known to her that Alistair was returning from Jamaica, where he made his fortune from a tea plantation that he had purchased six years before. His fortune secure, he had decided he should take a wife. This decision brought him to London for the season to look over this year's crop of debutantes. She didn't care why he was coming, only that he would be one more responsibility for her to oversee. His lordship would only add work to her constantly growing list of daily chores. She was already worked near exhaustion as it was.

Today put her one small step closer to the age when she could escape this life of drudgery she had come to know in the so-called care of her uncle. In his care, she was reduced to a servant in the household, treated quite cruelly by her relatives.

Her uncle and his wife Esmeralda, along with her cousin Diana, took pains to remind her daily of the imposition they had been made to suffer by providing her with their so-called protection. She scoffed at the notion. She wasn't sure what they meant by imposition, considering that they gained a free servant in the bargain.

She wasn't allowed to mix with the family or attend any parties or social functions that they so often engaged in. She suspected her guardians didn't want it known to the local bachelor population that she was a potential bride with a very sizeable fortune. That would be too much competition for her cousin, Diana. Esmeralda simply couldn't allow that. No, instead she was housed in the servant's quarters, a small room in the attic with only a cot, a small table and stool for her comfort.

It was a sad plight for an heiress of some considerable fortune to have to endure. Sadly, she was still three years away from being able to receive a monthly pension from her fortune. She hoped that when she did, she could leave this cursed place, though she didn't think her uncle would allow it. He would still be her guardian for another four years beyond that. Of course, she wouldn't be able to obtain her entire fortune before the age of five and twenty unless she married, which would give her husband control of her money … if she found a husband …

Even that was an unlikely possibility for her, with her uncle refusing to allow her to have a season where she could meet potential candidates. She suspected he rather enjoyed controlling her fortune and that he wanted to keep her from marrying until the last possible moment before being forced, by law to relinquish his custodial rights to her inheritance. She also suspected that by the designated age, she wouldn't have much left. Since her arrival, the family had been living in highly improved circumstances, all with the exception of her, of course. Alyssa didn't dare dream too often about escaping her reality. It was better just to quietly cooperate, making as little trouble as possible to get through it as best she could. Aunt Esmeralda was always quick to squash any attempts she ever made to improve her situation. The punishments were always harsh.

A few months ago, Esmeralda caught her thumbing through a book in the library. The consequences were quite merciless. She had been forced to go without food for three days. If it hadn't been for Cookie, smuggling small meals to her every day, the suffering would surely have been unbearable. Had Cookie been discovered, there's no telling what Esmeralda would have done to her, so Alyssa decided that it would be better to live as a servant should until which time she was old enough to escape her situation legally.

Cookie was the only real ally she had in the household. She told Alyssa on more than one occasion that if she ever wanted to escape her plight, she could help her. But she had to be truly desperate. The price for doing so would be costly. Alyssa told her she didn't have access to her money and couldn't pay any price, but Cookie assured her money wouldn't be a problem. That was confusing to Alyssa so she didn't dwell on the puzzling statement much. It would be better to tough it out here where she could keep an eye on her relatives as they spent her fortune. One day though, she would make them pay for what they had done to her. One day … she sighed deeply and finished putting the bed together. There was simply no sense in dreaming when she had so much work to do.

Alyssa continued preparing the room not realizing she was being observed. She was in the water closet now, down on her hands and knees scrubbing the inside of the copper tub when she heard a soft whistle behind her. She jerked her head up, instantly making eye contact with a very handsome man standing in the doorway admiring the view of her backside. Flustered from being taken unawares, she quickly stood up, faced the man, and blushed with embarrassment at being caught in such an unladylike position. Her curly auburn hair had fallen away from its bun in her struggles with the tub, causing her lace cap to become askew, leaving strands of her unruly hair hanging about her face, covering her eyes. She tried to blow at the offending strands only to have them fall right back into her eyes. She went to move them with her gloved hands but only managed to smear her face with suds, furthering her overall embarrassment. Alyssa was sure she must have made quite a comical sight.

"Don't let me interrupt you lass, please continue," the handsome man armed with a devilish grin said in a mild, Scottish brogue.

The tall, broad shouldered man was adorned with black hair cut in the popular Brutus fashion, which served to accentuate his intense black eyes. He had a strong jawline adorned with heavy side-burns, and a dimple in his chin that drew the eye to his wide-set mouth. The man's skin was bronzed, obviously from prolonged exposure to the sun, giving him a virile look. Alyssa calculated he must be close to thirty years old as his eyes were starting to show signs of age, with squint lines in the corners.

He stood there in his relaxed pose, leaning against the doorframe. He continued to look her over from head to toe, with an arched eyebrow and that same wicked smile. He was ruggedly handsome, in his state of half-dress, wearing only a white lawn shirt with the sleeves rolled up and his black breeches tucked in his Hessian boots. Alyssa was reminded of the pirates she had read about in her youth. He was the most handsome man she had ever seen, she decided. True, she hadn't seen many men outside of the household, but this one standing before her now had to be an exceptional representation of his gender.

It finally occurred to Alyssa that this must be Alistair. She quickly recovered her wits, "Forgive me my lord, I was just preparing your room and should only be another moment or two," she said, turning back to her task.

She became aware of movement behind her and was startled when he placed a hand on her shoulder to stop her from bending back down.

"What is your name, my lovely?" he asked in a husky voice.

Alyssa felt a warm sensation seep into her back, making her shiver in response. She swallowed hard, turning to face him.

"My name is Alyssa, my lord," was her timid

reply.

"Alyssa, ah … a lovely name for a beautiful maid," he said as his eyes devoured her.

His penetrating eyes bore into hers, causing her to become quite unsettled. She cast her eyes down, turned to go back to her chore, hoping he would leave so she could finish in peace. He was just too handsome that his being so near in such a small space was unnerving. She bent back over the tub, scrubbing again, but every fiber of her being was aware he remained behind her.

After a moment, she heard him turn to leave the water closet, allowing her to breathe a sigh of relief. When she was through with her task, she hurried to the mirror to tidy up her hair and return it to the confines of her cap. Once she had herself set back to rights, she picked up her cleaning supplies, taking leave of the water closet. Thinking she would be able to avoid the man, she quickly came to a halt when she spotted him standing with his back leaning against the closed bedroom door. Like a trapped animal, she stood frozen while he stared at her for what seemed like an eternity. She felt quite helpless to move. Finally, Alistair pushed himself away from the door. Slowly, ever so seductively advanced toward her. When he was standing directly in front of her, he raised his hand to her head. With a gleam in his eyes, he gently removed her cap as though he were unwrapping a gift. She tried to step back, but her attempt was feeble, allowing him to close the gap between them.

"Don't be frightened lass, I only want to see how beautiful you are with your hair down," he said as his eyes held hers captive.

Alyssa was afraid to move, so she just stood there while he removed the pins from her hair, causing the unruly mass to fall on her shoulders and down her back. Alistair gasped his appreciation and stepped back to admire his handiwork.

"A woman such as you should not be scrubbing bathtubs," was his conclusion.

Alyssa didn't respond to that. Instead, she cast her eyes down to the floor hoping he would quit toying with her so she could make her escape. It was embarrassing to have him gazing at her as if she were a prized cow. He startled her when he boldly took her by the chin to lift her face so he could look into her eyes. His captivating black eyes held her as he slowly leaned in to place a gentle kiss on her lips. Stunned by his audacity, she froze in place, afraid to make a move. She had never been in this situation before. It was daunting to say the least. She knew that he shouldn't be doing this, but more importantly, she knew she shouldn't allow it. Her mind reeled at all the trouble she could get in if she were to be caught, yet she was afraid that if she were to make an issue of it, things would go badly for her with Esmeralda, his mother, so she remained quiet.

"You taste like fresh honey," he said, ending the kiss.

Alyssa was slightly trembling now, but she remained quietly in place. He continued with his perusal of her person for another moment or two before she worked up the courage to ask, "May I be excused now, my lord?"

"I could take you away from here and give you everything your heart desires," was his response.

Alyssa didn't know what to make of this. What was he suggesting? She quickly got her answer when he took her silence as some kind of acquiesce, then took her in his arms causing her to drop her supplies. He dove forward, taking her lips in a searing kiss that quite stunned her. She felt his tongue probing between her lips, gasping in surprise at the intimacy allowing him to thrust it in slowly to mingle with her own. It was a strange sensation, though not entirely unpleasant. This man who dared to take such liberties with her smelled of brandy, bay rum soap mixed with sweat, causing his essence to overwhelm her as he continued with his domination of her mouth. Finally, she realized the precariousness of her situation and shoved away from him. breaking the kiss.

"My lord please, may I be excused," she said trembling.

When he said nothing, she grabbed up her supplies and quickly made for the door. Just as she opened it, she heard him say, "I will have you, lass."

She did not respond but rushed through the door and down the hall in escape.

*****

Alistair was in love. There was simply no other way to look at it, but that he was entirely besotted with the maid. He laughed at himself while watching her scurry out of the room like a frightened little rabbit.

Could you have botched that up any worse old boy? Yes, he had botched it up; he frightened the poor lass half out of her wits. He sighed deeply while running his hand through his hair, shaking his head in recrimination for his own behavior, but truly he had never seen a lass as beautiful as she in all his life.

Her eyes were the color of the sea, beautiful blue-green that went on forever in their depths; a man could drown when gazing upon them. She was enchanting with her mane of rich auburn curls with streaks of fire that perfectly framed her delicate oval face, which was accented with a light dusting of freckles across her perky little nose. She was petite in stature but shapely in all the right places, with full breasts and perfectly rounded bottom. She was so small that he had felt like a giant next to her as the top of her head barely reached his shoulder.

Disappointment settled in as the realization struck him that the minx was a distraction he really didn't need right now. He was here for the purpose of finding a wife. He couldn't take on a mistress in the midst of that, lest he be a considered a scoundrel. Oh, but she was so beautiful, he silently lamented. When she was bent over the tub, it was all he could do to ignore the invitation that her shapely bottom had offered as it wiggled back and forth as she struggled with her labor. His hands had ached to reach out to possess her then and there. It had been too long since he had lain with a woman, he decided, many weeks, in fact. That's all it was, surely. She was a tempting morsel that no man could ignore much less one who had been traveling in a state of celibacy for weeks.

Perhaps there would be no real harm in partaking of her before he actively started his search for a wife. She was just a maid after all; it wasn't like he would set her up as he would a real mistress. He smiled as the notion began to take hold in his mind. He would get her out of his system with a few good romps then he could start his search with a fresh unpolluted view of the field. It wouldn't do to go out in search of a wife all wound up in sexual frustration ending up with a toad because he wasn't thinking clearly. She would be therapeutic, now that he thought on it.

Too bad, he wouldn't see anything to equal her among the debutantes of the ton. What a man wouldn't do to have a wife like that. Sadly, he could never offer a servant such as her, his proposal. His peers would ridicule him if he were to marry such a woman. But then again, he would be going back to Jamaica. No one would have to know … he shook his head. Who was he kidding? The news would arrive there before he did. No, the best he could do was to have an affair with her for a week or two then be done with her. With that decided, he undressed and went to the water closet to prepare a bath. He would have her … if only for a week or two.

*****

Alistair sat at the dining table brooding about Alyssa. He hadn't seen her again since this morning upon his arrival. He was aching to get his hands on her. His mother was chattering away like a magpie. His stepfather was grunting his responses while consuming his meal. His half-sister, Diana was humoring her mother with nods and smiles as she regaled them all with all the latest gossip of the ton.

A thought occurred to him as he sat there thinking about Alyssa. He could ask Diana to make arrangements to send the lass to him tonight. He could contrive a complaint about something lacking with the readiness of his sleeping quarters. Yes, that would work, he reasoned.

He straightened up in his chair trying to look lively as he finished his meal. He wanted to bring a quick end to it so he could speak with his sister in private. A quarter of an hour later, he was put out of his misery when everyone finished their meal, moving to the drawing room. Just before entering, he pulled Diana to the side.

"I need a favor, dear sister," he said quietly.

Diana beamed at him, leaning in so she could hear his request. She was a very tall though somewhat slim, pretty young woman at the age of two and twenty, with black hair as a backdrop for her hazel eyes, which she had received from her mother. She had always adored her brother and would do anything for him, so she was eager to hear what he had to ask of her.

"Yes, Ali?" she encouraged.

"There is a maid here by the name of Alyssa. I want you to make arrangements to send her to my room tonight, I have need of her services before I retire," he explained.

Diana's reaction wasn't what he would have

expected. She burst into laughter. "Oh dear brother, what on earth could you possibly want with her?" she asked incredulously.

"That is not your concern, Diana," he said somewhat indignant. A gentleman didn't discuss such things with his sister, after all.

"I'm afraid you will have to find another maid. She is off limits," she told him.

"Off limits?" he asked.

"Yes, she is my cousin, you see, Papa's ward."

"You had better explain yourself," he demanded.

"She is Uncle Hugh's orphaned daughter, so of course Papa has taken charge of her until she reaches the age of five and twenty. She has been with us for the last five years since she was three and ten. She is an heiress you know, a vast fortune worth millions," she told him with a hint of jealousy in her tone.

Alistair was speechless. He stood there gaping at his sister as if she were speaking a foreign language. Finally, he found his voice, "What in the name of all that is holy is she doing scrubbing bathtubs if she is an heiress and family, no less?"

"Don't huff and puff at me brother, it's none of my doing. Papa says she has to pay for the privilege of our protection. Papa says she needs discipline, that she is strong-willed and would never make a good wife with her disposition. He says she needs to be brought to heel. That can only be accomplished through hard work and strict discipline," she explained with an air of utter disdain for her cousin.

Alistair couldn't believe what he was hearing.

He continued to stare at his sister in utter disbelief before saying, "Are you pulling my tail?"

"No, I am not pulling your tail, I am quite serious. It's true, all of it," she said, offended by his accusation.

Alistair looked over at his stepfather, whom he now completely loathed. He was shocked he could treat the poor lass in such a barbaric manner. He suspected that there was more to this than met the eye, and he intended to get to the bottom of it. He walked away from his sister, entering the drawing room. The wheels in his mind were spinning. He felt somewhat uplifted, knowing that Alyssa was now within his reach. If what his sister said was true, he could offer marriage to her and become a very rich man in the offing. Not a bad prospect at all.

*****

"Cookie?" she asked, "What do you know about the Earl of Keith?"

Alyssa had stayed hidden from view as best she could the rest of the day after her encounter with Alistair, but she couldn't quite put him out of her mind. That kiss had been so shocking to her senses that it had ruled her thoughts constantly since it occurred. She went down to the kitchen as she always did at this time in the evening to partake of her meal with Cookie and the butler Mr. Humphrey. She thought to take the opportunity to do a little probing about the man who had taken such liberties with her this morning.

"You must mean her ladyship's son. Well, I don't rightly know much but that he's been away for many years making his fortune in Jamaica on a plantation or some such; not sure exactly what kind. I know he was born in Scotland; seems a nice enough young man, though he must be close to thirty, if not already, I'd wager," she explained.

Cookie was a rather nice looking middle-aged woman with brown hair dusted with gray and soulful brown eyes. She was fairly educated for one of her class as her father had been a scholar and had taught her to read and write. How she ended up as a cook was a complete mystery to everyone. She had never divulged that information. She was known to have traveled to France where she learned the culinary arts. She was so good at her profession she could work for the king if she were so inclined. Indeed, she was a bit of a mystery. She adored Alyssa and always looked after her as best she could. Cookie was the only real friend she had.

"Why do you ask, love," she asked when Alyssa had remained quiet.

"Oh, no reason in particular," she responded with a blush that she felt all the way to her toes.

"Ah, what's this?" Cookie asked, taking in Alyssa's rosy complexion.

Alyssa ducked her head and squirmed on her stool. She did not want to discuss her condition with Mr. Humphrey sitting right there. Cookie seemed to realize the problem and said, "Henry, could you take your supper to your room, so I can speak to the child?"

Mr. Humphrey got up, doing as he was bid.

When he was out of earshot, Cookie pressed, "Tell me child. Did the earl do something he shouldn't have?"

Alyssa's blush deepened if such a thing were possible making it hard to look at Cookie, who was scowling at her now.

"H-He kissed me," she finally managed.

Cookie gasped. She reached out and took Alyssa's hands in hers. "You mustn't allow yourself to be alone with him again, do you hear me child?"

"He was very kind. He offered to take me away from here," Alyssa defended him.

"Aye," she said, "and to make you his mistress, no doubt," Cookie said, shaking her head in disgust. "Although, becoming his mistress could be the answer to your problems, my love. It wouldn't be so bad really. I'm sure he would treat you far better than you have been here," she added.

It was Alyssa's turn to gasp, "I could never allow such a thing. Why, I would never be able to marry if I did that, and I do plan to marry some day, you know," she admonished.

"Don't get yourself all riled up, dear. It was just a suggestion. Many a lady in your situation has done just that and worse to escape their plight," Cookie said, then quickly looked away. Alyssa saw she was blushing herself.

"Cookie, is that what you did?" Alyssa asked before she thought about her question with its implications.

Cookie was silent for a moment then turned back to Alyssa. She simply said, "Aye."

"I'm sorry, I didn't mean to pry."

"It's all right, love. My sister and I were forced to make tough decisions when our father died, leaving us in debt. Annabelle and I both found protectors, but when our beauty started to fade, we had to make another choice. Hers was to start a brothel. Mine was to become a chef, so here we are. I don't regret any of it," she explained.

Alyssa stared at her friend as if seeing her for the first time. She tried to imagine what she must have looked like as a young woman. She could clearly see she had been a beauty. It was a shame that fate dealt her the hand that it had. She could have gone on to find a husband and raise a family had her father not left her and her sister in debt. It was sad that women had so few choices in this world.

Alyssa took her friend's hands in her own this time, saying, "I love you, Cookie, and I thank you for sharing your story with me. I will take what you said into consideration with the care that it was given. It's true; he could probably offer me a better life than this, but oh, I would miss you so."

The two friends sat in teary-eyed silence for a few moments before Cookie gave a magnificent smile, saying, "How about one of my peach tarts and some creme?"

"That would be grand," Alyssa beamed at her in return.

*****

Alyssa was tired by the time she crawled into her cot that night. Her mind was reeling with the day's events, but try as she might she couldn't put Cookie's words out of her head. Her words mingled with Alistair's kiss until she was quite beside herself with indecision. Could she really swallow her pride and self-respect to become Alistair's mistress? She didn't know. Her situation was bad, but it wasn't as desperate as Cookie's had been. There were no creditors threatening to send her to prison, though she was in a prison of sorts, there was no real threat to her overall well-being. True, Alistair was a very handsome man and very wealthy, too. He could set her up quite nicely for the next few years until she started receiving her monthly allowance. Why, they might even fall in love and get married, she thought with a shiver.

Well, first things first. He has to ask me to become his mistress then I shall make my decision. No point in working myself up when the question hasn't even been put to me. He merely suggested he could provide a better life for me. Nothing has been set in stone.

Yes, she would wait to see what tomorrow would bring, she decided, making a vain attempt to fluff up her hopelessly flat pillow. Once settled, she closed her eyes and tried to sleep.

Chapter Two

"So tell me what this is all about Alistair," the earl said as the two men sat down in his library. His gray brows were furrowed, emphasizing his usual angry expression. He was a tall thick-set man in his sixties with an odd mix of gray and red curly hair. His appearance wasn't helped at all by his double chin and chipped front tooth.

"I would like for you to explain to me, why your niece Alyssa is living as a servant in your household," Alistair said, looking his stepfather square in the eyes. He was angry with him and his mother both for this atrocity. He meant to have an explanation.

The old earl glowered at Alistair for a moment, causing the tension in the room to become palpable. The earl didn't feel he had to explain himself to this young fop, but could tell by the look in his eye that he meant to have an explanation.

He drew in a breath of resignation saying, "The child is unruly if you must know, though I hardly see how it concerns you, but it is apparent she must be handled with the strictest of discipline. She has to be prepared for a husband, you see, for no man would take such a hellion as she. No, I do this as a favor to the girl as well as her future husband, whoever that poor unfortunate soul, may be," he repeated aloud, the lie he had told himself so many times before to justify his actions.

"I didn't get the impression she was an unruly child when I met her. Indeed, I found her to be quite obedient as well as respectful to me," Alistair shrewdly told him.

"There, you see, my methods are effective," the earl retorted with a gloating stare at his stepson.

"I have decided to take her as my wife. I need look no further. She will meet my needs quite admirably," Alistair told him bluntly.

The earl sputtered and coughed but quickly recovered himself. He glared at Alistair with his most formidable stare but realized that it was having little impact. Alistair glared right back, apparently he meant what he said. This was unacceptable to the earl of course.

"I refuse your offer. As her guardian that is my right," he stated bluntly.

"I don't see how you can refuse," Alistair countered. "She will be my wife. You will draw up the betrothal contract tonight. Once that is done, we will inform her of the decision, and you will start treating her accordingly henceforth,"

The earl was outraged by the unmitigated gall of his stepson. Of course, he would not cater to such a demand.

"I will do nothing of the kind, you overstep yourself, sir. The girl is my ward; it is I who control her future. I say who she will marry, and I say sir that it shall not be you," he stated with barely contained rage.

"Oh, you will consent to my demand dear father, and this is why. If you do not, I will go to The Times and tell them how you have embezzled the girl's inheritance while keeping her in near slave conditions for the last five years. When I am through with you, you will be cast out in shame.

None of your future works will make it through the House of Lords as your reputation will be complete and total rubbish. You will be ruined sir. Indeed, you will be vilified. Of course, as you say, it is your right as her guardian to refuse me. But deny me, and I will make you rue the day you were ever born." Alistair said, slamming his fist upon the earl's desk.

Alistair wanted to reach across the desk and choke the life out of his stepfather. He didn't have proof of embezzlement, but he felt reasonably confident in his assertions, noting all the improvements made in the house since he was last here. That he had spent lavishly on his mother and Diana was blatantly obvious as the two were dressed in queenly fashion. He could never have afforded it with his own meager resources, so he felt confident in his assertion.

The earl sat there in stony silence, considering the threat his stepson had issued. He believed Alistair would do just what he said he would. That would surely be the end of his career.

It was true he had dipped into the girl's fortune but only in the amount that was his due as her guardian to pay for her upkeep. One hundred thousand pounds compared to millions was hardly a crime. However, he had made the child a servant. He hadn't actually used any of the funds on her, so Alistair had him there. Once word got out, he would be ruined, indeed. Perhaps, he could make a deal with him in return for his acceptance. After all, he was entitled to a portion of her funds. His brother had only left him two hundred and fifty thousand pounds. He had used that to pay for improvements of his ancestral estate, nearly exhausting the funds. He couldn't afford to let go of her fortune outright, of course he should be compensated.

"I should be compensated," he said the thought aloud.

"Have you not already been compensated?" Alistair returned.

"I have not taken more than is my due. I should like a final settlement of say, two hundred thousand pounds for my consent of the marriage," the earl stated boldly.

Alistair considered the offer. Two hundred thousand pounds was a mere pittance in consideration to the millions she allegedly had, but he couldn't let him have the final say, so he countered, "One hundred fifty and we have a deal, payable on the day of the wedding, after the ceremony. Further, I would like to see her father's will as well as an accounting of that which you took," he told him.

The earl didn't like that part, but what could he do? He mulled it over for a moment, then went to his safe. He pulled out the will along with his ledger book, unceremoniously plopping them down on the desk in front of Alistair.

Alistair picked up the will and read it over. Immediately he was stunned. He couldn't quite believe what he was seeing. The lass was worth nine million pounds. She was the sole owner of Habersham Shipping. That paled in comparison to the six self-sufficient estates dispersed around the world. His future bride also held the controlling interest in a publishing company in New York, odd that. The publishing company was small and wasn't very profitable, making one wonder why her father would have bought into it.

Astounding! Alistair couldn't believe his good fortune. She was a veritable gold mine. He suspected that his stepfather had been well disciplined after all. With so much money to be had, that he only took a small portion, was truly amazing. Well, he could afford to be generous. He would allow him a settlement, he supposed. He would never be able to spend this much money even if he had ten lifetimes in which to do it.

Alistair looked through the ledger and was angered anew. The man hadn't spent so much as a farthing on his niece while his wife and daughter lived a life of luxury in high fashion. Unconscionable! That would change this very minute.

"I want her moved from the servant's quarters and installed in the room across from my own this very night. You will call in the very best modiste in London and have her outfitted properly as befitting her station, first thing on the morrow. You will provide her with a ladies' maid, as well, do I make myself clear?"

"As rainwater," the earl replied grudgingly.

*****

Alyssa was dreaming the sweetest dream she had ever had, when it was rudely interrupted by a familiar hateful voice, telling her to wake up. She didn't want to wake up. Morning came all too early for her, and she hadn't yet rested well enough. She opened her eyes to find herself looking into the face of Aunt Esmeralda, who was none too happy.

"Get up gel. You are to be moved this instant," she screeched. Esmeralda was a tall, attractive middle-aged woman with black hair with streaks of silver in the front. Her dramatically arched black brows accentuated her sharp hazel eyes, but her beautiful appearance was overshadowed by her ugly personality.

Alyssa sat up quickly, "Why am I to be moved?" she asked in bleary-eyed confusion.

"You are to be married to my son. He has commanded that you be moved to the room across the hall from his. I suppose you seduced or bewitched him somehow to get him to do your bidding," she huffed angrily.

"I did nothing of the kind. I have no idea what you are even talking about. What do you mean I am to marry him?" Alyssa asked defensively.

"I will take over from here, Mother," a deep male voice interrupted.

Alyssa was surprised to see Alistair standing there by the door with a soft smile on his face and an apology in his eyes. She didn't know what to make of this. *I must still be dreaming.* She shook her head and blinked several times, trying to shake off the dream, but it seemed all too real.

Alistair walked over to her cot then turned to his mother, "You may leave us," he instructed her.

Esmeralda glared at Alyssa, but relented, leaving the room in a swish of skirts and issuing a string of grumbling curses in her wake.

Alistair dropped down to one knee on the floor, taking her hand in his then placed a gentle kiss on her knuckles.

"Please forgive my family for all the wrongs they have done you, lass. I was shocked, to say the least, when I learned who you were and that you had been treated in such a deplorable manner. I would not have you suffer another moment of it and would beg you to do me the honor of becoming my wife," he said as his black eyes, lit with fire, held hers.

Alyssa was speechless. How could this be happening? She had only met the man this morning, and now he was proposing marriage to her! It simply made no sense. She had just started to try to reconcile her mind to the possibility of becoming his mistress, but his offer was so unexpected and far more honorable. She was flabbergasted.

"I—I hardly know what to say, my lord," she stammered.

"Tis simple lass; say yes." He smiled, delivering another sweet kiss to her hand.

"But my lord, we don't even know one another. Surely, you would like to take the time to have a proper courtship before you rush to such permanent judgment," she suggested.

"I have found the woman I shall marry. Your uncle is this very moment, writing our betrothal agreement. If you would like a proper courtship, you shall have it. But know this; we are to be married before the season is out. I must return to Jamaica in a few months. I cannot be delayed beyond what is reasonable for such an enterprise," he said sternly.

Alyssa was suddenly overwhelmed. She had no idea how to respond to such a command. True, he was a very handsome man. She did find him very desirable, if she were to be truly honest with herself, but to be betrothed so quickly to an absolute stranger was shocking to say the least.

"Can I give you my answer on the morrow? This is a lot to take in at such short notice. I haven't yet decided if I'm dreaming or not," she said with a nervous laugh.

Alistair didn't like that answer at all. He was determined to have her, but he didn't want to make her feel trapped either. He could afford to wait until morning, he supposed. He knew what her answer would be. How could she refuse? He was rescuing her from a life a misery. Of course, in her gratitude, she would say yes. He sighed deeply and planted another kiss on her hand.

"It will be as you have asked; you may give me your answer on the morrow as long as that answer is yes," he said with a teasing smile, but his eyes were deadly serious.

Alyssa managed a trembling smile in return as she became aware of her state of undress, the thought causing her to pull the sheet to her chin. It wasn't at all proper for him to be in her room with her wearing only her shift. He must have realized the course her thoughts had taken because he stood up and looked away.

"Take a moment to dress yourself, then I will escort you to your new quarters." With that, he left the room shutting the door behind him.

Alyssa watched him go with a mixture of thrill and trepidation. She jumped up, scrambling around for her frock, one of two that she owned. Having located it, she quickly donned it, barely making sure that it was on correctly. Her hands were shaking as she put her stockings on followed by her pitifully old shoes. Once she had herself clothed, she ran over to her little table, snatched up her hairbrush and furiously raked it through her hair before wrapping it in a haphazard bun. It would have to serve because she simply didn't care how it looked. That done, she stood with her chest heaving from her exertions, contemplating what awaited her on the other side of the door.

A new life! Yes, I will have a new life. I will become a countess. I will live in Jamaica. The thought was staggering. Would they really have to leave England? She didn't want to if she didn't have to. She would speak to him of it on the morrow when she accepted his proposal … she was taken aback by the thought. *I have already decided, haven't I? Yes, I suppose that I have. It would be reckless of me to refuse.*

She straightened her spine; she was ready for whatever the future would bring. She took a few deep breaths before opening the door and taking in the sight of Alistair, leaning against the wall, waiting for her just as he had promised. He smiled at her, offering his arm. She took it gracefully but halted as a thought suddenly occurred to her. She looked up at him saying, "Today is my birthday."

His smile was devastatingly beautiful. Her

heart thumped in her chest as he leaned over and planted a soft kiss on her forehead.

"Happy birthday, my love!" he said with a beaming smile. "How old are you this day?"

"Eight and ten; how old are you, my lord?" she asked with a blush.

"Nine and twenty; still young enough to please you, I hope," he said, still smiling.

Then he tugged her arm, gently leading her away from the life of drudgery she had endured for nearly five years. *Today is my birthday. What a fine present, indeed!*

*****

The morning came early when she was yanked out of bed by her new maid who told her to hurry and prepare for the modiste. The woman was due to arrive in approximately one-quarter of an hour. She barely had time to clean her teeth and take care of her personal needs before her door burst open with Esmeralda rushing in with the modiste and her two assistants in tow. The next thing she knew, she was stripped to her raggedy drawers while the women chattered as measurements were being taken. They fussed over her for four hours before they relented, only stopping to allow her to have lunch, which she took in her room alone while the others went downstairs to eat; she couldn't very well dine in her drawers, Esmeralda had told her.

After lunch, Alyssa was accosted once again for more fittings. By evening, she was completely worn out. She simply couldn't wrap her mind around all that was taking place. She hadn't seen Alistair again since the night before so she could give him her answer, but she would see him at dinner in about an hour. The modiste had three gowns with her that she altered to fit. Aside from shoes, she was well set for the evening and tomorrow as well. Esmeralda wasn't happy with the developments but was making an effort to get along. She monitored every decision that was made for her new wardrobe, using her influence when she thought something wasn't quite right. Alyssa hated to admit that her aunt had exceptional taste in clothing, but she did, so when she overruled her choices in fabrics and colors she kept her own counsel.

By the time the modiste left, she had ordered twenty-seven new gowns, twelve of which were ball gowns, three riding habits, four new sets of stays, seven new nightgowns and two dressing gowns. Of course, there was a need for warmth, so her new wardrobe included three cloaks, several wraps, fichus and shawls with matching reticules. She was told that on the morrow, they would go to the milliner to have her shoes ordered. While they were out, they would visit some other shops to buy some undergarments, gloves, fans, bonnets, ribbons and parasols. *This is exhausting work! Who knew high fashion could be so demanding?* Alyssa inwardly grumbled. Her mind was still spinning from it all as she sat before the mirror while her new ladies' maid Bea, fixed her hair. Esmeralda oversaw this, as well. That was a bit frustrating as she kept disapproving of the styles that Bea had tried thus far.

"It's only hair," Alyssa grumbled under her breath.

Of course, Esmeralda heard her. "If you are to marry my son, you will wear your hair, accordingly. You are to be a countess, after all," she said with a sneer.

"I won't have much hair left after this, ouch!" Her head was promptly jerked backward. Bea must have done that on purpose. Surely, there couldn't be any more tangles after all the fussing she had done so far? She glared at her in the mirror, but Bea didn't notice. She continued her task unfazed by Alyssa's outburst.

"Just braid the mess and roll it up in a topknot, Bea. Dinner will be served shortly. We no longer have time to dally. I will call a stylist to come out to see what can be done with the wretched red mass on the morrow when we return from our shopping trip," Esmeralda instructed with a sigh of resignation.

Thank God, Alyssa inwardly moaned. Maybe Esmeralda wasn't completely heartless, after all. Bea did as she was bid. The final result wasn't at all unflattering. To the contrary, Alyssa thought she looked quite lovely. The hairstyle complete, she put on her new gown. Then she and Esmeralda went down to the drawing room to wait for dinner.

*****

When they entered the drawing room, Alistair was pacing back and forth. He didn't hear them enter so he nearly jumped out of his skin when Esmeralda said, "Well, here we are, sadly this is the best I could do on such short notice."

Alistair walked up to her and stopped before her, taking her hand in his. He stared as if seeing her for the first time. He must not have liked what he saw because he was quite speechless. Alyssa became nervous. She cast her eyes down, sucked her bottom lip into her mouth and started chewing on it.

He lifted her chin up, "You look lovely, Alyssa."

Then he bent and kissed the hand he still held. A relieved smiled spread across her lips as he led her over to the sofa to await the announcement of dinner. It wasn't until Alyssa sat down that she noticed her uncle and her cousin Diana were staring at her with hostile glares. It was a little disconcerting, making it hard to sit still under their hostile scrutiny. She started fidgeting with her bodice, trying to relieve the discomfort from her new stays. Having never worn them before, she found them to be most unpleasant.

"Would you like a glass of sherry?" Alistair broke into her thoughts.

"That would be welcomed, my lord," she said in a barely audible response.

Alyssa really didn't like being here with these people. They didn't like her nor did she like them or the way they were staring at her. The situation unnerved her, making her want to shout at them to tell them what despicable people they were.

Alistair couldn't take her away from here soon enough. Surprisingly, Esmeralda was smiling. The woman must really be making an effort. She would have to make one in return, she supposed. It wouldn't do for her to lash out at her future mother-in-law and look like a shrew in front of her fiancé. Perhaps, Esmeralda would be an ally someday, well, probably not, but it was best to try to have a positive outlook. Her uncle was positively livid; she could tell. He must be lamenting the loss of her fortune.

Why, I wonder if I have any fortune left? She had no idea how much she had to start with. No one ever told her. For all she knew, it was gone, or they could tell her it was, and she would be none the wiser. She would have to speak to Alistair about this at some point, she realized. Perhaps he could help her reclaim what her uncle had taken. She didn't have proof that he had taken any of it, but she was sure of it nonetheless. When she had arrived, all their furnishings were shabby and threadbare, but now the entire house had been remodeled, redecorated and refurnished, complete with hot water plumbing. The ladies didn't dress as they did now, either. Yes, he was angry to be losing her fortune. That had to explain his sour expression.

Alistair brought her sherry, bringing her out of her reverie. She absentmindedly sipped at it, which was a mistake. She was wholly unprepared for its potency. She started coughing, trying to reclaim her breath. Alistair quickly assisted her by clapping her on the back. *Ghastly stuff, sherry!*

"Perhaps you would prefer some water," he suggested.

"No, this is fine, really. I just wasn't expecting

it to have such a kick to it," she told him.

Everyone but Alistair snickered at her comment. What was so funny? She had never had sherry before; she had no idea that it was so foul. She looked at Diana, noting she was fairly gloating at her inability to handle spirits. She wouldn't miss Diana, she decided. Perhaps it wouldn't be so bad living in Jamaica after all. The further she could get away from these parasites the better. Her rescue from the uncomfortable scene came in the form of Mr. Humphrey announcing that dinner was ready. She gratefully rose as Alistair ushered her to the dining room, which was through the adjoining door. It would be the first time she would have sat down at this table to dine. She was nervous as she wasn't sure she remembered proper etiquette. Esmeralda would point out any of her deficiencies, no doubt! However, there was no need to rely on the wisdom of her future mother-in-law as it turned out. When she couldn't remember which utensil to use, she simply looked to see what Alistair was using, allowing that small dignity to remain intact.

Cookie had outdone herself tonight. A clear message received. She would have to go speak to her later tonight after everyone went to bed. Her good friend was probably dying to hear all the details. After dinner, Alistair suggested a walk about the gardens. That sounded like a fine idea to her, so she gladly agreed. They needed to speak in private anyway so she could formally accept his proposal.

Once in the garden, Alistair impatiently came right to the point. "May I have your answer?" he asked, leading her to a bench and assisting her to sit before sitting down beside her.

"Of course, you know my answer is yes. How could I refuse? Look what you have done for me. I will forever be grateful to you," she told him.

"It's not gratitude that I want, Alyssa. I want a wife. A wife that will love and honor me," he told her frankly.

"Of course, I will honor you but I must be honest and tell you that it is too soon to say that I love you," she said, wishing she could take the words back.

She could have used a little more tact before saying such a thing. He wasn't upset by it though, saying, "Of course, love will come with time, lass. I realize this has all been rather sudden. It must be very unsettling for you. But I would have you know now that I simply adore you. I think we will have no trouble at all finding love between us."

She appreciated his words as they were rather comforting. She suspected that they really would find love. Indeed, she was rather smitten with him now. She was sure it would only grow with time. "Thank you for being so understanding, my lord," she said demurely.

He took her hand in his. Very slowly, he seductively placed a kiss upon the palm of her hand with heated breath. She didn't yet own a pair of gloves, so the warm contact on her flesh was like a bolt of lightning to her senses, causing her hand to jerk away in reflex to the intimacy.

"Do not be afraid of me Alyssa, I will never hurt you," he promised.

The look in his eyes reminded her of a hungry wolf. Suddenly she felt very vulnerable. She looked back at the house to make sure they were still in view, if anyone cared to view, that was. She didn't see anyone looking out the window, making her wonder if she should suggest that they go back inside.

"Alyssa, do you understand what is expected of a wife?" he asked.

Alyssa's attention was snapped back at he question he had asked. It seemed to her that he was being a bit forward. She knew that husbands prized virginity in their brides, but beyond that, she really hadn't a clue. Though she had seen animals mate on occasion in her youth before her papa died, she couldn't imagine that people would behave so. She shook her head that she didn't know making him laugh softly in response. He kissed her hand again, reaching up to brush away a stray strand of hair at her brow. She looked down at her lap, but he would have none of it; he raised her chin back up, kissing her softly on the lips. It was a sweet, tender kiss; not intimidating in any way. It was meant to reassure her, she realized. She inwardly thanked him for it. She tried to relax a little bit. He was to be her husband, after all.

"Shall I tell you what is expected?" he asked with a sweet smile that showed a dimple in his cheek that she had not noticed before.

"Should we not save that for our wedding night, my lord?" she ventured.

He laughed softly again, "Ah, sweet Alyssa, no we shall not wait for our wedding night, for what I am about to tell you, lass."

Alyssa felt like a trapped rabbit as the hungry wolf look returned. She shifted uncomfortably on the bench, casting her eyes back down at her lap.

"Alyssa, what I expect from you is that you call me by my given name. Call me Alistair, or if you would rather, you may call me Ali. There are some that even call me Sin, but I shouldn't like to hear that from your sweet lips," he said with a mischievous glint in his eye.

Alyssa raised a nervous laugh at his trick. He made her believe he was going to explain the birds and the bees, right here and now, but he simply wanted her to call him by his given name.

"Yes, Alistair, I shall call you by your given name from this moment forward," she said smiling.

"Good, I'm glad that's all settled," he returned. "There's more," he added.

Alyssa cleared her throat, "More my— Alistair?"

"Aye, lots more. On our wedding night, you will come willingly to my bed. I will make love to you as you have never imagined in your wildest dreams. I will not tolerate a frigid wife. I want you to enjoy the experience as much as I will. Promise me that you will never fear my touch," he said, giving her that look again.

She didn't know what he meant by frigid. Wasn't she just supposed to lay there and allow him to take his pleasure? She didn't know. Was this something she was supposed to know?

"I trust you will instruct me in these things Alistair because I have no knowledge of which you speak. I promise to be brave, but that's all I can say now as I have no understanding of lovemaking," she admitted.

Alistair was pleased by her answer. He smiled at her before gently kissing her lips again. Again, it was a sweet kiss making her feel warm all over. He pulled away from the kiss, caressing her cheek with his thumb.

"I should like to have our nuptials as soon as possible after the banns are read. I don't want to have to wait long to claim my bride," he told her with a fire in his black eyes that quite mesmerized her.

That was less than a month, she realized. She would become his bride in less than a month! She shivered at the monumental change her life had taken in the last few hours, but she wasn't scared. No, she felt free for the first time in her life; he had given her this. She would marry him tomorrow if it could be arranged, but she knew that would be impractical.

"It will be as you say, Alistair," she told him.

Chapter Three

Alyssa was tired from all the shopping, but she had everything she would need now to come out in society and take her place beside Alistair as his betrothed. He accompanied her along with Aunt Esmeralda on their shopping expedition, but his presence was somewhat disappointing as he didn't seem to approve of many of her purchases. Aunt Esmeralda overruled his complaints. He seemed to accept that he had little say in the matter. He did put his foot down, however, when Aunt Esmeralda suggested that she get her hair cut so her unruly locks could be better managed. She thought he and his mother were going to have a brawl right there on the street when the two of them started arguing.

Alistair was really angry. He shouted at her, but it was quickly diffused after a few moments. Esmeralda realized she had overstepped her authority. After taking measure of his hostile expression, she chose the prudent course of silence and relented. After the argument was over, Alistair apologized for his outburst, making a genuine attempt to compose himself so as to enjoy the rest of the outing. However, he still seemed a little out of sorts as his grip on her arm became rather painful when they were strolling down the strand. Alyssa noted that every time a gentleman tipped his hat in her direction, his grip would tighten a little more. It was almost as though he were jealous and didn't want other men to see her.

She was ready to go home now as she had finally had enough. "I think that I have all that I will need now, if you both wouldn't mind going home. I'm a bit tired. I would like to get off my feet. These new shoes are pinching my toes somewhat," she complained.

Alistair halted them as soon as the words left her mouth immediately whistling for their carriage to come fetch them. Within moments, she was ensconced within the carriage with Alistair removing her shoes to administer a to massage her feet. It was a little embarrassing but when she tried to pull her feet away, he tugged them right back into his lap giving her a look that suggested he would put up with no nonsense on her part. She resigned herself to the embarrassing massage and after awhile she rather enjoyed it. He really had a way with his hands as before long her feet were in absolute heaven.

Esmeralda had all she could take. She mentioned the impropriety of the situation but Alistair undaunted glared her into submission then sharply said, "I will not have a crippled bride, mother."

That was the end of that! Esmeralda resigned with a huff and looked out the window so as not to offend her eyes further by the situation. Alyssa had to admit she rather enjoyed seeing Alistair put his mother in her place. It was high time that someone did.

*****

When they arrived home, Alyssa was pleased to see she had several boxes from the modiste awaiting her. She was surprised that the modiste could have managed to have anything done so quickly, but Esmeralda informed her that they had paid extra to have them rushed; more of Alistair's persuasion she surmised. She had so many packages from her shopping trip, now the modiste too, that it took three maids to make sense of it all.

Alyssa was delighted by all her new things but simply didn't know when she would ever wear all of them. When everything was put away, Esmeralda told her she would have to model her new gowns to be sure they would be a proper fit. Alyssa eagerly agreed. With a word of advice from Esmeralda, she selected a lovely emerald green ball gown with a scandalously low bodice. She wasn't at all sure she ordered the gown. She didn't remember choosing anything with such a low bodice. When she donned the gown, Esmeralda told her to stay where she was and went to retrieve Alistair.

Alistair's reaction to the gown was shocking, to say the least. At first, he stood gawking at her then he turned really red. "You shall send that back to the modiste. I will not have my bride dressed as a trollop," he said harshly, then he promptly left the room.

Alyssa was stunned by his comments, standing there open-mouthed gaping at the empty spot that Alistair had just vacated. She blinked her eyes, trying to bring the scene into some clarity, looking to Esmeralda for some kind of support. She was smiling sardonically as she followed behind him, as though she were quite pleased by his reaction.

Clearly, she knew Alistair wouldn't like the dress and wanted to cause a scene. She wouldn't have put it past her to have ordered it herself for just such a purpose. Alyssa shook her head in exasperation; there was nothing to do but accept that this would be the way of things as long as they remained in Esmeralda's house. Resolving to salvage the evening as it was close to dinnertime, she selected a simple gown made of aqua blue muslin in a soft pastel tone. Though its bodice was far more modest, she tucked a fichu around the neckline, not wanting to cause another disturbance with Alistair.

Alistair was quite an enigma, she decided. One moment, he was sweet and attentive, then the next he was cross. She supposed that as her betrothed he had a certain right to command her in her choice of fashions, but his temper was being provoked by his mother, which she could sympathize with, but still, she wasn't at all happy about the way things were shaping up.

*****

Alyssa was quite relieved that Alistair seemed to approve of the gown she wore for dinner. When she entered the drawing room, he was once again pacing back and forth awaiting her arrival. When he realized she had entered the room, he rushed over, giving her a thorough perusal. After a moment, he smiled his approval before taking her hand in his and placing a tender kiss on her palm. Whatever was bothering him earlier seemed to have abated as his mood was once again pleasant. When they went in to dinner, he had the footman move her place setting so that she was beside him. Esmeralda had her at the other end of the table beside her. She was glad he made the change as she would much rather sit beside him. His mother didn't seem to appreciate being under-minded once again, but instead of commenting on it she glared at Alyssa as if it were somehow her fault.

Uncle Morley surprised her by saying how lovely she looked, but her pleasure at the compliment was lost when Diana snickered. "I think the gown clashes with her hair," she said with her usual smug demeanor.

Alistair gave her a look that suggested she should keep such observations to herself, and she made no further attempts. Alyssa wished she had the power that Alistair seemed to have over the family. His presence beside her soothed her feelings of inadequacy. He didn't seem to mind at all that she was so socially lacking. He reached for her hand under the table and began a slow rotating massage of her palm with his thumb while they were eating, shifting closer to her so that their thighs were touching. It was rather romantic, she mused. It was comforting to know she had an ally in Alistair. It gave her some much needed confidence and strength to face the villains who were her family.

Her thoughts were interrupted when Alistair made an announcement. "I have decided that we should have a dinner party to announce our betrothal," he said, smiling at her.

"That's a wonderful idea dear, but are you sure

she is ready for such a venture?" Esmeralda asked with an arched brow.

"Of course, she is ready, why would she not be?" he demanded.

"Well her manners are atrocious for one thing. For another, she has no idea how to socialize among the aristocracy," Esmeralda proclaimed with a smug attitude.

"Mother, you are speaking about my future wife. I will not have you speak of her in such an ill manner. There is nothing wrong with her etiquette. If she is lacking in anything, you only have yourself to blame."

Alyssa froze. Everyone stopped eating. They could have heard a pin drop in the deadly silence that followed.

Uncle Morley saved the moment by saying, "Your manners are fine, my dear. We shall be delighted to host a dinner party to celebrate your upcoming nuptials to my stepson."

Alyssa could have been knocked over with a feather. Of all the people to have defended her, he would have been the last she would have suspected.

She composed herself, saying, "Thank you Uncle Morley. I shall endeavor to live up to your fine compliment."

Alistair squeezed her hand, chuckling softly. Esmeralda was fuming. Diana was gaping at her father as though he had become some kind of stranger. It was rather unusual behavior, but it was a pleasant change from his usual sour attitude. This was Alistair's influence, no doubt. *Perhaps he can conquer his mother's bad attitude as well. One can always hope,* Alyssa thought.

"Then it's all settled. Shall we have it three days hence? I would like to put the announcement in the Times as soon as possible," Alistair said. "That should allow plenty of time for more of her gowns to be delivered. She needs to have a good selection for the dinner as well as all the balls we will be receiving invitations to, once the announcement has been formally made," he added.

Esmeralda refused to say another word, so it fell upon Uncle Morley to concur and set the date. "Three days hence will do nicely, don't you agree, Esmeralda?" the earl asked his wife with a look that told her she would be best served by agreeing.

She nodded her agreement, and the remainder of the dinner was spent rather quietly.

*****

After dinner, Alistair took her for another stroll in the garden. This time, he led her deeper into it so as to avoid prying eyes, she realized. She wasn't too worried since he was to be her husband, after all. As they strolled along, she thought it would be a good time to discuss a few things with him. She wanted to explain about the gown.

"Alistair?" she ventured cautiously, "About the green gown. I don't even remember ordering that gown. It was your mother's suggestion that I model it for you first," she told him.

Alistair didn't say anything for a moment then he sighed, "I suspected as much. I'm sorry that I overreacted to the situation. I was just so incensed when I saw you in it. Although, I do admit you were ravishing, but I could never allow my bride to dress in such a way."

His jaw tightened. There was a hardening in his eyes that unsettled her.

"Your mother is unhappy with the match, Alistair. Things will surely be better when we are married, and we leave her home."

She really was trying to view things on the bright side. She didn't want Esmeralda's behavior to influence Alistair's, causing trouble in the marriage before the ceremony was even held.

"Aye, things will be better when we leave for Jamaica. You will love it there, my sweet lass," he told her, draping his arm around her shoulder to draw her near.

It felt nice to be snuggled up to him as the evening was a bit chilly. She wasn't sure she really would like Jamaica. She had never considered leaving England before, but she would give it a chance for his sake. He had been so good to her, so it would be the least she could do to repay him for his kindness.

"We are to live in Jamaica, then?" she asked.

Alistair stiffened ever so slightly at her side, but after quiet reflection of her question, he stopped, drawing her into his embrace. He kissed her forehead, "You don't mind, do you?"

"I have never been anywhere before, so I have no idea what to expect. I understand that it is quite beautiful but rather hot," she told him, snuggling into his embrace.

"We don't have to live there year round, I

suppose. Perhaps, we can winter in Jamaica and spend our summers in England or Scotland," he suggested.

"That sounds lovely, Alistair."

They looked into each other's eyes for a moment; then Alistair took her mouth in an abrupt kiss. She was startled by the swiftness in which he lunged for her lips, but he didn't seem to notice. He simply increased the intensity of it. She felt as though she were suffocating. She tried to pull away to catch her breath, but he tightened his hold on her, refusing to relent. He pushed his tongue inside her mouth, then furthered his attentions, groping her breasts. Alyssa couldn't understand what had provoked him to behave in such a manner. She was a little frightened by his aggression. She tried again to push away from him, this time he let her go but he grabbed her by the face.

"I thought I told you never to fear me," he gritted out through clenched teeth.

He seemed angry now; his eyes were hard, his breathing ragged.

"I couldn't breathe," she pleaded, trying to move her face out of his grip.

He lunged for her lips again, this time more savage than before. He shoved his hand down her bodice, tearing the fabric in his wake, then began fondling her breasts with one hand while the other moved down her thigh gathering up her skirts. Once he had her skirt lifted, he shoved her drawers out of his way and began to caress her woman's mound. She began to struggle in earnest now, trying to shove his hand away from her private place. This simply wasn't acceptable!

"Alistair, you mustn't. We are not yet married. I cannot allow you to take such liberties."

His answer was to grab her by the shoulders, driving her down on the grass, covering her body with his. Once again, he began to kiss her with a savage hunger while his hands continued to rove over her body. In his frustration, he tore away her drawers then slid a probing finger inside her. In fear of virtue she jerked at the intrusion, squirming desperately to escape his touch.

He was relentless. "I cannot wait to have you, my sweet Alyssa," he rasped with a harsh, breathless voice.

"No Alistair, no please, you mustn't do this. Not now, not here. Please stop," she pleaded.

He stopped, then he buried his face in her neck as if trying to gain control of himself. She could feel the hard ridge of his arousal as it was pressed against her thigh. She had been apprehensive before, but now for the first time in his presence, she was truly frightened of him. She couldn't understand what had overcome him, causing him to behave in such a way.

"Forgive me. Forgive me lass," he quietly said.

Relieved that he seemed to have regained his senses but still unsettled by the whole episode, Alyssa wasn't sure she could forgive such behavior. It was possible that in her ignorance of the ways between husband and wife she had overreacted to his excited passions. He was to be her husband in less than a month, so perhaps this was the normal course of things; she wasn't sure. Now she felt a little guilty for thwarting him.

"I'm sorry Alistair. I was shocked by the suddenness of it and couldn't catch my breath. I began to panic, I suppose."

He still hadn't moved from on top of her, but she no longer felt quite as scared. He seemed genuinely disturbed by his own behavior as he lay atop her. He had a strange look in his eyes that seemed apologetic.

"I had an image of you in that green gown. I was quite overcome," he explained. "That's why you mustn't wear such things. Any men that were to see you dressed in such a way would think you were free for the taking."

Alistair shook his head, making a groaning sound, then rolled off of her. He stood up offering her his hand, pulling her to her feet. When he saw the condition of her clothing, a look of horror crossed his face. He began to try to right her clothing, but her bodice and her drawers were hopelessly torn. He picked the grass out of her hair, then took off his coat, draping it around her shoulders before pulling her into his arms and simply holding her. After a moment with nothing left to say, he escorted her back into the house, leading her to her room. He apologized again for his behavior and kissed her on the forehead, then turned, leaving her there. She stood watching him go with a deep sense of confusion, listened to him make his way down the stairs. She flinched at the sound of the front door slamming.

*****

Alistair felt like an arse. God's teeth, he had nearly raped his betrothed in the garden. In the garden! He stomped to the stables shouting at the groom to ready his horse. There was only one cure for what ailed him, he decided. He was going to have to go and get a whore. The frustration was driving him mad; he couldn't think straight like this. She had nearly driven him insane in that gown, even the memory of it made him behave like a savage. All day long he followed her and his mother around, watching as she picked out all her undergarments, shoes and other fripperies. He kept imagining what he would do to her in each and every article she picked up. When she caressed the fabrics of her hose and ribbons, he imagined she was caressing his shaft. It was not to be borne; he simply must have relief. If he didn't, he would hurt his beloved. The idea repulsed him. He would never hurt her intentionally but tonight, he very nearly had.

As soon as the groom brought his mount around, he jerked the reins from him and saddled up to make his way to the brothel. He had a certain amount of energy to expend. He wanted a whore that could handle his need. Alistair was feeling particularly angry and didn't plan on being nice. He went to his old favorite haunt, once inside he was met by Madam Comely, not her real name, of course; the woman was exceptionally vain. She may have been comely once, but she was an old crotch now. But she understood his needs; she always had.

"Lord Keith, it's been an age since you've graced my fine establishment," she preened.

He grunted his response. He was in no mood for this old trollop. He wanted a young piece with red hair and blue-green eyes. "What have you that might interest me?" he barked at her.

"You seem a little edgy, perhaps you have special interests tonight?" she hedged with a knowing look in her eyes.

"Yes, you could say that I have a particular need this night. Have you any redheads with blue or green eyes?"

"That, I do my lord. Will you require any special implements for your needs?"

"Some scarves, a gag … and something to spank her with, and tell her to put on an emerald green dress," he said.

"That will cost you extra, my lord," she shrewdly informed him.

"Yes, yes, see to it," he commanded.

"Go to the red room, I will send Marjorie to you. She specializes in such things. I believe she will satisfy you. Would you like two redheads? The more the merrier, I always say," she suggested with a wink.

"No just Marjorie. Are you sure she has red hair and blue or green eyes?"

"Yes indeed, she is very beautiful and … very talented, my lord. You shall not be disappointed."

"I had better not be, for I plan on keeping the wench the rest of the night," he said, turning to go up the stairs.

*****

Alistair's final orgasm was cataclysmic. His body shook and jerked for a full minute after his release as he still lay buried inside her. He had tied her to the bed face down, mounting her many times before, but this last time had been the most powerful. When she first entered the room in the green gown, he ripped it off of her and tore it to shreds. He grabbed her by the hair, dragged her over to the bed quickly tying her to the bedpost where he gagged her and set about spanking her bottom with the paddle that had been provided. She whimpered her pleasure, and the sound spurred him on into a frenzy to be unequaled. When he released her from the bedpost, he drove her to her knees and made her take him into her mouth until she was nearly gagging. She didn't seem to mind being called Alyssa while she worked. It increased his pleasure to scream out the name when he reached his first orgasm, filling her mouth with his seed.

He felt a little guilty about the bite marks, though. He would have to tip her something extra for that. Though, she had encouraged him to do it with her cries for mercy, he still felt bad. She lay there completely exhausted now with a smile on her face; she knew she had earned her coin well. He rolled off her, gave her bum one last slap and a pinch saying, "Good lass, Alyssa, you should always mind your master."

She giggled saying, "I shall always be yours to command my dear master."

He smiled; he liked that. He hoped that when the real Alyssa was in her place she would be just as submissive. That was the way he liked his women to be when he bedded them. He was master. They were to obey him. If not, then he punished them until they learned their place. It was the way it should be. He wasn't always as aggressive as this, but he had been provoked by that dress.

Sadly though, he must leave this accommodating wench now. Dawn had come. He needed to go home to his beloved. He was much relieved now, confident he could endure being in Alyssa's presence now without another incident like the one that had occurred in the garden. He would try not to feel guilty about that … or this. It couldn't be helped. He would make it up to her on their wedding night.

He untied Marjorie, offering his hand so she could rise. She was probably sore from the exercise, he certainly was. He walked over to the sideboard to clean her stench off him with soap and water. Then, he toweled himself dry all the while savoring the loose feeling in his once tense muscles. Once dressed, he pulled his coin-purse out of his coat pocket. He tossed her three guineas in addition to the usual fee. He told her to go buy herself something special. She thanked him, dropping to her knees, kissing him on his hand like a good little lass. He left there quite pleased, relaxed and whistling his favorite tune. It was going to be a beautiful day. If he hurried, he could get home before the household awakened, then he could break his fast with his beautiful Alyssa. He could hardly wait until the wedding when he would no longer have need of whores. He would make sure it was a special night for Alyssa. She would have to learn not to resist him though to avoid future unfortunate scenes such as the one that had occurred this evening. He felt like he could teach her properly with time. His stepfather had been right about one thing. She wasn't always obedient.

*****

Alyssa woke somewhat saddened by the events that had transpired the night before. Alistair had very clearly told her that he required her to go willingly to his bed, never fearing his touch, yet she had done just the opposite of what he had asked of her. It had happened so suddenly she was caught unawares. Surely, he understood that in her inexperience he would need to approach her a little more gently. She sighed deep, looking over her new clothes. She wanted to dress properly so as not to offend him in her choice again. He was right about the green gown. She would return it to the modiste first thing after breaking her fast. She would have to be sure none of the other gowns was so provocative.

Too bad about the gown last night; it had been one of her favorites, and now it was ruined. The more she thought about it, the more she wondered if Alistair's reaction to the gown wasn't a little overdone. Sure, the neckline had been scandalous, but to have him practically tear the other one off of her because of it had been a little much. She wished she could speak with Cookie about the incident, but she wasn't sure it was a good idea. She didn't want to cause Cookie any trouble by hanging about in the kitchens gossiping about her future husband.

Cookie would know if his behavior was normal. She had made her profession as a mistress in her earlier years. Maybe men were driven to high passions by such simple things as a low bodice. She wouldn't know, but one thing was certain, she could never ask Esmeralda about it. Yes, she would have to speak to Cookie about it, but it would have to wait. Maybe she could slip down to her room later tonight when everyone was asleep. She had meant to go speak to her the other night, but it had completely slipped her mind. She probably felt slighted that she hadn't been to see her.

She found a lovely day gown with peach stripes and a very modest bodice. It would serve. She still didn't have most of her new gowns yet. She hoped that some more would arrive today. Most of the other gowns she had would probably send Alistair into a tailspin with their suggestive necklines. She would definitely need several more fichus. Her gown decided, she rang the bell for Bea to assist her with her toilet, hoping that today would be a good day.

Chapter Four

"Cookie, I tell you he went berserk over that green gown. He told me he wouldn't have his bride dressed like a trollop. Then he attacked me later in the garden and ripped the bodice of the gown I was wearing," she explained yet again to her friend.

"I don't like the sound of this at all, love. What else did he do?" Cookie asked with a worried look in her eyes.

"Well, I don't really like to say, but he touched me there," she pointed to her lap, blushing.

"Well that's normal. Men like to sample the goods," she said with a grin.

"I don't know what you mean by that," she blushed deeper.

"Honey, when a man is amorous he likes to touch and fondle you all over. It's perfectly normal, but attacking you and ripping your clothes, well, that's a little scary," she explained with a grimace.

"He apologized! Oh, I could tell that he felt badly about it because I could see the shame in his eyes. To be truly honest, I felt quite guilty about it after because he told me that I should never fear his touch. I provoked him when I resisted his kiss. It had happened so suddenly that I couldn't breathe."

"The man should keep his paws off you until the wedding, but there's no real harm in kissing. Are you sure he wasn't just a little rough in his excitement; that's normal too. Some gents get a little aggressive when they're all stirred up," she explained.

"Yes, I think that's more the case; he was very

riled up. He said he couldn't wait to have me. I could tell he was aroused," she put her head down, giggling at her own audacity.

"Love, I'm sure everything is alright, but you hold out until the wedding, you hear? Some gents, especially lords, look unkindly upon a woman if she gives herself freely before the wedding, even though they pester them into it. It's not fair I know, but it's best to be wise. Keep your skirts down around your ankles until you say I do," she snickered.

"Yes, I suppose you're right about that. I did tell him that it wasn't right to take liberties with me before we were married. He has been so good to me. I want to return the kindness but not at the expense of losing him," she said with a furrowed brow.

Alyssa couldn't bear the thought of losing him. He rescued her. He was going to take her away and give her a wonderful life. She couldn't afford to do anything to mess that up. If what Cookie says was true, she must remain diligent in keeping his attentions at bay.

"Well love, you just stick to your principles and all will be well. But if he ever hurts you before the wedding, then there is something wrong. He should never mishandle you … ever. Oh, I know that the law allows it. It's encouraged even, but that doesn't make it right. You don't want to end up with a cruel husband. There are plenty of good men out there that appreciate a good woman and will never lay a mean hand on them. Do you understand me?"

"Yes, I certainly do. I have lived with enough

cruelty for the last five years to recognize it when I see it. I appreciate your advice and thank you for listening to me. I should get back upstairs and go to bed. Tomorrow is a big day. We are to have the dinner to announce our betrothal, and I want to be well rested so that I look my very best," she said. She got up and hugged her friend. "Goodnight Cookie. I love you."

"I love you too my sweet girl, pleasant dreams."

Alyssa left Cookie's room, quickly darting up the servants' stairway, then slipped quietly back to her room. She was glad she'd had her talk with Cookie. She wasn't worried about Alistair anymore. It had all been perfectly normal behavior on his part. She wished she knew more about what went on between a man and a woman so she wouldn't be so confused. Well, she would learn soon enough. With that thought, she smiled and climbed into her bed. She was feeling a little more optimistic after her chat with Cookie. There hadn't been any more strange incidents with Alistair; he had been a perfect gentleman since the night in the garden. He was very excited about announcing their betrothal and had already sent his notice to The Times so that it would print in tomorrow's edition. All was going well, so with a positive mindset she closed her eyes and drifted to sleep.

*****

Alistair waited impatiently in the drawing room with the guests that had started to arrive; Alyssa had not yet come down. He had hoped she would be ready sooner so he could approve of her gown before she was presented in front of so many men. There were to be fifty guests, half of which were men, many unattached bachelors. He didn't like the idea of so many men looking upon her. She was so beautiful, she would tempt a saint. He marveled at the effect she had already had on him, and he was a well principled man. She had nearly driven him to violence in just two days.

Without the aid of Marjorie for the last two evenings, he would never have survived. Just being in Alyssa's presence was more than he could endure. He needed to possess her body and spirit to leash his passions for her. He kind of liked Marjorie, though. He was considering keeping her as mistress and taking her back to Jamaica or sending for her upon his return. Of course, it would never do to have a mistress while courting a wife, neither would it be wise to have her travel on the same vessel with his wife, once married, he supposed.

He was more convinced than ever that he would need a new mistress. There would be times when Alyssa wouldn't be able to meet his needs; when she was with child, for instance. He didn't like the idea of copulating with a pregnant woman after she started to show; the child could be injured if he were to become too aggressive as he sometimes did. In fact, the more he thought about it, the more he realized that Marjorie would be ideal for medicinal purposes. Indeed, she would be the perfect prescription to avoid injuring his wife and child.

Alyssa was so precious to him that the thought of hurting her made him ill. He had truly scared himself that night in the garden. He didn't want to repeat such an action; the idea simply wasn't to be born. There were just times that a man such as he had to work out his aggressions. A woman of such a fine quality as his beloved Alyssa would never be able to endure the full weight of his passions when he was in one of his states. He had to bear this in mind at all times, so he never again risked hurting her. He really didn't like the idea of visiting whores, but if Marjorie were his mistress it would be perfectly respectable. All men kept a mistress for those times when they didn't want to offend their wives' delicate sensibilities. He could afford to keep several mistresses when he married Alyssa; he would be an extremely wealthy man.

Of course, he still had Batiste in Jamaica. She was a lovely half-breed native with green eyes and mocha skin. She enjoyed his passions as much if not more than he enjoyed giving them. He had regretted leaving her behind. He told her not to expect too much when he returned as he would be a married man, but now that he thought upon it, he really didn't see why he couldn't keep both Marjorie and Batiste. They could all three come together and share one another at times. The idea was beginning to gain merit. He liked to watch two women pleasure one another. The punishments he would dole out for their misbehavior would be delectable. He shook his head to clear away his naughty thoughts. Now was not the time for such fantasies.

His sweet Alyssa deserved his full attention tonight. He didn't want her to feel overwhelmed by all the guests. He wanted her to know she had his full support in all things.

He was so in love with her that it hurt. He couldn't wait until their wedding night when he would command her body and spirit. Tonight, however, he would introduce her as his betrothed. He would bestow upon her finger the symbol of his devotion in front of fifty witnesses. It was a romantic gesture that he felt sure she would appreciate.

*****

Alyssa was nervous as she descended the stairs for the betrothal dinner. She was running a little late because she couldn't decide what to wear. After much agonizing, she decided to go with the white muslin gown with puffed sleeves and a blue ribbon sash just below the breasts. The neckline was modest enough as not to offend Alistair; she was sure of it, but she tucked a fichu around the neckline to be safe in any case. She didn't want anything to spoil the evening. She was also nervous about being on display in front of so many members of the peerage, most of which had already arrived. There were to be many earls, countesses, marquesses, marchionesses, even a couple of dukes and a duchess. She hoped she wouldn't make any mistakes that would embarrass Alistair. It was all so overwhelming.

When she arrived at the drawing room door,

she asked the footman to retrieve Alistair. She didn't think it would be wise to arrive unescorted. She wasn't sure how these things worked, but she felt sure he would appreciate having the honors. A moment later, Alistair came through the door with eyes locked on hers. He stopped in his tracks, smiling. She could tell he was pleased with her choice. She breathed a sigh of relief when he approached her, taking her hand in his then kissing her gloved palm.

He was so handsome in his blue superfine coat with his tan breeches that she had to suppress the urge to throw herself into his arms and kiss him on the lips. She blushed at the thought. He tucked her arm into his, nodding to the footman to open the door. Together, they took a giant step toward their future. She got a chill down her spine at the thought of it. It was so monumental compared to her life less than a week ago. Alistair truly was her hero for he had saved her from a miserable existence. She felt so proud he had chosen her that she vowed to herself she would make him proud by being a good and dutiful wife.

The crowd grew quiet when she was announced. All eyes were on her. She clutched Alistair's arm just a little tighter, feeling soothed by his answering massage of her fingers. He escorted her in, stopping just in the center of the room. It wasn't long before she was crowded by well-wishers, people she had never seen before in her life. She did her best to meet and greet them with as much poise and dignity as she knew how to demonstrate, but inside her body was quaking with

nerves. Esmeralda broke the crowd up to take
Alyssa away from Alistair. She walked about the
room introducing her to the guests. Esmeralda acted
as though she loved Alyssa dearly. The effect was
nearly comical compared to what Alyssa knew to be
factually the opposite. She wondered if everyone
could see the falseness of it as she could.

She would never remember all of these names
and titles, some of which went on forever. Most of
the guests were gracious and kind, but some of the
ladies were looking at her as though she had no
right to be there. She supposed that a handsome
man like Alistair would inspire a certain amount of
envy toward her, so she tried to ignore their glares.
After she had been dragged around the room and
introduced to everyone, Alistair came to reclaim
her, bringing her back to the center of the room.

"May I have everyone's attention?" he said.

Alyssa was taken aback. She had no idea what
he was about to do. But she trusted him in all
things, so she patiently waited to see what was
afoot.

After everyone's attention turned to Alistair, he
said, "All of you have had a chance to meet my
sweet Alyssa. I'm sure you were all as charmed as I
was when I first saw her. So having said that, I
would now like you all to serve as witness as I
bestow the symbol of my devotion upon the finger
of this beautiful woman who has so graciously
agreed to become my countess." With a smile, he
took her hand in his, removing her glove.

All the females gasped at the scandalous nature
of it, but he wasn't disturbed as continued in his

course. When he had it removed, he brought her bared hand to his lips, kissing her knuckles sweetly. Then, without further ado he reached into his pocket, producing a huge pear shaped emerald ring, surrounded by diamonds and placed it upon her finger.

"A lovely jewel for an even lovelier jewel," he said before folding their hands together and raising them above their heads.

Everyone clapped, jeers and cheers were shouted, mostly by the men. Alyssa turned scarlet, nearly swooning from the shock of the gesture. She had no idea he would make such a spectacle, but he had. It was almost as though he were staking his claim, branding her, somehow. He should have done this in private. It would have been much more romantic. She felt tears of embarrassment stinging her eyes and tried valiantly to keep them from releasing.

Alistair noticed and bent to kiss her on the cheek saying, "Now all those present know that you belong to me, my sweet Alyssa. You are mine now; never forget."

Just as she had thought, he was branding her. She didn't like this at all, but she didn't want to hurt his feelings, so she decided she would keep her own counsel. She nervously looked around the room, noticing that all the ladies were staring at her while whispering behind their fans. She suspected she had just become the subject of the latest juicy scandal. She inwardly cringed, casting her eyes back on Alistair who seemed rather pleased with himself. The room settled down. Moments later a late arrival to the party was announced.

"Gabriel Hawkins, The Duke of Windhaven," the footman announced. The room quieted, all save Diana who rushed up to him and grabbed him by the hand, dragging him into the room. This must be her betrothed, Alyssa realized.

He was an exceptionally handsome man, though not as handsome as Alistair, with long dark brown wavy hair, kept neatly tied with a leather strip. His gray eyes almost looked silver. He was taller than Alistair and broadly built across the shoulders. His limbs bulged and rippled beneath the fabric of his clothing. His gait reminded Alyssa of a huge stalking panther. She could see why Diana claimed him so quickly as all the females were fluttering in his presence. He seemed like a jovial fellow. Alyssa had trouble understanding what a man like that would want with a shrew like Diana. *Opposites attract, I suppose,* she thought before dismissing him from her mind.

Dinner was announced soon after the duke's arrival. Alistair promptly escorted her to the dining room, placing her in the chair beside his. It seemed he was sitting awfully close to her compared to how the other guests were seated. Why, she was practically in his lap. Diana and the duke were seated directly across from her and Alistair. It didn't take long for Alyssa to realize that Alistair was unhappy with the seating arrangements. He didn't seem to like Diana's betrothed. The man was friendly with a wonderful sense of humor. She couldn't imagine why Alistair wouldn't like him, although as the meal progressed, it became a little clearer. The duke directed his gaze at Alyssa far too often; it even made her uncomfortable. Alistair reached under the table, gripping her hand in his, squeezing a little too tightly every time the man's gaze fell upon her. That was how she noticed he was even looking at her in the first place; Alistair's reaction to it was somewhat painful. She decided to keep her head down as much as possible, silently lamenting that the evening couldn't be over soon enough. It was becoming most uncomfortable.

*****

"You whore!" Alistair shouted just before he slapped her across her face. Alyssa fell to the ground, but he quickly grabbed her up by the hair, slapping her again.

It had happened so suddenly. All the guests had gone, and he escorted her to her room. Instead of leaving her at the door as he usually did, he pressed his way in, dismissing her maid. He locked the door behind her and commenced his assault. Alyssa had no idea why he was attacking her in this fashion. She had done nothing wrong. She hadn't had time to plead for him to stop before he jerked her up off the floor, delivering yet another blow, this one nearly knocking her senseless. She tried to crawl away from him, but he grabbed her by her hair again to hold her in place.

"Where do you think you're going, whore?" he breathed harshly in her ear.

Just then, he grabbed the fabric of her gown at the back of her neck, ripping at it savagely, tearing it beyond all possibility of repair. He pulled her to her feet by her hair, spinning her around, then grabbed at the front of her gown, ripping it in the same manner. The gown, now reduced to shreds lay about the room. She stood before him, shivering, wide-eyed in absolute shock, wearing nothing but her undergarments to shelter her modesty. Sadly, she was not allowed this simple protection. He then began ripping away her stays and chemise until she stood before him in only her drawers and stockings. Ruthlessly, he shoved her onto her bed, throwing himself on top of her causing Alyssa to remain in stunned silence. He was so vicious she didn't even recognize him. She put up no resistance when he grabbed her hand, roughly removing her betrothal ring, then held it close to her face.

"How can I allow a whore to wear the Sinclair betrothal ring? Answer me that!" he snarled.

"Alistair, please, I have no idea what has provoked you to do this. Please, tell me what I have done wrong?" she whimpered after managing to find her voice.

"You don't think I saw you mooning over the duke? You don't think the whole party saw you?" he demanded.

"I swear I don't know what you mean."

"Don't you?"

"I did not do this thing, I swear," she said through tear-filled eyes.

Alistair was a monster! How could she not have seen it before? She was terrified and didn't know what to do to placate him. He grabbed her cheeks between his thumb and index finger, squeezing hard before he lunged for her lips. He thrust his tongue into her mouth, making her gag from the depth at which he had plunged it. She choked and coughed, struggling to free herself. He started to grope her about her breasts, then he grabbed her breast hard in his hand pinching her nipple until she cried out from the pain.

"This is how whores are treated. Do you like it?"

He didn't give her time to answer, plunging his tongue back into her mouth in a punishing kiss. He continued to squeeze and pinch her breasts while plundering her mouth. She was terrified to imagine what he would do next. He drew back from her mouth, staring hard into her eyes, the intensity of the moment bone-chilling with its promise. As Alyssa imagined, he was hardly finished with her when he dove down, grabbing her nipple into his mouth, sucking and nipping with his teeth like a frenzied madman. Before she could process what was happening, he ran his hand down to her waist where in one savage move he tore away her drawers, thrusting his knee between her legs to drive them apart, not caring he would no doubt be leaving marks as evidence of his abuse. Alyssa gasped loud when he rammed his finger inside her private place in a deep, probing manner, but when he met resistance there which caused her to wince in response, he slowly pulled his hand away.

"You had better be glad that you are still a virgin. If you weren't, I would have killed you," he snarled.

His words sent a chill through her blood. She

could tell by the look in his eyes that he meant what he had just said. She felt violated and was crying in earnest now.

"I swear to you that I have never been with a man, Alistair! Until you, I have never even been kissed," she pleaded through choking sobs.

"You are mine, do you hear? You belong to me. You can just forget about any fantasies you have imagined with the duke," he said harshly.

"I do not know what you mean. I have had no fantasies, I swear," she sobbed.

Alyssa could feel the swelling starting around her eye and lip. She would have terrible bruises. She could taste blood in her mouth from her split lip. Her jaw ached from his assault. She feared it might be broken. There was a loud humming in her ears, causing her to feel dizzy. Her whole body was trembling with fear.

"I saw the way you blushed and fluttered when he looked at you. I saw the way you kept looking at him, sizing up his body as though you were a starving slut," he gritted out between clenched teeth.

He began to undulate himself against her hips, pressing himself against her. She could feel the hard ridge of his arousal pressing into her flesh and knew he was about to take her against her will. She was scared, really scared. She needed to stop him before he took her virtue in violent anger.

"Please Alistair, I only want you. You are the only man that I love," she said in an attempt to calm him.

She realized now, she could never love him or

want him for that matter. She only wanted to survive this with her virtue intact. The best way to achieve that end was to calm his jealousy and figure out how to escape him later. He lunged forward, plundering her mouth again. With all the calm she could muster, she reached up, running her hand through his hair, lightly massaging his head. He pulled back from her to unfasten his breeches. Then he pulled out his shaft. He roughly grabbed her, forcing her to wrap her hand around it then started guiding her into a stroking motion. Not understanding what he was about she didn't resist him as he did this. Soon, the motion became more rapid causing his body to jerk and shudder. His body soon relaxed and a moan escaped him as something warm and wet filled her hand. She was relieved that this seemed to have settled him down. He collapsed atop her then but still kept her pinned underneath him. She could hear his ragged breathing as his mouth was pressed up against her neck. Then, he started to cry, wailing like a wounded child as he continued to lie atop her.

"Look what you made me do," he sobbed.

Alyssa was stunned by that accusation. *I didn't make him do anything. He did this all on his own. I have done nothing to provoke him. Nothing!*

"Shhh ...it's all right Alistair. I am repentant," she lied.

Alistair pulled back, looking at her. He took her face gently between his hands, kissing her tenderly on her lips and forehead.

"I love you so much, Alyssa. We shall have to move the wedding up to one week from today. I cannot wait to have you. We must marry soon or I shall go mad, I fear. The thought of you with another man is driving me insane. The only thing that will save me is for us to be married right away and go home to Jamaica," he cried.

"One week?" she asked.

He must truly be mad. I wouldn't marry him in a hundred years, much less one week. What to do? The thought horrified her.

"Yes, or sooner if I can arrange it," he said before kissing her tenderly on the lips again.

He rolled off of her then, drawing her into his arms so that she draped across his chest, and he held her tight.

"No other man can ever have you Alyssa. You belong to me now. I will not be made to wait much longer to claim my bride," he vowed.

Alyssa wiped her hands on the bedding to remove the wet sticky substance from her hand. He didn't seem to notice as he continued to hold her close.

"We shall have a wonderful life Alyssa. I swear, once we are married things will be better. I have never behaved this way before. I know it's because the idea of losing you to another is making me irrational with jealousy. I would die before I would hurt you again, I swear. Please say that you believe me."

Is he jesting?

"Of course, I believe you Alistair. You are good and kind. I know that you love me," she cooed as though soothing an injured child.

"Good lass, my sweet Alyssa," he said, nuzzling his face into her hair.

They lay this way for what seemed an eternity until she realized he had fallen asleep. She was relieved; she wanted away from him but dare not move for fear of waking him, so she lay there quietly, waiting for his sleep to deepen. How could this have happened? She couldn't believe the turn things had taken. She would be jumping from the pan into the fire if she married this madman. She couldn't do it, no matter what he said. If he were behaving this way now, it would only be worse once they were married, and he had complete control.

This must be some kind of sick, twisted obsession he had for her, not love. If you love someone, you are not cruel to them. What he had done tonight was the most cruelty she had ever experienced at the hands of another. Even her Uncle Morley and Aunt Esmeralda had never beaten her like that. She had to find a way to escape, but how? Whatever she did, it would have to be soon. He said a week, maybe less, if he could arrange it. She had to come up with something fast. She had no access to her money. No jewels in which to pawn or sell. She was at the mercy of her relatives who were merciless people.

She sighed deeply, contemplating her dilemma. If she ran away without money, there would be no end to the horrors that could befall her. She must figure out a way to get funds and escape England where he could never find her. Perhaps she could go to the American colonies. She could be lost in such a place quite easily, so that Alistair and her family wouldn't ever find her. But she had to have money to book passage and to survive on until she could gain employment somehow. She couldn't sell her betrothal ring as he had taken it back. Even if he gave it to her again, it would be impossible to sell it as it was a family heirloom, probably entailed. She could possibly be hanged for that if she were caught. No, she had to come up with something else.

She remembered Cookie's words to her then. 'If you ever want to escape, I can help you, but you have to be desperate because the price is high,' she was sure that the situation was now desperate if not life-threatening. Tomorrow, she would go to Cookie begging for help. Whatever the price, she would pay it. She had to, otherwise she could be killed by this madman that would call himself her husband.

*****

Alistair woke up in the middle of the night confused about his surroundings. He remembered then, what he had done and where he was. He looked over and saw that Alyssa was sleeping beside him. He sat up, reaching for the candle on the nightstand and struck a flint stick to light it. He held the candle close to her face and saw the evidence of his rage, the sight causing tears to slide down his cheek. What had he done? Why had he done it? He reflected back over the evening, realizing that his beloved had been quite innocent. She had done her best to avoid the duke's attentions. She didn't converse with him at all, keeping her head down throughout most of the dinner. He shuddered at his behavior as he wiped away his tears. It had been the duke's fault. He was looking at his beloved with a predatory hunger. He wanted her for himself. The thought had been too much and driven Alistair to abuse his beautiful Alyssa.

Tears streamed down his face anew from his shame. He swore he would never hurt her, but he had. Her lip was split. Her eye and jaw were bruised and swollen. *What must she think of me now? She probably hates me.* He knew he must make it up to her. *I will treat her like a queen from here on out. I will give her everything her heart desires. She will learn to love me again. Oh my precious Alyssa, please forgive me,* he inwardly pleaded. He leaned over, kissing her tenderly on the forehead, then slid out of the bed. She wouldn't want to see him in the morning, he was sure of it. He would give her a day to recover before he pressed his attentions on her. He loved her so much that if he didn't marry her soon, he feared he would explode, likely killing her in the process. He shivered at the thought, he couldn't allow that to happen. He would have to see what could be done to move up the ceremony. His mother wouldn't like it, but she could go to hell. No one was going to stop him from possessing his sweet Alyssa.

Chapter Five

Alyssa woke with the dawn to find, much to her relief that she was alone. Alistair had gotten up and left her some time during the night. She didn't care as long as he was gone, and she didn't have to face him. She hadn't meant to fall asleep, but she was overcome with exhaustion from her ordeal. She needed to get dressed so she could go speak to Cookie. She wanted to escape this place today if at all possible. Bea wouldn't arrive for another hour, so she had time to speak with Cookie before she was expected to be up and about. She slid out of bed, gingerly standing and swaying for a moment before getting her strength. She was still woozy from the blows that Alistair had dealt her. Her jaw ached terribly, but she could move it fine, so she didn't think it was broken.

She walked over to the mirror to have a look at herself. The bruising around the eye wasn't as bad as she had imagined, but it was puffy. It would probably look worse as it healed. Her bottom lip wasn't as bad as she had imagined either, it wasn't even bruised, just split and swollen. She turned away from her image to go to her wardrobe where she halfheartedly chose a day gown of pastel yellow muslin. She donned it without her stays as she didn't plan on wearing the gown long. There was no one to help her with it, regardless. The gown she selected buttoned up the front so she could manage it on her own. She put on her slippers then went back to her vanity where she brushed out her hair, quickly rolling it in a simple knot. She stood taking a few steadying breaths before going to the door, cracking it open so she could listen for activity in the hall. She heard nothing, so she silently padded to the servants' staircase, making her way to the kitchen to see her friend. When she reached the kitchen, Cookie looked up at her and gasped, dropping the platter of bacon she had just finished cooking. She rushed over to Alyssa and grabbed her by the arms, hugging her fiercely.

"What has happened to you, my girl?" she asked, surveying the injuries.

"Alistair went into a rage last night after the party. He accused me of flirting with the Duke of Windhaven, Diana's betrothed. I swear I did nothing of the kind, but he couldn't be reasoned with. Oh, it was so horrible. He called me a whore and ripped my gown off and did things he shouldn't have," she relayed to her.

"Did he … take your innocence, child?" she asked with a worried look in her eyes.

Alyssa shook her head indicating that he had not. Cookie breathed a sigh of relief as she ushered her to sit down at the table. She poured her a cup of tea and handed it over. Alyssa sipped, wincing when it stung her lip.

"What are you going to do?" Cookie asked her.

"I have to leave here. I cannot marry that monster. He is a madman. I fear he will kill me in one of his jealous fits. You said that you could help me if I wanted to leave. I want to, and I'm desperate too, Cookie. Please, you must help me. I must leave today. He said he was going to move the wedding up to next week or sooner if he could arrange it, so I must leave here this day and not a moment sooner," Alyssa said in a rush.

Cookie listened, nodding her head.

"Tis true, I have a way for you to leave, but you may not like what I have to say," she cautiously ventured.

"Please, I will do anything. I must escape this place and him. I can trust no one to help me but you. The family will support Alistair. I will have no choice but to marry him if I stay. Then he will take me to Jamaica, where I will surely die at his mercy."

"I told you that my sister owned a brothel. Well, you have a precious commodity that is worth thousands of pounds in an auction," she told her.

"What commodity?"

Cookie looked down at her lap for a moment then returned her gaze to Alyssa. Taking her hands in hers, she softly said, "Your virginity."

"I'm not sure what you mean. How could I auction my virginity?"

"Annabelle would send out invitations to select clients who have a penchant for young virgins. She would make them bid for the right to deflower you. You would get most of the money. She would only keep a fee for assisting you. Selling one's virginity is done all the time with women in your circumstances. Many wealthy lords would pay thousands of pounds for such a beautiful virgin as you," she explained.

Alyssa thought about this. *Could I really sell my body to a stranger*? It didn't take long to decide she could, considering what was at stake. If she got enough money, she could book passage to America, disappearing until she turned five and twenty when she could shake off her uncle's yoke and claim her inheritance. If she sold her virginity, it was almost a certainty she would never be able to marry. No man would have a soiled wife. Then again, after seeing how Alistair behaved, she thought maybe she didn't want to ever be married. There was no need, really. She would have her inheritance. She could live her life as she chose. She could do this. She had to if she were to survive. She needed to do it quickly, but she was badly battered. Who would pay thousands of pounds for one such as her? She would need time to heal before she could do this, and she didn't have that kind of time.

"Look at me, Cookie. Who would want me, looking like this?" she asked.

"Tis a problem to be true, but I can speak with Annabelle. She could hide you until you are well then have the auction. She would do it for me, if I asked."

"I must leave today, I cannot wait," Alyssa insisted.

"Aye, we must remove you as quickly as possible, but it cannot be done until tonight, lest we draw suspicions. Tonight, after everyone goes to bed, meet me in my room. We will have Adam take us to Annabelle's. He won't tell anyone what we've done. He's a good soul and can be trusted."
She was referring to Adam the old stable master whom she had been having an affair with for the last ten years. Adam loved her. He would marry her today if she would agree to it. Cookie had told her

she didn't see a need to marry; she was too old to have children. Things were good as they were between them, and she saw no need to change it. Adam was devoted to her. He would do anything she asked of him. Alyssa was sure they could trust him. Alyssa was relieved that she had a way out. She could bear one more day here, knowing that tonight she would leave forever. She would just stay in her room today, taking all her meals in there. Then tonight she would escape. They wouldn't know she had gone until tomorrow. She would leave a note saying she had gone to Wales to stay with her old aunt, so they wouldn't think to look for her in London. It was a good plan. Her spirits were lifted, but she knew she had better return to her room before Bea came to attend her.

"I must get back to my room, Cookie. I will stay there all day. Then, when the household is asleep, I will come to you. You will go with me won't you?"

"Of course, love. I wouldn't send you off alone. I will see you safely settled before I leave."

The two women stood hugging one another. Then, Alyssa scurried back to the servants' stairs, slipping back into her room. She quickly disrobed and put on a nightgown, then crawled into the bed to pretend to be sleeping. She would escape tonight! The thought filled her with trepidation, but hope nonetheless.

*****

"I will be staying in my room today Bea. Just have

all my meals brought to me here. As you can see, I'm not feeling well, and I don't wish to see anyone," she informed her gaping maid.

"As you will, my lady, would you like for me to draw you a bath?" Bea asked her.

"No, I will return to bed after I have broken my fast."

"Very good my lady, have you any messages for Lord Keith?"

"No."

Alyssa thought that was a strange question. She wondered if perhaps Alistair had asked her to inquire. That was probably the case. It was good to know that Bea was his spy because she could turn her over to Alistair if she were to discover her plans. It was best to be safe and make no mention of anything to Bea. The maid stood there expectantly. Alyssa realized she had been too abrupt in her answer, so she said, "That is, send him my regards, of course."

Bea drew her eyebrows together as if trying to decipher her true meaning but quickly recovered and accepted the message. She tidied up the room a bit more then took her leave. Alyssa let out a long breath of tension. Tonight couldn't come soon enough. Alyssa sat at her vanity looking over her wounds, thinking about her plan. She would need to pack a small portmanteau, of course. What would one need for such an enterprise? Certainly she would need a gown that would display her attributes to their full advantage. A smile crossed her face; the emerald green gown, of course. How fitting, almost poetic in its irony. If the gown had drawn such a response from Alistair, then it would surely stir up the men at an auction. Yes, it was just the gown for such a thing. As luck would have it, she still had the gown. She had meant to return it but had not done it yet, she had simply been too busy. It would be perfect. Of course, she would pack two of her more practical gowns and some undergarments. She would have to make do with one pair of slippers that would go with everything.

After awhile she began to think about the mystery man that would take her innocence. She hoped that it was a handsome man, but feared it would probably be an old lecher instead. She hoped he was kind and not violent like Alistair. If she were to have to endure such behavior and lose her virginity too, it would be a living nightmare. She didn't know how she could endure such a thing. She was grateful that Alistair had fallen asleep last night and not taken her then and there. Where would she be now if he had? No, it was truly miraculous he had left her intact. She silently thanked her lucky stars.

She shuddered when she imagined his reaction to her running away. If he ever found her, he would surely kill her. She rubbed her arms from a sudden chill. She got up from her vanity and climbed into bed, pulling the covers up to her chin in an attempt to get warm, but it was a deep chill, one that couldn't be warmed. She regretted that Alistair had turned out to be such a madman. He had been so handsome and it had felt wonderful to have an ally in the house. Was what he said really true? That he had never before behaved in such a way? If so, then what had caused it now? Reflecting over their brief courtship to see where it had all started to go wrong, she determined that it must have been the shopping trip where it had begun. She remembered how he had gripped her arm tight when men passing by tipped their hat in her direction. Then he was pushed to boiling over the gown. Still, if he had acted so severely then, he had to have had symptoms of his madness before.

She wondered if he had ever kept mistresses, if so, how he must treat them. Was he rough and violent with them as well? She wondered if perhaps he was this way with her because his feelings were involved. Men didn't have feelings for their mistresses, did they? She didn't know. She was glad she would never have to learn more about his behavior with mistresses or otherwise. She closed her eyes, drifting off to sleep.

She hadn't been asleep long when there was a knock at her door. She jumped up to put her wrap on before answering, fearing that it would be Alistair. She pressed an ear and listened, but she heard nothing, so she timidly asked, "Who's there?"

"Diana," an unwelcome voice answered.

Wonderful! What could she possibly want? She sighed deeply to gather her strength and opened the door. Diana didn't wait to be invited in; instead she pushed past Alyssa, marching to the center of the room then spinning toward her. She didn't look very happy at all, Alyssa observed.

"What do you want Diana? I was resting."

"Yes, I see that you need the rest. You look like shite," Diana gloated. "I suppose my brother taught you a lesson for your wanton behavior last night," she added.

Alyssa stood where she was with her hand on the open doorknob, just staring at her incredulously. How dare this vixen come into her room and treat her in such a way.

"Cat got your sluts tongue?" Diana demanded.

"Get out of my room this instant. I will not stand here and be insulted by you," Alyssa shouted.

The two women stood glaring at each other for a moment before Diana broke the silence.

"I came to warn you to stay away from Gabriel. He is mine. If you dare think to have him, I will cut your tongue out," she snarled.

"I have no interest in the duke. You and your brother have fabricated this madness in your own minds. I want none of it, do you hear me?"

The door across the hall opened. Alistair stood half dressed and disheveled, with anger in his eyes. He walked into her room, going directly to his sister. "Get out!" he shouted at her.

"You just make sure that whore of yours stays away from fiancé, or I shall have her roving little eyes preserved in a jar and placed upon my nightstand," Diana snarled with a heaving chest.

Alistair grabbed his sister in a vicious hold on her arms and shook her violently.

"I will not have you speak about my beloved in such a way. She did nothing wrong. It was that rake-hell of yours, the duke, who is at fault. If I were you dear sister, I would have him gelded before he makes you a complete laughing stock among the ton. I can promise you this; if he ever looks at Alyssa again, he is a dead man."

Alistair dragged her over to the door and shoved her into the hall, slamming the door behind her. He turned to Alyssa, who was still standing in the same place in shock. He dropped to his knees in front of her, hugging her around her bottom. He seemed to be trembling as he drew her close, burying his face intimately against her person.

"Please forgive me, Alyssa. We shall be married right away and leave this place. I will never let anyone hurt you again. If I ever hurt you again, I will gouge my own heart out with my bare hands. Please say that you forgive me," he cried, hugging her.

Alyssa was stunned into silence. This was the Alistair she had begun to care for. *He truly does feel bad about what he did to me. Maybe ...* NO! She decided, she wouldn't be fooled by this. This was just another indication of the man's unstable nature. He was volatile and dangerous.

She ran her hand through his hair and massaged his head. "I forgive you Alistair. Tis forgotten too," she lied.

He held on even tighter than he had before, wailing like an infant while mumbling words of contrition. She couldn't make most of them out, but she did hear him say many times that he was sorry. *Yes he is sorry. Sorry indeed!* She continued to rub his head while he cried. After several moments, he wiped his face with her nightgown and stood up. His eyes were swollen and bloodshot from the tears of anguish he had displayed. She could tell he genuinely felt bad, but it wasn't enough. He could never make up for what he had done. Never! He gently placed a hand on both of her cheeks giving her a tender kiss upon the lips. He kissed her swollen eye and then her forehead.

"I love you, my sweet Alyssa. If I live to be a thousand years old, I will never deserve you. Thank you for your forgiveness. I will cherish it always and never again abuse your trust," he said with tenderness in his eyes.

Alyssa said nothing to this. She just stood and allowed him to kiss her wounds and hug her again.

"I want you to stay in bed and rest for the next two days, then we shall be married. I want you to be refreshed for our wedding day. Oh, sweetheart it will be wonderful. I will give you everything and you will have made me the happiest man in the world," he crooned.

Alyssa smiled at him and said, "Yes I do believe that I need the rest, Alistair. I have been quite dizzy this morning, and I would like to have plenty of time to heal so that I will look my best for our special day," she told him.

Alyssa realized that it wasn't hard to lie to Alistair. He seemed easily appeased. All she had to do was stroke his ego a little by telling him what he wanted to hear then he was like clay in her hands. Poor Alistair! He really was a tragic soul. She hoped that someday he could find happiness. It just wouldn't be with her.

*****

"We must hurry Alyssa. Adam is waiting for us out in the stables. We can go through the kitchen door.

No one will hear us depart. Do you have everything you need?"

"Yes, I have packed as prudently as I could, taking into consideration that I would only have one bag. I have two practical gowns, one for the auction and what I'm wearing of course," she told her.

"That should hold you over until the auction. Let us be on our way then, shall we?"

Alyssa drew in a deep reassuring breath and nodded her head. She was ready.

"I sent word ahead to Annabelle, telling her what to expect. Are you sure you can go through with this?"

"Yes, I'm sure. I have decided that I shall never marry, so my virginity is moot. If I can use the funds that I will gain to have a better life, then I shall do it gladly," Alyssa declared with conviction.

Cookie gave her a sad smile, "I'm going to miss you so much, my love. Perhaps when you gain your inheritance you can send for me so I can come to cook for you."

"Oh Cookie, I would love that. We shall see each other again, of course we will, you are family to me. You have been the only person to care for me since my father died. I could never forget you."

Alyssa meant that. She would miss her good friend with all her heart. She wished she could make enough to support them both at this auction but that was an impractical dream. They would be together again someday, she would see to it. They made their way to the stables. As expected, Adam was waiting in the unmarked carriage. She was glad he had chosen that one. She wouldn't want anyone to be able to trace her through the family crest emblazoned on the other carriage. Adam loaded them up, sending them on their way in record time. The tension was thick as he progressed slowly through the darkened road until he was a goodly distance away from the house. She realized she was holding her breath and let it out. Cookie grabbed her hand, squeezing it reassuringly as they rode hand in hand the rest of the way. It didn't take them long to cross town at this time of night. There was no traffic, allowing them to whiz right along the rest of the way.

"I have instructed Adam to go in through the back," Cookie told her.

Alyssa's stomach clenched as they turned down the street that would lead them to the brothel. She would be living in a brothel! She inwardly chuckled at the absurdity of it. She would have never pictured herself in such a scenario before today, yet here she was racing toward it.

"Oh my God," Cookie exclaimed.

"What is it?" Alyssa asked in alarm.

"It's Lord Keith. Get down," Cookie said, shoving her down on the seat.

Alyssa was shocked to hear that he was out in such a part of town. What was he doing?

"Where do you think he was going to?"

"He was going into a brothel. Not Annabelle's. I checked with her, he has never visited her establishment," she quickly assured her.

That was a relief. It would be horrific to bump into him at the auction. So Alistair had his little secrets does he? Well she didn't care. She was free of him now. Let him visit brothels and mistresses. It was none of her affair.

"Can I come up now?" she asked. Her neck had started to stiffen from the awkward angle she was laying.

"Of course, he is already inside now and won't see you. He didn't even look our way. What a blaggard! Betrothed to you and visiting a whorehouse," Cookie said indignantly.

"I assure you that I don't care in the least what he does. I am free of him now," Alyssa said with a nervous chuckle.

"That you are my dear; that you are."

Moments later Adam pulled the carriage into an alley. They crept along for a bit before the carriage came to a stop. Alyssa's heart fell in her stomach when she realized they had stopped. This was it! Her future awaited her at this very spot. She shivered at the thought of what lay beyond the door. Adam opened the carriage door assisting them out of the carriage before retrieving her portmanteau. After he ushered them to the door, Cookie knocked. A moment later the door opened. There they were whisked inside to be taken up a back staircase where they were led down a long hall and taken to a bedroom. Presumably this was to be her room during her stay here. They sat quietly waiting after they were unceremoniously deposited there by the footman. He had not said a word to them as he directed them here. Strange! Well, she wouldn't have liked an introduction anyway. It was best if no one knew who she was.

Moments later, the door opened and Annabelle

came into the room. She knew it was Annabelle because the two sisters flew into each other's arms, hugging one another. They kissed each other, crying as they held each other in absolute jubilation. After they had their cry, Cookie introduced her to Annabelle. Annabelle was a very handsome woman, she looked very much like Cookie. She could get a clear picture of what Cookie might look like if she were to take more care in her appearance.

"We are twins," Annabelle announced. Apparently she had noticed the line of Alyssa's thinking.

"I thought you two looked an awful lot alike. Cookie, you never told me she was your twin sister,"

"Oh? I felt sure I'd mentioned it before," Cookie replied with a smile at her sister.

"So this is your darling girl? Don't worry love; I shall take good care of her. She will never fall into that monster's hands again. Just look what he has done to her beautiful face. Don't worry dear girl, you will heal up nicely in less than a week," Annabelle said, inspecting her. "You will bring in a very fat purse, my pretty. Ah, to be young again," she added with a sigh.

Alyssa was glad to hear she would heal up quickly. She didn't want to stay in England any longer than she had to.

"You said she was beautiful, but you didn't tell me she was a living doll, dear sister," Annabelle admonished.

"She is beautiful. I wish she didn't have to do this. But those monsters that call themselves her family have forced her to it. They wouldn't help her if she begged or pleaded. She is an heiress, you know. Her uncle has kept her living as a servant since she was a child. Can you imagine? We thought that Lord Keith was the answer to her prayers, but he turned out to be the worst villain of them all," Cookie said with a tear sliding down her face.

"We'll make sure only the crème of the crop is invited to bid. No old men for this one. We will make it as pleasant as possible. Who knows? Maybe the gentleman will offer to keep her as a mistress," Annabelle suggested.

"Oh no, I want to go to America. I need to leave England so they never find me. I can't risk staying behind in London as a mistress. It would be suicide," Alyssa said in a panic.

"Aye tis true, I forgot myself for a moment. Well, you shall earn enough to get you there and then some," Annabelle assured her.

"Can you help me buy passage on a ship once the auction is over? I don't think it would be wise for me to risk doing it myself. They will be looking for me. I will have to use a fake name and a disguise."

"Oh yes, we can take care of that. Don't you worry about those details now my love; you let Annabelle take care of you," Annabelle said patting her on the shoulder.

"I should go now before they discover we are gone," Cookie interrupted.

"Yes of course. I can't thank you enough, Cookie. I will remember you always," Alyssa said, throwing her arms around her friend.

"You will write to me as soon as you are settled in America. Use your fake name of course; I will know it's you. I don't know anyone else in America," Cookie said with tears in her eyes.

The two women embraced. Cookie reluctantly withdrew. Adam held out his arm, and she took it as he led her away. Alyssa sobbed at the loss.

"There, there dear. You will see her again. Don't fret," Annabelle consoled.

"She has been my only family since I was three and ten. The only person who loved or cared for me. I wish I could take her with me."

"My sister is a wonderful woman. She saw something special in you. I see it, too. I shall take care of you now and protect you from that blaggard as well as your family," she assured her. "We need to come up with a name for you. Have you anything in mind?" she quickly added.

"Nothing comes to mind just now, what would you suggest?" Alyssa said with a sniffle.

Annabelle studied her for a moment, then said, "Cookie's real name is Audrey. How would that suit you? You could be Audrey Flowers. Yes, I like that; you shall be Miss Audrey Flowers,"

"Oh, I love it, thank you so much."

Alyssa was to be known as Audrey Flowers now. It was a fine name. She would carry it with her to America, into her new life.

Chapter Six

Gabriel was bored with his mistress; sick and tired of her, in fact. He rolled off of her, shoved away from her, sitting up on the side of the bed. He looked back at her, saying, "We are done here; I no longer have an interest in you."

"Oh come back to bed, you say that at least once a week," Melody told him.

"I mean it this time. There is nothing there between us anymore."

"Hawk, how can you say such a thing after what we have just done? Surely, I wasn't mistaken when you cried out your passion for me not three minutes ago," she said, sitting up in the bed.

Ignoring her comment, he got up, walking bare arsed naked to the window to look out at the street below. London was calling him, and he had a desire to answer. He wanted to go to his club to carouse around with his mates. He didn't want to be stifled here with her. She had become too demanding. He suspected she was angling for marriage. He laughed inwardly at the thought. They all angled for marriage to the duke. Yes, his title was too tempting to ignore. His mistresses could never just be happy to have him in their beds. No, they always wanted marriage. He wasn't about to marry anyone, least of all his mistress. Besides, he already had a fiancé that he needed to figure out a way to be rid of. There had to be a way to wriggle out of his betrothal to that virago, Diana.

Their fathers had arranged their betrothal when she was born; he had been just a lad of six years old at the time. He was eight and twenty now and was no closer to wanting to be leg-shackled than he had ever been. His father was dead now, so he didn't particularly care if he honored the arrangement. But Diana and her father were crafty devils. They would surely try to ruin him if he broke it off. There had to be some way out. He was determined to find it. He couldn't imagine his life with her as his wife. She was a horrible creature. Oh sure, she was beautiful, but that wasn't enough to make up for her ugly nature.

He cast off his dark thoughts as he walked away from the window. He went over to the sideboard to set about cleaning himself up. He wanted to wash away all traces of Melody before he left so he would be prepared for whatever the night might have to offer. He wouldn't miss Melody, he decided. Oh sure, she was great in bed, always adventurous just as he liked, but he was ready to move on. She just didn't excite him anymore. Once the lovemaking was over she always started to nag. It was hard to muster up enthusiasm when one knew the real price one had to pay the piper.

He cleaned himself up, donning his clothing without speaking further to her. Once done, he walked to the door, turning to look back at her. She was beautiful, he would give her that. She wouldn't have trouble finding a new protector. She was blonde and luscious, had arresting violet eyes and full pouting lips made for kissing and other many other wonderful things. Yes, she would do fine without him.

"You can keep the house. I will send my man

around tomorrow with the deed and a few thousand pounds to set you up for awhile until you find a new protector. Goodbye Melody, it's been fun, love," he said. He cast a devastating smile and left. He was free!

Gabriel Hawkins, or as his friends called him, Hawk, was a self-professed rake-hell of the first order. He knew what he was and didn't try to pretend otherwise. He loved the ladies and the ladies loved him. He had a great sexual appetite to go along with his more than ample manly endowments. He was a big man; able to give women great pleasure with his impressive size and skill. His friends envied him for his gift, but honestly, sometimes it was a burden. Word had spread around years ago about the size of his manhood. His endurance was legendary. Everywhere he went, ladies fawned all over him. It wasn't uncommon for him to be pulled away into a garden or a linen closet to pleasure some unhappy wife or wanton widow at dinner parties or balls.

He had been known to keep two or three mistresses at a time. He was well able to handle them all with enough energy to spare for the unhappily married ladies, or even the occasional whore. He was gifted, he knew this. In fact, he reveled in it. It wasn't uncommon for him to bed three or four different women in the course of a day. At times, all at once; it was just who he was. Why should he be ashamed of it? He wasn't married, after all, and he was a duke. Who would gainsay him?

One of the things ladies loved about him most

was his personality. He was a playful man in bed, always making it fun for the ladies. He enjoyed laughter and silliness during sex play; it always spiced it up nicely. Life was too short to be down in the mouth all the time. No, he embraced life with gusto, spreading cheer, wherever he went. Of course, they loved his body, too. He kept physically fit with rigorous exorcise, fencing, riding and bare-knuckle boxing at his favorite pugilist club, The Macintosh Slam. He was an active man, he was very healthy, too. That was well reflected in his stamina. He didn't waste time lying abed, sleeping until noon, like many of his peers. If he didn't make it home before dawn, he would go ahead and stay up. He always woke with the dawn.

Gabriel loved the mornings, when every day without fail, he took his gray Arabian stallion, Chester, for a ride in the park; he loved Chester. He bought him from a gypsy four years ago at a fair because he had seen him performing such tricks that he had fallen instantly in love. The gypsy didn't want to part with him, of course, but Gabriel had offered him a thousand pounds there on the spot. The gypsy was no fool, grudgingly selling Chester to him. Of course, his name hadn't been Chester then; it was something completely ridiculous that he couldn't even pronounce. Chester was ten years old now but still loved to perform. That was another thing the ladies loved. Chester knew how to court the fair sex, aiding him into many a lady's bed. He smiled at the thought. He returned the favor to Chester every chance he could by studding him out to friends here and there. Chester was in nearly as high demand by the ladies as Gabriel was. They really made quite a pair.

"There you are my fine handsome lad. Come Chester, let us leave this place and go see what the night has to offer, shall we?" he crooned to his horse.

He lovingly stroked his face, nuzzling his head with his own. Chester stamped his foot, snorted and bobbed his head in agreement. Yes, Chester was his best friend. He loved him dearly. With one last stroke of his face, he mounted up. Together they went into the London night heading over to Whites. His friends would be there, and they would be well into their cups by now. No doubt, the card games would be in full swing. He wondered how much Luther had already lost. Jasper had probably cleaned him out hours ago. Perhaps Dylan was watching out for ole Luther keeping Jas in check.

*****

"Ah, Hawk, you're just in time. We were about to leave this hole to go to Annabelle's for the auction. Dylan here has been invited to bid on a sweet piece named Audrey Flowers. We thought we would tag along to see how he fairs. We want to see if he gets the honor of deflowering the Flowers, pardon the really bad pun," Jasper said with his usual wicked grin. "Maybe while we're there we can take in some cards and wenches ourselves. Care to come along?" he added.

Jasper Townley, the Earl of Pembrook, was a

mischievous fellow of sorts, always up for some sport or a prank. He had golden brown hair with streaks of blond. His hazel eyes seemed always to be laughing at you. He was highly intelligent, most of the time and had a knack for inventions. He was always tinkering around with his gadgets, swearing that every one of them would be the answer to mankind's problems.

"Another virgin, Dylan?" Gabriel asked with a grin.

Dylan was Gabriel's favorite among the group of friends. He loved him dearly. The two men would do anything for one another, but he didn't like the recent changes in him with regard to females.

"Are there any left in London that you haven't already plundered?" he prodded further.

"Yes, my friend. You might want to start doing the same before your legendary cock turns black and rots off from all the indiscriminate rutting about that you inflict upon it. It's the only way to remain safe, my good man," Dylan Crenshaw, the Earl of Sumersleigh told him with an air of authority.

Dylan's older brother had died two years ago from the pox. With him, Dylan's sense of humor. It had been a life changing event for him. He told his friends that his brother's death caused him to examine his own behavior with the ladies. He changed his way of thinking as a result. He determined he would only have virgins in his bed from that day forward to avoid the same fate as his unfortunate sibling. He always said one could never be too careful in these times. He was still unmarried and planning to remain so for a good number of years, yet.

"Are you sure you don't have a fetish for young virgins to cover up your lack of skills?" Luther Rollins, the Marquess of Huntley verbally jabbed at him.

Luther was a happy-go-lucky, overgrown bloke with reddish blond hair that always looked as though he just crawled out of bed. His head was full of long unruly ringlets that went every which way. Boyish dimples accentuated his big green eyes. Though he was the tallest of them all, he looked much younger than he was. He wasn't the sharpest knife in the drawer, but he made up for his shortcomings through honesty and integrity. There was no better man to have at your back than Luther; he was huge, loyal and truly fearless.

"Put a cork in it, you bloody sod," Dylan jabbed back, accompanied by a swift kick under the table to Luther's shin.

"OUCH! Why did you kick me you, you … blasted bugger," Luther shouted.

"Come now, gentlemen this is no way to act. Luther, let Dylan have his pleasures, and we shall have ours. Dylan, it is way too early in the evening to kill anyone, so behave. I'm sure that Luther will be available later for a good pummeling. We don't want the wenches to see us all banged up yet," Jasper said in a voice of reason where reason rarely prevailed, to prevent another fracas between his companions.

When all four gentlemen were together and drink was involved, it wasn't uncommon for them to end the night, black and blue from their many skirmishes with one another. They loved each other like brothers, but they were all virile men with plenty of aggression to expel, often working it off on each other's skull. The four men became the best of friends while at Eton where they had formed their little club to protect one another from the older boys. They were pranksters for the most part as there wasn't a mean bone between the four of them. They were just fun-loving guys who never really hurt anyone in their escapades. Singularly, they had all been victimized by bullies, but together they were an unstoppable force. Many a rapscallion learned the hard and often embarrassing consequences of picking on a member of their ranks.

The first time they had teamed up was when Luther was badly beaten by a young marquess. He had been much smaller then; one would have never dreamed he would have grown into the mammoth that he was today. The four shared a room. When they saw his condition they formulated a plan of retaliation. It was a good plan, instantly becoming the stuff of legend. They took the young scamp and tied him naked to a post in the luncheon hall. He wasn't completely naked; no, he was covered with writing done in shoe polish. The boys wrote 'ninny' across his bum and on his back they wrote 'polish your knob for a shilling'.

Needless to say that the bully became the victim of his own brand of ruthlessness, ultimately leaving school in shame. The poor lad just couldn't seem to get beyond it. He was mercilessly teased and harassed by the other students who would hurl shillings at him as they offered up their knobs to be polished.

"To Annabelle's, eh?" Gabriel asked. "Why not," he said smiling at his friends. The night was still young. Annabelle always had lovely wenches, clean ones too.

"Then it's all settled. Shall we, gentlemen?" Jasper asked, standing up and tossing back his scotch whiskey.

*****

Alyssa was nervous, but resigned. She didn't really regret her decision to auction off her virginity … yet. She only hoped that it would be a fairly pleasant experience since it was likely to be the one and only time she would lay with a man. The most humiliating part thus far was the doctor's examination to verify her virginity for the certificate of authenticity. Annabelle said that when so much money was at stake the gentlemen would want a guarantee she was indeed a virgin. The worst part of this situation she now found herself in was that she really had wanted to marry one day and have children. Instead, she would become a spinster, living her life alone. What man would want damaged goods for a wife? Even if she could find a husband, how would she explain the loss of her virginity? She didn't think too many men would appreciate knowing that their prospective bride had auctioned away her virginity in a brothel at the tender age of eight and ten. No, she would likely never marry.

Annabelle assured her that only the crème of the crop with very deep pockets had been invited to attend, many of which were renowned lovers. There were no married men or old lecherous louts like she had feared there might be. For that, she was grateful. There were to be ten men in all competing for her virginity. The bidding would start at one thousand pounds. Annabelle told her it was possible she could fetch a king's ransom with her beauty. She had healed up quite nicely with barely a sign that she had been abused. Her eye was back to normal. Her lip was mostly healed with barely a scratch to hint at a previous injury and that was covered with lip color.

It had been six days since she fled her uncle's house. Word from Cookie had been sent to her saying that Alistair went into a tirade, nearly destroying the house looking for her. She said too, he hired three Bow Street runners to find her. She hoped her note, saying she went to Wales, would keep them off her trail long enough for her to escape. Poor Alistair! She did feel sorry for him in a way. He had such great potential before he let his obsession for her carry him away. It was an obsession, she realized. He couldn't possibly have loved her in so short a duration. He had decided he would have her. That was that, then he let his passions rule his reason. It was rather sad, actually. Perhaps he would give up looking for her after a week or two and start to participate in the remainder of the season to find himself a nice woman he could be happy with. She wished him well, harboring no ill feelings for him. He had been too kind to her in the beginning for her to believe he was irredeemable. She simply refused to believe he was a lost cause.

"Are you ready, child?" Annabelle's knock at the door broke into her reverie.

She jumped in response and quickly went over, opening the door to let her in.

"As ready as I'll ever be. How do I look?" Alyssa asked nervously.

"Aphrodite couldn't hold a candle to you."

Alyssa didn't know about that, but she appreciated the compliment.

"Do you remember everything I told you?" she asked.

"Most of it; I'm just nervous."

"Of course you are dear. But I can assure you that I have picked the very best clients, so it should be a pleasant experience for you. Just make up your mind to enjoy it sweetheart and you will. Lovemaking can be very pleasant after the initial penetration. Once that is done, if you relax you will enjoy it," Annabelle assured her.

Alyssa hoped she would. She hoped she could actually go through with it, too. But she wouldn't tell Annabelle that. It would be too tempting to take the money and run, but her conscience really wouldn't allow that. She was only as good as her word, and a deal was a deal.

"I don't really want to be introduced around to the gentlemen, though. I would rather just go to the platform and let them all view me at once. That way I don't dwell on any one individual. I don't know why, but it seems too personal if I go around greeting them first," Alyssa said frowning.

She hadn't liked the idea of that since Annabelle told her how it was done. She told her that the men would like to get to know her first to see if she was worth bidding on.

Annabelle looked thoughtful but said, "The bid could suffer from it and you want to make as much as you can, so I don't see a way around it, but it's up to you."

"I think I should like to remain mysterious, perhaps it will actually drive the bid up," Alyssa said smiling.

"You might have something there. We shall see won't we," Annabelle winked.

"Yes let us see what happens, shall we? It should prove interesting," Alyssa concurred.

*****

"Aye, she's a beauty, Dylan, but do you think she's really worth the coin?" Luther asked as they looked at the woman on the platform.

She was petite in height, but well rounded in all the right places, with auburn hair. Her big blue-green eyes offset her come-hither lips.

"A Pocket Venus," Dylan breathed in awe.

"Aye!" he agreed. "That she is! Look at her bosom; it's about to fall out of that gown," Luther said. He was staring at the woman as if by doing so he could will her breasts to actually fall out of the gown.

That gained the notice of Gabriel who had been

ordering a round of drinks for him and his friends. He looked up to see a true vision of beauty. She had to be one of the most beautiful women he had ever seen. As he continued to gaze at her, he couldn't help the feeling of familiarity. He just couldn't quite put his finger on it but she reminded him of someone. He shook off the thought, continuing to gaze at her. Too bad she was a virgin up for auction, or he would have pursued her himself.

"How much are you going to spend Dylan?" Jasper asked. He too was staring at the gorgeous woman.

"I don't know, but I suspect it will be a king's ransom," Dylan said, looking about the room at his competitors. "All of these men are very wealthy. Most would be able to spend a fortune without batting an eye, so it's anyone's guess," he added.

"That bastard Yarbrough is here," Gabriel remarked.

He and Sebastian Latham, the Duke of Yarbrough had had a long standing rivalry and the tension between the two men was palpable. "Don't let him win, Dylan," he added.

"Yarbrough can eat shite; she will be mine," Dylan replied with conviction.

Gabriel would hate to see the rogue end up with such an exquisite beauty.

"I wonder if it's too late to get an invitation to the bidding," he mused aloud.

"You would do anything to thwart Yarbrough, eh?" Jasper chuckled.

"True, I cannot abide the man," Gabriel sneered.

"It's too late, my friend. Just let me handle it. Yarbrough won't get his filthy paws on her," Dylan assured him.

"See to it," Gabriel commanded his friend.

"Gentlemen, may I have your attention?" Annabelle's voice cut into the din.

All the men quieted down giving her their full attention.

"I would ask all those who are not in the bidding, to please take your seats away from the platform so we can begin."

Everyone shuffled to their seats. The gentlemen in the bid took their places in front of the platform.

"Very good, now it is my pleasure to introduce to you all, the lovely Miss Audrey Flowers. I have here, her certificate of authenticity signed by Dr. Brownstone. I will pass it around for your perusal. Then, we will start the bidding," Annabelle explained, passing the parchment that she held in her hand to the first man in the front row.

Gabriel couldn't help but notice the woman on the auction platform was nervous. She looked terrified, in fact. He wondered what could have befallen one so young and beautiful that would have landed her here, in this situation. It's too bad that she didn't mingle with the guests before the auction. He would have offered her the role of his new mistress to help her avoid the humiliation of this process. Perhaps, when the night was over he could seek her out to discuss it with her, he mused. It would be a shame to let a beautiful woman such as she get away before he had an opportunity to sample her assets. He didn't really like the idea of bedding a virgin, so it was good that someone else would get the job. He hoped that it would be Dylan and not Yarbrough.

Melody had been Yarbrough's mistress four years ago, and he knew that he had been unkind to her. He had beaten her on more than one occasion during their brief arrangement. Gabriel didn't approve of men who beat their women; there was no need for it. He didn't like to think of this woman suffering at the hands of a cruel initiator. Melody had been a virgin when Yarbrough bought her at an auction, just like this one. She told him that he had beaten her the first time, then used her for about a month before casting her off and leaving her destitute for someone else. It stood to reason he might be looking for a new mistress and had set his sights on Miss Audrey Flowers. Aye, Dylan must thwart him, if at all possible.

All the men finished looking over the certificate, then handed it back to Annabelle. Without further ado, the bidding commenced.

"The bid starts at one thousand. Do I hear one thousand and one?"

The bidding progressed quickly. Soon it was a war between Dylan and Yarbrough as they had surpassed the eight thousand pound mark. Neither man was willing to concede to the other. The bid quickly shot to fifteen thousand pounds. Gabriel looked at his friend who had sweat on his brow and a defeated look in his eyes. He had reached his maximum allowance for the chit and could go no further. Yarbrough was smug. He won the bid at sixteen thousand pounds. Gabriel was sick at his stomach to realize what the poor girl had in store for her. It was not to be borne. He had to do something. The girl was whisked away from the platform and taken away from the room. Yarbrough stood at the center of all the men who had lost who were now bestowing their congratulations upon him. Yarbrough looked over at Gabriel and winked. The bloody sod winked! Gabriel lost all sense of reason, heading straight for him. He wasn't sure what he was going to do when he got there, but he couldn't let such a taunt stand. He simply had to do something.

"Hawk, have you come to congratulate me?" Yarbrough asked mockingly. Yarbrough was of an age with Gabriel. He was a tall regal man with blond wavy hair and green leonine eyes. He would venture to say he was a handsome man with his Viking looks, square jaw and muscular physique.

"No, I came to buy the girl from you," Gabriel found himself saying. He had no idea where it came from, but there it was; his course was set.

"You want to buy her?" he asked incredulously. "My good man I haven't even used her yet. I'm hardly ready to sell," Yarbrough said smugly, dusting an imaginary piece of lint from his lapel.

"Twenty thousand pounds," Gabriel stated.

"No, you can have her when I'm finished with her."

"Vingt-Et-Un! Best out of five; the winner gets twenty thousand and the girl," Gabriel challenged.

It was well known that Yarbrough, a seasoned gambler, loved the game above all others, since it wasn't played often in London he would jump at any opportunity to play. Gabriel watched him turning it over in his mind; he had him. Gabriel realized that his friends had come up behind him to see what was going on. If there was to be a fight, they were squarely behind him and wanted all to know it. There wouldn't be a fight, no. Just a good old fashion high-stakes game of Twenty-One, Vingt-Et-Un as it was best known in France.

"How do you propose to pay your losses?" Yarbrough asked.

"I have him covered," Dylan's voice came from behind Gabriel.

"That's very kind of you Dylan, but I am good for it, and he knows it. If I lose, I will write him my vowels, and my man will bring it around to him on the morrow," Gabriel stated; his gray eyes mercurial.

"We will need a dealer. Someone neutral," Yarbrough shrewdly suggested.

"I'm sure Annabelle can assist us, can't you love?" Gabriel asked the stunned Annabelle. She had been standing by, listening to the exchange with high anxiety.

"I have yet to be paid for the auction, your grace, and you would ask that I should now provide a dealer so you can use the girl in a wager?" she asked aghast.

"Thomas pay Annabelle," Yarbrough instructed his assistant, all the while staring at Gabriel.

The two men had yet to break eye contact throughout the exchange. Anyone looking on could see that this was a deadly serious proposition

Gina Rose

between two very intense rivals. The efficient Thomas quickly wrote out a bank note for sixteen thousand pounds. He handed it to Yarbrough for his signature. Yarbrough signed it and handed it to Annabelle.

"I believe that settles it. Now about that dealer, Annabelle," he said sternly.

"Yes your grace, Davis will deal for you, if you will follow me to the card room," she said nervously.

Gabriel and Yarbrough with their entourages followed Annabelle to the game room. Not a word was spoken by anyone, but all had concern in their eyes. This could end badly, and everyone knew it. These two men loathed each other. The situation could easily turn violent. The two men took their seats and Davis shuffled the cards. Annabelle explained the nature of the wager to Davis. He nodded his head that he understood that the house was not to be involved in the game. He dealt each man a card face down, then one, face up.

Yarbrough was on the dealer's left so he went first. His down-card was a four of clubs, his up-card was the queen of diamonds. He tapped the table to indicate he wanted another hit. He was dealt a six of spades and he held up his hand to stay. The dealer looked to Gabriel whose down-card was a three of hearts and his up-card was a seven of spades. He tapped the table, and he was dealt an ace of diamonds. Twenty-one! He stayed his hand and the dealer looked to Yarbrough. He turned his down-card up to show his hand. He had twenty. The hand went to Gabriel. He let out of sigh of relief.

112

Yarbrough's jaw tightened. Both men stared at one another while Davis shuffled the deck.

The next hand went to Yarbrough as Gabriel stayed at nineteen; Yarbrough made twenty. The tension in the room ratcheted up a few notches as some of the observers could be heard whispering side wagers on the final outcome. Gabriel didn't let that distract him; he had to beat Yarbrough. It was a matter of honor. Yarbrough was a cad of the worst order. He couldn't let him walk out of this card room the victor. He braced himself as the cards came down. His down-card was a five of diamonds and his up-card was a king of hearts. He drew in a breath, tapping the table. A six of aces came down; he inwardly smiled. Yarbrough went bust with twenty-three. Gabriel had won two hands now; he was almost there.

Yarbrough was an unhappy man. There was fire in his catlike eyes. The muscles in his jaw were tight to grinding. Davis shuffled the deck dealing them both two cards. The cards came down, one up, one down, just as the two hands before. Yarbrough had seven of clubs showing. Gabriel had a jack of spades. Yarbrough tapped the table and a ten of spades came down. Gabriel nearly shouted with glee when he saw the look on Yarbrough's face. He had him and he knew it. Gabriel stayed his hand. He had an ace of diamonds. Together with his jack, he made twenty-one. Yarbrough flipped his down-card up, and he had gone bust at twenty two. The room became chaos as Gabriel's crew shouted out their appreciation of their friend's triumph. Gabriel was too shocked to move. He had just beaten a legendary gambler at his own game. What were the odds?

Yarbrough very calmly got up from the table, straightening his jacket. He looked at Gabriel, snarling, "Enjoy the whore." Then, he looked at his assistant and said, "Pay the duke." Without further ado, he exited the card room.

Gabriel watched him go, realizing he was twenty thousand pounds and one virgin richer than he was less than a quarter of an hour ago. He inwardly chuckled over his sweet victory and ordered a drink.

Chapter Seven

"You lucky bastard," Luther proclaimed.

"If you don't want the task of deflowering her you can always give her to me," Dylan joked.

"Why don't you two play best out of five; the winner takes the girl," Jasper asked as if he had just had a stroke of genius.

"No, I will take the spoils of my own victory, thank you very much. I think I will even offer to let her become my new mistress. She obviously needs the blunt, or she wouldn't have come here in the first place," Gabriel said.

"You've cast off Melody?" all three of his friends asked in unison.

"Aye," he said, "just this eve, in fact. She took it rather well, I think," he added thoughtfully.

Gabriel thought about the task that lay ahead. It had been many years since he had a virgin, and he didn't relish the prospect. The last time he had been a youth of seven and ten, and though he wasn't as well endowed then as he was now, he had hurt the chit. He had always felt bad about that, swearing he would never again have a virgin until he married. He inwardly cringed at the thought of the task ahead, then quickly tossed back his drink. Perhaps he should order a bottle of brandy to take up there with him and get her to drink two or three glasses before the deed was to be done. If he could get her sauced then she might not feel the pain so much. He motioned for the waiter to come over to the table.

"Send a bottle of your best brandy to Miss

Audrey Flowers' room, with my compliments, my good man," he instructed.

Yes it was a good plan; he wanted it to be as pleasant as possible for the both of them. The poor chit would probably be offended when she learned he won the honors to her virginity in a card game, and it didn't cost him so much as a farthing and that he had gained twenty thousand pounds in the offing. He shook off the thought, mildly disgusted with himself. He would make it enjoyable for her. He would show her the joys to be had between a man and a woman, surely she would eagerly agree to become his new mistress. It was a win-win situation, really. He could help her out with her problems, whatever they were, and she could help him with his needs. It was a good bargain.

Luther and Jasper got up and left the table to woo the twins. Everyone loved the twins. They were adorable, fun loving girls, full of all kinds of tricks to drive a man crazy. They were best taken as a team, but as a small party of four the games would be endless. Lucky bastards!

Poor Dylan sat moping. The poor sod was left out in the cold. "You know Dylan, Annabelle keeps a clean house. Her girls are attended regularly by a physician, and you could always use a French-letter," Gabriel mused aloud.

Dylan didn't feel like discussing it; he tossed back his drink, "I think I'll just stay here and play cards," he said broodingly.

For a brief moment, Gabriel considered giving her to his friend, but he knew Dylan had too much pride to actually accept her now. So, instead, he stood up and saluted him, leaving to find his virgin.

*****

When Gabriel made it to the upstairs hallway, he saw Annabelle pacing back and forth in front of a door. She looked up when she heard him and dashed over to him.

"I have not yet told her of the developments, your grace. I'm not sure how she will take it. She is a very sweet girl. She has been through so much before now, and I fear this will devastate her," Annabelle rushed out.

"I shall be kind to her. Have no fear Annabelle," Gabriel assured her.

"But what will you tell her?"

"I will tell her the truth of course. It is always best to be truthful. I could not stand by and allow Yarbrough to win her. He is a scoundrel of the first order. I'm surprised he was even invited here. I thought you screened your clients better than that," Gabriel admonished her.

"I have no idea what you mean, your grace. I do run a clean establishment, and I do take care to screen my clients. I have never had any negative feedback about his grace.

"You remember Melody, do you not? He bought her at one of your auctions and beat her the first time as well as several times after when he took her as a mistress. He kept her for a month before leaving her completely destitute," Gabriel explained.

Annabelle was speechless.

"So you see, my love, it has all worked out for the better," Gabriel said with a smile and a wink.

"Yes, I suppose that it has. You will be kind to her, I know. Thank you, your grace," she said, with a curtsy before taking her leave.

Gabriel stood outside the door for a moment, thinking about what lay on the other side. He took a deep breath and knocked on the door. He heard a shy quiet voice bid him enter, so without further hesitation, he opened the door and went in. The girl was standing in the middle of the room facing the door. When she saw him, she gasped, "What is this? You are not Lord Yarbrough!"

Gabriel looked at the beautiful young woman with a sense of awe. She was still wearing the scandalous gown, and her hair was down, draping around her shoulders. Her eyes were huge with surprise and something close to fear.

"There has been a change in plans," he told her softly.

"I don't understand."

"I could not allow Yarbrough to have you," he told her bluntly.

"But he paid for the right to have me," she defended.

"Aye, and he lost that right to me in a game of Vingt-Et-Un. You see, he and I have a long history of rivalry. I could not ignore the opportunity to challenge him. I did, and I won, so here we are," he said, advancing toward her.

She took a step back, staring at him as if she didn't understand a word he had said. He closed the gap that she tried to put between them. He took her by the hand, kissing it softly on the palm.

She pulled her hand back as if she had been burned and said, "I should like to speak to Annabelle about this. Why should I take your word for it?"

"We could call for her if you like, but I assure you, she was there when the transaction took place; she witnessed it. Indeed, I just spoke with her outside your door and assured her that the better man has claimed you," he told her earnestly.

She was quiet for a moment, looking past him at the door. He could tell she wanted to flee, but she couldn't decide if she should. He stepped aside and bowed, sweeping his hand toward the door, to show she was not a prisoner and was free to leave if she wished to. That seemed to ease her mind a bit so she looked back at him and straightened her spine.

"I suppose you would not lie about such a thing. Tis a bit discomforting to know that a woman can be bought and sold, then bartered away in a card game like a piece of cattle," she said indignantly.

"He is a cruel man. I could not allow him to have such a lovely creature as you. I know of his habits, you see. My mistress was bought by him in just the same fashion as you were, and I know what he did to her. You are far safer with me, this I swear," he promised.

He watched her take in the information with what looked like relief. Her shoulders relaxed and she sighed softly. He reached out to touch her cheek with his thumb, and she closed her eyes in response.

"I think we should have some brandy. Did you get the bottle that I sent up to you?" he asked.

"Yes, but I do not handle spirits well, so I have not partaken of it,"

"You will like the brandy. It will relax you. Come, I shall pour you a glass. If you don't like it, you don't have to drink it, but I want you to try. I would have you relaxed so you can enjoy yourself."

She nodded her head in consent, so he went to the sideboard pouring them both a glass of brandy. He walked back over to her, handing her the drink. He watched her take a sip, then cough in reflex. But she was determined and took another sip, this one more tolerably. She smiled at him. He couldn't shake the feeling that he knew her from somewhere.

"Here is to a successful enterprise," he said raising his glass to hers, and lightly tapping it against hers. He tossed back his drink. She did the same. She coughed again but didn't otherwise complain.

He took her empty glass and went to refill them both. He brought it back to her and said, "Once more."

She looked at him incredulously as she accepted it but quickly tossed the brandy back. He did the same, then he took both glasses, putting them away on a nearby table. He took her hand in his and massaged her palm, bringing her forward, then without further ado he took her lips in a searing kiss. Her essence was like a punch to his loins. She smelled of lavender and citrus. She tasted like the sweetest honey mixed with brandy. He instantly became aroused, deepening the kiss. She returned

the kiss eagerly, beginning a slow caress of his
chest with her delicate little hand.

He broke away from the kiss. He ran his hand
along her cheek, then down her chest, where it
rested just under her lovely bosom. They stood
looking into each other's eyes for what seemed like
an eternity before she lunged forward, kissing him
as passionately as he had ever been kissed before.
Her kiss was unskilled, but he reveled in her
enthusiasm. He returned her kiss, probing her lips
with his tongue, urging her to open and receive him
fully. He gently thrust his tongue inside her mouth
and began a slow sensual mingling. She groaned in
response, the sound sent a jolt straight to his shaft.

He pulled away, turned her around and began
unbuttoning her gown. He slipped it off her
shoulders, his eyes roving over her body as it landed
in a heap on the floor around her ankles. He was
pleased to see she was unencumbered by a corset;
they were such tedious devices. He gently turned
her back around to face him and slowly removed
her chemise. He pulled it over her head, his eyes
locked with hers as she stood before him wearing
only her stockings and slippers. He took her by the
arm assisting her safely away from her fallen gown
and walked her to the bed. She sat down on the
edge, watching with eyes wide open as he began to
remove his own clothing.

When he was all but bare save for his breeches,
he bent to take her mouth in another passionate kiss,
pushing her back on the bed as he did so. He
encouraged her to wrap her legs around his buttocks
then began to plunder her breasts as though they

were a bountiful meal and he a starving man. She was so responsive and warm that he felt that if he didn't slow down he would surely hurt her in his eagerness. He had nearly forgotten her virginity, so he pulled back from her, staring into her eyes.

"The first time will hurt you, my love," he told her softly.

"I know; tis all right."

"Do you want some more brandy first?" he asked.

"No, I just want you," was her soft reply.

"I will need to ease the way first. Don't be scared, you will enjoy this," he said with a sexy smile.

He didn't give her time to respond before he dropped to his knees on the floor, pulling her hips forward, placing her legs over his shoulders. He smiled brilliantly at her once more before he dove forward plunging his tongue into her passage. He chuckled when she gasped at the sensation but gave her no quarter as he laved her tender folds and her sensitive nub. She whimpered, whined and twisted her hips in response, but he held on tight to her hips, continuing his sensual assault. He slowly inserted his middle finger, then began to move it back and forth, mimicking the penetration that was to come. He never let up with his tongue. He inserted yet another finger, causing her to cry out. She grabbed a handful of his hair so she could force his face closer, nearly smothering him with her flesh, squeezing him between her thighs. He laughed again at the knowledge that she was on the brink of her first climax. She was reaching for it like a hungry she-wolf, grinding her flesh against his mouth.

Then, her body began to jerk and shudder, so she went rigid with her spasms, her grip tightening in his hair as she rode the waves of her release. Her response had nearly been his undoing. His shaft strained to be set free as he reveled in the intensity of his own arousal. He was rock hard and ready to burst. He brought her down slowly and began to undo his breeches. She raised her head up and over her heaving bosom. She watched as he removed his manhood from its restraining garment. She gasped. Her eyes widened as she took in the size of it. She squirmed and scooted herself back, shaking her head.

"We will fit my love, fear not. I have prepared your body to accept me," he promised her before kissing her woman's mound once more.

She laid her head back, shimmying closer and lifted her hips to give his mouth access. He laughed at the greedy minx, but instead of obliging her, he grabbed her by the ribcage and hoisted her up and dragged her to the center of the bed, coming down over her.

He took her hand in his, guiding it to his shaft, "Feel what you do to me," he softly commanded her.

She nervously took his member in her hand, gently caressing it up and down, then whimpered again. He laughed out loud then kissed her lips and moved his hips into position. He moved her hand away so he could insert the tip of his arousal into her tight passage, stopping to give her time to adjust to the intrusion. He kissed her to demonstrate with his tongue his intentions and was pleased when she reciprocated.

He inched forward, freezing when he heard a knock at the door. "Do not enter," he called out to the intruder.

"Tis I, Annabelle. Please, we must get her out of here. Lord Keith has arrived, and he has Bow Street runners with him. They are searching for the girl," she pleaded through the door.

Gabriel froze anew; Lord Keith? He suddenly realized who she was. Oh my God! He jumped up, tucking his painful arousal back into his breeches, then buttoned them up. He looked down at her. She was frozen, too. She looked terrified, in fact. He pulled her up to a sitting position.

"Where are your things? We must get you dressed and get you out of here," he told her.

That brought her out of her shock. She jumped up, ran to the wardrobe to pull out her portmanteau and began rummaging through it. She pulled out a gown, quickly tossing it on and asked, "Please, can you assist me with the buttons?"

He rushed over to her, buttoned up the gown then quickly finished his own dressing. That done, he went over to the door and opened it to see a scared Annabelle standing there.

"You will have to go out the window, he has a man waiting at the foot of the stairs," she told them, thrusting an envelope at him. "That is her money; quickly take her and leave. Lord Keith will kill her if he finds her," she added.

Gabriel shut the door, ran over to the window

and looked down. It wasn't that far down, they could make it.

He handed her the envelope, and said, "Put that away in your bag. Let us be gone from here. I will jump down first and catch you when you jump. Don't be scared. It's not that far, and I am very strong. I will not allow you to be harmed."

She did as he bid, putting the envelope in her portmanteau. Then she grabbed it and ran to the window just in time to see him drop down. He landed on his feet with the agility of a cat and raised his arms up for her to jump. He was glad to see she didn't hesitate. Instead, she dropped out of the window like a stone with total trust in his ability to catch her.

*****

Alistair was livid as he searched the brothel for Alyssa. He had been told that there had been an auction of a virgin here tonight, and the woman described sounded exactly like Alyssa. He didn't really believe she would do such a thing, but he had to be sure. The woman's name was Audrey Flowers, a whore's name to be sure, his sweet Alyssa would never use such a moniker. He didn't understand why she had left him, but he didn't believe she had really gone to Wales as her note had suggested. All he knew was that he had to find her. She needed him, and he needed her. The thought of her out there alone in the world without his protection was more than he could endure. If she had ended up here tonight, it had to have been against her will. She would never willingly do such a thing.

The more he thought about it, the more convinced he was that maybe she had been kidnapped and forced to leave him. She simply loved him too much to leave him willingly. He would question the household staff again to see what they might be withholding from him. He wouldn't put it past that bastard stepfather of his to have taken her away from him. Aye the old bastard was probably behind it. He would cut the man's heart out with his teeth if he learned of it. But, in the meantime, he would turn this place upside down in search of his beloved. He could almost swear he smelled her sweet fragrance. He needed to find the proprietor to see what they knew.

He found the card room. There, he saw a lone young man with long, loosely curled black hair and ice blue eyes sitting at the table drinking. He estimated that the man, who was clearly a lord, must be of an age with him, perhaps a year or two younger. He seemed solemn, sitting there alone, almost sad. Everyone had fled when the word came that Bow Street had arrived, but this lone man sat calmly with his drink as though nothing unusual at all had occurred.

"You there, who is the proprietor of this hovel?" Alistair barked.

Dylan looked up at the angry man standing in the doorway. Who did this bloody arse think he was?

"You want Annabelle, but tell me, what is it you want with her, perhaps I can help," he asked calmly.

"There was a woman sold at auction this night. I would know who she was and where she can be found," Alistair stated with authority.

"Ah, you would be referring to Miss Audrey Flowers, an ugly wench if ever I saw one. Spots all over her face, truly hideous," he said with a mock shiver.

"Spots?" he asked.

"Aye, she must have had a bad case of the pox as a child for her face was covered with thousands of pits," he told him with another shiver.

Dylan wasn't about to give the man information to harm his friend with. So he quickly decided to lead the man astray with misinformation.

"Pox you say?"

"Aye, you couldn't really see the scars until you got up close to her. Pity the man who ended up with her because when she smiled, her rotten buck teeth with huge gaps were truly … gruesome," he said with yet another mock shiver.

Alistair was relieved. It hadn't been his beloved after all. "Can I buy you another drink, my friend?" he asked.

"No, tis piss. I've had my fill, but I thank you for your kind offer," he said with a smile.

"They told me she was beautiful … that she had auburn hair. I thought sure it was my fiancé who has been cruelly kidnapped from me," Alistair told him with tears in his eyes.

"Aye she had red hair, but it was most likely a wig. It slipped back at one point. You could see she had very little of her own hair underneath. Probably lost with the fever," Dylan calmly perpetuated his lies.

Alistair shivered this time. The woman sounded ghastly.

"I thank you for your information. If you see a petite woman, the most beautiful woman you have ever seen, with auburn hair and sea-green eyes, you will know you have found my Alyssa. I will reward you handsomely for her return. My name is Alistair Sinclair, Earl of Keith. I am residing with my stepfather, Lord Glenmont in Mayfair, should you need to find me," he said vehemently.

"I shall endeavor to keep vigilant, sir," Dylan said, feeling a tad guilty for lying to the poor sod, but he could see that the man was a wee bit unstable. Perhaps it was best that he not find the Pocket Venus.

Alistair thanked him and took his leave of the kind gentleman that had helped him call off the search of the brothel. He would go home and speak with his stepfather and the staff again. God help the bloody bastard that took his sweet Alyssa from him.

*****

Dylan watched him go with a satisfied smile on his face. He waited for five minutes, then got up in search of Annabelle. He wanted to be assured that Hawk was safe and find out what he could about the woman. He soon located her upstairs on the landing, pacing back and forth.

"They have gone, Annabelle. I gave Lord Keith some misinformation. Upon receiving it, he was sure that the woman you auctioned this night could not have been the woman he sought," he told her with his usual calm.

"Oh, thank God. How can I ever repay you, my lord?"

"You can repay me by telling me who she really was, and how she ended up here," he told her.

"Her name is Alyssa Habersham. She was brought here by my sister. She was betrothed to that evil man, and he beat her badly. She had to escape him and would receive no help from her uncle who is her guardian. The poor dear has been treated so badly by her own family. She had nowhere to turn. I told her she could auction her virginity for a small fortune and escape to live her own life. I believe she wants to go to America until she is old enough to receive her inheritance," she explained.

Dylan took in the information, then asked, "Who is her guardian?"

"The Earl of Glenmont," she stated.

Dylan could get a better picture of the situation now. Her uncle must have sold her to his stepson, which explained why she had no one to turn to. Poor girl!

"Is Lord Windhaven with her now?" he probed.

"They have escaped through the window, my lord. I warned them that Lord Kcith was here, and they quickly left. I have no idea where he took her, but I am worried sick. I swore to protect her. Now I don't even know where she is," she fretted.

"You have done very well, Annabelle. She will be safe with Windhaven, so put your mind at ease my dear lady," he assured her with a pat on the shoulder.

"Yes, he is a kind man, isn't he?" she said. Annabelle was grateful to him for telling her about Lord Yarbrough, so she would never again make the mistake of inviting him to one of her auctions. Had she known he was violent, he wouldn't have ever gotten through the door. She took great pride in screening her clients to protect her girls and wouldn't abide a man like that inside her establishment. She was grateful to Lord Windhaven too, for protecting Alyssa from Lord Keith. She hoped he would help her to get on a ship so the poor dear could start a new life in America.

"The very best!" he assured her.

She stood mute with sadness in her eyes. "I believe my two other associates are occupied with the twins right now. Will you pass word along that they should attend me in the card room as soon as they have concluded their business? I would like to inform them of the developments here so that we may offer our assistance to Lord Windhaven and the girl," he told her.

"Yes certainly my lord, it shall be as you requested."

Dylan turned and went back down to the card room to await his friends. He thought to formulate a plan in the event that things turned nasty with Lord Keith. The four men were well schooled in dealing with his ilk. All they needed to do was put their heads together to come up with a plan. He knew where Hawk would take her, so he wasn't too worried about him for the moment. They had escaped. That was all that mattered now.

Chapter Eight

Alyssa couldn't believe what was happening. How could things have turned out like this? She had resigned herself to being sold to one man, then found herself gambled away to another, Diana's betrothed, no less. That was shocking, to say the least, but she didn't see she had any choice in the matter after the deal had been made. He didn't seem to recognize her. For that, she was grateful. And then my word, the things he did to her. *Oh my heavens, I behaved like an absolute wanton in his arms*!' The man was so adept with his tongue that she had completely given herself over to him. She shivered at the memory of the intimacy. The size of the man was so intimidating, but she was just tipsy enough not to care. She was still a bit woozy, even after the shock of learning that Alistair had arrived. Alistair! Oh my God! He nearly found her! What was she to do now?

Lord Windhaven was pulling her along at breakneck speed behind him, and she could hardly think. She felt like a rag doll, flopping and bobbing along in his wake. Finally, they stopped at the stables. He went inside to retrieve a beautiful stallion. After he lovingly spoke to the beast, he grabbed her portmanteau, tied it to the back of his saddle, then grabbed her up and plopped her atop him, mounting up behind her. Now they were galloping through the streets of London at even faster speed than before. Her head was spinning. She wasn't sure she was going to be able to remain atop the animal much longer. She slid to the left and he reached an arm around her, hoisting her back into place.

"Hang on my lovely."

His voice was like a warm balm in her ear. What had she gotten herself into? She giggled at the absurdity of it all and hiccupped. The brandy had been really strong, and she was completely sauced. Her life was in danger, and she was being whisked away by Diana's betrothed, going God knows where, and here she was in a drunken stupor acting as though she hadn't a care in the world.

"Where are we going?" she thought to ask, hiccupping again.

He chuckled and squeezed her tight around the middle, "Don't worry, you will be safe. I will not let the bastard get his hands on you," he assured her.

She was mollified by that and leaned back against his chest. The bouncing of the ride was having a sedating effect on her, so she closed her eyes. She needed to sober up so she could deal with this crisis she now found herself in. She would never drink spirits again, she mused just before she drifted off.

Gabriel realized after a few moments that she had passed out. *I guess she wasn't kidding when she said she didn't handle spirits very well.* He laughed, kissing her on the temple. She was a tempting piece of baggage. What had he really gotten himself into, though? He had to get her out of London; that much he knew for certain. He would take her to Windhaven and hide her there. It was the only way to guarantee her safety. She needed to be protected, of that he was sure.

He thought about the first time he had seen her and remembered the possessive way in which Diana's brother had treated her at the dinner last week. He had been told of the ridiculous show of ownership he had displayed before his arrival. He was glad he had missed that. He wouldn't have been able to contain himself from ridiculing the man for his stupidity. The man had been insane with jealousy, he and Diana both. He knew he was making the man jealous, but he'd had a little fun toying with him by staring at his woman excessively. He probably shouldn't have done that in hindsight. Clearly, the man was unstable and probably took it out on her. Poor girl, he thought kissing her temple again.

He was beginning to get an idea of what had driven her to the auction. He must have abused her in some way, so she became frightened and was trying to escape the man. She must not have had anywhere else to turn. He didn't blame her. He would do all he could to help her. She would be well protected as his mistress. No one would dare harm her while she was under his protection. He was glad that the weather wasn't too cool as they made their mad dash out of London. He wondered if it would be safe to take her to an inn first, then travel on to Windhaven on the morrow. Windhaven wasn't too far away though; they could be there within two hours. Perhaps, he should push on while she was sleeping.

He drew her snug up against him, then encouraged Chester to top speed. She was lightweight and wouldn't tax him too badly.

Chester loved a good run. There was a full moon tonight, and the road was in fairly good shape along the way, so they shouldn't have any problems. He became painfully cognizant of her bottom nudging against his arousal that still hadn't gone down since they had been about to make love. It was right uncomfortable now, and he needed relief, soon. Unfortunately, relief was hours away yet. He shifted in the saddle so as to give his crotch a little breathing room, but it was impossible really. She kept slipping to the side in her slumber.

He smiled, remembering their little tryst earlier. She had tasted so sweet, and she had been so responsive to his lovemaking. She was so tight and untried that it had been almost painful trying to enter her. He shivered at the memory. Once he got her virginity out of the way, there would be no end to the pleasure they would find in one another. Thinking about how tight she had been, he knew he would have to be sure to get her to drink more brandy. He chuckled at the thought. *Poor chit would have to be completely sauced to be able to take me all the way in.* He was glad he had plenty of brandy at Windhaven; he had plans for this lovely chit.

He could still taste her on his lips. That with the motion of the ride causing her to rub against him was sheer torture. Maybe he should stop at an inn and relieve himself with her.

He was sure she wasn't so tipsy that he couldn't revive her for a quick romp. The thought made him feel like a bit of a heel so no, it was best to push on while they could. Keith probably had spies everywhere searching for her, no doubt. He tried to put the thought of bedding her out of his mind and will his erection into submission. Now was not the time to be ruled by his cock. Unfortunately his shaft had a mind of its own. It knew it had been shortchanged. Demanding devil! Gabriel inwardly chastised his wayward member.

"Chester, I'm afraid we are in for a frustrating two hours old friend," he told his horse.

Chester ignored him as his head was completely involved in the run. Chester was in heaven as he rarely got to let loose like this. Poor Chester needed to be back at Windhaven for a while so he could run free and mount a few of his ladies.

"You and me both, my friend," Gabriel mused aloud, snuggling Alyssa back against him.

Alyssa? Yes, I believe that's her real name. She was a rare beauty. It's no wonder Keith was so obsessed with her. Well, he wouldn't let that happen to him. No, there wasn't a woman to be found that could hold him if he didn't want to be held. Once he figured out a way to be rid of Diana, his life would be perfect. It wasn't that he never intended to marry. Indeed, he did, someday in the distant future. Perhaps, when he was five and thirty, he would be ready to settle down and take a wife. He wanted a house full of little brats running amok, turning his world upside down. He loved children; they were what life was all about. He just wasn't ready to give up his freedom yet. He certainly wasn't about to give it up to Diana. She was a vile woman with a black heart. He couldn't inflict a mother such as her upon his children. No, he wanted a woman with a sweet and sunny disposition; someone who loved children as much as he did.

He supposed one way to be rid of Diana was to put her off until she was too old. Maybe at some point she would realize that she would never have him and be forced to marry another. How long would she wait though? She was already two and twenty. She was practically a spinster now. If she didn't marry in the next two or three years, she would be fast approaching the end of her child rearing years, so it stood to reason she wouldn't want to wait much longer. Yes, he just needed to hold out for a few years, and she would become desperate and find another. It was a good plan, he supposed. The only one he really had.

He had often considered spreading a rumor about her that would be bad enough that, if he were to break things off, no one would look unkindly on him for it. But it wasn't in his nature to be so cruel. He had thought that if he waited long enough, her personality being what it was, would naturally produce a scandal of some sort, but she had been careful with her reputation. Perhaps he could get one of his friends to try and seduce her? Who would he willingly sacrifice though? It couldn't be a good friend. It would have to be merely an acquaintance. Stop dreaming Hawk! You are stuck with the virago … for now.

*****

"Alistair, get hold of yourself this instant!" Esmeralda commanded her son.

Alistair had his stepfather by the lapels of his robe, threatening to do violence to the man if he didn't tell him what he wanted to know.

"Tell me what you have done with her, you blaggard!" he shouted.

Lord Glenmont swallowed hard and cleared his throat as he trembled before Alistair.

"I tell you again, that I have done nothing," he rasped out as his throat was dry from fear of his stepson. He realized the man was dangerous and didn't want to provoke him further.

Alistair towered over him. He had fire blazing in his black eyes as he looked down at him.

"Why don't I believe you?" he said after a protracted moment. "You didn't want the lass to marry me because you coveted her fortune for yourself. You and that whore mother of mine have been bilking her inheritance. You had plans to take even more. I'm no fool. You have taken her from me out of spite, and I will see you destroyed before I allow you to succeed," he added.

"Alistair, he knows nothing, I swear. He has been out searching for the child too. Please believe me; he did not do this thing that you accuse him of. I told you the girl was no good and that you could do better. She has left you son. Why do you refuse to believe this?"

Alistair released his stepfather and turned on his mother. Her words nearly pushed him over the edge. He was angrier now than he was before. He stood before her, breathing hard. His fists were clenching as though he wanted to strike out. He realized he was about to hurt her and tried to reach for the control that threatened to elude him.

"Do not talk about my beloved, you bitch. You have no right. It is because of you and your husband that she has left me. When I find her, if she is harmed in any way, so help me God, I will kill you both!" he told her as calmly as he could.

He was shaking violently. The urge to kill them both was palpable. He had to get away from them before he did something he would regret. He turned away from her and stormed out of their bedroom. He met Diana in the hall, and she quickly got out of his way. He stopped, staring at her, causing her to swallow hard, fearing he would turn on her. He moved toward her, towering over her in an intimidating fashion.

"What do you know of this?" he gritted out between clenched teeth.

"N—Nothing, I swear," she stammered.

He shoved her aside and stormed down the hall to the stairway looking for Mr. Humphrey. He saw him standing in the foyer and called to him.

"Mr. Humphrey, I want you to send me each and every member of the staff for another interview. I shall start the interviews first thing on the morrow at seven sharp in the library. Is that understood?"

"Y—Yes my lord; it shall be as you command," he told him.

"Thank you, Mr. Humphrey. Bring a bottle of brandy to my room, if you please," Alistair told him.

Alistair went to his room and stripped out of his clothes. He was suffocating and needed to cool off. He had wanted to kill his stepfather and his mother.

He needed to relax before he lost all reason. He was standing there bare arsed naked when Mr. Humphrey arrived with the brandy.

"Mr. Humphrey, I would like you to send a groom over to Madam Comely's and tell her that I have an urgent need of Marjorie and to send her to me right away. No delays, do you understand me?"

"Madam Comely, my lord?"

"Yes, she is located at number 13 Haymarket Street. Be quick about it man," he growled.

Mr. Humphrey scurried out of the room and Alistair breathed a sigh of relief. He would feel better after Marjorie arrived. She would help him deal with this.

*****

"What's this about Dylan?" Jasper asked, still short of breath from his romp with the twins.

He and Luther had cut their visit short with the twins and came down barely dressed in a state of panic to see what was afoot. Dylan hadn't meant them to attend him so quickly. He had been prepared to wait an hour or two if need be.

"Hawk is in trouble. The virgin has skeletons in her closet that could get our brother killed," he told them.

"Skeletons?" Luther asked gaping at him.

"She is betrothed to Lord Keith and has escaped him. The man is looking for her. He showed up here with several Bow Street men. They were ransacking the place. I'm surprised you weren't disturbed," he said with sarcasm.

"The twins are a bit noisy at times," Luther blushed.

"Aye, well let me tell you what else you missed. Hawk escaped, with the girl, out of a second story window after Annabelle warned them that Lord Keith was here. I suspect he has taken her to Windhaven for her protection, but the three of us need to formulate a plan to deal with Keith," he told them.

"Where is he now?" Jasper asked.

"I fed him some misinformation that convinced him that the woman sold here tonight was not his fiancé. I think he actually bought it because he called off the search of the brothel and left. He told me there would be a reward for her safe return. He gave me his name and where he could be found. He is Glenmont's stepson. Glenmont is the girl's uncle and guardian. We need to learn more about this man and keep an eye on him as he searches for the girl. If he was to catch Hawk with her, he would try to kill him, I'm sure of it. I saw murder in his eyes. He is unstable. That makes him very dangerous, my friends. We must act quickly to aid our brother."

"Luther and I can take shifts watching his house round the clock while you see what you can dig up," Jasper suggested.

Dylan nodded his head in agreement. That was what he was going to suggest, as well. He had a good friend that worked for Bow Street, and he would see what could be learned from him.

"Alright, it's a start. I'll send word to Windhaven on the morrow to verify that Hawk did take her there and tell him to keep us abreast of his activities. You two, put yourselves in position to keep watch on Keith, starting tonight. He is staying at Glenmont's in Mayfair. See if you can talk to the staff to see what's going on inside, as well. Perhaps, we can learn what his plans are and head off disaster. Start with the stable master. They always have an ear to the ground. I don't like this, my friends. I don't like this one bit."

The three men were satisfied with their initial plan. They agreed to keep each other informed and headed out to perform their tasks.

*****

"Thank you Henry, I appreciate you informing me what all the commotion was about, goodnight dear," Cookie said, kissing her friend on the cheek. She closed the door and turned to Adam who was still lying in her bed. "What are we to do?" she asked him.

"What can we do, love?" Adam asked in return.

"We mustn't let Lord Keith find out what we have done. He will surely kill us," Cookie fretted.

"We stick to the plan; we know nothing. What can he do? Torture us all?"

"If he is mad enough to torture Lord Glenmont, then none of us are safe. I only hope that Marjorie, whoever she is, can calm him down. She must be the whore that we saw him going to that night," she said with a shudder.

"Aye, she must be one of them deviant sorts if she works at Madam Comely's," he said. "Not that I would know mind you, but I hear things," he quickly added.

Cookie gave him an admonishing look. The Devil! What would he know of deviant sorts?

"Perhaps I should send word to Annabelle that we are having trouble here so she can quickly get her on a ship. She must leave London right away," she suggested.

"Nay, we can't afford to do anything to bring attention to ourselves. We wait for her missive as planned. She will inform us how the bid went. When she does, you can return a message to her, but right now, we wait. Come back to bed, my pretty," he said, patting the bed in invitation.

Cookie was too worried to frolic around in bed. She needed to see her girl to be sure she was safe. With that villain after her, she was in peril. How could she possibly think of anything else? She didn't regret helping her escape, but she was so worried now that she was gone and out there on her own. She was so young and innocent of the world. How would she survive?

"She will be fine Cookie, don't you worry. Come back to bed and let me hold you," Adam said from behind her now. He took her by the hand, leading her to the bed. He was worried about the girl too, but what was done was done. All they could do was wait and hope that crazy bastard didn't find out what they had done.

*****

Morley lay in his bed, thinking about what had transpired. Alistair was right about one thing. He didn't want him to have her, more now than ever. He was a madman. It was his responsibility to protect her from him. He was her guardian. Though he wasn't the one that took her away, he would have, given what he knew now. Where could a young girl have gone without money? She had to have had help from someone, but whom? She had no other family aside from her old aunt in Wales, but how could she have gotten to her without money? There was only one person in the household that would have been able to help her. Aye, Cookie would have helped the girl. Tomorrow he would speak to her to see what he could find out. She would be hesitant to tell him anything, but he would assure her he only wanted to assist the poor child. He wanted to keep her away from that madman. If the child needed money then, she would have it.

He had an old cottage near his estate in Kent. He could send the girl there. She could hide out until Alistair returned to Jamaica. He realized now he had given the child a bad turn. He shouldn't have listened to his wife and treated her in such a way. She was the only real family he had left. Aye he had no one else in the world. He had no sons, so Diana was his heir. She would be a countess in her own right upon his death. He wasn't even sure that Diana was his daughter. He had been married twice before, widowed both times with nary a child from either marriage. Esmeralda had been quick to urge marriage between them after he bedded her. Then when Diana came along seven and a half months later, he had become suspicious. She didn't look anything like him, not even a hint. True, she looked just like her mother, but if she were his, there should have been a hint of it somewhere. Look at Alyssa; she looked just like his brother.

He would give his right arm to be able to make Alyssa his heir. She was his blood and his only living relative. He hoped that God would forgive him his sins and allow him one more chance with the child. He would do right by her this time. He just had to find her first. When he did, he would make sure she lived like she should have all along. He would get rid of Esmeralda and Diana, send them away somewhere. He didn't love them, and they didn't love him. They were money grabbing harridans; two of a kind. He didn't blame Lord Windhaven for trying to avoid marriage to Diana. Perhaps he should do the man a favor and tear the betrothal agreement up. Aye, he could tear it up and send Diana to a convent. The thought had possibilities.

He could probably petition for divorce. He was sure he could prove Diana wasn't his by virtue of his first two marriages being childless without a single pregnancy. Aye, he was sterile, even his mistresses throughout the years had never become pregnant. He had never taken precautions, nor had they as far as he knew. That ought to count for something. He would speak to his solicitor about it. There had to be a way. First thing though, he had to find his niece. She was in danger and needed his protection. To think of that poor child alone in London with no one to look after her was disturbing to his soul.

"I'm sorry, Hugh … forgive me!" he said quietly.

"What did you say, dear?" Esmeralda asked.

"Nothing, go back to sleep," he told her.

Esmeralda was sleeping with him for the first time in ten years. Even she was afraid of her spawn now. The madman had nearly attacked her too. Esmeralda had always claimed he was just like his father, but he knew where he got his evil from; his mother, even a blind man could see that. He should have the constable come take the lot of them away. He didn't think that would work, though. Alistair was an earl after all. Any law officer would think twice about arresting him. He would have to bide his time and see what developed in the search for Alyssa.

Chapter Nine

"Your grace, what is that you've got there?" Harvey asked Gabriel as he burst into his bedroom with his burden tossed over his shoulder. Harvey slept in a small room off to the side of Gabriel's. Waking to the sound of his master's footsteps, he hurried to his room to be of assistance.

Gabriel faced his valet and trusted friend. He was in his nightdress and sleeping cap, with a look of complete surprise as he stared at him and Alyssa's delectable bum. She was still passed out when they had arrived, so he slung her over his shoulder like a pirate raider and hauled her up two flights of stairs to his chambers.

"Ah Harvey my good man; I would like to introduce to you Miss uh … Alyssa … uh … I don't know her last name, Harvey but she will be staying with us a good while. No need to prepare her a room. She will be sharing mine," he said with a devilish grin.

"Your grace, it's a bit awkward addressing her bum, so perhaps you could put her down so I may speak to her face," Harvey said, rolling his eyes heavenward in exasperation.

"You may quit staring at her arse, Harvey. I suspect she wouldn't like that," he said, walking past the old man to unceremoniously plop his prize down in the middle of his huge bed.

"Where did you find her, your grace?" Harvey asked, gazing upon the lovely creature.

"At a brothel," Gabriel stated while removing her slippers.

"I dare say, if you found her in a brothel, she is quite used to men staring at her arse, if I may say so, your grace."

"How many times do I have to tell you to stop calling me 'your grace'? Call me Gabriel, Hawk or even 'Hey You' but stop 'your gracing' me," Gabriel huffed as he lifted her into a sitting position and began unbuttoning her bodice.

Harvey only called Gabriel, your grace when he was angling for something. Gabriel knew this, but usually refused to play his games. Tonight, however, he was impatient. Being randy for two hours with the subject of one's randiness rubbing about your arousal the entire time was a bit vexing.

"Shall I bring her some tea your grace?" he said, looking at the unconscious woman.

"What is it Harvey? What do you want now?" Gabriel asked, letting Alyssa fall back on the bed once he had her bodice undone. He started removing her gown past her shoulders, then stopped, looking at Harvey.

"Well are you going to stand there gawking or are you going to tell me what all this 'your grace' nonsense is about?"

"Far be it for me to complain, your grace, but it's time for my yearly wage increase. You keep me rather busy, your grace. I am entitled to compensation. I'm getting rather old, you see. I need to be sure I have enough to live on in my dotage," he said, showing Gabriel his knobby knuckles.

Harvey was plagued with rheumatism. He liked to use it as a weapon to gain sympathy from Gabriel when he was trying to manipulate him into something.

"Didn't you just get a yearly wage increase last month?" Gabriel asked.

"Aye, sure but it wasn't nearly enough. I have an eye on the widow Burley in the village. I wanted to be able to impress her, you see, by buying that cottage on the hill," Harvey explained.

"If I buy you the cottage, will you stop calling me your grace?" Gabriel asked.

"Oh sure, Hawk I would be most grateful to you if you did that for your poor old valet," he said with a toothy grin.

Gabriel had been manipulated again. He knew it, but he didn't really care. He loved Harvey. He would give him the moon if he could. The old man had been with him since he was a small lad. He had pulled Gabriel out of many a bad situation, so he quite literally owed him his life. If the old bugger wanted a cottage, by God he would get him a cottage.

"I won twenty thousand pounds in a card game along with this virgin here, and its yours Harvey … the twenty thousand, that is; the virgin, however, is mine," he told him, fishing in his coat pocket. He pulled out Yarbrough's banknote and handed it to him.

"I don't know what to say Hawk. I think, I'm going to cry," he sniffed. "This is far more than I need to buy the cottage. Why, I could buy the widow a fine wedding ring. I could buy some new breeches too. Maybe a few of those coattails made of superfine and some silk cravat's. Maybe even a carriage too. What do you think Hawk?"

"I think I've been swindled, you old scoundrel. Now if you don't mind, I would like to undress the lady here, and I would like to do it alone … and Harvey, bring me a bottle of brandy and two glasses before you go to bed, would you?"

Harvey smiled, then spun on his heel and went about his errand with new life in his step. Gabriel sighed and scratched his head. He thought about the scene that had just taken place. He burst into laughter and plopped himself down on the edge of the bed. Somehow Alyssa had slept through it all. Well, he would wake her up soon. He looked her over as she lay there splayed out on his bed. A little peek under her skirt wouldn't hurt, he decided. He lifted up the hem of her skirt. When he saw her shapely creamy thigh, his shaft practically screamed in response. He quickly put her skirt down before Harvey came back.

He got up from the bed and started removing his clothes. He didn't really want Harvey to see the state he was in, so he began undressing himself instead of allowing him to assist. He didn't want the old bugger to drop dead from shock when he saw his angry erection. He quickly donned his robe, then put on his slippers. Ah, much better. He went to the water closet and cleaned his teeth. He thought about shaving but decided against it. He could have fun tickling Alyssa with his evening beard. He went back in his room just in time for Harvey to return with the brandy.

"Thank you Harvey. Go back to bed, my good man. Feel free to sleep in on the morrow. I think I shall be rather busy and will not need your attendance," he said with a huge grin and a wink.

Harvey snickered and went to his small room. Gabriel went back over to Alyssa and set about removing her clothing. *Damnation, she's a beauty*, he thought, gazing upon her naked body. He would leave her stockings on in case her feet were cold. He liked them on her anyway. There was nothing sexier than a naked woman still wearing her stockings. Something about it just made him turn into a mindless fool. After his perusal, he shifted her into the bed properly, then went to his desk for a quill. He walked back over to the bed and climbed in beside her. Time to wake her up to finish what they'd started, he decided.

*****

Alyssa was having a strange dream. A talking fly kept landing on her nose. He was a silly talking fly, saying the most provocative things as he buzzed about her nose and ear. She tried to swat at him several times, but he kept coming back. The fly could use some lessons in dealing with a lady. Why, the things he said were most inappropriate. He kept laughing at her, too. Finally, the fly went away then her dream changed. She was with a pirate. He was telling her how big his sword was as he rubbed his hands all over her. They must have been on a beach somewhere because it was getting awfully hot. The pirate was tickling her now. She had just about had enough of him when that naughty fly came back, landing on her nose again. She reached out and slapped herself on the nose. Suddenly, she was awake. She was disoriented and confused, she wasn't sure if she really had woken up at all. Diana's betrothed was lying next to her. He was wearing a robe and a wicked smile.

"Ah my sweet Alyssa, you have returned to me," he said just before diving for her mouth.

At first she was convinced she was still dreaming, kissing him back with wild abandon. It was all right to kiss him in her dreams. The kiss was so warm and delicious. He tasted of mint and brandy. She closed her eyes, deciding she was indeed still dreaming and allowed him to ravish her mouth. But then that talking fly came back. She swatted at it and was startled into reality when she heard him cry out. It was then she realized that Diana's betrothed was rubbing his jaw. She struggled to sit up, feeling bewildered now, she truly needed to make sense of the situation before her. *Ah, I remember now. He won me in a card game.* She lay back down, looking him over smiling; it all made sense now. She remembered the things he had done to her, and she blushed. She heard him laugh again, and she shot him a look.

"What are you laughing at?" she demanded.

"You have a mean right hook," he told her.

"I was trying to swat a fly … a talking fly that kept saying naughty things, just before the pirate started tickling me," she explained.

He rolled over on his back, roaring with laughter. Why, he was making sport of her! She didn't like that at all! He continued with his laughter for a moment. Despite herself, she began to laugh too. His laugh was so infectious that she began to giggle. Before she knew it, the two of them were nearly in tears with uncontrollable laughter. The laughter died down, and he rolled back on top of her and began to kiss her again. *Wait a minute! He has already claimed my virginity; what more does he want?* She pushed him off of her.

"Just what do you think you are doing?" she demanded.

"Why, I was kissing you," he told her.

"There has been enough of that already," she told him.

"My dear, I am just getting started," he told her, lunging for her lips again.

She shoved at him, scooting out of his way before he made contact. Jumping up and out of the bed, she left him kissing the pillow. She started looking around the room then realized she didn't recognize her surroundings at all. Where was she? She looked back at him. He was smiling at her and looking at her bum. She realized then, she was naked. She gasped and dove down beside the bed to hide her nakedness from his eyes. She heard him laughing again. Just what was so funny? She didn't see anything humorous about this situation at all. She was completely naked, in a strange room with a strange man who was her cousin's betrothed, who had won her in a card game, no less. *Oh, how I have fallen!*

"What is so funny?" she demanded, remaining hunkered down beside the bed.

She heard him sliding around on the bed then

suddenly she was face to face with him. He was hanging his head off the side of the bed.

"You are," he boldly stated, then reached out to tweak her nose.

Alyssa gasped and felt herself turn beet-red. She would have no more of his nonsense, she decided.

"Where are my clothes? Where are we?" she demanded.

"We are in my room and your clothes are over there on the chair, but you don't need them, come back to bed so we can finish our business," he told her with his head still dangling off the side of his bed.

She jumped up, frantically looking around for said chair, quickly spotting it. She made a mad dash for her gown then clumsily donned it. Just then, she felt his hands on her shoulders as she pulled the gown over her head. She spun around glaring at him. He dropped his hands, taking a step back as though he thought she were about to pummel him senseless.

"I should like to return to my room, if you please," she told him with her shoulders squared for battle.

"I don't understand," he told her, looking truly perplexed.

"Tis simple, I should like to go back to my room to collect my things so I can leave this place," she said indignantly.

"But we haven't finished our transaction," he told her, a bit miffed at her now.

Alyssa didn't know what he was talking about.

Of course they had finished their transaction. He took her virginity and now they were finished. There was no need to continue any further association with this dratted man.

"I would remind you that you have already taken my virginity, which you didn't even pay for, might, I add," she said with exasperation.

He looked at her as if she were daft. He scratched his head, blinking his eyes as he looked at her. He was the one that was daft!

"Would you kindly button up my gown?" she asked, turning to give him her back.

He didn't move to assist her, and she turned huffing at him before giving him her back again. He reached for her shoulder, spinning her around to face him.

"I think you are confused," he told her.

"What do you mean?"

"I mean that you are still a virgin. We still have to remedy that," he said with a smile.

Alyssa was aghast. Who did he think he was fooling? She knew good and well she was no longer a virgin. She remembered that they … she gasped again, really remembering now. They had been interrupted … by Alistair. She began to tremble, the action causing her knees to buckle. She nearly dropped to the floor. He caught her by the elbow to steady her with a look of concern on his face. Alistair was here in the building; she had to run.

"Please hurry and button my gown. I must run before he finds me," she pleaded.

"He won't find you. Don't you remember what happened?" he asked incredulously.

She closed her eyes tight, going back over everything that had happened. They had jumped out a window and got on a horse. She looked around the room, realizing there were no rooms as grand as this one at Annabelle's.

"Where have you taken me?" she asked with a trembling voice.

"You are at my home, Windhaven. Gabriel Hawkins, The Duke of Windhaven at your service," he said with a sweeping bow.

"I know who you are, you are Diana's betrothed," she shouted while stomping her foot.

Then she began to cry. She dropped to her knees in a heap on the floor blubbering like a baby. She was in a sorry state. How could things have gone so wrong? How could she ever hold her head up again when word got out what had happened. He dropped down on his knees beside her, taking her into his arms. He was patting her on the back, stroking her hair.

"There's no need to cry, love," he crooned.

She sniffed back her tears and looked at him. His eyes were so kind. He was so handsome. Then she had a sudden memory of what they had done. She blushed scarlet all the way to her toes, bursting into tears anew. Oh, this was horrible! What was she to do? He stood up, lifting her to her feet and walked her over to the bed, sitting her down on the edge. He walked over to the sideboard to pour her a brandy, then walked back over to her, thrusting it in front of her.

"Drink this, it will settle your nerves," he told her.

She took the brandy, sipped it, then started coughing. She remembered how tipsy she had gotten before and handed the brandy back to him. He refused to take it, so she held onto it but didn't sip anymore.

"What am I to do?" she asked him.

"You are to stay here with me so I can protect you," he told her.

"I couldn't possibly do that. I need to get to the docks. I have to purchase passage to America. That is the only reason I went through that horrible ordeal in the first place. I must leave England before they find me and force me to marry Alistair. I cannot marry Alistair; he beat me, you see," she said in a rush of hysterics.

She was trembling at the memory and very scared. He took the hand that held the brandy and lifted it to her lips. She didn't resist as he insisted she drink the cursed stuff. It did seem to warm her, so she sipped it some more on her own.

"I will protect you, Alyssa. Trust me," he said.

"How can you protect me? What would Diana think about such a thing?" she demanded of him.

"I don't give a shite what Diana thinks, forgive me for swearing, but really I don't care what she thinks. As soon as I can find away to break off our betrothal, I will. Our fathers arranged it when she was born. I have no interest in tying myself to such a creature as she," he told her with vehemence.

So he didn't love Diana? It was a relief to know he didn't love her. Then perhaps he wouldn't tell her of this, and no one would ever have to know.

"You won't tell her about this will you?"

"You have my word on it as a gentleman. This is between you and I. No one will ever know. I will take care of you. You will stay here with me until we can find a way to rid you of Alistair. You shouldn't have to leave England for that," he told her.

"I couldn't possibly stay here. I have money to make it on my own now," she said with a blush.

He took the brandy from her hand, placing it on the table beside the bed and lifted her to her feet. He drew her in his arms, taking her in a passionate kiss that nearly made her swoon. He slid her gown off her shoulders and started gently massaging her breasts. For a moment, the feeling had been so soothing, she allowed it. Then she realized the implications of his words, and she pulled away from him.

"I cannot allow these liberties, your grace," she told him.

He sighed in exasperation and walked away from her, scratching his head again.

"You are a confounding woman, Alyssa. How can you say that you cannot allow me these liberties when we have yet to conclude our business?"

"I don't owe you anything. I owe Lord Yarbrough, if I owe anyone. You merely played a game that I had no say in at all. I owe you nothing," she argued.

"Lord Yarbrough would have beaten you. That's what he does. He beat my mistress when he bought her from Annabelle's auction. He would have done the same to you. I couldn't let him have you, I just couldn't. So yes, you do owe me. I intend to collect," he insisted.

"So you would skip the beating and go straight to the rape?" she asked with fire in her eyes.

"Rape? Who said anything about rape?" he too had fire in his eyes.

"You would take what I do not wish to give, your grace. To my mind that is rape."

"Good God woman! I have no intention of raping you. I have never forced a woman to have sex with me in my entire life. I resent the insult madam," he shouted.

He walked over to the sideboard and poured himself a drink this time. He tossed it back angrily then poured another, tossing it back, too. Alyssa realized she had indeed insulted him, but she was going to stick to her principles.

"I meant no insult. But I refuse to go through with this ridiculous scheme. I want no part of it. You won me in a card game at a brothel, for goodness sakes. Not to mention you are betrothed to my cousin. And you have a mistress, too. What could you possibly want with me?"

"You truly are an innocent, aren't you? Let me just tell you what I want with you," he said, advancing toward her.

He took her by the shoulders saying, "You are the most beautiful woman I have ever seen, and my body aches to be inside you. I have tasted your sweetness, and I want more. I want to feel your sheath wrapped around me as I drive myself into you with every ounce of power that I possess while I take us both to an extraordinary release such as you have never imagined in your wildest dreams.

Then I want to do it all over again and again until our bodies ache and collapse in complete and glorious exhaustion," he told her, his eyes silver like mercury.

Alyssa stood speechless. Her mouth had dropped open. They stood staring into each other's eyes for a suspended moment, then he leaned forward ever so slowly and kissed her again. Oh, he can kiss so very well! She gave herself over to the moment, and he deepened the kiss. He pulled her close against him. She could feel the huge ridge of his arousal as it was pressed against her stomach. She remembered how large he was now, and she quickly pulled away in fear.

"I can't!"

"Yes you can, it will be wonderful, I promise," he pleaded.

"No, please, you don't understand, w—we won't f—fit," she stammered.

He laughed again, then he opened his robe to show her his manhood. It was the most shocking thing she had ever seen. She stood there like a frightened deer, gazing upon it.

"Come now, he's not a beast. He won't hurt you," he smiled. "Touch it!" he said with a sultry voice.

She shook her head no, but her hand had a mind of its own and reached out for it. She stroked it once along its length. It jerked in response. It looked painful as it was angry red with blue veins bulging on its side. She jerked her hand away and looked up at him. "Does it hurt?" she asked.

He nodded his head that it did. She reached out

touching it again, but this time he put his hand over hers and wrapped her hand around it in a snug grip. He began to move her hand back and forth. With his other arm he drew her near.

"He has been very upset ever since we were at Annabelle's, and he was denied his pleasure. The trip from London nearly did me in as I suffered his complaints for two hours without relief while he was teased by your luscious bottom grinding against him," he whispered in her ear with an ache in his voice, beginning to thrust himself in and out of her grip.

She felt sorry for him now, not wishing him to be in pain, but neither did she want to allow him to put the thing inside her. It was simply too large. It intimidated her. She knew it would hurt badly. Wanting to ease his suffering, she continued to massage him there as Alistair had made her do. She found herself mesmerized by his response. His whole body tensed, and his breathing became harsh. His moan traveled down her spine, warming her to her very core. Suddenly he pulled himself away from her and ran into the water closet, slamming the door behind him. After a moment, she heard an agonized groan come from inside, causing her to worry he had been harmed. What had happened? Did she hurt him? She could hear water running. After another moment the door opened, and he came out, looking flushed about the cheeks. He looked rather embarrassed, so to spare him she dropped her eyes and looked at the floor. Was he angry at her?

"Forgive me," she heard him say.

She looked back up to see him advancing toward her again.

"I was quite overcome. I didn't want to make a mess all over your lovely hand," he said sheepishly.

Alyssa realized what had happened then. The same thing had happened with Alistair. She was embarrassed, so she averted her eyes back at the floor. He lifted her chin to look at her. He seemed more subdued now as if a great deal of pressure had been released. Strange the way men behaved when they were aroused. She was glad she was a woman and wasn't burdened with one of those things.

"I can think straight now. I'm sorry if I upset you," he said calmly.

Alyssa felt relieved too now. Perhaps he wouldn't pester her anymore. Maybe he would now help her gain passage on a ship.

"Will you button my gown now?" she ventured.

He laughed softly, gently spun her around and deftly began buttoning up her gown. He turned her back to face him, then kissed her tenderly on the lips. It wasn't a passionate kiss this time, just one of affection.

"Now, why don't you tell me about Alistair and how you ended up at Annabelle's?"

*****

Gabriel listened as she relayed her story. He was angry now. He hated Diana and her uncle more than ever before. He realized while she was talking about Alistair, that the man was completely unstable. She truly was in danger. The man clearly became obsessed over her and lost control of his senses. He had seen it happen before. Sometimes men lost all reason where women were concerned. He looked at her, realizing she was even lovelier than he first thought. She was so petite and adorable that it was all he could do not to reach out to kiss her voluptuous lips. She had a cute little dimple in her left cheek. Her eyes were big glass orbs of blue-green like the sea in the tropics. Her hair was so lustrous as it draped over her shoulders and down her back in loose curls. Her little nose was dotted with freckles. He ached to kiss each and every one of them.

He could see how Alistair had lost his mind over her, for he too wanted her desperately. He had to convince her to stay with him somehow. She seemed determined to go to America. He just couldn't allow that. He would take care of her if she would let him. He felt guilty for pressing himself on her the way he had. He had been so consumed by his prolonged arousal he couldn't think straight and desperately needed relief. He hadn't meant to do what he did, but he was overcome by the moment and her beauty.

When he had succumbed to her touch he realized he was about to be unmanned, so he ran away to relieve himself. She must think that he was some kind of perverted monster, after all she had already endured at the hands of a man. He would make it up to her, somehow. He would get her to agree to become his mistress. If there was any way possible to be rid of Diana, then maybe he could make an honest woman of her … someday. She was a delight to be around obviously being a lady of quality. If he were to ever marry, she would be most ideal. He thought about how confused she had been when she woke up and inwardly laughed. He had teased and fondled her while she was sleeping. He told her he was a randy fly while he tickled her about the nose and ear with the quill, whispering naughty nothings in her ear.

Then, he had changed tactics, telling her he was a pirate who wanted her to play with his gigantic sword. He tried to tickle her awake. He would have liked to be in her head to see what her dreams had showed her. He liked to play games in bed. Her reactions to his teasing had been worth his aching jaw. He sighed. He realized that sooner or later Alistair would find them, but he wasn't scared of him. He was well skilled in self-defense and the arts of war, but still, if Alistair was truly a madman he could be dangerous to anyone.

She finished her story looking at him with expectant eyes. She wanted him to take her back to London. She wanted to be on a ship to America. He sighed again, shaking his head. He couldn't send her on a ship alone. It was too dangerous. He had to convince her to stay here with him at all cost.

"I cannot put you on a ship to America," he told her.

Chapter Ten

"What do you mean; you cannot put me on a ship?"

Gabriel knew she would be unhappy about this, but he was determined to convince her to stay here where she would be safe.

"It's too dangerous for such a young woman as you to travel alone on a ship without proper escort. Anything could happen. You would be at the mercy of God knows who. No, my love you must stay here with me until we can rid you of your problem with Alistair. If, as you say, he will be returning to Jamaica, you simply have to wait him out. You can do that here in comfort and security."

He watched her turn his words over in her mind. He hoped he had appealed to her good sense and she would reach the logical conclusion that she should stay here.

"It would be improper," she finally said.

"It would be no more improper to stay here than it would to go off alone on a ship. Have you any idea what would be thought of you or the attention that you would attract. A woman alone on a long voyage at sea would be prey to the ship's crew or any other scoundrels aboard. You would never make the crossing with your virtue intact," he told her earnestly.

"I don't think I will survive here with my virtue intact either," she said indignantly.

He laughed softly, took her hand in his and lightly kissed her palm.

"'Tis true that I want you, my sweet Alyssa, but I would never force myself upon you, I swear."

Her huge eyes were locked on his and her luscious bottom lip slightly trembled. He released her hand, and she tucked it primly in her lap averting her eyes to the floor. Looking at her now, he could see she lacked self-confidence from the way her life had been. He regretted the loss of who she could have been, had her father never died.

"Trust me," he told her softly.

"If Alistair finds us, he will kill us both," she said, still looking down at the floor.

He tipped her chin up so he could look into her eyes and said, "I will protect you."

She wanted to believe him, he could tell but she couldn't allow herself to trust, yet. He sighed deeply and said, "Think about it; you don't have to decide anything now. Go to sleep. We will discuss it in the morning."

"Where am I to sleep?"

"Here with me," he ventured mischievously with a sexy grin.

"I couldn't possibly sleep here with you. Surely, you must have a guest room that I could sleep in."

"Aye, but they have not been prepared to receive guests, and the staff is asleep. You will be safe here, I promise. I won't do anything to you that you don't want me to."

He watched her considering his words. He had left himself a big loophole and hoped she wouldn't see it. He had every intention of trying to bring her around to his way of thinking, but he would have to go slowly to keep from frightening her.

"We will sleep with our clothes on. You will

sleep on top of the blankets," she consented.

That's my girl, he smiled inwardly. "Of course, it will be as you say. But you don't have to sleep in your gown, your chemise will keep you covered … or you could wear one of my nightshirts," he suggested.

"Tis true, I would ruin my gown if I slept in it, I suppose. Alright, I will wear one of your nightshirts, but you must put some breeches on," she said with admonishment in her tone.

He nodded his agreement, removing himself from the bed. He went to his wardrobe to pull out a nightshirt for her to wear.

"You may change behind the privacy screen or in the water closet if you would like to freshen up before you come to bed."

She reached for the nightshirt and scurried to the water closet. He sighed. He put on his breeches but took off his robe. He lay down on the bed to await her. He wouldn't try to take her tonight. He would convince her to stay and start wearing her down on the morrow. He smiled, rolled over on his side and closed his eyes. There was nothing wrong with a few kisses or some caresses he reasoned. He could give her another release to show her the joys she could have with him as her lover. His musings were interrupted by a sweet, shy voice calling from the water closet.

"Excuse me, your grace, but could you please come and unbutton me?"

Gabriel smiled, got up and went to the water closet to steal a peek inside the partially opened door. He saw her standing there biting her thumbnail and laughed softly.

He pushed the door all the way open and said, "I will unbutton your gown for a boon," he told her with a cheeky grin. She looked at him with something that looked like a mixture of fear and hostility.

"Tis not what you think," he assured her. "I will unbutton your gown if you will please call me Gabriel or Hawk, if you prefer, but no more of this 'your grace' nonsense," he told her.

She smiled, turning a lovely shade of pink. She nodded her head before presenting him with her back. He slowly unbuttoned her gown and was sorely tempted to caress her lovely back, but he resisted, instead removing himself from the water closet when he completed his task. He climbed back into the bed, closing his eyes to await her. He knew she would be nervous when she came out wearing his nightshirt, and he didn't want to unsettle her. Moments later, she tiptoed out of the water closet and slipped quietly into the bed as close to the edge as she could get without falling off.

*****

Alyssa couldn't help herself; she was charmed by the duke. He was so different from Alistair that she was completely drawn in by him. Where Alistair was serious and angry, Gabriel was full of laughter and mischief. A rogue to be sure, but it was sort of endearing. Of course, she didn't try to fool herself for even a minute about the man's true nature. He was a philanderer. Engaged to her cousin, keeping a mistress and gambling for virgins in a brothel didn't say much for his character. But he did it all without the least bit of shame. He had such playfulness that you couldn't really be angry at him for it.

A man like that would never be faithful to his wife if he were to ever marry. Of course, she really shouldn't care about that since she certainly had no plans to marry him. The idea was completely ridiculous, but he was so handsome and tender that she couldn't help but imagine what it would be like to be with such a man. He had given her amazing pleasure such as she had never imagined when they were at Annabelle's, but that was then, when she thought she had no other choice in the matter. She had been lucky to survive the night with her virtue intact yet still accomplish her objective to gain money to start a new life with. Now, she could still marry if she chose to, some day. She closed her eyes, trying to settle down to go to sleep.

After several moments, she realized she was having trouble going to sleep. She looked over at Gabriel, who was snoring. She grumbled when she noticed he had forgotten to put the lamp out before he fell asleep. She sighed with annoyance wondering if she should do it herself. Perhaps he always slept with the lamp burning. Surely, he wasn't afraid of the dark. His snoring seemed to increase. It was really loud and annoying. How could I ever fall asleep like this? She threw back the covers, slipped out of bed, carefully tiptoeing around to his side so she could put out the lamp.

"He must have simply forgotten to do it. Anyone snoring like that, wouldn't care whether the lamp was burning or not," she grumbled aloud.

When she reached the nightstand to put out the lamp, she startled as suddenly his eyes opened and he grabbed her arm, pulling her down on top of him.

"Got you!" he said, tickling her unmercifully on her ribcage. She twisted and squirmed. Despite herself, she was overcome by his playful assault, bursting into uncontrollable laughter.

"Stop!" she managed to shout between giggles.

He stopped but only to roll over, pinning her beneath him just before he lunged forward kissing her soundly. She was stunned by the sudden change in her situation and allowed him to ravish her mouth. He smelled so good, and her senses were overwhelmed by his essence; before she knew what she was about, she found herself returning the kiss. Oh, he was wickedly delicious as he deepened the kiss. His tongue was massaging hers, making her feel warm all the way to her toes. She found herself quite helpless to end it. A little kiss wouldn't hurt would it? Tomorrow, she would be gone, bound for America, but they could have this now as long as she didn't allow him to go further.

He moved his hand to her breast and started a slow sensual caress. He gently kneaded, making her nipples tighten in response. Somehow, he managed to untie the drawstring of her nightshirt without her knowledge. His lips found their way inside. He began to suckle at her breast. Oh, the feeling was divine. She felt a heating at her private center. It began to ache, causing her to squirm as it was beginning to feel uncomfortable the way it made her feel restless. He seemed to understand her distress as his hand lowered to lift the hem of the nightshirt where he began a slow sensual of her woman's flesh.

He slipped a finger inside, gently thrusting it in and out. He began a slow rotating motion of her sensitive nub with his thumb. He continued his ministrations all the while maintaining the pleasure at her breast. She was held captive under his sensual assault, she couldn't end it even if she wanted to. She began to lift her hips, undulating as the feeling grew so very intense. She was on the verge of fracturing into a million pieces as she had earlier at Annabelle's. He certainly knew his way around a woman's body. He performed his task with the skill of a master. Slowly he lifted from her breast and began to plunder her lips with an assured intent.

"Let yourself go, Alyssa," he breathed into her mouth.

The sound of his voice had an immediate response as she did as he bade her. It was with devastating tremors and a tightening of her passage around his finger that she could feel the pulsing as her body gripped and released around him. The moment seemed to go on forever. She was lost to it, swept away, riding the tide of ecstasy. He laughed softly then slid his way down so he could lave her belly with his tongue as he continued to go lower. Soon she felt his breath on her woman's mound as he nudged her legs apart with his chin. Then he thrust his tongue inside her and began to feast upon her as if he were feeding from the juices that were flowing from her center.

She was so overwhelmed by the sensations of

his sensual ministration that she found she was helpless to resist as he once again brought her to another powerful release. She clung to his head with her thighs, grinding herself against him to savor the feeling as she rode the waves of her ruthless climax. Finally, she was released from the tidal wave, and she relaxed her hold, allowing him to slide back up her body, whereby he kissed his way back to her lips. Her breasts were heaving as she was quite out of breath. She pulled back from the kiss with a gasp, drawing in the precious air.

"That was wonderful Alyssa. See how good we are together?" he asked, gazing into her eyes.

His words brought her back to reality, and she pushed him off of her, sitting up in the bed.

"What have I done?" she cried out, then hid her face in her hands, weeping.

"You enjoyed yourself; that's all. It was beautiful. You shouldn't be ashamed. I loved watching you as you reached for your release. It was the most erotic thing I have ever seen," he told her.

His words made her cry harder. A witness to her sin was not something she wanted to consider.

"I am a wanton trollop, that's what I am. How could I have fallen so low, so quickly without even a thought to propriety?" she said with a wail.

He sat up, drew her into his arms and stroked her hair and her cheeks.

"Shhhh, I don't ever want to hear you say such things about yourself again. You are a woman with a woman's needs. There is nothing to be ashamed of," he said soothingly.

A woman has needs? What does he mean by that? Women aren't supposed to enjoy such things or even want them, are they? She didn't know about other women, but she sure seemed to have wanted it. There must be something wrong with her, she decided.

"Am I still a virgin?" she asked timidly.

He held her tighter, laughing softly in her ear.

"Much to my regret!" was his soft reply.

The thought comforted her, and she began to relax. All was not lost as long as she still had her virginity. She pushed him away and scooted herself to her side of the bed, drawing her knees to her chest so she could wrap her arms around herself.

"Don't be afraid, Alyssa. I told you I would not force you to do anything you didn't want. Believe me when I tell you that you wanted that, or I would have stopped," he told her without an ounce of shame for his behavior.

She dropped her face to her knees, refusing to look at him while considering his words. She had wanted it and he knew it. How could she ever show her face again? She was one of those women that you hear about. A slut! She sighed deeply and continued to keep her face buried. She felt him moving on the bed. Then he was beside her, lifting her chin up.

"I will take good care of you Alyssa. I will set you up in a nice house. I'll give you everything you could ever want. You will stay here until we deal with Alistair. Then, we shall move you back to London where I will buy you a nice house, and we will make mad passionate love there, every day," he said with a sultry voice.

What was he saying? Why would he buy her a house and give her things? Is he … she gasped when the realization of his words struck her.

"I will be no man's mistress," she boldly stated.

"You will be my mistress, Alyssa. We still have much unfinished business between us, you and I. We will be perfect together, you shall see. I will show you things you haven't ever dreamed of. Wonderful things between a man and a woman such as you cannot even imagine."

She shivered as his voice washed over her. He was so persuasive as he told her of his plans. He was so handsome and kind. The things he had already shown her had shaken her very soul. What more could he teach her? She wanted to know, but she didn't want to be a whore. She wanted marriage and children. She could never have those things if she were a mistress.

"I cannot," she told him with little conviction behind her words.

She wanted to, she did. She had to get away from him before she fell so low that she was irredeemable. She needed to get on that ship and soon. Tomorrow wasn't soon enough, but it was the middle of the night now. She could go nowhere.

"You can and you will. You want it as much as I."

"No, I want marriage and children. I cannot have those things if I become your whore. I won't do it. I must leave here on the morrow. Take me to London. Put me on a ship, I beg you," she cried out.

"Alyssa I have already told you that it is too

dangerous for a woman to travel alone. I will not do this thing you ask of me. You will stay here with me. I will leave you alone if that's what you really want. I will have a room prepared for you on the morrow, but you will stay here with me. Is that understood?"

No, she didn't understand his stubborn refusal at all. However, if he were to put her in her own room she could stay here for awhile, she supposed. It was this constant pressure he put on her that made her want to flee. She really didn't want to leave England if she could help it, but if she stayed here with him, like this, she would be lost.

"You will give me my own room and leave me alone?" she found herself asking.

"You have my word as a gentleman," he told her solemnly.

His behavior hadn't been very gentlemanly, but she felt she could believe him, despite it. A man was only as good as his word, after all. She knew he was a good man beneath the surface.

"Go back to sleep Alyssa. I will bother you no further," he said after a moment.

He leaned over and blew out the lamp, settling himself down with his back to her. She sat there for a moment longer, decided that it was best to just go to sleep and think about it in the morning. That decided, she shimmied under the covers and closed her eyes.

*****

What have I done? Gabriel asked himself, trying to

command his body into submission. He felt like a
cad for pushing his attentions on her the way he
had. He had promised she would be safe from him,
but he had showed her otherwise. He suppressed a
groan. He grabbed his shaft through his breeches,
angrily pressing against it in an effort to bring it
under control. It was raging at him once again, and
he wanted relief. He would have no relief this time
as he didn't want to scare her further by relieving
himself, yet again. It was his just desserts to suffer
this condition for his actions, he decided. He was
ashamed of his behavior, but he had been quite
unable to relent.

He had pretended to be asleep and hoped she
would get up to blow out the lamp so he could do
just what he had done. He wanted to seduce her into
accepting him as her protector but, instead, he had
probably ensured the opposite. He didn't want to let
her go for reasons he couldn't quite come to terms
with. He couldn't offer her marriage as she
deserved because of his contract with Diana. He
really didn't want to marry anyway, so there was no
point in dwelling on the issue. But he wanted her so
bad. He knew that would likely be the only way to
have her. Despite finding her in a brothel, she was a
lady, the niece of an earl. She deserved to be treated
with deference due her station—but marriage—he
wasn't sure he was ready. She was a beautiful
woman no doubt, anyone would be lucky to have
her as his wife. He was deeply attracted to her in a
way that he had never been to another, but
marriage? He had had many lovers, but none of
them had moved him the way she had. When her

body was lost to the throws of passion it was the most phenomenal thing he had ever witnessed. Her responses were wild, unhindered. She became quite aggressive when she reached for her release. He had never had a woman clutch him between her thighs and grind herself against him as she had. Most of his lovers were passive by comparison. He wondered now if any of them had ever really found release or if they had been faking.

No, he refused to believe that. He knew when a woman reached climax, but none had ever gone after it with such a hunger. He wanted more; he had to have more. He would have more if it was the last thing he ever did. He could still smell her essence upon him. It was making it difficult to control his arousal. Her very being had crawled beneath his skin until he ached to join with her. She had bewitched him just as she had bewitched Alistair, he realized. The woman was dangerous to a man. She was a menace to his peace of mind. She could enthrall a man, making him become a mindless animal. She had no idea the power she possessed, he was sure of it. The combination of her innocence and her savage hunger for passion was a potent formula to enslave a man.

He couldn't let her go to America or out of his life. He needed to convince her anyway he could to stay with him. He could see he had offended her with his suggestions, but he had been sure he could appeal to her passion through seduction and bring her around. Perhaps he couldn't offer marriage now, but someday he could, he just had to keep her satisfied in the interim. He would do whatever he had to do to rid himself of Diana so the way could be cleared for Alyssa. She had all he would ever want or need in a mate. He would change his ways. He would be the man of her dreams if he were free to offer for her. He would change his ways whether he could offer for her or not. From this moment onward, she was the only woman for him. He needed to be with her as he had never before needed another.

He rolled over onto his back and looked over at her silhouette. She seemed to be sleeping. Her breathing had become rhythmic. He slowly reached out and touched her hair. It was so soft, luxurious. The color was unlike he had ever seen before; deep red with streaks of fire. Maybe it was true that redheads were full of fire and passion. She certainly was. She was lightly snoring now. He smiled, his sweet Alyssa was exhausted. He knew why and was pleased he was the cause of it. He had brought her to climax two times, one right after the other, not to mention what they had done before, at Annabelle's. Greedy minx, he mused. His erection flinched in response to his thoughts. He pressed it harder in his grip. The stubborn devil was not cooperating at all. He wouldn't be able to sleep in such a state. If he allowed it to go on like this, there was no telling what would happen during the remainder of the night.

With a sigh, he slid from the bed and silently went to the water closet, quietly closing the door behind him. He decided he would need to cool off, so with reluctance he ran a cold bath. He would kill the problem then maybe he could sleep. He was amused though surprised with himself by this action. Normally, he would have simply relieved himself, but he didn't have the heart to do it. It felt wrong somehow to take things into his own hands, with her sleeping just in the other room. If he couldn't share himself with her, then there was no point in sporting such a monument to his prowess. He quietly laughed at himself, he truly was bewitched. He was ruined for all others, including his own hand.

With that thought, he removed his breeches, slid into the frigid water and winced at the shock of it. He laid his head back, thinking about his life and the woman who lay sleeping in his bed. He had lived such a life of unrestrained debauchery with little thought to the future. For the first time, he found himself considering matrimony as a real option. He was eight and twenty now, a good age to think about settling down to start a family, he supposed. He knew many men younger than he that had been caught in the parson's trap, but they seemed completely miserable and sought solace with their mistresses. He wondered why that was and thought about their wives. Most of them were cold, stern creatures with no sense of humor. His Alyssa was nothing like them, she was unique in every way. He didn't think he would be miserable with her. She would make a beautiful duchess with her glorious hair and spellbinding eyes. She had cast a spell on him with those eyes, he was sure of it. When he looked into them, he was completely lost to her power. It was a bit like falling helplessly into their depths but never fearing the fall as the landing would be quite pleasurable.

He closed his eyes, imagining the future with her by his side. The children they would have would be beautiful and strong. His sons and daughters would probably have her hair and eyes, he mused. He imagined himself down on his hands and knees, giving them rides on his back while the giggles of his offspring sang in his ears. He could see himself teaching his sons to fence and ride, and his daughters to be little hoydens. He would make sure his daughters knew how to defend themselves against men such as Alistair and Yarbrough, so they would never find themselves at the mercy of such a brute and have to make a decision like their mother had.

Their mother … yes he would marry her, he knew that now. It was his destiny, it had to be. Why else had things worked out the way they had. He had beaten a renowned gambler at his preferred game. It was the hand of fate; it could have been nothing else. Yes, they would marry, but he couldn't give her false hope, just now. He was betrothed to another. It wouldn't be easy to get out of it without a huge scandal. He should just take her to Gretna Green and be done with it, Diana and her father, be damned. He had had his fair share of scandal. One more wouldn't hurt, there were the legal consequences to consider, though.

However, if he were to make it known how she and her family treated Alyssa, no one would blame him for crying off. They had treated her like a virtual slave. Slavery was thought poorly of here in England. He supposed that would take care of the

problem with Alistair, as well. Once she was
another man's wife, what could he do? Alyssa had
not signed a betrothal agreement with him. It would
be within her rights to cry off for the abuse he dealt
her. Besides, he had completely compromised her
by bringing her here, it was his duty to marry her.
He sat up in the tub as it occurred to him that there
really was nothing in the way of their marrying. He
lifted himself out of the tub, happy to see his partner
in crime had given up the ghost, he was quite
relieved now. He toweled himself off, put on his
breeches. With a smile of satisfaction that he had
reached a decision, he climbed back into the bed
and pulled her sweet, sleeping body into his arms,
promptly falling into a peaceful slumber.

Chapter Eleven

Alyssa woke with her nose pressed against a wall of flesh. She realized then that it was Gabriel's chest and that she was wrapped within his embrace. She looked up to see he was smiling at her and she blushed.

"Marry me," he said.

Alyssa wasn't sure she had heard him correctly. She looked at him, bewildered.

"Yes, marry me," he said just before placing a tender kiss on her lips.

She struggled to free herself of his embrace, but he held on and wouldn't let her go. She stopped struggling and thought about what he had said, and suddenly she was offended. Marry him indeed! She would never marry such a rogue.

"I will not marry you," she defiantly told his chest.

He rolled her over onto her back so he could lean over her and stared into her eyes. She could tell then, he was serious about this and that she had hurt his feelings. His gray eyes reflected the pain of her rejection.

"Why?" he quietly asked.

"When I marry, it will be for love. It will be to a man that loves me in return, one who will be faithful to me. You could never be that man, Gabriel. You shouldn't even be proposing to me at all, considering you already have a fiancé and a mistress."

"I no longer have a mistress, and I don't care about Diana. I have no plans to marry her; I have already told you this. Marry me," he insisted.

"But you would not be faithful. We do not love each other," she softly responded.

"I will be faithful to you Alyssa. We would learn to love one another in a very short time. I already feel a deep attraction for you and have decided that you are the only woman for me. I would change my profligate ways for you. I will be the man you deserve, I swear. Besides, I have compromised you. My honor demands that I marry you," he said with passion laced in his voice.

Alyssa was stunned by his words. He seemed so sincere. His offer was tempting, and one she should consider seriously, she knew, but right now her bladder was about to burst. She wriggled away from him and sat up.

"I have need of the chamber pot. Please excuse me," she said, slipping out of the bed.

She looked back at him, seeing pain in his eyes. She had not responded to his tender words of affection, but she wasn't ready to. She needed to relieve herself and have a few moments to collect her wits. She stared at him, unsure how to tell him to leave the room so she could have privacy. He took the problem away by saying, "You will have privacy in the water closet."

She turned red with embarrassment then twirled around to take care of her needs. When she was finished, she washed her face and teeth, all the while thinking about his proposal. Was he serious? Did he really want to marry her? Or was he offering out of a sense of duty. He hadn't really compromised her; she had done that to herself.

They didn't even know each other, so how could they possibly marry. Look what had happened with Alistair after agreeing to marry him so quickly. What if Gabriel became like him and hurt her? She didn't really think he would because they were so different. For all she knew, all men were like Alistair, though Cookie had told her that was not the case.

Perhaps Gabriel was one of those men she had spoken of. Gabriel said that he saved her from Yarbrough because he would have harmed her. He had not done anything to harm her. Instead, he had protected her from harm. Sure, he was a randy sort, but he hadn't forced her to do anything she didn't want to do. She had been a willing participant in all that had occurred between them. Could he be faithful? That was another question entirely. She didn't want to marry a man that would cavort with mistresses and frequent brothels, gambling for virgins.

She cast away the thought with a sigh and looked at herself in the mirror. Her hair was a mess. She was a mess. How had all this come about? She thought she would have been on a ship by now, but here she was considering marriage to a man who won her in a card game the night before when she had thought to auction away her virtue. She used his brush, running it through her hair, trying to force her unruly locks into a sense of order. She thought about last night and the wonders she had found at his hands. Why should she deny herself a future with this man? Would she ever meet anyone to equal him? She didn't think so, but neither did she think she should rush into anything. There were simply too many things that must be dealt with first. There were Diana and Alistair to contend with. She didn't think they could be gotten rid of so easily. With another sigh, she put down the brush and straightened her spine. She would consider his offer. She would be a fool not to. With that decided, she opened the door and went back into the room. He was sitting on the edge of the bed with his face in his hands. He looked up when he heard her footfalls with uncertainty in his eyes. She would have to tell him of her decision.

"I will consider your offer, Gabriel, but I don't want to rush. It was rushing that put me in this situation to begin with. Had I taken the time to know Alistair, I would have never agreed to marry him, knowing what I do now," she told him.

He stood up and walked over to her, embracing her gently. He stroked her hair and caressed her cheek, leaned forward and kissed her lips tenderly, then slowly pulled away.

"I am nothing like Alistair. I will never harm you. I will be a good husband to you, Alyssa, but we mustn't wait too long. We could go to Gretna Green so that you wouldn't have to have permission from your uncle. If we leave now, we could be married in just a few days," he said softly.

She believed him, but still, she had to be careful. She was alone in the world and had no one to guide her. She needed to go slowly to see how things went between them for a few weeks. A lot could be learned about one another in a few weeks.

She would stay here with him as he suggested. If it turned out that they wouldn't suit, well then she would go to America as she planned before.

"I can only promise to consider it. I would like to take a few weeks to get to know you better. Can we not do that first?" she asked.

"No, I don't think it would be wise. We need to do all we can to rid ourselves of Diana and Alistair. What better way than by our marrying? It's the perfect solution, really," he insisted.

"I need some time to consider this Gabriel. Please do not rush me so, I beg you," she pleaded.

He sighed and scratched his head as he often did when he was frustrated.

"Three days," he said.

Three days? How could she possibly learn about him in three days? However, she learned quite a bit about Alistair in that amount of time. Perhaps it would be enough. She didn't know. She wished desperately she had someone to advise her.

Reluctantly, she nodded her agreement.

"Three days. We will decide then if we should suit. If not, you will put me on a ship to America."

He pulled her close, kissing her on the forehead. It dawned on her then that she needed to set some rules.

"You will still provide me with a room of my own, and you will keep your hands to yourself until you have my final decision," she told him.

He roared with laughter, hugging her tightly. "My sweet Alyssa, you will be my undoing," he told her. "But I will do my best to adhere to your dictates. I don't know if I can keep my hands off of you, but I do promise not to try and bed you again until you have consented to be my wife," he added.

She smiled at him, saying, "I suspect it is I who will be undone."

He pulled her tighter in his embrace and kissed her soundly with a passion that stunned her. Yes, she would most likely be undone.

*****

Gabriel was pleased by the morning's developments. For a few agonizing moments, he thought she really would refuse him, but she had surprised him when she returned from the water closet, saying she would consider it. He would give her every reason to determine that marrying him was for the best. He would do as she asked and behave himself. It would be hard, but he felt sure he could do it for her. She had been pleased with the room he provided her, even though it was the duchess' apartments and adjoined with his own. He assured her that the lock was in working order, giving her both keys, which he noted, put her at ease.

After they had bathed and broken their fast, he went to his library to take care of some correspondence. He needed to send word to his secretary to have him send money and the deed to the house to Melody to complete their business arrangement. He was glad to have that behind him so he could look to the future with Alyssa without any problems cropping up later. He didn't think there would be any problems because Melody was a good sort. He had treated her fairly.

The only real problems remaining were Diana and Alistair. He was reasonably certain that once he married Alyssa, put word around about the cruelty she had suffered at their hands, no one would look unkindly on them for crying off their engagements and marrying one another. Everything would work out fine. He eagerly anticipated his nuptials.

He opened a missive from Dylan.

My good friend Hawk,

I hope this message finds you well. I am writing to you, to let you know that after your great escape from Annabelle's last night, I had the displeasure of meeting one, Alistair Sinclair, Earl of Keith, also known as the fiancé of the fine piece you absconded with by way of the upstairs window.

It was clever of you to leave by that route. He had Bow Street men searching the premises. He had been informed of the auction and was sure that the description given him matched her and that it could have been none other than she.

I, of course, fed the man some very convincing misinformation whereby he promptly called off the search, leaving with the belief that it had not been the woman he sought, after all. I confirmed the young woman's identity with Annabelle and in case she has not told you already, her real name is Alyssa Habersham. She is niece to Morley Habersham, Earl of Glenmont. That's right Hawk, she is cousin to your fiancé, Diana.

It is likely that the earl sold her to Sinclair. He is Glenmont's stepson. Annabelle said that the family has mistreated her and that Sinclair physically abused her, which led her to the pitiable plight she found herself in at Annabelle's.

I learned this morning, through my man at Bow Street that Alyssa is an heiress of some large degree, though the amount is not known as it is a closely guarded secret by Glenmont and his solicitors. The knowledge of her wealth might lend to Sinclair's zealot-like determination to recover her.

I have decided that this Sinclair is dangerous and bears close scrutiny. With the help of our brothers Luther and Jasper, who are at this very moment, keeping round the clock surveillance, I hope to head off any potential threat to your health and that of the girl.

My friend, you must speak with her. Find out all that you can about the man and report your findings to me so that we may better assist you. I, of course, will report all of my findings to you as soon as I learn of them.

As in all things, you may count upon myself and the others to alert you of any new developments as well as lend arms to defend you should the need arise. I don't want to be offensive, but I hope that she has been worth the trouble I feel she is bound to bring upon your head.

Sinclair is unstable. He is determined to find her. He is offering a reward for any information that will return her to him. He believes she has been kidnapped and wouldn't have willingly left him.

I saw madness in his eyes, dear brother and would caution you strongly to remain vigilant so as not to be taken unawares.

I strongly urge you to reply to this missive so I will know that you are safe. We must keep in close contact my friend if we are to keep you and the girl safe.

If you would like, I could come and stay with you at Windhaven until the matter is resolved. Just say the word and it shall be done.

As always, your loyal friend
Sumersleigh

Gabriel wasn't surprised by anything that Dylan had told him, but she hadn't mentioned being an heiress. She only said she had an inheritance due upon her twenty-fifth birthday or upon her marriage whichever came first, but that she didn't know how much or even if she had any left after her uncle got his hands on it. He suspected too that it must be rather substantial for her uncle and his solicitors to keep the sum secret. It mattered not to him whether she had a million pounds or ten shillings, he wanted her regardless. He had his own fortune and would be able to provide for them quite lavishly for the rest of their lives and beyond.

What was important to him was her safety. It sounded like Alistair would tear London apart until he found her. If he ever got his hands on her, there was no telling what he would do. They needed to marry quickly. It was the only way to ensure that he had no further claim upon her. He had better inform Dylan of his decision to marry her, right away.

My good friend Dylan,

I thank you for the information, most of which I already knew or suspected. I should probably inform you that I am to be married within the very near future. I cannot in good conscience let matters stand as they are and leave Alyssa unprotected.

I have quite compromised her after all, though not the way you would imagine. She is deserving of fair and honorable treatment. That's right dear brother, I have yet to lay with her, but her being here alone with me is compromising enough in and of itself. It would certainly solve the dilemma of Diana and Alistair as once we were married they would have no claim to either of us.

She has consented to consider the matter over the course of the next three days, but I suspect she will reach the conclusion that we would suit quite admirably. I, however, plan to apply pressure to make her see that we need to act more swiftly. Time is of the essence.

She is a wonderful woman. I am quite smitten with her. She fills my soul with joy. Every moment that I am with her convinces me that she is the one woman in this world that could inspire me to be a faithful and loving husband. I want to share the rest of my life with her and raise a very large family with lots of little red-headed sons and daughters.

Did you ever think you would live to see the day where I would be considering marriage? It is surprising even to me, I can assure you.

She finds it rather hard to trust after her experience with Sinclair, but once she has given her consent, we shall elope to Gretna Green with all possible haste.

I appreciate all that you and our brothers are doing to ensure the safety of Alyssa and myself. Truer friends could never be had.

Of course, you are always welcome at Windhaven. I will leave whether you should come now to your own discretion.

I am forever in your debt,
Hawk

*****

His correspondence complete, Gabriel left the library in search of Alyssa. After an exhaustive search of the house, he located her in the kitchen assisting the cook with luncheon. This wouldn't do; his future wife should not be working in the kitchen.

"Alyssa what are you doing?" he pleasantly inquired. She looked up from chopping carrots and smiled.

It was a magnificent smile that lit up her eyes. She seemed quite content to be right where she was, doing what she was doing, and apparently saw nothing wrong with it. How could he chastise her for doing something she so obviously enjoyed?

"I thought you might like a tour of the gardens," he improvised.

"That would be lovely, but I am quite busy now," she told him.

"Yes about that; you shouldn't be doing such menial tasks. I have a staff for that; one that I pay quite handsomely too," he said with a smile.

She looked over at the cook Otto as if to ask his advice on the matter. He nodded his head that she should go with him. She stood up, wiped her hands off with a cloth and removed the apron she had donned.

"I suppose it wouldn't hurt for me to walk with you in the gardens," she said begrudgingly.

Gabriel inwardly laughed at her comment. She was a silly goose, if ever he saw one. She would learn in time what was expected of a duchess and act accordingly, so he wouldn't make further issue of it. He just wanted to spend time with her and try to encourage her to consent to his proposal so they could make haste for Gretna Green.

*****

Alyssa was enjoying herself in the kitchen. She wasn't exactly thrilled to have been taken away. Otto was such a nice man and didn't mind her assistance at all. She just felt out of place and needed something to occupy her mind. She knew she couldn't hide from Gabriel long before he sought her out.

They walked along in companionable silence in the garden. Alyssa thought she had never seen a lovelier day. It was cloudless and the temperature was pleasant. The birds were busy searching for grubs. Butterflies were fluttering about the flowers. She inhaled deeply. The smell of roses stimulated her senses. She smiled, remembering the roses in the garden of her childhood home. She missed her home and hoped that someday she could return.

"Have you given any more thought to my proposal?"

Alyssa blinked as she was brought back to the present and smiled at him. She could see he was nervous and probably feared she would reject him.

"Not really," she replied.

Gabriel stuck his hands in his coat pockets and looked down at the ground in contemplation of her words.

"I'm not refusing. I think that I shall probably marry you, but as I told you before, I don't want to rush to the decision," she told him kindly.

"About that; we should not waste a moment as it is to both of our benefits. I received correspondence from a friend this morning; one that was at Annabelle's. last night. He said that Alistair had been tipped off that you were there. Dylan, my friend, led Alistair astray by convincing him that it couldn't have been you, but he felt that the man still remained a threat."

Alyssa went over to a nearby bench and sat down. Gabriel followed her and sat next to her. They sat in silence for a few moments while she mulled over this information. Alyssa knew he was right. Alistair wouldn't give up. The only real protection she could have would be to become the wife of another. He would have to give up then, wouldn't he? She thought so. She resented the constant pressure she was placed under by men and wondered if the world would ever change to make life easier for women. She hoped so, but wishing didn't solve her dilemma. Could Gabriel be a faithful husband to her? That was the question that plagued her mind the most.

How could a man such as he go from rake-hell

to saint as he had implied he would do? He promised he would be faithful to her, but she just wasn't sure she believed that he could. What would she do when he took a lover? Would she be able to look the other way? No, she didn't think that she could. What if she wanted to take a lover? The thought made her giggle.

"What's so funny?" he asked.

"I was just imagining the future," she improvised.

She didn't want to tell him what she was really laughing about. He would think she were a woman of low morals. Of course, she wouldn't take a lover, but neither did she want him to. She wanted a marriage founded in love that would endure through the good times and the bad.

"We will have lots of laughter in our future Alyssa. I have a fondness for life, and I am rarely in a foul temper. When our children are born our house will be filled with love and joy. I will endeavor to make you the happiest woman alive."

Alyssa thought that was sweet. She was glad to hear he would like children. She too loved children and couldn't wait to have at least a dozen. Well not really a dozen, but she wanted a house full.

"I will marry you Gabriel," she found herself saying.

Gabriel sat quietly as if he had not heard her words. He was looking down at the ground as if trying to figure out a way to convince her. She laughed.

"Did you hear me?"

"Yes but I can't believe it. I thought you would

put up more of a fight," he said with a tender smile.

"Do you want to fight?" she asked playfully.

"I would love to wrestle with you," he said with a sexy smile.

Leave it to Gabriel to think of sex. The man was incorrigible. She could tell she would have her hands full with him. Suddenly he jumped up, grabbing her by the hand, starting to spin her around as if they were dancing a waltz. "Whewhooo!" he hollered.

Then, as quickly as he had started the dance, he stopped it, drawing her into his embrace. He kissed her with a searing passion that warmed her very soul. The kiss went on for a spellbinding moment before he broke away.

"We shall leave on the morrow with the dawn. We must make haste," he said.

"Can we not wait a day or two at least?"

"My love, please do not torture me so. I want to claim my bride as soon as possible," he said with a pained expression in his eyes.

"I have agreed to become your wife; can you not allow me a day or two to become accustomed to the idea?" she pleaded.

"You can become accustomed to it on the way to Gretna Green. It will take a few days to get there. Please, we cannot afford to delay."

Alyssa realized that she was quibbling over minor details. She supposed that it didn't really matter whether she became accustomed to it here or on the road.

"I suppose that it must be as you say. We shall leave on the morrow with the dawn," she consented.

"That's my girl!"

Chapter Twelve

Cookie crumbled her sister's missive and threw it in the waste-can after learning what had become of Alyssa. She was surprised by the turn of events, now she found herself quite concerned. She couldn't have ended up in a worst situation if she had tried. To have been whisked away by Diana's betrothed would certainly cause additional problems. She wished she could get word to her, but she didn't dare risk it. She left her room, heading for the kitchen, full of worry about her girl. Lord Keith was interviewing the staff again this morning. He would call for Adam soon and then her. She wished the man to the Devil and hoped that they would see the last of him in the very near future. Perhaps the duke could assist them with that.

*****

Diana decided to watch Cookie closely. She, above all others would have information about Alyssa's whereabouts. Cookie and Alyssa were very close, always taking their meals together, so it stood to reason that she would have information. She waited for Cookie to leave her room, then slipped inside. She was aware that a messenger had come for her this morning which she found highly suspicious. She needed to see that message. She searched the room thoroughly and had given up hope of finding anything when she spotted the crumpled up paper in the wastebasket as she was leaving. She reached in,

took it out and read it. Her eyes nearly bulged out of
their sockets at what the message contained.
Why, that whore was with Gabriel! Oh, she would
pay for this; she would kill her. Better yet she
should give Alistair the message and let him deal
with her. He had already put the tramp in her place
once before; he would do it again. Unsure what she
should do to take her revenge, she stuck the
message in her bodice and scurried out of the room.
She had to decide how best to handle this, but one
way or another Alyssa would pay.

*****

"I have had enough of your lies Mr. Quigley, tell
me what you know, or I will brand you like the pig
you are," Alistair roared at Adam, holding a hot
poker from the fire near his face.

"I tell you, Lord Keith that I know nothing. If
the girl left here, she left without doing so by way
of the stables. There are no horses missing, and the
carriages had not been used on the night she left.
She must have left on foot. I swear that is all I
know, my lord," Adam said, looking fearfully at the
red hot tip of the poker.

Alistair was starting to believe the man. He had
consistently stuck to his story, even under the threat
of violence that he had used. He growled low in his
throat as he rubbed his aching head. He didn't
believe Alyssa had simply walked out of here, on
her own. Someone had to have assisted her or taken
her against her will. But who could it have been?
Everyone he had interviewed so far seemed to be

telling the truth. Even his stepfather seemed to be in the dark as to the whereabouts of his Alyssa. He had been told by the other servants that Alyssa was particularly close to the cook. He would speak to her again when he was done with Mr. Quigley. If the old crotch didn't know anything, then he was at a loss as to what to do next. Even the Bow Street men had had no success tracking her down; she'd simply vanished.

He had gone over the details again of what he knew so far without reaching any substantive conclusions. She left with one small bag, a couple of frocks, undergarments and very few of her personal items. That seemed to indicate premeditation on her part, but he refused to believe she had willingly left him. But who had reason enough to want to take her from him? He could only think of two people. They were his mother and stepfather. Neither wanted the match but for different reasons.

Morley didn't want to let go of her fortune. His mother simply didn't like Alyssa. He couldn't imagine why she would feel that way. Indeed, Alyssa was sweeter and more docile than any woman he had ever encountered. He was worried out of his mind about his beloved, fearing that every day that she remained out there alone meant he would never see her again. He feared for her life as London was a dangerous city. A young lass traveling alone would be prey to every type of hardened criminal imaginable.

He didn't know how he could have made it this last week if he hadn't had Marjorie to lean on. She was a good soul too, despite being a whore. He had quit pretending she was Alyssa because it felt wrong somehow, now that she was gone. The pleasures had increased between them as a result. He had called for her last night. She had dutifully come to attend him. He had taken her with a savage need, and she seemed to thrive and relish in it. No matter how rough he handled her, she seemed to enjoy it and beg for more. She was a good whore; she would make a good mistress when he and Alyssa married. She was delighted when he told her of his plans to take her to Jamaica where they could share their passions with Batiste. The light in her eyes would have lit up all of London. She cried and kissed his feet in supplication. He felt a hardening of his cock in response to the vision of her and Batiste being naughty. He needed to take her again and soon, or he feared he would become more violent against his family and the staff. He didn't want to hurt anyone if he could help it. But when he got his hands on the villain that took his sweet Alyssa away from him, he would kill them with his bare hands.

He shook his head to clear his mind so he could concentrate on Mr. Quigley, who was now looking at him as if he had gone daft. He had nearly hurt the poor man. He had slapped him many times and choked him, too. He felt a little bit ashamed of himself, but it had been necessary.

"I think we are finished here, Mr. Quigley. You may go back to your station, but if I hear anything to contradict what you have told me, we shall meet again. Next time, there will be no mercy," Alistair told him.

"Thank you my lord," Adam answered, scurrying for the door.

Before he was able to make his exit, Alistair halted him.

"Stop by the kitchen, and send the cook to me. I am to meet with her next."

The man looked at him with fear in his eyes. It made him wonder if the old stable master didn't have a relationship with her. She was still a fine looking old woman, though certainly not to his tastes at all, but he could see how Mr. Quigley might enjoy the occasional indulgences with her.

Moments later the cook arrived. She had a defiant look in her eyes. She must be upset over what he had done to her lover. Well, he would make it up to her by handling her more gently.

"Sit down, Madam," he instructed her.

She did as she was bid and put her hands primly in her lap but maintained the defiant look in her eyes with a tilting up of her chin. She had been a beauty in her youth; she was educated too. He wondered how she found herself in such a lot in life. It wasn't his problem though. He needed to concentrate on the business at hand.

"How may I help you my lord?" she calmly asked.

"I would like for you to tell me what you know of the disappearance of Alyssa. I understand from other servants that you and she were particularly close and that you have often served as a mother of sorts to my beloved, for which I thank you kindly," he told her sincerely.

He owed much to this woman who had taken Alyssa under her wing and guided her into being the lovely woman she was. It spoke highly of the cook that she would have been so kind and generous to the lass.

"My lord as I told you before, I have no knowledge of her disappearance. She had come to me that morning. She was deeply distressed by the treatment she had suffered at your hands. I tried to calm her down and told her that was the way it was between a man and a woman. She seemed to have accepted it, then went back to bed so as not to be seen with so many bruises," she told him with fire in her eyes.

She was angry at him for treating her as he had. He didn't blame her. It had been wrong of him, and he deeply regretted it.

"I know that I was wrong. I am repentant. If I could find her, I would never again harm her. I love her, you see. She means the world to me. I shouldn't have to explain myself to you, but I know that you love her, too. I feel that I owe it to you to let you know that I have only the best intentions toward her. So please, if you know anything at all, tell me because I am afraid she could be in danger, alone in the world as she is."

The woman's eyes softened, and she relaxed her shoulders. She was worried, too.

"My lord, if I had any information, I would share it with you. I want my girl home safe and sound where she belongs. But I know nothing that would help you find her," she told him with tears in her eyes.

He wanted to believe her. He was tired and needed to go to Marjorie for comfort. He stared at her for a good long while before gently saying, "You may go."

She quickly took her leave. He went to his room to see Marjorie. He needed to be restored as only she could restore him.

*****

Morley was waiting for Cookie when she returned to the kitchen. He caught her by the arm the moment she crossed the threshold and gently put his hand to her lips for silence. He urged her to follow him through the kitchen until they were outside.

"I have to speak with you Cookie. I know you have no reason to believe me or trust in me, but I need to know what you know about the whereabouts of Alyssa. She needs my protection. I must find her before that dastardly spawn of Esmeralda's does. Please tell me what you know," he implored her.

Cookie looked at him incredulously. Indeed, she didn't trust him, but he felt sure she knew something.

"I know what you are thinking, but you are wrong. I will not allow that animal to get his hands on the child. You must help me with this, I beg of you. I realize now that my treatment of the child has been shameful. I fully intend to rectify it and have her take her rightful place among the family. I should never have let my wife guide me as I have. It will forever be my shame. I can only hope that I am not too late to repair the damage. Please tell me what you know, so that I may rescue the girl and make amends."

Cookie had tears in her eyes as she looked back at him. She wanted to believe him, but she was afraid of being betrayed. The girl needed protection that was true, but could she trust the earl to do as he said? She didn't know, but someone had to do something. She was just a cook. She had no power to help the child. She needed her family. Sadly, the earl seemed to be the only one caring enough to offer aid.

"Alyssa trusts me not to betray her," she ventured.

"I will not let you down. You have my word of honor."

"You will want to have me discharged when I tell you the whole of it," she said with her head down in shame.

She should never have advised that poor child as she had. She, too, would have to carry the shame of knowing that she failed the girl.

"I will not discharge you if you tell me now what you know," he persisted.

Cookie chewed on the inside of her cheek, contemplating what she was about to do. She wasn't worried about being discharged so much as she worried that she would never see Alyssa again. She could always take a place with Annabelle to survive.

"I know where she is."

"Please Cookie, tell me."

"She is with the duke. The Duke of

Windhaven," she said quickly.

The earl sucked in a gasping breath. He stared at her as if she had gone mad. He rubbed his hand through his hair and shook his head as if by doing so he could reshuffle her words to have them make more sense.

"Pray, how did she end up with Windhaven?" he asked.

This was the part she didn't want to tell him, but she must. He deserved to know the whole of it.

"Lord Keith beat her the night before she left. She came to me the following morning, begging for my help. I took her to my sister's and …" she couldn't finish.

"And?" he calmly prompted.

"There was an auction held for her virginity last night. She was bid upon by several wealthy lords. Lord Yarbrough won her, but Windhaven was there. He didn't want him to get his hands on her, so he challenged the man in a game of cards for her. He won, and he took her away when Lord Keith showed up with the Bow Street men to search the place. I am not sure where he took her, but he has her. Annabelle was assured by one of his associates that he would take good care of her and protect her from Lord Keith. She wanted to take her earnings and go to America, but I don't know if she succeeded."

Morley was mortified. His niece had auctioned herself to get funding to escape her life. *Why couldn't the child have come to me? Of course, she wouldn't have even considered it.*

"This is a tragedy," was all he could manage to

say.

"Aye, tis indeed, and we are all to blame. We have failed that sweet girl, and she was forced to go out and fend for herself. Shame be upon us all," she cried in heaving sobs.

Morley reached out, pulling her close in a comforting embrace.

"We will retrieve her and protect her from now on Cookie. This, I swear," he told her. "We must hope that Windhaven behaves honorably and has not …" now he couldn't finish.

If Windhaven had taken her virginity, he could force him to do the honorable thing and marry the girl. That would certainly send Alistair into a tailspin, but what could he do once the girl was married to another? It might just be the answer to this dilemma.

First thing was he would have to try to find out where Windhaven had taken her.

"Do you know who the associate that your sister spoke to was?" he asked.

"I believe it was Lord Sumersleigh," she told him with a sniff, blotting the tears from her eyes.

"Thank you, Cookie. You must go about your business now. Don't tell anyone of our conversation. We must do all we can to protect Alyssa now," he told her.

He turned, going back inside with a mission to complete. He felt good about himself for the first time in years. He would make sure Alyssa was protected. If he could manage it, he would secure a husband for her as well. Diana and Esmeralda would be livid when they learned of it, but he didn't care. He would be rid of them soon as well. He went to his library, opened his safe and pulled out the two betrothal contracts. He was glad he hadn't made a copy of the one with Alistair and Alyssa, but Windhaven would have a copy of the one between him and Diana. He didn't think Windhaven would mind at all what he was about to do.

He went to the fireplace, stoked up the flames and tossed the two documents within. He stood there watching them burn to cinders and felt a huge measure of relief. That done, he left the house to locate Lord Sumersleigh. He hoped the man would tell him what he needed to know, and that he would be able to put an end to this nightmare once and for all.

*****

"There goes Lord Glenmont, Jasper. Where do you suppose he's off to in such a hurry?" Luther asked while watching the man quickly hop into his carriage. It took off like a shot as soon as the door closed.

They were tucked away behind some bushes in front of Lord Marvin's home, which supplied them with a perfect view of Glenmont's home. They had told him that they were on a mission for the Duke of Windhaven, and he allowed them the use of his shrubs and stables. He was a good sport and didn't ask any questions. Jasper, too, had watched the man and noticed he seemed to be in a very happy state. Odd that, considering his niece was missing.

"Perhaps we should have followed him," he

suggested.

"Too late now; he is long gone. We would never catch up to him," Luther told him.

It wasn't often that Luther was the voice of reason, but it was true they would never be able to catch him now. The carriage had already rounded the corner and could have gone any number of directions from there. Besides, they were to stay and watch Lord Keith's activities, Jasper decided and gave the matter no more thought.

"Don't you think it's interesting that the doxy never came out?" Luther changed the subject.

"Aye, it is," Jasper agreed.

When the wench showed up the night before they had wondered why she would have shown up here in the first place, but that she had stayed this long was curious.

"Perhaps when she comes out we can speak with her," he mused aloud.

Luther grinned. "I have more than talking in mind for that one."

"Get your mind out of the gutter, Luther. She isn't your sort anyway," Jasper chastised.
"What do you mean? They are all my sort, my friend," Luther continued with the same silly grin.

"Not that one; trust me in this."

"How do you know about her?" Luther asked with anticipation of what would surely be a nice story overflowing with juicy details.

"She likes it rough," Jasper said solemnly.

"Well now, do you mean she likes to be rough or that she likes to get roughed up?" Luther asked, waggling his eyebrows.

"She likes to be the one to get abused. Why does it matter? It's sick either way as far as I'm concerned?" Jasper stated emphatically.

"Well now, that's a matter of opinion, I would say. There's nothing wrong with playing a little rough," Luther defended.

"No, there is nothing wrong with being a little rough, but what she likes is a whole different ball of wax. She likes to be beaten and restrained."

Luther looked aghast at that.

Jasper snickered. "You are so naive sometimes," he said rolling his eyes at his friend.

"Me, naive? I'll have you know that I have played all sorts of games in the sack, but I draw the line at beating a woman for my pleasures," he said horrified.

"Most of us do, but there are those that like it and can't be stimulated otherwise. She is one of them. I would wager that our friend Lord Keith is the sort she enjoys," Jasper said in his all knowing tone.

"No wonder that poor girl ran away and auctioned herself," Luther said with sympathy in his voice.

"Aye," he agreed. "She must have felt she had nowhere else to turn. Lord Keith probably gave her a taste of what their married life would be like, and she decided it wasn't her cup of tea."

"We should tell Dylan of this. But tell me, how do you know so much about the doxy?"

"She wasn't always a doxy. She is a countess; the widow of Lord Barclay. She was married to him at the age of three and ten; can you believe it? He was an old man in his sixties, and her but a child," he told him with a shiver.

Luther was looking at him with shock on his face; he was clearly offended by such a prospect. "I had an affair with her once after the old bugger cocked up his toes but quickly ended it after she continued to insist that I beat her," he admitted with a measure of shame and disgust.

Luther thought about that for a long time. "Did you beat her?" he finally asked.

"I don't want to talk about it."

Jasper was ashamed at what he had done with her. She obviously had been mistreated by her husband and thought it was the only way between a man and a woman. He had indulged her a few times, but he found that it took his pleasure away. He could not bear the idea of continuing on with her. It made him feel like a monster, but she had clearly enjoyed it; always begging for more and harsher abuses. He shook his head to clear out the memories. He didn't like seeing her as it reminded him of how sad things were for women sometimes. Luther was like a dog with a bone, however. He wanted to keep discussing her.

"Wasn't Lord Barclay deep in the pockets? Why would his widow have to be a whore?" he asked.

"To feed her needs, I would imagine," was Jasper's simple reply.

"That's disgusting," Luther said.

"To each, his own I suppose. Let us not judge her, shall we?" Jasper said with finality.

Luther got the hint and dropped the issue.

Together they sat in quiet contemplation as they continued sentinel.

*****

Diana was pacing in her room, trying to decide how best to handle the piece of information she now found herself in possession of. Her first reaction had been one of murder, but she knew that if she were to kill Alyssa, she would be caught and hanged. Then, she thought the best thing to do would be to tell her brother, but he was closeted with his whore again. Who knew when he would emerge? She would have to wait for him, and she was growing impatient. She didn't like to be made to wait. She was used to getting her way in all things. She pondered whether or not she should tell her mother what she had learned but decided that too should wait. She didn't want to overplay her hand and have the whole thing come crumbling apart.

Her mother would fly into a rage and insist that she break it off with Gabriel. That, she would never do. She would have Gabriel no matter what. He had belonged to her since the day she was born. She wouldn't let her mother or that slut of a cousin stand in her way. She had to fight the urge to get in the carriage and go to Windhaven to take care of matters herself. She wanted to gouge Alyssa's eyes out with her bare hands. She couldn't do that, of course. What would Gabriel think of her if she were to do such a thing? She would have to play the role of sweet innocent fiancé so as not to fall out of his favor.

She would have to be clever and make sure he never knew of her involvement when Alyssa was punished, and punished she would be. She should make a deal with her brother to allow her to have a few minutes alone with the bitch. Her hands clenched into fists at the prospect. *Oh how I want to kill that whore. Yes that's what she is now.* She had lived in a brothel for a week. She had probably been had by dozens of men. She looked forward to telling Alistair that his precious was a whore. That would surely be the end of Alyssa; he would kill her himself. Then they could have her entire fortune for themselves. *Think of all the things we could do with such a sum of money*! She smiled. Yes, the possibilities would be endless.

*****

After several hours of exhaustive searching, Morley finally located Lord Sumersleigh at Whites. He was sitting by himself, brooding over a Scotch whiskey. Morley took a deep breath and walked over to his table.

"Lord Sumersleigh?" he ventured cautiously.

"Ah, Glenmont! How are you my good man?"

"I am well but I have an issue of utmost urgency that I must speak with you about. May I join you?"

"Please do."

Morley sat at the table. A waiter immediately came over to take his order. He ordered a whiskey. After it was brought to him, he looked at Lord Sumersleigh, noticing then that the man was looking at him with restrained hostility. This wasn't going to be easy, he realized.

"Perhaps I should just come right to the point," he stated with determination.

His cause was just. He would make him see that he was serious. It didn't give him comfort to know that this man would have knowledge of his crimes against his niece, but he would rectify it as best he could.

"Yes, the point would do quite nicely," he said, raising his glass to his lips and tossing the contents back.

"I understand you were present at an auction last night at Annabelle's, where my niece was the … how shall I say this? Er, the subject of much interest."

Lord Sumersleigh's eye twitched. There was a tightening of his jaw, but Morley pressed onward.

"It has come to my attention that a mutual acquaintance of ours is now in possession of my niece. I would like to know where he might have taken her. I am told that you would know those whereabouts, and I would implore you to assist me in this. I need to protect her you see, from that animal who would call himself her betrothed."

Dylan couldn't believe what he was hearing. This man, who had more than likely mistreated that poor child, which led her to put herself in such a position, would now ask him to betray her to him. He wanted to take him by the collar and shake him until his head dropped off.

"Why do you suppose she would have placed herself in an auction to sell her virtue when she had a loving uncle such as you?" he asked him, sarcasm dripping in his speech.

Morley dropped his head in shame. He understood the implications. He had mistreated the girl. She felt she had no other choice when Alistair had attacked her.

He sighed deeply and looked Sumersleigh squarely in the eyes. "I have done the child wrong. I have failed her to my everlasting shame. But I am here to rectify that now sir. I have only her best interests at heart. I swear to you now that if you will provide me with the information, I will endeavor to treat her as she should have always been treated. She is my brother's daughter. She deserves a caring guardian. I was influenced by my wife and became greedy. I kept the girl tucked away in my home living the life of a servant while I spent her fortune. God may never forgive me for my sins, but I hope that while there is still breath in my body I am given a chance to repent. I can only do this if I find her," he said with passion in his voice.

Dylan was impressed that he would admit such abuses. He thought that perhaps the man was genuine. Surely, he wouldn't have admitted such a thing if he intended to remain a villain. Dylan could ruin him quite easily after such an admission.

"I could ruin you with such an admission," he spoke the thought aloud.

"Yes, you could. I give you leave to do it if you find that I am playing you false," Morley told him with passionate conviction.

Dylan believed him. The man was an active member of the House of Lords who was noted for all his many bills promoting good works for the poor working class. If he were to tell the press what he knew, he would be finished. He fished in his pocket, withdrawing the letter he had received from Hawk about an hour ago. He laid it on the table but kept his hand on top of it.

"You may not like what this says."

"I just want to know that she is safe. Please sir, may I read it?"

Dylan slid it over to him. Glenmont quickly grabbed it and began reading it. The man smiled and a tear slid down his cheek. For a moment Dylan was confused by his response. His daughter's fiancé was about to marry another woman.

"This is wonderful," Glenmont said.

"Your daughter is losing her fiancé," he pointed out.

"She has already lost him. I have burned the betrothal agreement. She is undeserving of him, and I would not have him suffer such a shrew for a wife. I have destroyed the one and only betrothal agreement between Alistair and Alyssa as well, so there is nothing standing in their way. They are free to marry with my blessings."

"I am to go to Windhaven after supper. I have a feeling they will need a witness to their nuptials and an extra eye at their back," Dylan said with a smile.

"Perhaps I should join you. I wouldn't mind a trip to Scotland. However, I should stay and keep an eye on Alistair. He has become volatile and has taken over my home. He has brought his whore there, and she has yet to leave. He is terrorizing my staff for information. He has threatened me and his mother as well."

"What will you do?" Dylan asked.

"What can I do? I have to let it run its course. Once he gives up on Alyssa, he will find someone else and go back to Jamaica. It was my plan to hide her at my estate in Kent, but this is much better. I will be rid of him sooner. When they are married, I will inform Alistair that it is too late and that he has lost her. Then, all will be well."

"That sounds a bit optimistic to my ears. I don't see him going away quietly. Perhaps we can arrange to have him removed for you. Hawk and I have two other friends. Together, we can take care of the matter. But first we need to assist Hawk and Alyssa with their plans to marry. I will leave for Windhaven immediately and write you of my findings when I arrive. I'll keep you abreast of any changes. The two other gentlemen I spoke about are this very moment watching your home to keep track of Sinclair's movements. We shall not let any harm come to Alyssa," Dylan told him.

Morley was relieved. "I can't thank you enough for all that you have done. I had no idea Alyssa had such devoted protectors. I have aged ten years in the last week. I am much relieved now."

"I will send word to Luther and Jasper to tell them of these developments. Then, I'll be on my way to Windhaven," Dylan told him.

Chapter Thirteen

Alyssa was more comfortable with her decision this evening than she had been in the morning. Gabriel had been a paragon of gentlemanly behavior. He had danced attendance on her, treating her with the utmost respect all day long. He hadn't once tried to seduce her, for which she was a little disappointed if she were to be honest with herself. She supposed he wanted to demonstrate that his feelings for her were deeper than the superficial ones of lust. Oh, but when he looked into her eyes, she was reminded of the things they had done, and she wanted more. She would wait, however because nothing was set in stone as of yet. Who knew what tomorrow would truly bring. Everything could be ripped out from under her feet in the blink of an eye. She couldn't take anything for granted. The last week and a half of her life had been one of turmoil. It taught her that you truly never knew what would happen from one moment to the next.

She felt she had grown considerably within that time as well. She was quickly learning the ways of the world, as well as the ways of men. She wished that life was easier for women and hoped that as Duchess of Windhaven she would be able to make a difference in the plight of women; especially those of the common class. Perhaps when she received her inheritance, she could set up a shelter of sorts for females in need. There were many women suffering from domestic abuses and they had nowhere to turn. She knew this first hand now. It needed to change, they were a civilized country after all.

Gabriel had told her he hadn't really taken his place in the House of Lords, but she hoped that with her influence, he would. He was in position to do great things if he would apply himself. She smiled, looking over at him. He was looking through his selection of poetry and was planning on giving her a reading. She thought that was very sweet and anxiously awaited.

"I have found one by Abraham Cowley that I think you will enjoy," he told her with a mischievous grin. He walked and stood before her. The tome was propped upon his forearm as he prepared for his recitation.

"The thirsty earth soaks up the rain,
And drinks and gapes for drink again;
The plants suck in the earth, and are
With constant drinking fresh and fair;
The sea itself (which one would think
Should have but little need of drink)
Drinks twice ten thousand rivers up,
So fill'd they o'erflow the cup.
The busy Sun (and one would guess
By 's drunken fiery face no less)
Drinks up the sea, and when he's done,
The Moon and Stars drink up the Sun:
They drink and dance by their own light,
They drink and revel all the night:
Nothing in Nature's sober found,
But an eternal health goes round.
Fill up the bowl, then, fill it high,
Fill all the glasses there—for why
Should every creature drink but I?

Why, man of morals, tell me why?"

Alyssa giggled at his silly performance. He was such a goose as he had read the poem with mock drunkenness, complete with hiccups and slurring speech.

"I certainly shouldn't drink," she said with a blush.

Gabriel roared with laughter and he bent to kiss her upon her cheek. "'Tis true, you do have trouble with spirits, but you are oh so funny when you imbibe my dear. Please don't deny me the pleasure of your future inebriations," he told her with a wicked grin.

Alyssa blushed deeper; the man was shameless. But it was rather endearing, so she found herself playing along with his game. "I shall not serve myself up for your amusement, sir," she told him with a wicked grin of her own.

"How you wound me," he said with mock sadness.

She giggled again. She loved his sense of humor, naughty though he was.

"Forgive me for the intrusion your grace, but Lord Sumersleigh has arrived," Mr. Mosby said, sticking his head around the open doorway of the library.

Alyssa looked up, shocked to see the man who had bid so fiercely against Yarbrough for her virtue just last eve, entering the library. She felt ashamed, quickly looking down in embarrassment. Lord Sumersleigh strode into the room. He and Gabriel embraced, each of them oblivious to her humiliation.

"Dylan, I am so happy that you have come and just in time, too. We are to leave with the dawn to Gretna Green. You may be the first to congratulate us on our upcoming nuptials," Hawk proudly told him.

"You have my most heartfelt congratulations of course. Might I also commend you on your fine performance of Abraham Cowley's—Drinking," he said with a smile. "I became quite misty in remembrance of the days of our misspent youth when I heard you reciting it," he added.

The four friends had grown up with that poem as their mantra, so he was well familiar with it.

"Where are my manners? Dylan may I make known to you Miss Alyssa Habersham, my fiancé? Where are you going Alyssa?" he called after her as she bolted upright and ran out of the room.

He stood there dumbfounded for a moment, then it occurred to him what the problem was. She remembered Dylan and she was embarrassed. This could be problematic.

"You should go after her my friend. She feels humiliated and needs your comfort. I shall remain here and help myself to your Scotch whiskey until your return. I have much to tell you my friend," Dylan advised him.

Hawk didn't hesitate; he ran after her. He caught up to her in the hall leading to her chambers. "Alyssa wait!" he called to her.

She stopped but kept her back to him. He quickly reached her, took her by the elbow turning her toward him. She had tears in her eyes that were threatening to spill over, but she was trying to be brave and hold them back. He wrapped his arm around her and held her close. He could feel her give way and begin to tremble with her sobs.

"Shhh … it's all right love. You should not be embarrassed. Dylan is my best friend in the world and will be like a brother to you soon. He understands how you must feel and pointed it out to me. I feel like such an arse for not seeing it myself at first. Please love, you mustn't cry," he said, lifting her chin so he could see her eyes.

"How can I ever show my face again? He knows of my shame!" she cried.

"He is a compassionate man. He understands what drove you to it. He will not judge you, nor will he tell anyone of it. Please, you mustn't let this upset you. You are to be a duchess soon, and you will hold your head up high with pride, do you understand me love?" he told her sternly, but with love laced in his command.

He wrapped her tight in his embrace once again, gently rocking her from side to side as they stood in the hallway. He was falling in love with this woman, he realized. It was a wonderful feeling, too. He would do anything to shelter and protect her. She cried her tears until she was gasping, so he started walking her toward her chambers.

"Why don't you have a nice hot bath and go to bed my love? The dawn will come early, and we have an assignation to keep," he told her gently.

When they reached her door, she looked up into his eyes and nearly broke his heart with the words that followed. "Are you sure that you really want me, Gabriel?" she asked with a trembling lower lip.

He couldn't help himself, he had to kiss her. He leaned forward taking her lips with his, putting all the passion for her that he felt behind his kiss. She reached around his neck with her arms and kissed him back with an equal passion that was nearly his undoing. He would prove to her now how much he truly wanted her, but she deserved to have a proper wedding night. He reigned in his desire, pulling away.

"Never ask me that again; 'tis blasphemous," he told her with mercurial eyes.

She smiled shyly at him and turned to go into her room. Once inside, she gave him one last longing look and slowly shut the door. He stood there for a moment with a desperate need for this woman, such as he had never known. It was all he could do to convince himself to walk away.

*****

"Do you believe him?" Gabriel asked after Dylan relayed to him what Glenmont had said.

He was astounded that the man had a change of heart about his niece. He was even more astounded that he destroyed the betrothal contract with Diana and gave his blessings of their marriage. It was a bit like being in a dream, a very pleasant one. He had longed to be rid of Diana all of his life. Now, he was truly free of her.

"Aye," his friend told him. "He gave me leave to destroy his reputation if he were playing me false," he added.

"That is something, isn't it?" he said thoughtfully. "I believe this cause for a celebration!" he added with a beaming smile.

Gabriel poured them both a whiskey. They tapped their glasses together and tossed them back. He poured them both another, and they both sat in quiet contemplation for a moment as they nursed their drinks.

"She will make a beautiful duchess," Dylan mused aloud.

"She is a beauty isn't she? But she is so much more, Dylan. I can't explain the effect she has had on me. I feel quite enchanted by her. It's as though she has bedazzled me with her charms," he said, his eyes soft.

Dylan looked at his friend. He knew he was falling in love, if he hadn't already. He was totally besotted with his Pocket Venus. Who would have thought he would have been so easily taken down by such a woman? He laughed inwardly and wondered which of them might be next; this could be an omen. Hawk had been their leader. Now he was willingly being leg shackled. They were surely all doomed to follow his lead.

"I wonder which of us will fall next," he spoke his thoughts aloud.

Gabriel laughed, pointing his finger at Dylan.

"You shall be next my friend. You need to stop fooling around with all these virgin auctions and marry yourself a nice girl. Just make sure you find one that you can love. Don't marry a shrew," he said soberly.

"I have given it some thought of late. It gets

tedious being around you fellows while you frolic at will with all the wenches as I sit idly by playing cards. I have had enough of cards and the ghastly practice of bidding for virgins. I shall never do so again. They are real women with real problems. I will never forget that now," he told him.

"Perhaps you should attend one last virgin auction to find yourself a bride. I'm sure she would welcome being rescued by such a handsome man as you."

Dylan didn't reply to that. He had actually considered doing just that after last night. Had he won Alyssa, he would have offered for her, too. She was a rare beauty. He suspected it would be a long time before he found one to equal her, but he would keep his eyes open. He didn't want a silly debutant from Almack's, he wanted a real woman like Alyssa. He wouldn't covet his friends betrothed, but he did envy him his good fortune.

"What time shall we leave in the morning?" he asked him.

"You will come with us?"

"Of course!" he stated with conviction. "You need a witness to your upcoming bondage and an extra pair of eyes while you travel. Luther and Jasper have things well in hand watching Sinclair's movements. So I find myself quite idle and in need of an adventure," he told him with a cheeky grin.

"Good! We shall leave with the dawn! We will put Alyssa and her maid in a carriage. You and I can travel by horse. Did you bring your pistols?" he asked.

Dylan opened up his coat to show he was

wearing two pistols, one strapped on each side of his ribs.

"You know I never leave home without Lester and Hank," he told him with a wink.

"Let us hope that we shall not need your two fine friends, but it is good to be prepared. I will have mine as well. The coachmen and groom will be armed, also. I will leave nothing to chance with the safety of that woman upstairs. She has quickly become very dear to me."

"I find it hard to believe that you have managed to abstain with her," he found himself saying.

He probably shouldn't have said that aloud, but Hawk's reputation was well known. It was difficult to believe he hadn't already taken her, many times. He certainly would have if he had been in his shoes.

"I very nearly did, but we were interrupted by Keith's arrival at Annabelle's. However, after knowing her now, I find that I am prepared to wait for her as is proper. She deserves to be treated with respect," he told him with a seriousness that was out of his character with regard to women.

"You are in love," Dylan said softly.

"I think that I must be."

*****

Alyssa was in love. What else could it be? Gabriel had moved her moments ago like she had never been moved in her life. She would have given herself to him then and there had his friend not been waiting for him in the library. She was soaking in her warm bath remembering his tender words. She suspected he might be falling in love with her too, but she couldn't be sure. *Should I tell him how I feel*? She shivered slightly as thinking of the pleasures he had given her sent jolts of lightning coursing through her blood. Alistair's attentions had been frightening, but Gabriel was warm and kind. He never handled her with anything but tenderness. She tried to imagine the act of making love with Gabriel and became aware of an aching between her legs. She had felt that same aching when she was in his embrace as well and knew that it was the need that he spoke of.

Women must have needs just like men; why else would she be in such a state. *It is odd that I never considered it before my encounters with him.* She didn't really think it meant she was immoral, but she couldn't help but wonder why women were taught that they should simply endure the man's needs as a duty and not be allowed pleasures of their own. She shook her head and decided she had better get out of the tub before she turned into a prune. Besides, it did her no good at all to sit there naked thinking of him. She would never be able to sleep if she didn't get it off her mind.

She rose from the tub, reached for the luxurious bath towel and began to dry herself off. She reached for her chemise and put it on, then wrapped herself in the robe that Gabriel had given her to use. She felt warm and secure enveloped in his robe, breathing in his familiar scent. On the morrow, they would leave for Gretna Green to be married. A few days after that she would become his wife, a woman in every sense of the word. She smiled at the thought, putting all doubts about herself out of her mind. She would be a happy bride. She would enter her marriage with her head held high and embrace the passionate things that he would teach her. She climbed into her bed and shimmied under the covers. Aside from Gabriel's bed, this one was the nicest she had ever slept in. She turned over on her side, sank down into the fluffy pillows and continued her reverie.

I'm to be a duchess in a few days. Who would have ever imagined that she, an orphan and a lowly servant would have found herself in such a situation? She certainly wouldn't have. She thought about Diana then, and her heart thudded in her chest. She quickly sat up in a state of panic feeling isolated and alone. She looked over at the open window and wondered if she should shut it. Her room was on the third floor, and no one could scale the wall to get to her, so she sank back down, trying to relax. Alistair wouldn't be the only one they had to worry about as Diana would surely become irate and would want to harm her as she had told her she would. Diana was a cruel person. She wouldn't blink an eye at the thought of harming her. She must remember to caution Gabriel about this.

Gabriel had probably already considered it. Surely he had a plan in mind to manage the issue. She shouldn't worry now. He would protect her. The thought was comforting. She closed her eyes and attempted to clear her mind of her concerns. Moments later, she drifted off to sleep and soon lost herself to dreams of the future with Gabriel, and though she wasn't aware of it, she was smiling as she slept.

*****

Gabriel and Dylan said their goodnights to one another, and Gabriel took himself off to bed. He stopped when he passed Alyssa's door and placed his hand upon the door-handle. He stood there considering whether or not he should turn the knob, then thought better of it. With mild regret and great anticipation of days to come, he went into his room. He had to walk away, otherwise he would have not been able to resist taking her now. He would do the right thing, no matter how much it hurt. He had to show her how much he respected her. Ravishing her outside of wedlock was not the way to go about it.

"Ah, Hawk!" Harvey greeted him upon entry.

The old man was donned in his nightgown and sleeping cap as was his usual habit. He looked somewhat somber while assisting Gabriel out of his clothes.

"What's wrong Harvey?" Gabriel asked him.

"I'm losing me boy," he said with a quivering lip.

"What say you Harvey? You're making no sense," he told him.

"I'm losing you to the virgin from the brothel," he sobbed.

Gabriel laughed and clapped the old man on the shoulder.

"You are not losing me, Harvey. I will still have need of you after I am married," he assured him.

The old man was truly overcome with emotion at the thought of Gabriel marrying. He hadn't considered how he would feel about it.

"You have become a man now Hawk. I never thought I would live to see this day. 'Twas only yesterday that I had to clean and powder your arse, and now you are getting married," he continued to cry.

"I haven't needed my arse powdered in a very long time, Harvey. What else is troubling you," he asked him.

Harvey sniffed and tried to reclaim his manhood by ridding himself of the unmanly tears. He straightened up to his full height and looked Hawk squarely in the eyes.

"The widow Burley has accepted me, Hawk. I too am getting married as soon as the banns have been read," he told him with a toothy grin.

Gabriel roared with delight and grabbed the old man in his arms, spinning him around. He set him back down gently when he realized that he was probably making him dizzy.

"This is wonderful Harvey! Why did you not tell me sooner?" he asked.

Harvey swayed, trying to regain his bearings after being twirled around like a whirligig. Gabriel kept a steadying hand on him until his eyes stopped darting back and forth.

"Forgive me Harvey, I quite lost control of myself. Are you alright now?" he asked him.

"Aye, but remind me to stand on the other side of the room next time I have something to tell you, so I can make a run for it in case you are inclined to lose control again," he admonished him.

"Is this what you meant when you said that you were losing me? Do you wish to retire now and enjoy your married life?" Gabriel thought to ask.

Harvey looked down at the ground as if ashamed by the question. Gabriel understood then that it was indeed the case.

"I release you, Harvey, if that is your wish. You have served me well. I am quite prepared to deal with life now without your guidance," he assured him.

"Thank you Hawk," he told him. "I would stay if you needed me to; you know that don't you?"

"Of course I do, but I wouldn't have it any other way Harvey. I won't have time in the morning to deal with it, but I will speak to my man when I return from Gretna Green and have him prepare you a severance. I want you to retire in the style in which you and the widow Burley deserve. You shall never want for anything, Harvey, and I congratulate you on your upcoming nuptials," he told him warmly.

"I will be just upon that hill whenever you have need of me you know," Harvey told him with new tears in his eyes.

"Go to bed Harvey. Fear not, we shall always be family, you and I." Gabriel told him.

Harvey nodded his head, then turned and went to his room; Gabriel watched him go with a smile. He was happy for the old codger, but he would miss him being around to fuss with. Funny how things work out, he mused as he finished undressing himself. Good old Harvey was getting married too. Small wonders never ceased. He hoped that the widow would be good to him. She was considerably younger than him, but that was what he needed; a strong healthy woman to care for him in his old age. Why he might even be able to father a child with the widow; she was still young enough. He smiled at the thought.

He was still a nice looking bloke in his mid-fifties. He would have many years yet to enjoy his bride. He was pleased for his friend. They were both headed in the direction of a new life. Though he was happy for them both, he couldn't help but feel a little melancholy for days gone by. He laughed softly, remembering he had told Dylan that he would be next to fall but the crafty old devil had beat him to it and with a woman nearly half his age.

Chapter Fourteen

Diana rose before the dawn, anxious to speak with her brother. He still had not left his room by midnight, so she had resigned herself to sleep, but it was a fitful, restless sleep. She wouldn't be able to rest fully until she told him what she knew. She quickly dressed and brushed out her hair. Her maid had not yet risen to aid her, so she wore something simple that she could manage herself. She only needed to wear it long enough to speak with her brother anyway, so it wouldn't matter. She was a bit nervous about what his reaction would be. She knew he would be angry, but she didn't know to what extent it would be. She hoped he wouldn't take it out on her. When she finished dressing, she went out into the hall and down to his room and pressed her ear to the door. She could hear muffled voices speaking, so she knew he was awake, too. It wouldn't be long before he would want to break his fast, so with that in mind she went to the breakfast room to await him.

*****

"Wake up Luther," Jasper said with a yawn. It was time for them to get up and take up position at their post. Jasper's back was stiff from sleeping in the hay, but he would loosen up as soon as he started moving.

"Mum?" Luther cried out.

"I'm not your mother fool; get up! We have a job to do," Jasper said, nudging him in the ribs with his boot.

Luther stretched, groaned and curled back up into a ball to renew his symphony of snorts and snores. Jasper sighed and went outside to relieve himself. He would be glad to have his own bed back after this mission. He missed his mistress, too. In a way, he was glad that things were turning out the way they were. After reading Dylan's missive yesterday, his first reaction had been shock. He couldn't believe that Hawk was actually going to marry the chit, but doing so seemed to be the logical solution. She had been truly compromised. He quickly saw the benefits and realized that it would put an end to the problem of Keith sooner, and everyone could go back home. But Hawk getting married? Who would have imagined it? The fool must have been bewitched by the red-headed minx.

After the much needed relief of his bladder, he went back into the stables and knelt down beside Luther. He watched his child-like friend in his slumber, wondering what it would take to wake him. They hadn't had much sleep in the last two days. He was still exhausted himself, but they had to get back out there and resume their post. He had a feeling that something would happen today to alert Keith to the new developments. They needed to be alert and ready for whatever may come. There hadn't been a lot of activity with Keith thus far as he seemed to be holed up with Marjorie. She must be keeping him busy, and he hadn't had time to dwell on the missing girl. Jasper reached out and pinched Luther's nose to stop him from snoring. Luther sputtered, swiped at his hand and opened his eyes when he realized that it wasn't a monster but someone holding his nose.

"Get up you lazy arse!" he told him with a grin.

Luther looked at Jasper with eyes crossed and groaned. "Let go of my nose, or I'm gonna piss on you," he told him, struggling to sit up.

Jasper stood and looked at him as if he had gone daft.

"Why would you threaten to piss on me of all things?" he asked incredulously.

Luther stood up, grunting as he straightened up to his massive height. "Because I've got the Thames backed up in my pipes, and I'm about to whiz all over myself, you …you …it's too early to know what you are," he grumbled, then stumbled and staggered toward the stable door.

Jasper snickered, watching him go. At least he was up and on his feet now. He dusted the hay out of his hair and off his clothes, then went over to see to their horses to make sure they had plenty of grain and water.

Luther returned and was eyeing the horses like a hungry wolf. "Do you think Lord Marvin will give us some food? I'm hungry enough to eat your horse," he told him while rubbing his stomach.

"Eat your own horse, you savage beast," Jasper returned with an expression of mock horror.

"You have hay in your hair," Luther told him with an air of indignity.

"You should look at that mop upon your own head before you criticize mine. You look like Medusa after a nasty fight with a porcupine, which you lost, I might add," Jasper said. He reached out to pluck hay from his friend's unruly curls.

Luther returned the favor. Together they stood and served as valet to one another until they were satisfied that they were once again presentable. Neither man had an extra suit of clothes as they had gone straight to Glenmont's to take up their assignment. They were fast acquiring the look of two impoverished bums.

"You smell like shite, Luther; did you step in it or something?" Jasper asked.

"You don't smell like fresh spring rain yourself," he complained. He examined the bottom of his boots. "Blast and damnation!" Luther cursed. "Would you look at this? I have horse shite on my new Hessians. This was not part of the deal Jasper!" he griped. He started scraping the bottom of his boot on the ground.

Jasper rolled his eyes heavenward. Then he thought to check his own boots. He hadn't stepped in shite, thank God, but he knew he smelled ripe nonetheless.

"Don't feel bad; we both stink like a couple of animals. We shall have to endure my friend. Later, one of us can go and get us a change of clothes, but for now, we just have to reek."

*****

Alistair was whistling a friendly tune as he entered the breakfast room. He walked over to the sideboard, still wearing his robe and started preparing a plate. He hadn't yet seen his sister. He was preoccupied with visions of a naked and subdued Marjorie dancing in his head. He had left her tied to the bedposts. He was planning on taking his plate to her and making her beg to be fed in between sexual favors. She liked it when he did that; she was such a good girl. He didn't think he would ever get enough of her.

"I have news for you, brother."

Alistair gave a start, then turned to look at Diana. She looked tired and agitated, but clearly she was about to burst at the seams with her news.

"What is it?" he asked.

"You may want to sit down before I say what I am about to," she told him cautiously.

"I am in a bit of a hurry this morning, Diana, why don't you just tell me now what it is so that I may be on my way," he said, somewhat irritated by her tone.

"As you wish, but don't say that I didn't warn you."

"Yes yes, out with it!" he snapped.

"I know where your betrothed is."

Alistair dropped the plate and rushed over to her, glowering at her.

"What say you?" he demanded.

Diana drew back from him. He was snarling like a wild beast, and she felt as though he would attack her at any second.

"She is with Windhaven," she told him.

"Windhaven?" he asked in confusion. "Your fiancé?" he clarified.

"The very same," she told him. "It seems the little slut has been living in a brothel all this time and for whatever reason has run off with my fiancé.

What do you propose to do about this?" she demanded, now feeling somewhat emboldened.

Alistair was reeling as he tried to absorb his sister's words. How could this be? Why would she do it? She wouldn't; he refused to believe it.

"You lie!" he thundered after having collected his wits.

He reached out for her, grabbed her up by her shoulders and shook her hard. "Why would you say such a thing?" he yelled.

"Calm yourself, brother, I have proof," she told him.

"I'll have this proof or your neck," he shouted before releasing her.

Diana reached inside her pocket, drawing forth the crumpled up note she had found in Cookie's room and handed it to him.

Alistair read the note.

Dear Sister

Our girl fetched a very good price at the auction last night in the amount of sixteen thousand pounds and should now be able to live freely in America as she had planned. There was a bit of a problem afterward, however.

Lord Yarbrough won the bid, but Lord Windhaven challenged him to a game of cards with her as the prize. I tell you, I was quite offended by it but was powerless to stand against two dukes of the realm.

That was not the end of it, I am sad to say. Lord Keith turned up with Bow Street in tow just moments after the game was played. Lord

Windhaven and our girl fled by way of an upstairs window, and I have no idea where he might have taken her.

I was told by one of his associates she was in very good hands and that she would be well protected. I believe he is an honorable man and will indeed protect her from Lord Keith and her dastardly family.

I shall tell you more as I learn of it and would ask that you do the same. I am worried about the poor dear as I am quite fond of her now.

I love you dear sister, please stay safe.
Annabelle

Alistair was stunned. His first reaction was to deny what he had read, but he couldn't. He had gone to Annabelle's that night, and there was no way his sister could have known it. Why would Alyssa have done this thing? Why would she whore herself out for money to escape him? Had she been lying when she said she forgave him? She must have; how else to explain this? Had she been playing him false all along? She must have because she had run off with Windhaven and was at this very moment whoring herself to him. The thought made him shake with rage. He was suddenly unable to contain the emotions that were storming inside him. He roared at the top of his lungs and grabbed the end of the huge breakfast table, hurling it over on its side. He grabbed a chair, smashing it against the table and then another and another, his chest heaving from his exertions. He stared at his sister then as she was still there, smiling at him now.

"What have you to smile about?" he demanded.

"I think you will take care of my problem quite nicely dear brother. I want the bitch killed, and you shall do it for me," she told him in a sing-song voice.

She was mad, he wouldn't kill Alyssa. He wanted her still; even now he would take her back. Besides, she and her fortune had been promised to him. She belonged to him no matter what she had done. So what if she had become Windhaven's whore; he would punish her, yes, but she still belonged to him. It was Windhaven who would die.

"Oh, I will kill all right, but it won't be her. You have miscalculated if you think I would give her and her fortune up for you or anyone else. Yes, I will kill, but it will be your precious Windhaven that dies," he vowed. He turned and left the room.

He was still shaking violently as he made his way up the stairs. His anger was coursing through his blood like lava as it rushed forth from a volcanic eruption. He made it to his room and flung the door open, slamming it behind him. He saw Marjorie there with fear in her eyes. She had clearly heard the noise from below and was now in fear of her life. Being in her presence soothed him even now, and he walked over to the bed and untied her. He didn't want to hurt her. She had been too good to him to take his rage out on her.

"Get dressed and get out; I must leave you now. I have found Alyssa and must go to her."

She quickly got up and went to stand before him. "What will you do to her?" she asked, her expression a mask of fear.

Alistair didn't like being questioned by anyone, but somehow, by Marjorie, he didn't mind. Even in the anger he felt now her very presence was a comfort. He grabbed her by the back of her neck, pulling her angrily to his lips, then delivered a punishing kiss. She whimpered at the pain of it, and the sound of her distress excited him.

He pushed away from her, nearly sending her to the floor and yanked off his robe. "Get down on the floor on your hands and knees like a bitch in heat, Marjorie. I have an animal need within me that only you can satisfy," he told her.

*****

"What have I done?" Diana fretted.

She had not planned on things turning out the way they had. Alyssa must die. She had counted on Alistair being the one to do it. She quickly gathered herself, fleeing the breakfast room and dashed up the stairs to her room. She had to warn Gabriel. She would go to Windhaven with all possible haste. She would deal with Alyssa herself somehow, but first she had to protect her betrothed. She stopped by Alistair's door and heard the grunts and cries of him and his whore as they copulated. She was relieved that the woman was there to distract him long enough so that she could get a lead on him to Windhaven. "Keep him busy Marjorie. Don't let me down," she whispered.

*****

"Did you hear that?" Jasper asked Luther in response to the sounds of violence coming from Glenmont's.

"He must know now," Luther said.

"I think he must; either that, or there is a wild animal loose over there," Jasper concurred.

"What should we do?"

"We wait and watch. If he leaves, we follow him," Jasper told him.

Both men were poised and ready for battle as the adrenaline of anticipation rushed through their bodies. This was what they had been here for, and they would not fail their friend.

*****

Morley was startled awake by the sounds he heard below stairs. His blood instantly turned to ice. There was no doubt that Alistair had somehow learned where Alyssa was. He jumped up and quickly dressed himself so he could be ready to act swiftly. He had to warn Windhaven somehow so that he could protect Alyssa. He went over to the window, looked out and saw the two men that Sumersleigh had mentioned. They were looking closely over at the house as they too must have heard the outburst below stairs. It gave him comfort to see them there. He went out into the hall and down toward Alistair's quarters. He listened at the door and heard the grunts and growls within indicating that he was busy with his whore. This was good; perhaps it would buy him some time.

*****

"Isn't that Diana?" Luther asked as they watched the woman jump into the carriage that quickly left thereafter.

"I believe so yes," Jasper said calmly.

"Something is definitely up. It's strange that she would be leaving so early in the morning. The sun is just barely rising, where could she be going?" Luther asked perplexed by this development.

"I suspect she is on her way to Windhaven," Jasper mused aloud.

Luther looked at him quizzically.

"Why do you suspect that?"

"Where else would she be going? Her fiancé is being taken away from her by another woman. I suspect she has learned of it and is now on her way there to try to prevent them marrying," he told him.

"Should we follow her?"

"I suspect we too shall be on the road to Windhaven very shortly. We stick with our target of observation. What harm can a woman do? Let her run to Windhaven if she wants to," Jasper said with a snicker.

"Should I ready the horses?" Luther asked.

"It would be wise. Try not to step in any more shite, would you?"

"Oh you would love that wouldn't you?" Luther asked appalled.

"Why pray tell, would I love such a thing? You already stink to high heaven, Luther. Use some sense man and avoid the shite, that's all I ask," Jasper chided him.

Luther puffed up his chest, preparing to fire back some witty retort, but no matter what he did he couldn't outwit Jasper, so he turned on his heel and went to ready the horses. Jasper watched him go and shook his head at his lack-wit friend. He loved him, but sometimes he wanted just to shake some sense into him.

*****

Alistair's release had been nearly painful as he poured himself into Marjorie with an agonized heart. It hurt to know that Alyssa didn't love him, but she belonged to him. That was all that mattered. He would have her, and he would kill Windhaven for the insult that he had given him by taking her away from him. He rolled off of Marjorie, collapsing beside her on the floor. He drew her into his arms and lay there contemplating the situation. He still had her at least; she wouldn't leave him.

"I must go after her now," he told her solemnly.

He didn't relish the task ahead. Once he killed Windhaven, Alyssa would surely hate him. She could never love him after he killed her lover.

"Must you?" Marjorie asked timidly.

"Alas, I need to get her back so we can be married. Then we can all go to Jamaica. You want that don't you?" he asked her.

"Yes, you know that I would do anything you ask of me Alistair. But …" she grew silent.

"But you want me for yourself?" he prompted.

He didn't know what made him say it, but the words had just come out. He knew that Marjorie was becoming very fond of him. How could she not?

"I don't mind sharing you Alistair, but if she doesn't love you, why not just let her go. I love you and I want you. Isn't that enough?" she boldly asked.

"She is mine, just like you are mine, and what is mine, I keep. You must endeavor to understand this Marjorie. You are a whore and will be one of my mistresses. She will be my wife; you must respect that," he said with finality.

Marjorie didn't say any more. After a moment, he got up from the floor and assisted her up.

"I want you to leave now, Marjorie. I will be in touch with you upon my return. You are to see no one else but me from now on, is that understood?" he told her.

"I understand Alistair, and I will await you at my home in Grosvenor Square. I don't live at Madam Comely's. I have my own home. I am a widow you see."

"You never told me of this," he stated with surprise.

"You have not asked," she said with her eyes on the floor in submission.

"Tell me of it," he commanded her.

"My father sold me to Lord Barclay when I was three and ten, and he died a few years ago. There isn't much to tell really. He taught me everything I know. I am grateful to him. He left me very well off when he died,"

"You are a whore by choice?" he asked aghast.

She tucked her chin down and wouldn't meet

his eyes. She had wanted to show him that she was as good as Alyssa, but it was going all wrong.

"Answer me Marjorie!" he commanded.

"Yes, I am a whore by choice," she calmly stated.

"Go home and wait for me until you hear from me, Marjorie. You will think about how naughty you have been, and I will deal with you appropriately upon my return," he told her.

Marjorie smiled, dropped to her knees and kissed his hand. She jumped up quickly and started getting dressed. *It is possible … just possible … Oh I mustn't think it.* Alistair watched her getting dressed. When she was finished, he pulled her into his arms and kissed her ardently. Then he turned her toward the door with a slap on her arse and sent her on her way. His Marjorie had been naughty indeed; he smiled, watching her go.

*****

"Look Jasper, the doxy is leaving," Luther said excitedly.

"I see her. You stay here. Watch for Keith. I'm going to speak with her to see if she can tell us anything. If he comes out, whistle three times real loud and I will come," Jasper said over his shoulder. He had already begun to follow her.

She was on foot, and he wagered that she would try to hail a hack at the corner, so he began to run to catch up with her.

"Marjorie!" he called out to her just as she was about to round the corner.

She stopped and turned back to look at him. Her eyes grew round in surprise. She turned and started to walk faster.

He quickly caught up to her, grasped her by the shoulder and turned her to him. "I need to speak to you, Marjorie," he said sternly. He knew that she would be more cooperative if he were to be stern.

"I am not to speak to you Jasper; my new master wouldn't like it. He has instructed me to see no one else but him," she told him pleadingly.

"I won't tell Keith of our discussion," he said soothingly.

"How do you know of Lord Keith?" she asked confused.

"I have been watching his house for the last two days as a favor to a friend. We may be able to help each other Marjorie," he told her as a thought occurred to him.

"I don't know how I could possibly help you Jasper. I shouldn't even be talking to you now. I must go."

"You will hear me out first Marjorie," he said once again trying to be stern.

She blinked her eyes, then looked around nervously.

"Relax. I have a man watching for him, and I will know when he has come out," he told her.

She seemed to relax then, so he forged ahead. "You love him don't you, Marjorie? But he loves her, doesn't he?" he asked her.

"I don't know what you mean," she said with a blush.

"I know all about you and Keith and his search

for Alyssa. I know that Alyssa doesn't want him and is planning to marry another. I know that you want Keith for yourself. Am I wrong about that?"

She didn't answer, but he knew he was right.

"Tell me, what is going on in the house, Marjorie? Lives may be at stake," he commanded her.

"He has found out where she is and is going after her. He was very severe when he learned of it. I fear he will try to do harm to her or whoever took her from him."

"Is he leaving today?" he asked.

"Yes, he sent me away so he could go after her. He said he would marry her then we would all go back to Jamaica upon his return," she told him.

"Wouldn't you rather go with him to Jamaica by yourself?" he asked her.

She nodded her head but looked down at the ground.

"I will help you, but you must trust me."

"I do," was her timid reply.

He heard the whistles then. "Wait right here for me. Hide behind that bush over there, but don't go anywhere else. You shall come with us. Together we will secure Keith for you and you alone," he told her.

"He wouldn't like that; I cannot," she told him.

"You must Marjorie. I don't have time to argue with you about this. You must do as I say if you are to have him for yourself. We mustn't let him find Alyssa," he told her.

Luther impatiently whistled the signal again. He was forced to leave her there and trust that she would do as he instructed. He doubted that she would, but he had to try. An idea was forming in his mind about how to deal with Alistair, but he wasn't sure. He needed to have more time to speak to her to be sure if he was on the right path. The only way to do that was to bring her along. He reached Luther and saw that he had both horses ready and waiting.

"It's about time; he is getting away," Luther said angrily.

"We know where he is headed. It is okay if he has a bit of a lead. We don't want him to see us in pursuit of him anyway," Jasper told him.

"What took you so long?"

"We are going to bring Marjorie along with us," he told him.

"Are you daft?"

"No, an idea came to me while I was talking to her, and I need time to speak with her to see if I am correct in my thinking. I must bring her along so that I can probe her for details about Keith."

"Then what?" he asked.

"After I get the information I need, we will drop her off at a posting inn and send her home on a coach. Relax and trust me; I just need time to speak with her."

Luther didn't like the sound of it at all, but he knew that Jasper was brilliant. He would trust him in this. "She doesn't have a horse," Luther pointed out.

"She can ride with me," he told him.

"Excuse me!" a man's voice interrupted them. Jasper turned to see Lord Glenmont approaching them. This was unexpected, but Dylan had informed them of the man's change in attitude so it would probably prove interesting to see what he had to say. "Lord Glenmont, how are you sir?" Jasper asked.

"I am distressed! Lord Keith has found out where Alyssa is. I'm almost sure he has gone after her. We must prevent it with all possible haste. The man is dangerous. My niece and the duke could be in peril," he told them.

"We were just leaving to pursue him. However, you might be interested to know that your daughter left ahead of him by nearly an hour. We suspect that she, too, is headed to Windhaven," he told him.

Clearly the man had no idea that his daughter had left. He looked alarmed by the prospect.

"I should like to come with you," he told them.

"Of course, we cannot stop you from joining. Since your daughter could be in danger as well perhaps you should," Jasper told him.

"I will get my horse and meet you here in ten minutes," he told them, then quickly turned and scurried away.

"What a debacle," Luther groaned.

"You stay here and wait for him. I will go and pick up Marjorie from the corner. I shall return momentarily," he advised.

Chapter Fifteen

Alyssa wished that she too, could ride a horse alongside Gabriel and Dylan, instead of being cooped up in the carriage with the snoring Wishy, who Gabriel had assigned as her maid. She must not have gotten much sleep last night because as soon as the carriage was underway she promptly fell asleep. Wishy was a pretty young woman of an age with Alyssa, perhaps a year younger. She was the niece of the head housekeeper, Mrs. Timpson and was pleased to be brought up from the village to become Alyssa's ladies maid and companion. She was very efficient as maid went and quite friendly too; far more pleasant to be around than Bea had been. She was eager to please and very good with hair, having quickly fixed hers in a beautiful style, which was no easy feat.

Alyssa didn't really think she needed a maid, but Gabriel insisted that it was necessary since she was to be a duchess now and should have her own personal maid. She was quite used to doing for herself and didn't have a lot of clothes with her that needed to be kept up with. She only had three frocks in total, the one she was wearing and two spares. She had left the shameful green gown behind at Annabelle's in her hurry to escape. Gabriel had promised her that he would have all of her new gowns retrieved when they returned. If that proved impossible, he would call out a modiste to have new ones made. That would be a terrible waste of money so she truly hoped her uncle would allow her to have her wardrobe.

She was surprised when Gabriel told her of her uncle's change of heart and that he actually gave his blessing on the marriage, but she wouldn't really believe it until she heard him say so himself. Gabriel assured her that it was genuine, and that he had actually destroyed the betrothal contracts for his and Diana's marriage as well as the one for her and Alistair. She wondered what had brought about this sudden change of heart. It was all rather suspicious, but as Gabriel had told her, it must be true as he gave Dylan leave to go to the press to tell them how he had treated her thus far if he should be proven false. She would try to think positive on it and hope that he really had changed his heart toward her.

She shook herself out of her musings, deciding she wouldn't worry about her uncle, but instead keep her attention on her maid. She couldn't help but notice that Wishy seemed to like ogling Lord Sumersleigh. She hoped that it wouldn't become a problem later on. When they were waiting to depart in the foyer this morning, she seemed to have been overcome with the giggles in his presence. He, however, seemed not to notice. When Dylan was with Gabriel, he was open and friendly. So far, he had been very respectful, even kind to Alyssa. However, when Wishy was near, he clammed up and became solemn. Perhaps he didn't want to encourage the girl. For that she was appreciative. She was glad he didn't seem to take note of the silly girl because she didn't want him to think he could take liberties with her maid.

When she had first noticed the girl's behavior, she

immediately became concerned. She quietly spoke to Gabriel about it before entering the carriage. He assured her that Dylan was not a man who frolicked indiscriminately with the ladies. He told her, he was a very selective man who preferred to stay clear of women of easy virtue. Was Wishy a woman of easy virtue? How would Gabriel know it? She hoped not and didn't want to dwell on the possibility that Gabriel would have personal knowledge one way or the other. She decided that she would just trust Gabriel and Dylan to be gentlemen and stay clear of the girl. She liked the girl so far and hoped that they could have a long-term relationship. In so doing, perhaps she could improve the girl's circumstances. As a ladies' maid and companion to a duchess, she could ensure that the girl could one day find a proper husband if she were inclined to have one.

She was pulled from her reverie when the carriage slowed and came to a stop. Wishy came awake and started fussing with her hair. After a moment, the door was opened, and Gabriel was standing there smiling.

"We shall stop for lunch. Dylan and I are starving, and this is the last inn for quite some time," he said offering his hand to assist her out of the carriage.

She was hungry and glad to have a chance to stretch her legs. She wasn't sure of the time, but she was sure that the hour for luncheon had passed at least two hours ago, but she wouldn't complain. She knew Gabriel wanted to keep a tight schedule. They probably wouldn't stop again until well after dark.

"I'm starved as well," she said beaming at him

with her own smile.

She gave him her hand and disembarked, then he assisted Wishy down as well. She was looking around wildly. Once her eyes found the subject of her frantic search she relaxed and fell into place beside Alyssa. Dylan had taken his and Gabriel's horses to the stables and was giving the stable man instructions. The Sword and Stone Inn seemed clean. She hoped that they would provide pleasant victuals for their hungry crew. Inside was just as nice as the outside, and they were quickly greeted by the innkeeper, an elderly lady who introduced herself as Mrs. Harper.

"What can I do for you my lord?" she addressed Gabriel.

"I would like to have a private dining room for four. Of course, our horses and our coachmen will need to be tended as well," he told her.

"Very good, my lord, follow me."

She led them to a small dining room that was situated directly off the tavern room. The three of them took their seats at the dining table. Mrs. Harper took their order, and before her return, they were joined by Dylan. He quietly sat down as close to Gabriel as he could get without appearing strange, presumably to keep distance between Wishy and himself. She didn't seem to notice. She was all aflutter in his presence once again. Gabriel and Alyssa looked at one another, and he winked at her. She blushed and looked down at the table. He quietly snickered at her reaction, and she blushed even more. The man was incorrigible.

"How are you ladies fairing in the carriage?"

Dylan asked conversationally.

"Fine I suppose, but I would dearly love to be riding on a horse. Though I confess, it's been years since I have ridden and probably wouldn't do very well. I would still find it preferable to being cooped up inside on such a lovely day," Alyssa told him.

"Perhaps you would like to ride for an hour or two when we get back on the road?" Gabriel suggested.

"Oh, but we haven't a spare horse," Alyssa said.

"You could ride with Chester and I. We would both enjoy the company of such a lovely lady. Chester is quite the ladies' man, you see," he told her with another wink and a devilish grin.

Alyssa grinned at him in return. The only time she had ridden Chester, she had been asleep and missed the adventure almost entirely. Gabriel had told her about his horse, and she would dearly love another opportunity to meet him.

"That would be lovely, Gabriel. Thank you," she told him.

"You haven't seen Chester perform I gather," Dylan said.

"No, but Gabriel has told me all about him. I look forward to seeing it very soon," she said.

"Oh! Me too, I would love to see him perform," Wishy blurted out.

Everyone became quiet and looked at her. She was staring wide-eyed at Dylan.

Her brown eyes were round with excitement, and her cheeks were flushed. This could be a problem indeed, Alyssa realized. She would have to speak to her tonight when the men were out of hearing. This wouldn't do at all. Gabriel must have been thinking the same thing because he looked at Alyssa then quickly at Wishy, who was still staring fondly at Dylan. She nodded her head that she understood his silent message.

"Hawk, perhaps you could arrange a quick exhibition for the ladies before we resume our trip. I don't see how there would be any harm in taking a few minutes for a little entertainment," Dylan suggested.

Dylan had yet to make eye contact with Wishy but seemed uncomfortably aware of her gaze upon him. He was a gentleman put in a difficult situation, she realized. She would certainly have to take her maid in hand; this could not be allowed to continue.

"Yes, we shall arrange a small demonstration before we set out again," Gabriel agreed.

*****

"Take a bow to the ladies, Chester," Gabriel commanded.

Chester lowered his head and the front half of his body in a very gentlemanly bow.

"Now Chester, show your appreciation for their beauty," Gabriel once again commanded.

Chester raised himself from the bow and whinnied. He stomped his right foot and bobbed his head up and down several times.

"Very good Chester, now show the ladies how well you can dance," he told him.

Chester strutted around in a sweeping circle

about ten yards in diameter before them, then reared up on his hind legs and bounced three times before coming down. He lowered his head, swaying it from side to side. Then, he raised it up and began to take a few crisscrossing steps in one direction, quickly shifting back in the other.

"Very good, Chester, now take your bow and bid the ladies adieu."

Chester slowly went before the ladies, bowed gracefully again and whinnied loudly before turning about and walking away, falling into step beside Gabriel.

Alyssa and Wishy were both enthralled. Chester had been a sight to see. She could tell he truly enjoyed performing.

Dylan had stood by the carriage while Chester was giving his demonstration. He was smiling at Gabriel. When they reached him, he very lovingly stroked Chester's face and gave him a treat.

"Did you see that My Lady?" Wishy asked.

"Yes, he is delightful isn't he?" Alyssa said, still marveling at Chester's prowess and grace.

"Oh yes, My Lady, he truly is. I have never seen anything to equal him in my life," she breathed with elation.

"Are you speaking about the horse or Lord Sumersleigh?" Alyssa thought to ask.

Wishy tucked her head and looked at the ground.

"You need to control yourself around him Wishy. He is a lord. You must respect his station. I will not have you fawning at him in such a way. It's unladylike, and it doesn't become you at all. It wouldn't do for you to gain a reputation as a light-skirt," Alyssa chastised her.

"I'm sorry, My Lady, but I have never seen such a fine looking man in all my life. I realize he is too far above me, but I cannot help but admire him," she said honestly.

"As long as it's from afar, you may do so, but you must stop flirting with him," Alyssa stated.

"Yes, My Lady, it will be as you say."

Alyssa felt better having told her that Dylan was off limits. Perhaps now there wouldn't be any more trouble. She felt a bit hypocritical chastising her maid when she herself had been of the working class, but she knew that it was improper behavior and could never come to a good end.

"Will you be alright in the carriage alone for a couple of hours?" Alyssa thought to ask.

"Yes My Lady, don't worry about me. I always fall asleep in a carriage; I will be fine. You go along and enjoy yourself," she responded.

"Very good; I shall join you again in no time."

They joined Gabriel and Dylan. After Gabriel assisted Wishy into the carriage, he turned to Alyssa, offering his arm. He guided her to Chester and propped her upon him, then mounted up behind her, and they resumed their journey.

"I saw you scolding your maid. I hope it went well," he said quietly in her ear.

Dylan was up ahead of them a pretty good pace. He wouldn't have been able to hear them, but she kind of liked him speaking quietly in her ear, so she didn't remark upon it.

"Yes, I told her she needed to behave herself.

She promised she would. I hope Dylan isn't too upset by it all."

"He is mildly amused by the chit, but fear not, he is the consummate gentleman. She will come to no harm by his hand," he assured her again.

"I think he is in more danger from her than the other way around," she said with a giggle.

Gabriel laughed too and snuggled her closer to him. He placed his arm just under her breasts to keep her securely against him, and the warmth traveled deep within her. She liked being close to him like this and never wanted it to end.

*****

Dylan was more than mildly amused by the chit; he was having trouble keeping his eyes off of her. He knew he shouldn't be so interested in her, but he couldn't help himself. He had gone too long without a woman. He saw her being chastised by Alyssa. He thought he should probably make himself as scarce as possible to avoid causing the girl further trouble with her mistress. It was going to be a long week or so if he was going to be forced to endure being around her all the while. She was simply far too tempting. She wasn't a raving beauty by any means, but when her come-hither lips stretched into that magnificent smile that showed her deep dimples, she became quite adorable.

The girl had a natural charm that he found refreshing and quite irresistible. She had big doe eyes, the color of cinnamon and honey. Her hair was a rich dark brown that was nearly black. Loose curls fell softly about her cheeks, but the bulk of it was kept tucked under a lace cap as was proper for one of her class. She was a very shapely piece of baggage with big bouncing breasts and well rounded hips. She was too young, of course, but she would no doubt be a willing participant in her own seduction if he were inclined to pursue her. He wouldn't pursue her. He was an earl and she but a servant. It would be frowned upon for him to take advantage. He suspected she was probably still a virgin. She had an obvious innocence about her despite her giggles and fawning at him.

He thought about the gap in their classes and felt a brief pang of loss. Two years ago, he wouldn't have thought twice about taking advantage of one of her class, but now that he was titled, he couldn't bring himself to do it. However, Hawk was marrying a woman who had been a maid, but she was, in fact, the niece of an earl and an heiress in her own right. Their situation was more acceptable by societal standards but would at some point cause a certain amount of cruel speculation and gossip. He hoped that it wouldn't, but he knew how cruel the gossips could be.

He would have to be selective in his future bride. He was the heir to a dukedom. His grandfather, though nearing the end of his long life and mostly bedridden, was the Duke of Blackstone. Since he and his father were his last surviving male heirs, the title would fall upon him someday as the title of Earl of Sumersleigh had upon his brother's death. His father was still alive too and was the Marquess of Wentworth. But as his health was increasingly failing, it wouldn't be long before he passed on as well, making Dylan the last in line for the dukedom. He found that regrettable as he didn't want to be titled at all.

He wished his brother hadn't died so he would be free to pursue such a sweet girl as Wishy. It would have been more acceptable had he still remained untitled. Untitled gentlemen could get away with marrying a girl such as her far easier than a duke or even an earl, so it was best for him to put her out of his mind. He shook his head as he realized he was thinking of the girl in the terms of marriage and was a little startled by it. True, he had already decided he would start searching for a bride, but he had no intentions of marrying a servant.

*****

Long after dark, they stopped at the Gray Horse Inn to take supper and rooms for the night. It had been a long day, and Alyssa was exhausted. She had ridden for several hours with Gabriel before returning to the carriage. She felt like she had used muscles she didn't even know she had. She ached from head to toe and decided that when they set about on the morrow she would remain with Wishy in the carriage. She would have to re-accustom her body to riding again, but she had better do it at a lesser pace than she had today. Gabriel told her she would have her own mare when they returned to Windhaven, and that they would take up riding together in the mornings.

After they ate their dinner, Gabriel could see

she was exhausted and ordered her a hot bath. She was grateful to him for noticing her discomfort and was now sunk to her neck in the hot scented water. He and Dylan took connecting rooms across the hall from her room, which shared a connecting room with Wishy. She was worn out from traveling, too, so Alyssa told her to go and rest. She would tend to herself. Wishy gladly took her leave and went to bed. She didn't know how the girl would possibly sleep tonight as she had slept most of the day, but she assured her that she was exhausted and would have no trouble at all. The men, however, opted to take a few drinks in the taproom before they turned in for the night. Alyssa realized that she was about to fall asleep in the tub, so she reluctantly got out, dressed herself for sleep and crawled into the small but comfortable bed. It didn't take her long to succumb to the exhaustion that she felt. She soon drifted off to sleep.

*****

"Well my friend, I believe that about does it for me. I shall see you at dawn," Gabriel said, standing up to bid his friend goodnight.

"I believe I will have another before I turn in," Dylan told him.

"In another day and a half, I shall be a married man and need to accustom myself to turning in early," Gabriel grinned.

"Yes, you will be expected to spend your nights with your bride soon; you had better get into the habit of behaving now."

The two men shook hands, and Gabriel went upstairs to find his bed. Dylan leaned back in his chair, stretched out his long legs and sipped his ale, considering the future of his group of friends. They would be losing Gabriel. With any luck, he would soon follow. What would Jasper and Luther do when left to their own devices? He couldn't imagine either of them settling down, especially Luther. He was such a child-like fellow that he probably wouldn't get married for years yet.

Jasper, on the other hand, would possibly follow suit once he realized he wasn't getting any younger. But what woman could put up with such a man. When he wasn't with his friends, he became obsessed with his inventions to the point of near madness. When his mind clapped onto an idea, he was like a bloodhound and would nearly work himself to death until he had satisfaction. He and the others would often have to rescue Jasper from his obsessions because he would forget to eat or sleep. Once, he had nearly starved himself to death. He was convinced he could create a device whereby men could communicate with one another even when miles apart. Such an idea was insane, but he was sure it could be done. He gave the idea up when his friends intervened and took him on holiday to Italy. He never returned to it.

They had found him emaciated and dehydrated. He was so weak he couldn't stand up on his own power. It had scared the men. They decided that they would have to look after Jasper better and not allow him to disappear for more than a two or three days at a time before they investigated his whereabouts. They never again wanted to find their friend in such a state. No, it would be most difficult for Jasper to marry successfully. Whoever he married would have to have the patience of a saint to endure his eccentricities when he was in one of his inventing moods.

His thoughts were interrupted by a sweet, soft voice that he recognized immediately. He looked up to see Wishy standing before him. She looked like an angel sent down from heaven. Her hair was down and she was dressed in a white nightgown with a soft blue wrap. She was looking at him with her big doe eyes as if he were the most handsome man she had ever seen.

"What are you doing here? You should not be in the taproom in such a state of undress," he admonished.

He looked around the room, realizing that they were essentially alone. Only the barman was there, and he was reading a book.

"I couldn't sleep," she told him.

"This is most inappropriate, Wishy."

She looked down in embarrassment. He had a twinge of regret that he had to be so severe with her. She looked so pretty, standing there. He knew that if he didn't send her away and soon, he couldn't be responsible for the outcome. He was just a man after all, and she was so lovely and apparently more than willing to bestow her charms upon him.

"I would like to sit with you for a little while. I know I shouldn't be here, but I can't stop thinking about you. I saw Lord Windhaven return without you. I was concerned that you might be lonely," she told him with a sweet, seductive smile.

He stared at her, and his jaw tensed. She was most likely a light-skirt, despite her young age, and she had set her sights on him for a little sport. "I am not interested in spending time with a woman of your sort."

Her bottom lip quivered, but she didn't turn away. He hadn't wanted to believe that the girl was this way, but apparently he had been wrong. He should teach her a lesson here and now, but he lacked the will to truly be cruel to the chit.

"If you are not going to leave, then sit down before you draw any more attention to yourself," he barked at her.

She hesitated, but then sat down beside him. "I am not what you think; I am not a light-skirt," she told him quietly.

"What would you have me think of a woman that comes to a taproom dressed in her nightclothes to talk to strange men?" he asked her bitterly.

"I have never been with a man. I only came down because …"

"Because what?" he snapped, cutting her words off.

"I don't know why I came," she said timidly.

"Did you have grand visions of losing your virtue to an earl?" he asked chidingly with a sardonic smile.

She looked down at the table. Her bottom lip began to tremble again.

"Do you even know what that means?" he demanded.

She shook her head, refusing to look at him.

He could tell he was scaring her and that she probably was having second thoughts about her irrational behavior now.

"Shall I tell you what it means?" he asked with a deceptive softness.

She looked up at him, her eyes wide, but didn't respond.

"You want to lay with me and spread your lovely thighs to allow me to plow your untouched field with my staff. You want me to sew my seed within you and have it take root and grow," he said with a measure of seduction in his voice.

"Soon after, I will abandon you as you will become swollen with my bastard. I will no longer have any use for you. Then, you will bore my bastard with the aid of no one and become reduced to poverty as no one will employ you when they find out that you are a woman of easy virtue," he continued with anger filtering into his words.

"You will then be forced to service ten maybe twenty men a day just to scrape up enough coin to feed and clothe the unwanted brat. Having to do that, you will become old and worn out before your time and die in some dark stinking pit of poverty and disease. That's what it means Wishy; now go back to bed," he finished, tossing back the last of his drink and slamming the glass upon the table.

She had a look of horror on her face. She jumped up. Instead of running up the stairs as he had intended her to do, she ran out into the night.

"Damnation!" he growled and got up to give chase.

He hadn't intended to be so crude and harsh,

but he was angry at her. He was also fighting an inner voice that was telling him to take what she was offering. He couldn't allow himself to do it, so he had to try to scare her away for her own good. It was dark outside, and he couldn't see his hand in front of his face. She had been quickly swallowed up by the night. He had no idea in which direction to search for her. Where could she have gone to? The only other building was the stables, perhaps she had gone inside. He quickly ran over there, but it was dark within. He couldn't see a thing.

"Wishy?" he called out.

There was no answer, but he truly believed she had come here. The stable man must be asleep because there appeared to be no one about, so he ventured inside.

"Wishy? I'm sorry; I didn't mean what I said. Please come out," he called.

He heard a very soft whimper up ahead and knew that he had found her. He felt along the wall. Eventually, he found a lantern and some flint sticks. He lit the lantern and began to seek her out. Soon he found her hunkered on the ground in the corner of an empty stall. She was hugging her legs close to her body, she was hiding her face on her knees. He could tell she was crying. He felt like an arse; he was an arse. Blast and damn! Why did he have to hurt the girl like that?

"Wishy, it isn't safe for you to be out here. You must come back inside. Come now!" he softly commanded.

She lifted her head, glaring at him with eyes full of glittering fire. "Go away and leave me be.

You are a cruel man, and I don't want to ever speak to you again," she shouted.

She was right; he had been cruel, but it was only to be kind. He had to make her see this. "Don't you understand why I said those things?" he asked.

She ignored him and continued to glare at him as if he were a monster.

"I had to make you see that your actions were wrong, putting yourself in danger where no good could come from it. I didn't mean you any harm. I was only trying to teach you a lesson," he said.

Her eyes softened. She sniffed in an attempt to control her tears and put her head back down on her knees to avoid looking at him. "Just go!" she said softly.

Dylan wasn't about to leave her out here alone. He ventured into the stall, sitting down beside her. He didn't understand what made him do it, but he reached out and stroked her hair. It was soft like silk. The contact sent a current coursing through his blood. He wanted her, he did, but he knew he mustn't give in to his carnal desires. He was now faced with an agonizing decision. Should he listen to his conscience or give her what she wanted; what they both wanted.

He sighed, then sat down beside her and pulled her into his arms and held her. "I'm so sorry Wishy. Can you forgive me?" he asked.

She buried her face in his chest because she was still embarrassed by what had been said. He began a soothing caress of her back and felt his loins responding with a vengeance. She began a slow caress of her own upon his chest, looking up into his eyes. He was lost then; he kissed her with a desperate hunger. She kissed him back with an equal need. Her kiss was unskilled, but she was eager. Soon he had her on her back, and he was on top of her. His hands were desperately roaming over her luscious curves. Her whimpers of pleasure spurred him onward. He tugged apart the strings of her night dress, seeking out her breasts with his lips. Her nipples were tight little rose buds. He eagerly laved them with his tongue, trying to give equal attention to them both. He growled in frustration when he couldn't.

He settled for the one on the right. She arched her back and pressed him closer to hold him in place. He reached down, gathering up the hem of her gown and found his way to her woman's mound. He began a slow, circular caress at her tender bud of flesh. She thrust her hips up to encourage his ministrations. It was that move that brought him to his senses. He pulled his hand away, raising himself up and off of her.

"This is madness!" he said with a groan.

"Tis wonderful madness," she said.

He ignored her and stood up. He couldn't allow this to go on, he simply couldn't.

"Please do not stop now, my body is on fire," she pleaded.

"I cannot! Put yourself back together. Go back inside before we both do something we shall regret!" he demanded.

She refused to listen. Instead she removed her gown from her shoulders, further exposing her breasts to him. She stood up, letting it fall to the floor. She stood before him in all her naked glory. He found himself as if pinned in place, unable to look away. There was no way she was a virgin behaving this way. She had to be a skilled woman, intent on bedding him. He had to get away from her, but he couldn't leave her here unprotected. He looked away, but she had become emboldened by her nakedness. She walked up to him, pressed herself against him and started kissing his neck.

"Vixen!" he shouted, then shoved her away. "What game are you playing? You said you were a virgin, but you act the whore. Do you think I would want a whore?" he asked with anger blazing in his eyes.

"I have never known a man, this I swear. But my body aches to know you, Dylan," she purred softly, walking back to him. Once again pressed her body against his.

He didn't believe her, but he wanted to. He wanted desperately to throw her down on the ground and ram his cock into her with a vengeance.

"Please don't do this to me. I am weak. I cannot resist you much longer, Wishy. Get dressed. Go back to bed, I beg you," he pleaded.

"No," was her soft reply.

She reached up, unbuttoning his shirt with swift efficiency. She pulled it out of his breeches, spreading it open to expose his bare chest. She started unbuttoning his breeches next until his erection sprang forth from its restraints. He growled and grabbed her by the shoulders, then drove her down to the ground. With a savage need he mounted her with a hard thrust, but stopped cold at her cry when he plunged through her barrier of innocence. She hadn't been lying; she was a virgin. He was stunned by her virginity, but he was too far gone to care anymore. He lunged forward, kissed her deeply and wrapped her legs about him so he could slide deeper within to begin a slow, deep thrust in and out. He had never known such a feeling. It felt so ... right, and she was so warm and tight. He feared he wouldn't last much longer as he had been deprived of a woman's body for so very long, giving him no control over his own. He didn't want her first time to end without completion, but he couldn't help it, his thrusts became urgent. When he was about to release, he pulled out of her with a roar of ecstasy, allowing his seed to spill out onto her legs.

He collapsed on top of her. His body quaked as he tried to get his breathing under control. Suddenly it felt all wrong. He began to question her actions. Why had she done it? Why had she thrown herself at him despite his begging her not to do it? Hadn't she believed him when he told her what would happen? He desperately tried to avoid it, but she had been so relentless that he had become overwhelmed. He truly had not believed she was a virgin, but she had driven him so mad, he could no longer ignore her attempts to seduce him. Aye, this was madness unless ... she had calculated the whole thing. Aye, she had set her cap for him, thinking to trap him into marriage. At that thought he quickly sat up and began to right his clothing.

"I won't marry you, Wishy, so all your calculations have been for naught, but you need not worry that I have left you with child. Believe me when I tell you that this will never happen again," he told her coldly.

She lay there looking up at him with hurt in her eyes. He had been an arse again; he knew it and hated himself for it. Not only did he not even try to make it pleasant for her, but after he had finished, he had become cold and callous. What did she expect? She had thrown herself at him. This was what she had been looking for; well, she found it. Knowing it did little for his conscience. He was even angrier now for succumbing when he should have showed more restraint.

"Get dressed!" he barked at her. He left the stall and went outside the stable to wait for her.

Chapter Sixteen

Dylan was angry at himself for taking advantage of the girl the way he had. Sure, she had asked for it, but he knew better than to fall for the seductions of a light-skirt and one so young. True, she hadn't really been a light-skirt, but you would never have known it from her behavior. He stood sentinel outside of the stables waiting for her now, brooding over what had occurred. What would he say to her? What would he say to Gabriel? He sighed deeply, running his hands through his hair. He was a pig for the way he had treated her. He would have to find a way to make it right. How could he unless he married the girl, though? Aye, that was the only way he could possibly make it right. It wouldn't be so bad really. She was a beautiful girl. She had been just as attracted to him as he had been to her. So what if she was only a maid? She would make him a fine wife. He would be proud to have her. He would tell her he was sorry and propose to her. All would be set to rights.

He heard her footsteps coming forward, and he braced himself to tell her of his change of heart, but found he couldn't say the words. He quickly decided that it would be far better to discuss it after they have both had time to think on what had happened between them. She was probably so angry at him that she would reject him now so he would wait until tomorrow, hoping that with a new day they would be able to start over. He didn't want the rejection, he realized; he wanted her, his titles be damned. He found the notion surprising.

"I am ready," she said, stepping up behind him.

He held out his arm to escort her back to the Inn. She hesitantly took it.

"Hold it right there!" came a commanding male voice. He couldn't make out who it was as they were shining a lantern in his eyes. He didn't recognize the voice, but he quickly pushed Wishy behind him, so he could shield her with his body then held still as he had been commanded. He didn't think he could successfully reach for his pistols before they fired at him. So he stood still, waiting to see what would develop.

The next thing he knew he felt a sharp pain at the back of his head. He dropped to his knees, falling into darkness. Wishy screamed, but her cry was quickly muffled by a very large hand over her mouth.

"Don't make another sound or I will kill him," the man commanded her.

"I'll handle it from here, John," said an unfamiliar female voice.

Wishy was terrified of what they were planning to do. She was worried about Dylan as he lay on the ground. They had hurt him badly. He needed her to tend to him. Fear for him made her whole body begin to tremble as she waited to see what would happen next.

"Another lord and a maid … when will sluts like you realize that it is fruitless to try and trap them? He won't marry you, you know," the woman chided.

Wishy didn't speak. She was too scared to breathe. She wished she could see who they were.

"Wishy is it?" the female prompted.

Wishy nodded her head that it was but remained silent. She didn't want to do anything to provoke the angry woman.

"Well Wishy. I have a job for you. You will do it for me without mistake, or I promise you that I will kill your precious lord. Is that understood?" she asked.

"Y—Yes miss," Wishy meekly responded.

She didn't want them to hurt Dylan further so she would do whatever they asked. But she had to figure out a way to help him somehow because he was bleeding, and he wasn't moving at all.

"You have a message to deliver to that other slut, Alyssa, who also thinks that she too, can trap a lord into marriage. You will tell her that her good friend Cookie is awaiting her in the stables. Tell her she must come with all possible haste. You are not to tell her anything else, do I make myself clear?"

Wishy nodded her head that she understood.

"Make one mistake, and John here will slit his throat. Then he will seek you out and slit yours too."

Wishy trembled. Her knees nearly gave out from under her. Who was this woman? Why did she want Alyssa? Surely she wasn't really a friend as she had said she was.

"Now go. Do as you were bid. You have ten minutes to convince her, or he is a dead man."

Wishy shot off like a speeding bullet and ran inside the inn. She raced up the stairs, went into her room, then quickly ran through the connecting door to Alyssa's room.

"My Lady, you must wake up," she told her, shaking her by the shoulder.

"What is it, Wishy?"

"Your friend, Cookie, awaits you in the stables. She said you must go to her with all possible haste as she has a very urgent message for you," Wishy told her as convincingly as she could.

Alyssa quickly sat up, swinging her legs over the side of the bed.

"Please get my wrap Wishy and my slippers. I shall go to her immediately."

Wishy was relieved for Dylan, but she was worried too. What if this woman wasn't really a friend but wanted to hurt her mistress? She already had Dylan and meant to do him harm if she didn't cooperate. She had to do something, but what could she do? She would go with her mistress to try to protect her as best she could, but she didn't know how she would manage it. Then suddenly, she remembered she had a knife.

"Wait right there, miss; I will come with you, but I need to get something from my room first," she told her.

Wishy ran back into her room, plundered through her bag and found her knife. Maybe she could protect her somehow with it. She dashed back into Alyssa's room. They quickly went down the stairs and out into the night. She led Alyssa to the stables. Her mistress was immediately grabbed by the man and held in restraint. Wishy panicked. She lunged for the man, but he threw Alyssa into the arms of yet another man. Then he grabbed her by the arm, nearly breaking her wrist as he forced her to drop her weapon. Once he had her subdued, he savagely struck her on the head with something hard, and she, too, fell into cold darkness.

"What is going on? Why have you harmed my maid?" Alyssa cried out in horror.

She couldn't see who her attackers were because of the blinding light of the lantern they held in front of her, but she was beginning to have her suspicions. Alistair must have found her.

"Get her and put her in the coach," a familiar female voice commanded.

Diana had found her, not Alistair. What was she to do now? What did Diana plan to do with her? She didn't know, but she feared the worst. The men forcefully dragged her away. She was tied at the wrists, knees and ankles. They placed a gag in her mouth and a blindfold around her eyes then threw her into the coach. Just then, she heard the sound of a horse thundering toward the carriage. It came to a stop right outside. She heard him then and began to tremble violently. Alistair was here.

"What are you doing here, Diana?" he shouted in anger.

"Oh dear brother, I have come to take care of that bitch because you were too busy with your whore to do it for me. I am a resourceful woman, after all. I have decided to kill the slut myself," she told him tauntingly.

"You will do nothing of the kind," he growled.

There was some kind of a struggle. A shot was fired. Alyssa jerked at the sound, whimpering beneath her gag. Had someone been killed?

"What have you done with Alyssa, Diana?" she

heard Alistair ask with barely restrained rage.

"She is in the carriage. If you make one false move, I will have John shoot you. This time he will not miss."

"What do you want?" he asked her.

"I want her dead as I have already told you," she said to him.

"You're insane!" was his incredulous response.

"Of course, I would be willing to make a deal with you for her life," she told him as though a thought had just occurred to her.

"What kind of a deal?" he asked in a cold harsh voice.

"Spare Gabriel, and you can have her here and now."

"Done!" he quickly agreed.

"What goes on out here?" a man's voice called out from the doorway of the inn.

"We must be away quickly as your man's gunshot has drawn attention to us. Give me Alyssa now, and I will spare your precious Gabriel. You have my word."

"Take her! She is all trussed up nicely for you inside the carriage," she told him gloatingly.

The carriage door flung open, and Alyssa was grabbed and slung over Alistair's shoulder. He threw her across the back of his horse, mounted up behind her and quickly fled.

*****

Gabriel was just about to drift off to sleep when he was jolted by the sound of gunfire. He jumped up, put on his boots and grabbed his gun. He went over to Dylan's door, opened it and saw that he was not within. He cautiously went down the stairs. The barman stood at the open doorway leading outside, holding a lantern in an attempt to see what had happened. Gabriel rushed past him. In the darkness, he couldn't see what the commotion had been. He saw a lit lantern over by the stables and ran toward it.

"DYLAN!" he shouted.

"Dylan is sleeping now, dear Gabriel," an all too familiar voice purred in the darkness from behind him.

His blood chilled. He realized he hadn't thought to check in Alyssa's room before he rushed out. He slowly turned toward Diana.

"What are you doing here Diana?" he asked with barely contained anger.

"I have come to claim my betrothed. You have no more worries now as I have rid you of your whore. There is nothing standing in our way of our being married," she said proudly.

"What do you mean you have rid me of her? What have you done?" he demanded while advancing toward her.

He got within inches of her when he heard a gun cock at the side of his head. He froze in his tracks.

"He won't hurt me, John; he is my betrothed," she told the big man wielding the gun.

"Where is Alyssa?" he demanded.

"She is gone with my dear brother, as is proper. She is betrothed to him, after all, so fear not; he shall take care of her. You needn't worry; he will only beat her a little for her impudence," she told him smugly.

"Your brother has her?" he asked as fear struck deep in his heart.

"Yes, you see, I had to trade her life for yours. Of course, I was prudent and chose you, my dear," she bragged seductively.

He didn't think; he just acted. He lunged for her but came up empty. He was quickly grabbed from behind and slung away from her. He reached for his gun, taking aim at the man who had accosted him, but his arm had been grabbed by another man he had not been aware of before. The shot went wild and harmed no one. He was spun around from behind and was slammed in the face with a vicious punch by the man he presumed to be the one she had called John. He reeled from the blow, but quickly recovered, throwing one of his own. He made contact with the man's nose, sending him flying backward, onto his back where he did not move again. Just then, a shot was fired near the stables and everyone froze as they heard another familiar voice; a voice that relieved him immensely. Dylan had come.

"Make one more move, any of you, and I will drop you where you stand. I have another pistol and it is primed and aimed at your head, Diana. I am an excellent marksman, so I suggest that you call your men off now," he told her.

Everyone stood still as Dylan advanced toward them. He went to the other man still standing and relieved him of his gun. Then he went to the man lying on the ground and relieved him of his.

"Diana do you have any weapons?" he asked her.

She glared at him, refusing to answer. He calmly walked past her and handed the weapons he had collected to Gabriel. Gabriel trained the one he was sure was still loaded onto the one uninjured man. John was still lying on the ground. He seemed to be unconscious. He didn't take it for granted, so kept a wary eye on them both. Dylan started patting Diana's person, looking for weapons. He found one strapped to her thigh. He relieved her of it, sticking it in the waist of his breeches. Gabriel was relieved that the group was no longer a threat. He needed to find out which direction Alistair had gone so he could pursue.

"Which way did Alistair go?" he growled at Diana.

"I shall tell you nothing," she spat.

He cocked the weapon and pressed it to her remaining henchman's head.

"Which way?" he asked the man.

The man pointed north, and he swiftly struck him on the head with the butt of the pistol. He went down in a heap.

"Do you have things in hand here Dylan?" he asked his friend.

"Go! I will stay behind and have the innkeeper call for the magistrate," he told him.

Gabriel headed toward the stable and stumbled over something lying on the ground. He knew it was a body, but he couldn't see who it was. "I need a lantern, there is a body here," he shouted.

The barman rushed over with his lantern, shining the light down on the body. It was Wishy. Her eyes were open. One look into her vacant stare confirmed she was dead. He heard an agonized wail behind him then. The sound of it sent his blood to curdling. He turned around just in time to see Dylan fire his weapon into the head of the man that Gabriel had fought with. He had a cold relentless look as he took the gun he had taken from Diana and fired into the head of the other man. He started advancing on Diana.

Gabriel ran toward him just in time to prevent him reaching Diana. He grabbed him around the arms from behind, pinning them to his sides. Dylan was like a wild man that couldn't be contained. He thrashed and kicked as he tried to free himself from Gabriel's hold, but he hung on for all he was worth, trying to wear him down. He struggled with his friend for what seemed like an eternity until finally he collapsed to his knees, groaning like a man who had been utterly defeated. Gabriel released him then. He sat there and sobbed as if he were in agony while he held the sides of his head in his hands. Gabriel was torn between consoling his friend and going after Alyssa. He turned to look for Diana and saw that the barman had her firmly in his grasp. She had a look of utter horror on her face.

Just then, he heard the thunder of horses approaching. He couldn't make out who the riders were, but it sounded like there were at least three. Indeed three riders approached. Gabriel was very relieved to see them. Luther, Jasper and Glenmont with some woman Gabriel didn't recognize had arrived. They quickly jumped down from their horses and with wild eyes took in the scene before them. Bodies were lying about. Dylan was on his knees pouring out his heart like a man who had just been through hell. Jasper rushed over to Dylan and immediately started trying to console him. Luther stood dazed, trying to take it all in. Glenmont approached Gabriel, but before he made it to him, Diana cried out for him.

"Go to her," Gabriel told him solemnly.

He ignored his daughter's cries and Gabriel's command.

"What has happened here?" he asked with a grave voice.

Gabriel wasn't sure about all that had happened here, but looking at the scene before him it was fairly easy to piece together. He squeezed the bridge of his nose, closing his eyes tightly for a moment. He composed himself and looked at Glenmont, then began to relay what he knew or thought must have occurred.

"Diana came. She somehow managed to kidnap Alyssa from her room, after which Alistair arrived. She turned her over to him in exchange for my life, or so she says. At some point, her henchmen must have killed a woman, Alyssa's maid, whom my friend Dylan was apparently very fond of."

"He went mad with grief upon the discovery of her body and killed the henchmen in turn. I just barely managed to stop him from killing Diana. Alistair has escaped with Alyssa, and I must go after them now before any more time elapses."

Glenmont stood before him with a mixture of

many emotions on his face. When he turned to look toward his daughter, his expression changed to one of absolute loathing.

"My friends will take care of Dylan now. Do what you will with Diana, only make sure I never see her again, or I will kill her myself," Gabriel told him with a coldness that surprised even him.

He turned to leave, going into the stables to retrieve Chester. He saddled him up, quickly mounted and raced off in the direction that Alistair had taken. He prayed he would find them and that he wouldn't be too late to stop the madman from harming her.

*****

Alyssa was terrified. She remained trussed up, lying on her stomach on top of Alistair's horse. He hadn't spoken to her yet, but he was driving his horse forward at top speed like a man with the fires of hell at his heels. She knew that Alistair would be beyond any kind of reasoning after what she had done. He would view the whole ordeal as a personal insult and would deal harshly with her. She wasn't so much worried about her own life as she feared what might be happening now at the inn with Diana and her thugs. She saw what they had done to Wishy and hoped that the poor dear would be all right. She was worried that they would try to harm Gabriel too when he learned what had happened. Diana was just as mad as her brother, she realized. The woman had wanted her dead because she had dared to be with Gabriel.

She wondered where Alistair was taking her, hoping that at some point she could try to escape him. She didn't think it very likely as he would watch her closely to make sure that she didn't. She shivered at the prospect of what he might have planned for her. She knew it wouldn't be good whatever it was. He was an unstable man who didn't deal with anger very well. Her head was beginning to pound. She was very dizzy, being bounced around the way she was. She didn't know how much longer she could hold out before she swooned. She wanted to try to remain alert, but she didn't think she would be able to much longer.

As if he could hear her thoughts, he seemed to become aware of her discomfort. He suddenly stopped his horse, untied her legs and ankles then sat her up before him. However, he didn't untie her wrists or remove her gag and blindfold. Once he had her settled before him, he quickly spurred his horse into action again. She was grateful for the small kindness he had just shown her, but she didn't expect many others would follow. At least she didn't feel like she was going to swoon anymore, but she didn't like the feel of his arm around her waist. He had her in a very tight hold. She could hear his ragged breathing in her ear. She almost wished he would say something so she could get a feel for his mood. His silence seemed very foreboding. It struck fear deep within her. She wondered if she should try to encourage him to remove her gag so she could speak to him. Perhaps it was best not to poke the angry bear anymore than she already had, she quickly decided. She would just have to be content to wait until he decided to do it on his own.

He brought her back against his chest. She didn't resist when he did. She would have to appear to be cooperative as best she could because she knew he could be appeased if he thought she was repentant. She remembered how easily she had fooled him before, hoping she hadn't made him wise to her ploys to deceive him. Of course, he would be wise. Who was she trying to fool? She sighed in despair, realizing she would probably never escape him. He would probably whisk her away to the nearest ship leaving for Jamaica. He would force her into marriage or worse. He had probably surmised that she would have given Gabriel her virginity and would be ruthless in his punishment. Didn't he tell her he would kill her if she were not still a virgin? The thought scared her on one hand but on the other she realized that it might put her in a position to try to negotiate with him somehow. If she could convince him she was still a virgin, perhaps he would go easier on her.

Again she must be trying to fool herself. He would never believe her now. She shuddered when she remembered how he confirmed that she was still untouched before. She hoped that it would come to that again. She didn't want him to touch her in that way ever again. He was obviously an evil man. She couldn't bear the thought of him touching her so intimately again. She would fight him to the death before she allowed him to touch her that way. She would rather die than be violated by such a man as him. She thought of Gabriel and how gentle and loving he was with her. Sadly, she regretted that she had not given herself to him. She would probably never know his sweet, gentle touch again. The thought plunged her into deep despair. Instead, she would most likely be taken by this animal with no thought for tenderness or kindness. No! She would not allow it; she couldn't. She would try to escape him if she could, but if she must, she would fight him with all of her strength before she allowed him to succeed.

*****

"I will deal with my daughter. You all need to go after Gabriel before the magistrate arrives. He will need assistance dealing with that madman. There is no telling what might happen. He will need your help," Glenmont told Jasper.

The magistrate had been called for but had not yet arrived. He wanted the men to leave so they would not have to stay to answer questions. He would handle it from here. He was disgusted with Diana. He would have the magistrate deal harshly with her. She was responsible for all these lost lives. Three people had died because of her greed and vengeance. Now Alyssa was in peril.

"Yes we need to get moving; however, I'm not sure what's to be done with Dylan. I cannot get him to leave the girl. Who was she?" he asked.

"Lord Windhaven told me she was Alyssa's maid and that Lord Sumersleigh must have been fond of her. That's all I know," he said with sadness.

Jasper was at a loss on what to do. They needed to follow Gabriel, but they couldn't leave Dylan behind in such a state. He supposed he could leave Luther behind to help Dylan. He and Marjorie could go on after Gabriel. What else could he do?

"I will leave Luther with him. He will stay with him to make sure he comes to no harm. What about Diana?" he asked him.

"She will be held responsible for all these lost lives. I will tell the magistrate that she is solely to blame," he said gruffly.

"She is your daughter; she will hang!" he told him incredulously.

"She is the daughter of an earl … she will not hang. But she will be tried for her crimes. That is to be expected," he said soberly.

Jasper didn't have time to argue with the man so he left it alone. "I shall go speak with Luther and Dylan. Then I'll be on my way," he told him.

He turned away and walked over to his friends with a heavy heart. He didn't like seeing Dylan this way. He wondered at the nature of his relationship with the girl.

"Luther, I shall take Marjorie and trail after Gabriel. I want you to take care of Dylan; don't let him out of your sight. Do you think you can handle that?" he asked him.

"He is my brother, as you are Jasper. I will protect him with my life," he told him with tears in his eyes as he looked at his friend.

Dylan was holding the girl's lifeless body in his arms, rocking her back and forth as though she were only sleeping.

"Dylan?" Jasper softly called to him.

Dylan looked up at him. Jasper nearly lost his breath when he saw the pain in his friend's eyes.

"When the magistrate comes, you need to give the girl over and leave with Luther. Let him take you home, all right?" he told him.

"I cannot leave her alone like that. She will have to be taken home and buried properly," he told him.

"Lord Glenmont will see her home to her family, Dylan," he gently told him.

"No, I shall," he said vehemently.
Jasper knew there was no convincing him otherwise so he let the matter rest.

"As you will my friend, as you will," he told him.

He turned to Luther. The two men exchanged nods of communication. Jasper's nod said, stay with him no matter what. Luther's confirmed that he would. No more words were necessary; they would take care of their friends, even if they had to die trying. Jasper turned and went in search of Marjorie. She had been inside the inn taking a cup of tea.

"It is time to go, Marjorie," he told her when he found her sitting alone at a table.

She stood up stoically and followed him out. His plan had better work, otherwise he feared that there would be more bloodshed.

Chapter Seventeen

Gabriel pressed Chester like he had never pressed
him before. Every minute that Alyssa was in the
hands of that madman tore at his sanity. He was
sick with worry and felt deep dread in his heart. He
had to get her back before the blaggard hurt her. He
realized that there was significance in the direction
that Alistair had taken her. He had taken her north
on the Great North Road as he himself had been
taking her. Alistair must be planning to force her to
marry him over the anvil in Gretna Green. It would
happen over his dead body before it happened like
that. Alyssa was his woman now. He wasn't about
to lose her to a monster like Alistair. She was
everything to him. He would protect her with his
life.

He estimated that Alistair had a good fifteen
minute lead on him and that he was probably
pressing his horse as hard as he was. Gabriel's
mount was rested, whereas his mount probably
hadn't rested since dawn. He would have to stop
soon or his horse would collapse and die. The
thought reassured him that he could catch him
before the night was out. There was another town
up ahead, but it would take at least another two
hours riding hard to reach it. He knew Chester could
make it, but he doubted seriously that Alistair's
mount would.

He wished it wasn't so dark so he could see
further ahead. The moon was hidden behind heavy
clouds. It looked like it might rain. The road so far
had been smooth, but there were bound to be pits

that his horse could take a tumble in. Then he would be in a fine fix. Dawn was still at least four hours away he estimated, and the night was cool. He hadn't had time to dress properly before he left in pursuit. He only had on a thin lawn shirt and his breeches and boots. He hadn't fully disrobed before going to bed as he usually would have because he was on the road and wanted to be prepared for just such an event. He was glad that he used what little foresight he had, otherwise he would be racing after them without a stitch of clothing on.

He took a mental assessment of his weaponry. He knew that he had already fired his gun, and since it was a single shot dueling pistol, it was basically useless except to bash Alistair on the head with. He did, however, have a rather large knife strapped to his calve; it would have to do. He was glad he hadn't removed it when he had taken off his boots. Perhaps he could locate some ammunition in one of the towns along the way if he hadn't located them before dawn. He truly hoped he wouldn't have to wait that long.

*****

Alistair had driven his mount as hard as he dared for two hours. He had to get them off the road to rest before he killed his horse. He could see faint lights ahead signaling a village. He hoped he would be able to find a room at this time of night. Alyssa had long ago fallen asleep. His arms were tired from trying to keep her atop the horse. A couple of times she had slid down. If he hadn't been holding her so tightly she would have fallen. He had to get her out of this cold night air before she became ill with the ague. It wouldn't do at all to have a sick bride. He wanted her to be hale and hearty for what he had planned for her.

He slowed his horse as he neared the village. There were several inns and they looked to be still open for business. They didn't look very reputable but that didn't matter. He just needed a bed and maybe some ale and some tea for Alyssa. He hadn't spoken to her yet because he hadn't been sure he could control his temper. He didn't want to make any mistakes. He had to win her back. The only way to do that was through kindness.

He was very angry at her for doing what she had done, and he planned on punishing her, but he would do it with as loving a hand as he could manage under the circumstances. He would bed her when he got her in the room to show her that she belonged to him no matter what she might have done with Windhaven. She belonged to him. She would just have to come to terms with it and realize she would never see her lover again.

He would have preferred a virgin bride because he didn't want to raise another man's bastard, but for her and her fortune, he would risk it. Perhaps their first born would be female. It wouldn't matter if she were a bastard. He would be able to tolerate that, he supposed. He could always abstain from her until she proved to be with child or not, but he didn't want to wait. He had to establish ownership over her, or she would continue to try to escape him.

He stopped in front of the Red Bull Inn and shook her awake. He must have startled her because she nearly jumped out of his arms. He held tight to her with one hand and removed her blindfold and gag with the other.

"You will behave now Alyssa, or it will go badly for you," he told her.

She reached up and rubbed at her mouth with her bound hands. He was upset to see that the gag had left indentions around her lovely mouth. He felt bad about that but knew her young skin would quickly spring back. She would be beautiful once again. He untied her wrists next and dismounted then assisted her down. He took her by the elbow, leading her inside the inn.

The place was a stinking hole, was full of rough looking men sitting around drinking and playing cards. When they entered, the whole room quieted down. Everyone stared at them. He grasped her arm more tightly in a demonstration of ownership and moved forward to the bar where he presumed the old man standing behind it was the innkeeper.

"I need a room and care for my mount," he told the man.

"You're in luck milord as I 'ave one room left an it's the 'oneymoon suite, it is," he said with a snicker.

"I'll take it," he told him.

"I'll 'ave the stable boy take care of your 'orse. Will you an' the missus be needin' any refreshments?" he asked, eyeing Alyssa.

"Ale and some tea," he told him.

"I 'ave ale milord but we aint go no tea."

"Just ale then and the key if you please," Alistair snapped.

Alistair dug into his coat pocket and slammed a crown down on the counter.

"Keep the change. If anyone comes around asking, you haven't seen us," he told the man.

The old innkeeper looked Alyssa up and down one more time. He made a clucking sound with his tongue and handed Alistair the key.

"Last room on the left an' we don't want no trouble round 'ere, milord," the old man told him.

"There won't be any trouble if you do what I have asked of you," Alistair said over his shoulder while leading Alyssa up the stairs.

He located the room and removed the candle from the wall sconce so he could better see to open the door. He shoved Alyssa inside then closed and locked the door. He was going to leave the key in the door until he saw how Alyssa had looked at it. That decided him to put it in the small pocket of his breeches.

"You will not escape me again Alyssa, so don't even think about it. I have been a very patient man, but my patience has reached an end so you must mind me now, or I will deal harshly with you," he told her. He lit the lamp on the table by the door.

She didn't respond to his command. She just stood there shaking and looking at the ground. He was glad to see her being so submissive; it would certainly make things easier for both of them.

"I think I am owed an explanation for your

disobedience," he told her.

She kept her eyes on the floor and shrugged her shoulders in answer.

"You don't have one?" he asked her.

She shook her head no.

"Was I not good to you?" he asked, lifting her chin to look into her eyes.

She shrugged her shoulders again in answer.

"Was it because of our last night together?" he asked.

She nodded her head that it was but said nothing, keeping her eyes averted as if she were repulsed by the very sight of him. That wounded him so deeply that he could feel his heart wrenching. He supposed he deserved it, but it wouldn't do. He had to make her understand he wasn't a cruel man; that he would still make her an excellent husband. She just needed to learn her place, and they would get along fine. How to proceed? he wondered.

"I would never willingly hurt you, Alyssa. I explained this to you, and you told me that you understood," he said almost pleadingly.

"You did hurt me, Alistair," she said, finally finding her voice.

"I didn't mean to. I will never do it again. How could I when I love you so very much?" he said taking her by the hand.

He felt her trembling beneath his touch and let go of her hand. She didn't believe him. She was scared of his touch. He didn't want that. He wanted her to embrace what they would have together. She stood there in the middle of the room looking down at the floor again, wringing her hands nervously. He wasn't sure what to say to her, so he decided it was time for action.

"Remove your gown and get into to the bed Alyssa," he told her sternly.

She quickly looked up. There was terror in her eyes. She darted her eyes around the room. They rested on the bed, and she began to tremble violently. He reached for her, drawing her to him so he could sooth away her trembling, but she cried out, shoving at him to try to get away.

"I'm not going to hurt you," he shouted at her, clinging tightly.

She was making him lose his temper. He didn't want to do that. He swore to himself he wouldn't lose his temper and hurt her again. His thoughts were interrupted by a knock at the door. He released her, cautiously walked over to it and pressed his ear to the door to see what he could hear.

"Who's there?" he called out.

"Tis the maid an I 'ave yer ale," was the surly reply of an old woman's voice.

He fished the key out of his pocket, opening the door just enough so he could take the tray from her. He quickly shut the door and locked it again, placing the key back in his pocket. He took the ale over to the table by the bed and poured himself a cup which he quickly guzzled down. He poured another, offering the cup to Alyssa. She turned her head in refusal, so he quickly drank the contents of it too.

"Get undressed," he told her again, then wiped his mouth on his coat sleeve.

She didn't move. He knew she wouldn't. He sighed deeply, walked over to her and reached out to untie her nightgown. She slapped his hand away and tried to move away. He grabbed her by the shoulders to subdue her. She froze in place. He stared hard into her eyes to show her he would brook no more refusals from her. Convinced that she would give him no more trouble, he reached out again, untied her gown and slipped it past her shoulders exposing her breasts. The sight of her lovely breasts took his breath away. He stood there gazing at her for a protracted moment. He had forgotten how perfect she was. He was truly enthralled by the vision before him. He lifted his gaze to her eyes, flinching when he saw the pure hatred there.

"You hate me, don't you, lass?" he found himself asking.

"Yes, I hate you. If you think to take me against my will, I will kill you or die trying before I succumb," she told him with absolute conviction.

Her words battered his heart and his mind. He didn't know what to make of this behavior; it wasn't at all how he imagined their reunion. He simply couldn't allow it to continue.

"I will take you. I will take you right now in this bed, and you will enjoy it, Alyssa. You will not miss your lover when I am done with you. I can promise you that," he told her with raw heat of passion in his voice.

He swiftly grabbed her by the arm, dragging her over to the bed. He pushed her down onto it, daring her to move with his heated stare while he began to remove his clothing.

"I didn't want it to be this way for us, Alyssa, but you leave me no choice. I will have you. There is nothing you can do to stop me. Our betrothal contract makes me your legal husband. Did you know that? All that remains is for the official ceremony before a parson. Even though you are my legal wife, I will overlook the fact that you have defied me and taken a lover, but you will not escape your fate. You belong to me. I will have you!"

He angrily jerked off his coat and then his boots. He had wanted it to be special, but she was forcing his hand. He started undoing his buttons on his shirt all the while never taking his eyes off of her. She boldly stared at back at him. If looks could kill he would be a dead man standing where he was. This was not going to be pleasant at all. The thought made him feel ill. He removed his pistol from his waist, setting it on the table beside the bed so he could remove his shirt from his breeches. He tossed off his shirt, let it land on the floor, and then he lunged for her.

She fought wild and hard like a crazed animal. She kicked and thrashed and tried to bite at him. It was all he could do to keep her pinned underneath him as he struggled to unbutton his breeches. He would have to take her hard and swift without benefit of any foreplay. He really hadn't wanted to do that. She had driven him to this; he had wanted to woo her; show her how good it could be between them but she wanted to fight and resist. He simply could not let it stand.

She took advantage of his distraction with his

breeches to try to gouge his eyes out with her fingers, temporarily blinding him. He reared back in pain, covering his eyes. She took further advantage, quickly squirming out from under him. His eyes were blurry. He could barely see through the tears that his eyes were rapidly producing in response to her attempt to remove them from their sockets. She hadn't succeeded, but she had certainly incapacitated him for the moment. He reached out for her as she jumped from the bed, but he was too late. She had already grabbed his pistol and was holding it to his head. He froze, not from fear of her actually killing him, but with fear she might accidentally harm herself. He would be destroyed if she were to harm herself.

"You do not know how to use it," he told her as calmly as he could.

"I am well aware how to fire a gun, my father taught me, and I have never forgotten. Doubt me at your own peril," she told him, with steel in her voice.

He froze anew, closing his eyes in fear that she might actually hate him enough to do it.

"Give me the key to the door," she told him.

"If you want it, you shall have to reach inside my pocket and get it yourself," he said defiantly.

She growled in frustration but didn't move to dig into his pocket. Instead, she did what he expected least; she struck him on the back of the head, sending him into darkness.

*****

Alyssa reached inside Alistair's pocket, retrieved the key and stuck it between her teeth. She realized he probably wouldn't be out long so she grabbed up his boots and his shirt, opened the window and tossed them out below. She decided since it was cold, she would keep his coat and quickly put it on. It was big and cumbersome, but it would keep her warm. She stuffed the pistol in the coat pocket and set about leaving. She opened the door slowly, sticking her head out into the hall to make sure no one was around to see her. She could hear the rowdy laughter of the men below as they continued to drink their spirits and play their cards. The thought of them trying to capture her made her tremble in fear. It was going to be tricky getting past them without being accosted, so she took the pistol out of the coat pocket, holding onto it tightly as she made her way down the stairs.

She decided to just make a run for it, hoping she could get by them before they had time to react to her presence … before she was safely outside. Drunken people weren't known for their quick reflexes, so when she hit the bottom step of the stairs she ran as fast as she could for the door. She nearly made it, when a man stepped in front her and she collided into him. She looked up at the man. He would be trouble.

"Slow down there lass, an' let me 'ave a look at ye." The man purred seductively.

He wasn't an ugly man, but he looked unpleasant nonetheless. He was dirty, grimy and had a hungry wolf look in his eyes as he raked them up and down her body. She lifted the gun, pointed it at him, and he quickly put up his hands, stepping out of her way. She dashed past him, into the night and started running down the street as fast as she could. She had no idea where she was going, but she hoped she was headed in the direction from which they came. She was sure someone would have come in pursuit of her by now. If she could go in that direction, there was a possibility of rescue.

She had been blindfolded when they arrived, so her sense of direction was useless. But she didn't let that slow her down. She continued to run wildly through the streets. She heard men chasing her, so she tried to run even faster. In her attempts to run faster, her slippers came off of her feet and she quickly became aware of the painful ground beneath her. She started crying now from the pain on her feet and the fear of the men behind her. She could tell they were gaining on her. If she didn't keep going, they would catch her. She had one bullet to fight off a horde of men intent on doing what only God knew, and she most certainly didn't want to know. She could hear the beating of their feet now even closer than before. She cried out in alarm and dared a look behind her.

The man she had run into was leading the charge. There were at least half a dozen men with him. She stumbled then, falling to the ground. The man quickly reached her before she had a chance to get up. She had dropped the gun when she fell and had no idea where it was, but she couldn't have reached it even if she knew where it was as the hungry-eyed man had her tightly in his grip.

"Look what we 'ave 'ere," he sneered.

She struggled to get away, but his fingers were digging into her flesh. She couldn't break his hold. He started trying to remove her coat, and she was terrified of what he planned to do … what they all planned to do to her. She continued to struggle, but he slapped her, leaving her momentarily stunned and defenseless. She felt the coat being torn away from her body. Then, his hands began to squeeze her breasts. He became excited and ripped her gown, exposing her to their view. She shrank in horror at the shouts and hollers of the men as they cheered their friend on in his assault of her.

She recovered from the stunning blow that he had dealt her. Once again she began to struggle and fight. She bit his arm, clawing at his face, and it gave her an opening to run. She didn't get far before he jerked her back into his arms and recommenced groping her body. Her heart was thundering in her chest now. Her fears were about to be realized.

She didn't hear the horse approaching, however, but she screamed out in pain at the wrenching of her shoulder when she was suddenly jerked up by the arm, out of the man's grasp and tossed up onto a horse that barreled through the men, sending many of them flying to the ground in different directions.

"I've got you, love," Gabriel told her, gripping her hard about the waist.

She sobbed when she realized he had found her and that she had been rescued. She clutched at him and cried, her body heaving from the gut-wrenching outpouring of emotions she was having. Chester continued through the small town like a lightning bolt. Soon they were out on the highway to safety. Gabriel couldn't believe his luck. He had found her and just in the nick of time. When he saw the crowd of men and the red hair at the center, he knew it couldn't be anyone else but her. She had somehow managed to escape Alistair, fled into the night and ran into the ruffians. He shuddered to imagine what would have happened if he would have been even seconds later. He held her close, kissing her temple while she continued to cry hysterically. He couldn't take time to console her now. He had to put as much distance between them and Alistair as he could. He didn't think he would give up easily and knew that he would come after them again. In an attempt to throw Alistair off, he circled back around the town, heading in the direction he had come from, back to the Gray Horse Inn.

Alistair would probably question those men, and he wanted to send him on a false trail. He hoped by doing what the man would least expect, he could buy them some more time. Alyssa was practically naked in any case and would need her clothing. He was forced to go back to the inn that they had stayed in to retrieve her clothing. He hoped that Alistair wouldn't think of that and take the same route. His heart went out to her. He knew she must be freezing in her sad state of undress. Her feet were bare, her gown was torn, and if he didn't get her into shelter as soon as possible, she could become very ill. He tried to envelope her in his body as best he could to offer his warmth, but he too was sadly under-dressed. It would have to serve. It was the best he could do; he only hoped that the rain would hold off. He pressed Chester as much as he dared. By now the old boy would be getting tired and would need to slow down to preserve his strength. He would have to get off the main road soon, but he wanted to go as far as possible before he did.

"I'm sorry Chester, but I need you my friend. When we get back to the inn, you can rest for a whole day before I take you out again. Just don't let me down now, please," he told him.

Alyssa looked up at him with concern in her eyes. He shouldn't have voiced his worries for Chester as now she was even more upset thinking they may be caught again.

"We'll make it, don't worry," he assured her as he brought her face back to the warmth of his chest.

She snuggled close. He could feel her trembling. She was chilled and needed to be warmed up; this wouldn't do. He had to get her out of the elements and soon. He was torn by what he should do. Should he look for a house or should he press on back to the inn?

"Can you hold on for a couple of hours, my love?" he asked her.

She bobbed her head up and down, so he decided he would do the best he could and continue on back to the inn. If she became too chilled, he could always find somewhere off the road to build a fire to warm her.

"Just stay as close to me as you can and let my body warm you. If at any point you think you are too cold, let me know. I will find some place to go and build a fire," he told her.

"Just keep going Gabriel, please don't stop now."

That decided it for him. He had been giving his marching orders. He would follow the command. She was one hell of a woman. He wouldn't let her down now.

"Do you want to tell me what happened? It might help to keep your mind off the cold," he suggested.

She relayed all that had happened at the Gray Horse Inn when she had been taken. He surmised from her telling of it that Dylan must have been with Wishy in the stables and that was how they got to her. They must have knocked Dylan out, sending Wishy inside under threat of violence, if she didn't do as they bade her. The poor child probably was scared to death and torn in between helping Dylan and protecting Alyssa. She had died a heroine in defense of them both. The thought moved him deeply. He wasn't mad at his friend, but he was quite disappointed that he had dallied with the girl. He didn't think he would do it, but the proof seemed indisputable. He must have been quite taken by her to have succumbed and ignored his better sense. He decided that it was probably wise not to tell Alyssa about Wishy just yet. He didn't want her to have anything more to be distressed about just now. She would probably take it very hard, and he was not looking forward to the telling of it.

She got to the part where Alistair had taken her into the room and tried to force himself on her. He hugged her tight thinking that she was about to tell him that he had succeeded. He was determined that it wouldn't matter; he would love her still, regardless. He had plenty of time in route to find her to come to that decision. It hadn't been a hard one really, but he had worried she would be disturbed after having been raped, and that she may not ever be the same after. But she had surprised him when she told him of the way she had fought him off, gaining the upper hand. And she impressed him when she told him how she had thought to slow his pursuit of her by ridding him of his clothing.

"Clever girl," he told her with warm and genuine affection.

His heart swelled with pride knowing that his woman was a fighter. She would never allow a man to take her by force. He was proud of her and knew at that moment he would love her until his dying breath.

"I'm very proud of you Alyssa. You are a remarkable woman and will make the most beautiful duchess in all of England," he told her with a loving kiss upon her temple.

She smiled wide, then snuggled into his chest again. It wasn't long before she fell asleep from pure exhaustion. His woman had been through hell. She had come face to face with the Devil. She fought brave and strong with defiance, defeating him in his own playground, then managed to escape with her life and her virtue intact. He was the luckiest man alive to have such a woman. He would love and protect her with his life from this day forward. Never again would Alistair or any other villain get their hands on her.

Chapter Eighteen

Gabriel's sigh of relief about a half an hour into their return journey had been audible when they encountered a man who Alyssa recognized as one of his friends, and a woman on the road. She had never seen the woman before and couldn't imagine why he would have brought her out into the night like this. Alyssa was glad to see friendly faces, as well, but she was terribly embarrassed by her sad state of undress. She placed herself as close to Gabriel as she could so as not to reveal her plight. She supposed there was nothing she could do except to endure the moment with as much poise and dignity as she could muster.

"I am glad to see you my friend," Gabriel said as they came to a stop.

The man immediately assessed her situation, shrugged out of his coat and offered it to Gabriel, who in turn draped it around her shoulders. She gratefully put it on and became aware of a terrible odor. It smelled as though he had wallowing around in a pigpen. She wouldn't complain about the barnyard stench. Her teeth had been chattering from the cool night air, plus it was an improvement over nothing at all. Her feet were still ice-cold as she had no shoes, but it was better than nothing.

"How did you manage to get her back so quickly?" the man asked.

"She is an amazing woman, Jasper. She managed to rescue herself. I came along and found her fighting off a group of seven men, single-handed and scooped her upon my horse. We fled quickly," he told him proudly.

"What of Keith?" Jasper asked.

"He shall no doubt be in pursuit of her, so we must make haste back to the inn. I have no idea how long it will take him to retrieve his clothing and gain a fresh mount before he can follow, but we mustn't be complacent. I laid a false trail to try to throw him off, but I suspect he will see through it and quickly come to retrieve her," he explained.

"How did she manage to escape him?" he pressed.

"She fought him like a tigress, gained the upper hand and managed to grab his pistol. She struck him on the head, rendering him unconscious and threw his clothing out the window before fleeing into the night. That's where I later found her being accosted by a group of men intent on doing her harm."

Jasper made a whistling sound and arched his brows skyward as he took all the information in. He looked at her, and she could see he was genuinely impressed with her.

"Miss Habersham, I am honored to make the acquaintance of such a brave and daring woman. I am Jasper Townley, Earl of Pembrook at your service," he said with a bow from atop his horse.

"I remember you from Annabelle's, my lord, though I did not know your name," she said, with a blush.

"Jasper is another of my dearest friends, Alyssa, and like Dylan, he too will be your brother as well as Luther whom you have yet to meet," Gabriel told her, to reassure her that she should not be embarrassed.

"I always wanted brothers," Alyssa said, smiling.

"Well, you have them now in great abundance," Jasper told her with a big, cheeky grin.

"I am afraid that I have not met your friend, my lord," she said after realizing they were being rude to exclude her from the greetings.

"Please call me Jasper as you are to be my sister; this is Lady Marjorie, the Countess of Barclay. She has come to offer her assistance with Lord Keith. She is a very close acquaintance of his, and it is my hope that she could become quite useful, should he become … unmanageable," he told her.

Alyssa looked at the woman and could see she was nervous by the meeting.

"It is very kind of you to offer your assistance. I am in your debt, Lady Barclay," she told her with sincerity.

She wasn't naïve. She knew what Jasper was implying. This was Alistair's mistress. She had come to help, though she couldn't imagine how she could. Neither could she imagine the woman's real motives, but she wouldn't turn away an offer of assistance if it would truly help her be rid of Alistair once and for all.

"I am very sorry for all the trouble that you have had. Please call me Marjorie," she told her with a timidity that Alyssa found a little disturbing.

The woman kept her eyes cast down as though she were afraid to meet anyone's gaze. She had spoken so softly that she could barely hear the words. If she were indeed Alistair's mistress, then she must have been handled roughly by him many times. She felt a moment of sympathy for the woman, but then quickly cast it aside. *She must like being treated that way if she is so eager to be of assistance*, she concluded. *Jasper must have brought her here as bait and she has willingly allowed it*. Alyssa shivered at the thought, but quickly recovered.

"Thank you Marjorie. You are very kind. You may call me Alyssa," she said in earnest.

Jasper cleared his throat, and Gabriel took it as a signal to end the greetings.

"Shall we be on our way then?" he said.

"Yes, let's," Jasper said sardonically.

Both men had clearly become uncomfortable about Marjorie's presence. They must have wanted to break up the discussion before it became any more awkward than it had been. Alyssa appreciated it. and she was sure the other woman did, too. They urged the horses forward to resume the trip back to the Gray Horse Inn where they continued on at a fairly good pace, though no longer at top speed as before. She was glad that Chester would have a reprieve from his arduous task now that they had the added protection of Jasper. Alyssa listened as the two men discussed what they knew of the events thus far. At one point, Gabriel tensed up and shook his head at Jasper who very quickly quit speaking. It was something about Wishy and Dylan that Gabriel didn't want her to know.

"What is it?" she asked, with a sense of dread.

The two men were quiet. The tension suddenly seemed very high. She realized they were trying to protect her, but she would not have it. She wanted to know what had befallen them.

"You must tell me. Has something happened to them?" she asked.

Gabriel's hold around her waist tightened. He leaned down so he could speak quietly into her ear.

"I didn't want to tell you this until we were back at the inn, but Wishy … didn't survive her wounds from the attack," he said softly.

Alyssa cried out at the news. She turned to bury her face in his chest and began to sob. That poor child had tried to save her and was killed for her devotion. She lifted her face and looked up at Gabriel.

"When they grabbed me, she tried to defend me. They struck her on the head very hard. I knew she wasn't moving, but I hoped she had only been unconscious," she said, then continued to cry with heaving sobs.

"She died instantly Alyssa; she did not suffer, I promise you," Gabriel told her, stroking her back to comfort her.

It was a small comfort to know that the child hadn't suffered but did nothing to lessen her sorrow at the loss. She had liked Wishy and would miss her dearly. Alyssa cried for a few minutes, then she realized there was more to the story, that something had happened to Dylan too.

"What of Dylan?" she asked.

"Dylan is alive, but he is very distressed about Wishy," was all he told her.

She was comforted to know that Dylan was alive and unharmed, but she still sensed that there was more he was not telling her. He was obviously still trying to protect her. She appreciated his efforts, but she needed to know all that had occurred.

"There is more that you are not telling me Gabriel. I will have the whole story, if you please."

Gabriel sighed deeply and began to relay to her what he knew. Jasper agreed with Gabriel's assessment that there had to have been deep feelings on Dylan's part for him to act as he had. He killed two men in the blink of an eye without thought and went after Diana, too. Then he became inconsolable and clutched the poor dead girl in his arms and wailed like a broken man.

Poor Dylan! She was deeply saddened by all that they had told her and cried silent tears the rest of the journey.

*****

Alistair came around with the blinding light of dawn. She was gone, he realized; she had escaped him again. He staggered to his feet, wincing at his aching head. She had knocked him in the back of his head with his pistol, he remembered now. Feisty minx! It had been a while since he had to deal with such a spirited lass, but he looked forward to the taming when he got his hands on her again. He would get his hands on her again. This was just a minor setback. He looked around for his clothing and boots but couldn't see them anywhere. She must have taken them with her when she fled in an attempt to slow him down. He laughed at how easily the clever lass had escaped him and felt like a fool. He looked around, noticed that the window was open and thought perhaps she had used it for escape. He went over to it, looked out and down. There, he saw his boots and shirt on the ground. He was relieved to see them, but his coat was still unaccounted for.

He quickly went downstairs to retrieve his clothing. Once he had them in his hands, he looked around for any signs of her and noticed something black lying up ahead on the road. He put his shirt and boots on, then went to investigate. Perhaps it was his coat. Along the way, he found her slippers. The sight of them offered no comfort. They must have come off in her flight, and she didn't take the time to stop to retrieve them. He continued on to retrieve what he was sure would be his coat.

When he reached it, he picked it up and his heart fell in his stomach when he saw that it was ripped to shreds. Had she used it to stay warm and then been attacked by someone in her attempts to escape him? He started shaking with fear that his beloved could be harmed, looking around frantically for any other signs to indicate what might have happened. He noticed something small and silver under a bush and walked over to it. His pistol must have been thrown clear during the struggle as it was still loaded! She hadn't even been able to defend herself with it. His blood turned to ice, and he quickly ran back to the inn.

Once inside he noticed some men lying about the taproom sleeping off their spirits from the night before. He went over and shook one man to wake him. The man must have passed out, face down on the table from an intoxicated stupor while he sat in his chair. He was startled awake, with an angry look in his eyes.

"What do ye want?" he growled.

Alistair wasn't intimidated by the man's anger. He would gladly face ten angry bears to find his Alyssa.

"Did you see a woman with red hair leave here last night?" Alistair asked him.

"Aye, ye be the bloke that brought 'er 'ere," the surly man said.

"That's right I brought her here. She is my wife. I need to know where she is," he barked at him.

"If she be yer wife, how come 'er to run out into the night to get away from ye?" the man had the nerve to ask.

Alistair's reaction was swift and unyielding. He grabbed the man by the collar, hoisted him out of his chair, slung him up against a nearby wall, pinning him there with his body.

"What do you know of it?" he demanded.

The man didn't seem scared at all by Alistair's tactics. He just stood there sneering at him. Alistair gave him a savage blow to his stomach to show the man that he wasn't to be trifled with. The man's wind left his body in a whooshing sound, then he coughed and gasped, trying to regain the air that had been knocked out of him.

"Tell me what happened to her or there will more where that came from," he shouted. "Why did I find her shoes in the street and my coat torn to shreds?" he added in demand.

The man still didn't seem too concerned by the situation he found himself but began to cooperate nonetheless.

"She were a nice piece an' some of the fellows decided to 'ave a little sport wiv 'er," he said with another sneer.

Alistair's mind reeled with horror at the man's words. He grabbed the man tight around the collar bringing his face so close they were nearly nose to nose.

"Where is she now?" he demanded with a snarl.

"She got away before they could 'ave their fun. Some bloke came barrelin' through on a white 'orse and snatched 'er right away from 'em," he said with a snicker.

Windhaven, thank God! He didn't think he would ever be relieved to know that Alyssa was with him, but at least he had gotten there before they had time to harm her. She was safe with her lover at least.

"Which way did he take her?" Alistair asked.

"North."

Alistair released the man and sat down at a table to think about what the man had told him. He didn't think for a moment that Windhaven would have taken her on to Gretna Green with no shoes and her being in her nightgown. No, he must have laid a false trail, going back the way he had come. It was the only logical conclusion to make. He went back upstairs, cleaned himself up as best he could under the circumstances, then quickly took his leave of the Red Bull Inn.

*****

Gabriel knew there was no hope for it; he was going to have to call for a doctor to come attend Alyssa. By the time they had returned to the inn, she was shivering with chills. Now she had a full blown fever and had become quite delirious. There was no way he could move her in such a condition, so they would just have to stay here until she recovered. Jasper had given her some of his laudanum, and she was resting better now, but the fever was still a great concern.

Dylan and Luther left with Wishy's body at dawn to return her to her family for burial, but Lord Glenmont stayed behind to deal with the magistrate. They arrested Diana. She had to be taken away in restraints because she had become quite violent. Gabriel was sad to see it happen, but he was glad she would no longer be a problem. He had assured Glenmont he would speak on her behalf at her trial It was the least he could do to keep the wretch from hanging. She was obviously quite mad and would probably end up in Bedlam when all was said and done.

After Glenmont's telling of events, the magistrate had concluded that Dylan had acted in self-defense when he killed the two men. No one contradicted the story. Gabriel was glad that Dylan wouldn't have to deal with a trial after what he had already endured.

Dylan was still a great concern to him. He had

never seen his friend so grief stricken before. Even when his brother had died, he didn't act the way he did over Wishy's death. He must be feeling a great sense of guilt over her death and maybe something a little more. He hadn't spoken of what had transpired between them, but Gabriel wasn't a fool. He truly believed he had lain with her in the stables shortly before she was killed. They must have planned an assignation after everyone else went to bed. It seemed to be the only assumption he could draw from his behavior. It filled him with a deep sadness.

Dylan must have really been taken with her to compromise his convictions the way he had. For her to be snatched away from him so soon after must have been truly devastating. He supposed when he was ready, Dylan would tell him what had occurred. They never held secrets from each other. When the time came, he would offer him his support; they were brothers after all, even if only in spirit.

Gabriel had much bigger problems to worry about now, however. There was still the issue of Alistair to deal with. He had no idea when he would re-surface. It was noon now. More likely than not, Alistair was out there lurking even now, watching their movements. It was a troublesome thought, particularly since Alyssa was so ill.

Jasper instructed Marjorie to stay out of sight. She didn't seem to mind at all. In fact, she was keeping vigil over Alyssa, working very hard to bring her fever down. She was really a godsend as Alyssa was without a maid with the death of Wishy. She would have personal needs that she wouldn't want Gabriel to tend to himself. He sighed deeply, thinking about all the things that had happened since last night and where they were to go from here. He supposed it would be impractical to push on to Gretna Green now as Alistair would no doubt dog their heels the entire time. He would have to be dealt with. He supposed that it might as well be here instead, out on the open road. At least here they had shelter and a warm bed for Alyssa. He breathed heavily, taking another drag from his ale.

Gabriel looked up to see Jasper coming down the stairs. He looked refreshed as he had finally bathed. With the use of Gabriel's clothes he was quite presentable again. Of course, Jasper was much thinner than Gabriel, but they were of the same height respectively; it would serve for the time being. The innkeeper assured Jasper she would have his own clothes cleaned and pressed. They would be returned to him on the morrow.

"You smell better," Gabriel told him.

"Aye, nothing like a bath to remove the smell of horse shite and three days of my own personal stench," he told him with his usual cheeky grin.

"You were rather malodorous, this is true. Poor Luther smelled worse though. Did you guys roll around in the stuff?" he teased.

"Luther did; like a hound wallowing in a mud-hole," Jasper said with a chuckle.

The two men laughed at Luther's expense, then Gabriel quickly sobered. "Alyssa will need a doctor. Her fever continues to grow worse. I fear it would be unwise to move her, so we shall have to hunker down here until she is recovered," he told him.

"I suspected as much. I have already asked the innkeeper to send word out to the local doctor," Jasper told him.

"You are always thinking ahead, aren't you?" Gabriel mused aloud in admiration.

"Simple deductions, my friend," Jasper said with a nod.

"I should have deduced it myself, but I am grateful that you had foreseen it and handled the matter. Do you know when he might arrive?"

"The innkeeper said that he lives about five miles out to the west, so hopefully he will be here later this afternoon," Jasper told him.

"I wonder when Alistair will make his presence known," Gabriel said, taking another drink of his ale.

"Soon I would imagine. He is no doubt watching us at this very moment. It might be unwise to sit in the window like that," Jasper admonished him.

"I am sitting here with the intention of being seen. If he wants to, he can come in here. We can settle this thing once and for all," he told him.

"Are you proposing what I think you are?" Jasper asked with a raised eyebrow.

"I think that I am," Gabriel said with sincerity.

"It may be the only way," Jasper agreed.

"I suspect that is."

*****

About four in the afternoon, Dr. Swanson arrived. He determined that Alyssa had the ague. He gave her some willow bark tea for the fever and recommended bed rest for three or four days. He said he would come back in two days to see how she was progressing as he was concerned about the possibility of pneumonia. Gabriel was worried about that too but hoped it wouldn't come to it. Alyssa was young and strong. With proper care she should recover quite nicely.

There still had been no sign of Alistair, but Gabriel had the feeling a time or two that he was being observed. He had been sitting at the table in the window and the hairs on the back of his neck stood on end, causing him to look out the window. The first time he had seen a young man standing across the road, he seemed to be observing the inn quite closely. Gabriel surmised that Alistair might have paid him to have a look about. Gabriel decided he would have to post one of the men at Alyssa's door at all times.

Now that Glenmont had returned from dealing with the magistrate, there were three of them in total, so they could easily guard her round the clock. Jasper took the first shift. He was up there now in a chair outside her door. Gabriel would take the next shift as it would be during the night when he suspected that Alistair would make his move if he were inclined. Glenmont could take the day shift as the inn was a rather busy place. Aid could be had quickly in any event.

Gabriel was very tired. He thought he had better get some sleep before his shift came about. He was now lying in his bed trying to relax enough so he could sleep. It was difficult as his mind had been racing, trying to make sure he had everything well in hand. He wished Alistair would go ahead and make his move so he could put the matter behind them. At least, he had his ammunition now. He would be well equipped to deal with any crisis.

He was still perplexed as to why Jasper felt so sure that Marjorie could be of aid. When he asked him to explain, he said he couldn't really, but that he had a feeling she would be needed. She had been needed indeed, though not in the way Jasper had envisioned. He only hoped she wouldn't become a liability at some point. He had expressed that concern to Jasper who told him not to worry; that he had already planned for that contingency.

Gabriel didn't ask him what he meant by that. He trusted his friend's intelligence. He knew that whatever measures he took would be the right ones. Where would he be right now without the aid of his friends? he wondered.

*****

Alistair had been watching closely all day as it turned out. He had a room at another inn just across the way with a bird's-eye view of the Gray Horse Inn. He had hired a young man to see what he could find out about Alyssa and Windhaven, but what he had learned so far upset him. Alyssa was ill. She had to be seen by a doctor, and Alistair couldn't help but feel responsible for her condition. He wanted to kidnap her during the night, but if she were truly as ill as he was told then it could be perilous to try to move her. He would have to wait for her to recover before he could even attempt it.

He had learned that Windhaven was not alone as he had hoped he would be; that he had the aid of another gentleman as well as Alistair's own stepfather no less. The other man was a tall thin fellow that didn't look like much of a challenge for someone as big as he was. His stepfather wouldn't represent a challenge either as he was an old man. He could be easily dealt with. Of course, with his stepfather there to bolster his case about the betrothal agreement, the old man might actually prove useful. For all intents and purposes, Alyssa was his legal wife, and Glenmont knew it.

There was nothing to stop him from going over there and claiming his bride, except for Windhaven. He didn't think he would just hand her over, particularly since she had tried so desperately to escape him, not once but twice. They were lovers now, and he probably intended to marry her, so he felt he too had rights. But Alistair was the one with a marriage contract. The law would be on his side.

He considered calling for the magistrate to force Windhaven to hand her over but he didn't have the contract with him to prove she was his wife. Nor did he want to involve the law in any of his business. It was bad enough that Diana had gotten herself arrested. He certainly didn't want to end up as she had. He would just have to wait a couple of days before he could make his move. Though he had given his word to spare Windhaven's life, he still wanted to kill the man for the insult he had given him.

Perhaps he should just openly challenge him to

a duel. That would serve his purposes quite nicely. He was a very good shot with a pistol, making him feel strongly he could defeat Windhaven. He didn't know of the man's reputation in that regard, but he had enough confidence in his own skill to assure victory would be his. Still, that would have to wait, as well.

The important thing now was for Alyssa to recover. The rest could be easily managed afterward. He would reclaim his bride. Nothing would stop him. One way or another, she was his. She belonged with him.

Chapter Nineteen

On the third day, Alistair's patience had reached an end. There had been a lot of strange activity going on over at the Gray Horse. Even a parson was called for. He feared that Alyssa might have taken a turn for the worst and was in need of a parson to pray over her. The idea that she may be lying there dying was more than he could endure. He would wait no more; he had to have her with him one way or the other, even if it was only to be as she lay dying.

With that thought in mind, he called for a bath, changed into his new suit of clothes and marched over to the inn. He would not let anyone stand in his way; pity the poor soul who tried. It was time to confront Windhaven once and for all. The man had been in custody of his wife long enough. He pushed his way through the door and immediately found Windhaven, Glenmont and the other gentleman, whom he still did not know, sitting at a table near the stairs. The men looked up at his entry. Windhaven quickly stood up and advanced toward him.

"Where is my wife?" Alistair demanded.

The two men stood face to face for the first time. Both had a look of deadly determination in their eyes. Each was poised; ready to strike the other man down if he so much as made one false move.

"I was not aware that you had a wife?" Windhaven said with cold, calculating calm.

Alistair glared at him, but the other man didn't even blink as he returned the stare. The tension in the room was intense. Each man was primed and ready for violence.

"Do not play games with me, Windhaven. You know very well that you have abducted my betrothed, who is by virtue of contract, my legal wife," Alistair gritted out harshly.

Alistair hadn't noticed that his stepfather had risen from his seat along with the other man, coming to stand beside Windhaven. He had been so intent on the man before him that he had blocked all else out.

"There is no betrothal contract, Alistair," Glenmont said.

Alistair snapped his gaze upon his stepfather. He had to fight to control the impulse to reach out and grab hold of the old earl's neck. The old man was smug, standing there under the protection of the other two men.

"What say you?" he demanded with steel in his voice and fire in his pitch black eyes.

"You failed to have the document legalized. As I retained the only copy, I took it upon myself to have it destroyed. There is no contract; she is not your legal wife. You have no claim upon her now or in the future," Glenmont boldly told him.

Alistair's mind was stunned. He tried to rationalize what the old man had just told him. Once all the cogs and gears of his brain finally fell into place, he didn't think, he just lunged for his stepfather. He missed him, however, and found himself face to face with the other man who had quickly jerked the old earl out of harm's way, blocking him from having access. They stared at one another. Alistair could see the unwavering determination in the other man's eyes. He could clearly see the message in the man's eyes. He would have to go through him, and no doubt, Windhaven as well to get to Glenmont.

He decided that it wasn't worth the effort it would take, so he calmly faced Windhaven, saying, "It hardly matters that he has destroyed the document; there is still the verbal contract, not to mention the formal notice in The Times which is also binding. I will have my wife now, or I will kill any man that stands in my way," he told him.

"I cannot hand her over to you Keith, for you see, she has just this morning become the Duchess of Windhaven, courtesy of special license by the local bishop," Windhaven calmly informed him.

Alistair staggered back at his words as if he had been struck, making him double over as if in pain. He clutched his head, roaring in anguish. Then, with the speed of lightning he turned, lunging for Windhaven. The impact caused both men to fall to the ground ,and Alistair had an iron grip upon Windhaven's throat. They struggled with one another for several seconds before Windhaven managed to pry his grip away from his throat, then the two men began to wrestle with one another in earnest. Alistair was taken aback at the other man's strength. He was soon overtaken in a choke-hold that he could not release himself from. Windhaven had managed to wriggle out from under him to position himself behind him where he subdued Alistair firmly by the crook of his arm.

"Give up Keith, you have lost her," he growled.

Alistair could barely breathe, but he managed to respond in a strained voice.

"I shall never give her up; I demand satisfaction."

Windhaven released his hold. He quickly stood up, allowing Alistair to, as well. He dusted himself off, looked at the men standing before him. Then his gaze rested on Windhaven.

"Name your seconds," he gritted out through clenched teeth.

"Lord Pembrook will be my second," Windhaven quickly replied, indicating his friend with a nod of his head in his direction.

"I shall second Lord Keith as he has no other available, unless he wishes to postpone until we all remove to London," Glenmont suggested.

"I thank you stepfather for your kind offer as I do not wish to wait," Alistair returned.

Clearly the three of them had already planned for this outcome. All that was left was the formalities. That suited Alistair well enough. He eagerly looked forward to killing Windhaven now.

"Your choice of weapons?" Windhaven asked.

"Pistols at dawn," Alistair barked.

"Very well, I shall meet you at dawn with pistols. We'll leave it to our seconds to name the place and the terms," Gabriel consented.

Alistair took one last hate-filled look at Windhaven, then turned for the exit. "I can be found at the inn across the way," he said over his shoulder upon reaching the door.

*****

"That went rather well," Jasper said after Alistair made his exit.

"Aye, it did," Gabriel agreed.

Each man fully expected as well as planned for this outcome. Yesterday morning, the three men had sat down, deliberating all the possible outcomes and had reached a consensus. At Jasper's suggestion, it was decided that Gabriel should seek the aid of a local bishop to have him issue a special license so he could marry Alyssa without delay. The license had arrived this morning. The village parson was called for. He quickly came, and the two were married at Alyssa's bedside. This was to provide further protection for her in the event of Gabriel's death. As his widow, she would be less likely to fall prey to Alistair's machinations or at least, that was their hope.

Alyssa had greatly improved during the night. This morning her fever had gone completely. She would still require a couple of days bed rest before she could be transported back to Windhaven, so Gabriel truly hoped he would still be alive to see her safely there. Jasper had assured him that if anything were to happen to him, he as well as his other friends would step in to protect her. He knew that they would and wasn't too worried on that score, but he would like to live long enough to make love to his new bride. Her illness would prevent them from consummating their marriage for days yet. With that, as well as her safety in mind, he was fully motivated to defeat Alistair.

Gabriel would have preferred to fight with swords, but there were none available, so pistols would have to serve. He wasn't as good a shot as Dylan, but he was very good nonetheless. He felt confident that he could certainly hold his own in any case.

The men sat back down at the table. Glenmont ordered Scotch whiskey for them all. Their nerves were tight, so they could all benefit by having a couple of shots.

"Do you think he will try and come back during the night and kidnap her?" Glenmont asked.

"No, he wants to kill Hawk so he can have Alyssa for himself. He will wait to do the deed by meeting him on the field of honor," Jasper answered.

"Try not to sound so cheerful about my death Jas," Gabriel said sarcastically.

"I shall marry your bride when you die brother, of course I am cheerful," Jasper teased.

"Why would she want a lunatic for a husband?" Gabriel retorted with a wicked grin.

"This is true; she did escape one lunatic and probably wouldn't want another in his place," Jasper conceded with mock disappointment.

Glenmont looked at the two of them as if they had both gone daft, causing Jasper and Gabriel to burst into laughter at his expression.

"Don't worry Glenmont, we jest," Jasper assured him.

"How can you possibly jest about such a thing?" he asked him incredulously.

He shifted his gaze to Gabriel, staring him in

the eyes with a fatherly scorn. Then, he lifted a chastising finger, waggling it at him, then promptly let into him.

"You had better take Alistair serious young man. He is an excellent marksman. It is highly unlikely that he shall miss. Not only do you need to bear your own safety in mind, you have my niece's to consider as well. No, my friend, this is no laughing matter, you had better sober up," he chastised.

"Fear not! I take him plenty serious. I am just venting a little steam. It serves no purpose to be consumed with anger. I will be at top form when I meet him at dawn. I will defeat him with calm deliberation," Gabriel said a little defensively.

He hadn't been chastised as if he were a small child in many a year. It wasn't a very good feeling. Of course, he knew the old man was right, but he was a man who knew how to defend himself. He would not, could not fail.

"It is not at all unreasonable to plan a marriage between Lord Pembrook and Alyssa, just in case. I could draw up a betrothal contract this very minute," he put in seriously.

"Oh, ye of little faith, Glenmont! I shall not fail. There will be no need to draw up any more contracts. I am her husband, and I shall remain so until I am a very old and happy man," Gabriel told him with a sardonic grin.

Glenmont grunted in disapproval but said no more on the matter. Gabriel was relieved that the matter was settled. He didn't like the idea of another man marrying his bride, so he didn't want to discuss such an absurdity further.

Jasper realized that the jesting had turned serious, so he moved to change the subject. "Should we tell Alyssa?" he asked.

"I don't want to upset her, but she will know something is wrong if I do not. She seems very intuitive when something is afoot," Gabriel explained.

"Aye, she must be prepared for the worst," Glenmont put in.

Gabriel gave a deep sigh. The old man was truly convinced he would die. He needed to get away from him before he began to believe it himself.

"I think I shall go spend some time with my bride. After you have spoken with Alistair about the particulars, let me know," he told them, standing up to leave.

"You should rest as well, so I shall not disturb you. I will take your shift tonight so you can sleep all the way through. I am quite accustomed to going without sleep for days on end with no ill effects, but you need to rest so you will be sharp at dawn," Jasper told him.

"I will take you up on your kind offer," he told him, heading for the stairs.

*****

Gabriel entered Alyssa's room and stopped in his tracks at the sight before him. Alyssa was bathing with the assistance of Marjorie. His first reaction was one of lust, but then he quickly realized she could be doing herself harm bathing so soon after her fever had broken. He shut the door rather hard, and they looked up at him in surprise.

"What are you doing Alyssa?" he asked a little too loudly.

Marjorie quickly moved away as he advanced in their direction. When he got beside the tub, he stared down at her, immediately enthralled by her nakedness. She too, seemed enthralled by his presence. They stared into one another's eyes for a suspended moment before Alyssa remembered modesty and covered her breasts from his view.

"I wanted to wash the smell of illness off of me. It is my wedding day after all. I didn't want to offend my new husband," she finally said with a brilliant smile.

He realized then he could not stay mad at her, but he was still very concerned for her well-being.

"I want you to get out of there this minute. Come, dry yourself before the fire. Thank God you did not wash your hair," he told her.

He looked around for Marjorie, but she had somehow managed to slink out of the room unnoticed, so he grabbed up the linen, holding it out for her. She stood up, got out of the tub, and he quickly wrapped her up. Then he scooped her up into his arms and took her over to the fire, where he sat down with her in his lap.

"You shouldn't have risked your health, Alyssa. I adore you even if you did stink," he teased, then kissed her on her temple as he began to remove the pins from her hair.

He ran his hands through her long tresses,

bringing a strand to his nose to breathe in her scent. "Your hair still smells nice," he said with a wicked grin.

She giggled, snuggling closer to him, and he was in heaven. He never wanted to move from this spot, but he knew he hadn't dried her properly so he reluctantly shifted her and slipped out from under her.

"Stay there, I am going to get more linen to dry you properly," he told her.

She smiled but said nothing. He turned to retrieve the linen and the gown that had been placed nearby. He went back to her, knelt down before her and removed the linen he had wrapped her in. He began to dry her off using slow circular motions, causing his tongue to become thick in his mouth as he gazed upon her body. Her nipples had become puckered. They seemed to be begging for his attention. He tried to shake off the thought because he knew he shouldn't be thinking such things. She was still too ill for lovemaking. He didn't want to do anything to risk her further than she had already done to herself. He swallowed hard and picked up the pace of his efforts until he was satisfied he had removed all the excess water. He turned to pick up her gown but she stayed his hand. He looked back at her and nearly lost his breath by the wanting he saw in her eyes. He forgot about the gown, lunging forward to kiss her passionately. She wrapped her arms about him to deepen the kiss.

Knowing where this was leading and wanting to prevent it from going further, he picked her up from the chair, walking her over to the bed. He pulled back the covers, laid her down, then pulled them over her, tucking them around her to keep out the chill air. He knew he shouldn't, but he crawled in the bed beside her, draping his leg and arm across her in an attempt to provide additional warmth.

"We cannot Alyssa," he told her with regret thick in his voice.

Her luscious lips pouted, and she struggled to move her arm out from under the covers. Once her arm had been freed, she very tenderly cupped his cheek with her palm. Her eyes were warm, full of wanting. He found he could not look away and was soon lost in their depths.

"Please Gabriel, I feel fine, and this is my wedding night. You promised me a proper wedding night, and I shall have it," she told him with complete determination.

The minx had clearly decided to undermine his good intentions. How could he deny such an importuning from her sweet lips? He cradled her head in his hands, brought her closer, then placed his lips to hers. As soon as contact was made, he knew he was lost. He could feel the tension in his loins and knew that he was sporting a massive arousal that would not be denied. Would it really hurt her if they were to make love so soon after her recovery? He didn't want to be the cause of any more problems, but he didn't see how he could resist her.

His decision made, he broke the kiss, pushed himself away from her, then stood up and began to disrobe. She lay there staring at him with hunger in her eyes, her cheeks flushed with excitement. Her eyes were sparkling orbs of blue-green fire as she watched him undress. He nearly groaned when she licked her lips in anticipation. She wanted him as much as he wanted her. The knowledge of it was nearly his undoing. He couldn't get out of his clothes fast enough. He quickly kicked off his boots and stripped away his shirt, not caring when two of the buttons went flying across the room. He undid his breeches with equal speed, slid them off and stood there before her in all his naked glory.

As he knew it would be, his arousal was huge and throbbing, standing at full staff. He watched her expression go from one of hunger to one something close to panic. She shrank back into the pillow and pulled the covers up to her chin but didn't say anything as he pulled the covers away so that he could join her. Once settled, he took her into his arms.

"Fear not my love, we will fit," he assured her.

He began to caress her back, leaning in to slowly plunder her lips and mouth. Her passions seemed to reignite. She whimpered, trying to pull him closer. She opened up to receive his tongue. With a growl of approval, he began to massage hers with his own in an imitation of the act of making love. She moaned in response, pressing her body against his. She caressed and squeezed his buttocks, and the feeling made his erection twitch with anticipation.

He pulled back from the kiss, looking into her eyes. "Greedy minx," he purred before returning to her lips.

He wasn't worried about her being chilled

anymore. Her body had quickly heated up. She had become desperate, groping and grabbing at his body. She seemed frustrated when she couldn't feel his skin through the material of the bed covering. She growled and started jerking and tugging on the covers, trying to move them out of her way. Gabriel laughed at her predicament, then offered his assistance until they were both unencumbered by the bedding. Once she was unrestricted, she shoved his shoulders down on the bed, quickly positioning herself on top of him. She straddled his loins and launched into a sensual assault that stunned him. He was riveted by her hunger and didn't try to resist her, allowing her to continue to lead the way.

Emboldened now, his little vixen began to kiss her way down his body until she reached his shaft, where she halted, looking up at him for a suspended moment. He didn't know what she saw in his eyes, but whatever it was must have convinced her she was on the right path. She wrapped both her hands around it in a tight grip, starting a slow exquisite massage. The feeling was intense, and he wasn't sure how wise it was to allow her to continue. He closed his eyes and reached for control to allow her time to continue her explorations. He didn't want to do anything that might inhibit her because he was fully enjoying this side of his wife.

When he groaned in pleasure, she halted instantly. He opened his eyes and found her gazing at his erection with intent. Then, without warning, she slid down to begin kissing it lovingly. Soon, she was bathing it with her tongue. His whole body tensed in response. After a moment of her tender ministrations, he knew he would soon spill his seed if he allowed her to continue. He placed his hand under her chin, forcing her to stop. She looked at him as if she feared she had done something wrong. In assurance, he took her by the shoulders, dragged her back up and brought her face to face with him.

"Careful my love, or I will not last," he warned her.

He reached down, placed his hand at her warm, moist center and found she was already slick with the evidence of her own arousal. He leaned in, placed his lips upon hers and began a slow sensual kiss while guiding her hips to encourage her to take him inside her. She ground her heated flesh upon his arousal. The motion soon excited her. She reached between them, took him in hand and moved his shaft into position. The tip was poised at her entrance. He began to push her hips down slowly upon him. She tensed up at the intrusion, but she didn't stop the slow decent until she met the resistance of her barrier. He leaned forward, drew the tip of her breast between his lips and lightly bit down while thrusting himself fully into her passage. She cried out, shoved him back against the pillow, then leaned forward and buried her face in the side of his neck, going very still.

"It will only hurt for a minute. I promise you that our joining will never cause pain again," he whispered in her ear.

She whimpered in response, and he reached up to gently guide her face toward his so he could look into her eyes. They were still wild blue-green blazes, and he was glad to see that the passion had not died with her discomfort. She surprised him when she lunged forward to kiss him again and started moving her hips in a slow undulating motion. She broke the kiss, sat up and threw her head back, increasing the rhythm.

"Better now?" he asked, rubbing her beautiful throat with his palm.

"Mmmm," she responded in ecstasy.

He laughed softly and began to thrust himself deeper within. They both groaned in reaction to the increased pleasure. She continued to ride him until they both became frenzied, reaching desperately for completion. He slid his hand between them, placed his thumb upon the nub of sensitive flesh at her woman's mound and began a slow rotating massage. The response was immediate. Her whole body tensed up and began to tremble. He could feel the pulsing of the walls of her passage as they gripped around his member.

While she was still in the throes of her release, he quickly rolled her onto her back, slid his hands under her bottom, lifting her upwards before plunging himself to the hilt to deliver deep, hard penetrating thrusts. She grabbed onto his shoulders, digging her nails into his flesh, crying out in response as another wave of release ripped through her body. It was all he could take; he quickly succumbed to his own climax. Together their bodies pulsed and jerked until they were limp and exhausted. He collapsed over her when he felt the last of the aftershocks of his release. He rolled over onto his back bringing her with him, resting her across his chest, he kissed her on her temple.

"You were amazing Alyssa; I have never before released so hard or so fast. You reduced me to the control of a green lad," he told her.

She giggled, nuzzling his chest with her nose, and he squeezed her closer to him in response.

"Where did you get the idea to mount me?" he asked her.

"Marjorie," she whispered.

Gabriel laughed as he envisioned the ladies discussing strategies. He was glad that Marjorie had been there to counsel her. He realized she had no one else to do so, and the advice had been excellent. He wished he could thank Marjorie but that would be very inappropriate.

"She said it wouldn't hurt as much if I was on top," she explained.

"And did Marjorie instruct you on the other?" he couldn't help but ask.

He felt her blush as her face heated up with embarrassment.

"I loved it Alyssa; do not be ashamed of anything that we will do during our lovemaking. Our bodies belong to one another now. There are no limits to how we can pleasure each other," he told her.

She quietly giggled and snuggled close. He brought the blanket up over her shoulders to keep her warm. Soon they both fell into a peaceful slumber. The sleeping didn't last, however as they kept waking up intermittently to make mad passionate love again and again. His woman was just as insatiable as he was, and he reveled in it. By the time midnight came they were truly exhausted.

After cleaning themselves up, they fell into a deep and satisfied slumber. Gabriel hadn't told her about what was to happen with the dawn. He didn't know how. He hoped she wouldn't even wake, and that he could slip back into bed unnoticed when it was over.

Chapter Twenty

Alyssa was awakened by a soft knocking at the door. She sat up in bed, shaking Gabriel to wake him as well. She couldn't imagine who would be knocking at such an hour, but she suspected that whoever it was must be carrying some bad news.

"Gabriel you must wake up, there is someone at the door," she told him.

Gabriel jumped up quickly, slid into his breeches and went over to the door. He opened it up a crack, then after seeing who it was he stepped out into the hall, closing the door behind him. She could hear the muffled voices as they discussed the issue at hand and felt a sense of foreboding creep over her body. She lit the lamp beside the table, then sought out her nightgown, quickly putting it on. She had just finished the task when the door opened and Gabriel re-entered the room. She was about to go to him until she took in his grave expression. It stopped her in her tracks.

"What is it?" she asked with a trembling voice.

"Go back to sleep my love," he told her.

She wasn't about to go back to bed until he told her what was going on. She knew something was happening. By the expression on his face it was a very serious matter. She stood her ground, refusing to move.

"Tell me what is happening Gabriel," she calmly asserted.

Gabriel sighed deeply, running his hands through his hair but didn't answer her. He began dressing as if she weren't there, or had even spoken to him. Anger coursed through her as he ignored her while he finished dressing. He clearly had no intentions of telling her what the situation was. That infuriated her. Well, she would have her answer, or he would not be leaving this room, she grumbled to herself.

She walked over and stood before the door, crossing her arms over her breasts and waited for him to finish dressing. When he was done, he removed his pistol from the nightstand, then looked it over before sticking it in the waist of his breeches. He turned to face her then. She winced when she saw his hardened expression. His gray eyes were like silver ice as he stood there facing her. She felt a chill sweep over her and she began to tremble.

"You must go back to bed my love," he told her once again.

The coldness of his eyes belied his tender words, but she was not going to allow herself to be intimidated. She searched her mind, trying to figure out what the trouble might be. Quickly, she realized that Alistair must have finally arrived, and that he was going to have a confrontation with him.

"I cannot allow you to go out there, Gabriel," she boldly told him.

He closed his eyes, squeezing the bridge of his nose for a moment before casting his hard gaze back upon her.

"I must go," he softly told her.

"Why must you go?" she demanded.

"He has challenged me for the insult of marrying his intended. I have accepted. It is a matter of honor now that I must go and meet that challenge out.

Alyssa's mind screamed with fear as she listened to his words. She couldn't let him do this, she just couldn't. He could be killed or maimed for life; she simply couldn't allow it.

"Damn honor and damn you if you go out there Gabriel!" she shouted at him.

He flinched at her curse but stood stoic as he defied her. He made to move her so he could leave. She stomped on his foot, and he yelped, stepping back.

"Why did you do that Alyssa?" he shouted at her.

His eyes pooled with tears from the pain that she had caused, or maybe it was something else that had caused it, she didn't know. She wanted to go to him, to wrap herself around him to comfort him, but she refused to leave her position at the door.

"I will do whatever it takes to keep you from making such a foolish mistake," she calmly told him.

"Is it foolish to want to protect you Alyssa?" he demanded.

She didn't have an answer for that, but she was determined he would not get past her so she continued to stand her ground in defiance.

"Is it foolish for me to want to rid you of a menacing madman?" he continued.

She remained silent, staring at him in her continued defiance, with complete determination. He slowly closed the distance between them, then touched her cheek with his palm. Tears were still in his eyes. One had escaped to roll slowly down his face.

"Is it foolish for me to love you?" he asked softly.

Her heart clutched with those words; he had said he loved her. It was the first time he had even so much as hinted that he did, and he waited until now to tell her. That thought made her angry. She puffed up her chest and glared at him.

"You wait until now to tell me that you love me?" she asked incredulously.

Hot tears began to form in her own eyes. She stood there looking into his eyes. His eyes had warmed to mercurial pools as he returned her gaze.

"Aye, tis true that I wait until now to tell you that I love you. I would have you know without a doubt, that when I go to meet him on the field of honor, I do it out of my love for you," he softly spoke.

She burst into sobbing cries, and her knees buckled beneath her. He caught her by the shoulders just as she would have fallen. He took her into his arms, holding her tight while she cried. There was nothing honorable about what he was planning to do. They would try to kill one another in her name. That, she simply couldn't stand for.

She drew in a breath with renewed anger, and began to pound upon his chest. "You would dishonor me to find honor for yourself," she shouted her accusation.

He gripped her hard around the waist, pulling her to him, in an attempt to make her attempts to thrash him ineffective. She struggled to break his hold, but he had the strength of a bear as he held on to her. She began to kick and stomp her feet upon him. When that proved just as futile she cried out in anguish, then went limp in his arms. Her body was shuddering, and she was wracked by more heaving sobs.

"Shhhh," he said, caressing her back in an attempt to soothe her.

"Please do not do this thing, I beg you," she cried.

She had her head against his chest. He took her by the chin, lifting her face so he could look into her eyes. She jerked and hiccupped from her exertions. Her ears were ringing, the sound of which was making her head ache with a vengeance.

"I must Alyssa; please try to understand. It is the only way to settle this between Alistair and myself. It is the only way to be rid of him once and for all. He will never quit. You know this as well as I," he calmly told her.

She stiffened in his arms and tried to pull away from him to no avail.

"I know nothing of the kind, sir. If you go through that door and commit this deed, I will leave you, I swear," she threatened, her own eyes hard with resolve.

Gabriel quickly released her after she issued her ultimatum. He walked away from her grumbling an oath such as she had never heard before in her entire life. Such things were never spoken aloud in front of women. He paced back and forth for a moment, then he turned to her. His eyes were once again cold as ice.

"As you will, but I am going to meet him; I

would be labeled a coward if I didn't. I would never be able to hold my head up again with pride. The world would think that I was …"

His words trailed off, and he didn't complete the thought. Instead, he stiffened his back and went to the door. Without looking at her further, he opened it. He stopped briefly just before he went through it, slamming it behind him in his wake. The sound went through her stomach like a piercing blade, but she quickly recovered and ran after him. Just before he reached the landing at the stairs, she jumped up on his back and started pounding savagely upon him. He whirled around and tried to grab her to get her off of his back, but she clutched him tight with her legs and grabbed him by the hair.

"You will not do this thing," she screamed.

The next thing she knew a pair of strong hands grabbed her around the waist and jerked her off of his back. She kicked and thrashed wildly as Gabriel and Jasper tried to wrestle her into submission. They finally pinned her to the floor on her back. She found herself nose to nose with Gabriel. He sat straddling her midsection with a firm hold on her hands out to the side of her head. She was panting and her chest hurt from the effort of simply trying to breathe.

"Stop this now, Alyssa," he told her.

"Get off of me; I hate you," she growled.

"You don't hate me! You wouldn't be acting this way if you did. You love me with a grand passion Alyssa, just as I love you. After what we have shared all throughout the night, do not even try to deny it," he softly said before lunging forward to deliver a punishing kiss.

Alyssa tried to struggle against his kiss, but he released her hands, cradled her head, and deepened it. Hot tears flowed from her eyes and down the side of her head. She sobbed into his mouth, returning his kiss with a desperate passion. His lips were so soft and warm that she began to melt beneath him. She wrapped her arms about his neck and clung tightly as they lay there, continuing the kiss. She hadn't given another thought to where they were or that Jasper was there, witnessing her behavior. All she knew was that she held the man she loved in her arms for what could be the last time, and she never wanted it to end. She began to try to remove Gabriel's coat so she could feel his skin. That was a mistake because he hadn't forgotten where they were or who was standing by. He broke the kiss and took hold of her wrists to stop her from removing his coat.

"Naughty minx," he purred in her ear.

Sanity returned, and she tried to buck him off of her. He had tried to distract her; seduce her into forgetting what he was about to do. She continued to buck and thrash. When she couldn't move him from her, she cried out in frustration.

"Please, please, please don't do this Gabriel," she wailed.

He got off of her then, brought her to her feet and started leading her back to her room. She wasn't going to have that. In the blink of an eye, she twisted out of his grip. She ran for the stairs for what, she knew not, but she was quickly retrieved and swept off her feet and into his arms. He carried her to her room, kicked open the door and walked over to the bed, where he laid her down. She tried to come back up, but he pushed her down by the shoulders.

"You will stay here Alyssa, or I will lock you in," he told her sternly.

How dare he think to treat her in such a way; the brute! She was mad all over again. She rolled away and quickly jumped out of the bed at a dead run to block the door again. But she hadn't been fast enough. He grabbed her from behind, whirled her around and quite literally threw her on the bed.

"Alyssa, you must stop this madness; I do not have time for it," he admonished.

She reached for her gown, ripping it away from her body to expose herself to him, causing him to gape at her in stunned disbelief.

"Stay with me, Gabriel; make love to me now," she implored him.

She could tell that for a brief moment he gave the thought serious consideration, but he stiffened his back, turned away from her and went for the door. She flew out of the bed, threw herself at his feet then wrapped herself around his leg causing him to topple over onto the ground. She straddled him this time and started kissing him about the face and neck with desperate urgency. She didn't know what had come over her; she only knew she had to stop him from going any way she could.

He quickly relieved her of her advantage and rolled her over onto her back. "Do I have to call for Jasper and have him help me tie you to the bed?" he asked her.

She had been stunned at how quickly he had turned the tables on her. All she could do was shake her head in answer.

"Good. Now, I have had enough of this. You will do as your husband commands, and stay here until my return," he told her.

She didn't speak. He sat there a moment looking into her eyes, and she could see the pain behind them. He didn't want to go any more than she wanted him to, but he was resigned in his resolve to do it.

"Make love to me one more time Gabriel," she said softly.

"Alyssa I cannot; please don't ask it of me. The dawn will soon be here. I must go and prepare," he pleaded.

"You have time to love me one more time Gabriel, please," she begged.

He shook his head in denial just before lunging for her lips. His kiss had been desperate and hungry when he pulled away from her and began to fumble with the buttons on his breeches. He got them undone, grabbed up the hem of her nightgown and shoved her legs apart with his knee with near brutal force, plunging himself inside her. He took her with swift determination that took her breath away. He lifted her bottom off the ground and roared out an agonized cry, plunging deeper within her. He pounded himself into her with a desperate urgency, not caring whether he was hurting her or not.

She had made him angry because he could no longer deny her pleas, she realized. Though she wasn't sure if he was punishing her or himself for being too weak to resist. She didn't care. She just wrapped her legs about him, hanging on for dear life. If this was the last time she would ever hold him in her arms, she would embrace it with all her strength.

It was over rather quickly. He spilled his life-giving essence deep inside her and collapsed atop her with a mournful groan. He lay there for a moment before rolling off of her to keep from suffocating her with his mass. She lay there numb from the experience and didn't fight him when he got up to start putting himself back to rights. When he had himself put back together, he lowered his hand to her. She placed her hand in his, and he lifted her to her feet. He had shame in his eyes and wouldn't look at her when he turned and left the room without so much as a word of farewell. She stood there, staring at the empty space where he had been in stunned silence until she heard the click that locked her in the room. She immediately came to her senses and started pounding on the door.

"DON'T GO!" she shouted over and over again until she was hoarse and wrung out with exhaustion.

"I love you Alyssa, and I shall return to you very soon, I promise," she heard him say after she had quieted.

And then he was gone, and she could hear footsteps descending the stairs.

*****

Gabriel felt like a part of his soul had been ripped out and left behind in the room with Alyssa. He was shaken and ashamed to his very core from all that had just occurred. He had never taken a woman with such brutal force before, and upon the floor, no less. How could he have lost control like that when that might have been the last time he ever held her in his arms? He shook his head in disgust as he and Jasper went into the taproom of the inn. What if he had hurt Alyssa just then? The thought made him feel sick in his heart and his gut. He shouldn't have allowed her to provoke him the way that she had. He was a big man and she but a frail woman. He should have handled her with more care. Though, she hadn't seemed frail when she had attacked him, he still should have taken more care. His duchess was fierce when determined in her course. He began to get a picture of how she had defeated Alistair. Despite what had happened between them, he felt deep respect and pride for her.

He understood how she felt. If the situation were reversed, he would have fought just as hard to prevent her from such a mistake. Was it a mistake? Was she right in what she said? He didn't really think so. He was doing what must be done. He had to protect her from Alistair. The only way was to defeat him utterly. He didn't want to kill him, but he must if they were to ever live in peace. It was not in his nature to kill, and he wasn't sure at all he really had it in him to do. Perhaps he could just wound him and that would be enough. Alistair was a gentleman after all. He should respect the code of the field of honor.

"What are the terms?" he found himself asking.

"To the death," Jasper said soberly.

Gabriel exhaled deeply and a sense of dread passed through him. He had hoped that it would be one shot, and whoever remained less injured would be the victor. If it were to be to the death, it could require multiple shots until the conclusion was reached. It would be a bloody battle that was brought on by a man who refused to face reality. He had lost Alyssa. He needed to accept it gracefully like a gentleman should. Instead, he put both their lives in jeopardy with this nonsensical challenge.

"Alyssa is quite the tigress," Jasper said in an attempt to distract him from dwelling on what lay ahead.

Despite himself, he smiled wide, saying, "Aye; that she is."

"At least you will never have to doubt her feelings for you," Jasper said with an elbow to his ribs.

Gabriel laughed then quickly sobered when he had a flash of memory with her begging him not to do this. He put his face in his hands, making a woeful sound.

"I have to do this thing, but she will not understand it," he said with great sadness.

"She will forgive you when this is over and you are safely delivered into her loving, though somewhat, wild embrace," Jasper said with a facetious smile.

"Let us hope that will be the case," Gabriel allowed.

He looked at his friend, who looked just as miserable as he felt, as if he could provide an answer to the madness. Of course there was no answer for why things had come to this other than they were dealing with an unstable man. They were being forced to play his game by his rules. Just then there was a calamitous crashing from upstairs and the two men snapped their heads and froze as they continued to listen. Alyssa had gotten a new wind and was in the throes of another raging tantrum. He shook his head in amazement, hoping she didn't tear the place down around her ears.

"You had better let this be the last time you get on her bad side," Jasper told him.

The two men chuckled, listening a moment longer as she shouted curses and hurled objects at the door.

"Shall we go?" Gabriel asked.

"Thats sounds wise. I would not want to find myself in the path of that storm again," Jasper said.

Gabriel had a pang of guilty conscience as they moved to leave. He stopped and placed a hand on Jasper's arm to stop him from going through the door.

"Jasper?" Gabriel called to his friend.

He was going to meet his fate, and he wanted to be sure that Alyssa would really be taken care of. He had made out his will, leaving her all of his fortune and property that was not entailed. But could he do more for her?

"You need not ask it of me; there shall be no need," Jasper told him as if he knew what he had been about to say.

Gabriel was going to tell his friend that if he didn't survive, he had his blessing to marry Alyssa. But Jasper would probably do it, whether he had it or not. If he didn't, one of his other friends likely would. It was just as well that the possibility of his death not be spoken of any further as he was about to put it into the hands of fate and a madman. He needed to go into this duel with a positive mindset. He did not want to think of the woman upstairs and what she meant to him now, or he might turn coward and refuse to fight the duel. His honor demanded it of him. There was nothing he could do now except to go there like a man and see it done.

*****

Alyssa had broken everything that could possibly be broken in the room. Now she sat on the floor amongst all the rubble. How could he have just walked away like that, locking her in her room? Didn't he know what this was doing to her? The idea that he was going to face Alistair in a duel was agonizing. Not being able to get to him to protect him was maddening. There was no way to escape the room. She was in a room that didn't have a window, so she was a prisoner until someone came to let her out. She had hoped that the innkeeper would have come by now, but perhaps they didn't want to get involved with a woman who was capable of such violence. There had to be a way to get out of this room. This simply would not stand.

She thought about her hairpins then, quickly searching for one. There was no telling where one would be in the mess she had made, but she knew they had to be around somewhere. She sifted through the evidence of her tantrum with diligence, finally locating a hairpin. She quickly went over to the door, inserting it into the lock. She fiddled around with it for several moments and realized she would probably never succeed. She threw the pin across the room, beginning to weep again. She was about to lose the man she loved by the man she despised, and there was nothing she could do to stop it. Then she heard the lock on the connecting door. She snapped her head up to see Marjorie standing in the doorway. She jumped up and ran to her, but Marjorie quickly stood in her way and blocked the door.

"You must listen to me," she told Alyssa.

Alyssa stopped before her, glaring at her. If this woman thought she was going to stand in her way she was sadly mistaken. It had taken two men to subdue her before, and she knew that she could handle her; they were very close in size.

"Get out of my way," she told her.

"No, you must listen to me first," Marjorie implored her.

"What is it?" she snapped.

"You must quickly dress and follow me," she told her.

That brought Alyssa quickly to her senses. Marjorie was going to help her stop the duel! She quickly found a gown and put it on, but she still had no slippers because she had lost her only ones and had been too sick to seek out a new pair.

"I have no shoes," she told her.

"We are not going far. You can do without them. They are to duel in the field behind the inn about two hundred yards out," Marjorie told her.

"Why are you helping me?" she thought to ask.

Marjorie stood there for a moment before speaking. "I do this for myself; I want to marry Alistair, so I must try to stop them from killing each other, or I will lose him forever," she told her.

"You're certainly welcome to him if we can stop this madness, but what do you plan to do?"

"We do not have time to discuss it now; I shall tell you on the way," she told her.

That would have to do, she supposed. Alyssa grabbed her wrap, threw it around her shoulders, and the two ladies fled the room and out of the inn. It was still very dark. Alyssa couldn't see where she was going, but Marjorie led the way as if she had prior knowledge of the path. Alyssa thought it was strange but didn't question it. She followed closely behind her. When they rounded the corner of the inn, she could see two lanterns lit about two hundred yards away. And she could see the silhouettes of the men. Two men were already there by the lanterns. Two others were still in route. There was still time, thanks be to God.

"We should run so we can catch them," Alyssa suggested.

"No, keep your voice down; it has to be timed just so," Marjorie told her.

"What do you mean?" she whispered.

"Jasper has told me of a way to allow them their honor but to prevent them from killing one another by the same token. He has instructed me when to start counting. When I reach the number five, I am to call out to Alistair," she told her conspiratorially.

"It sounds too dangerous. Why can we not run after them and beg them not to do this," she asked.

"Alistair has no idea that I am here. That gives me the element of surprise. It will guarantee his immediate attention," she explained.

"How can you be sure?" Alyssa asked.

"I cannot, of course, but it is the only hope we have. They will not listen to us if we try to stop them. I think you have already unsuccessfully tried several tactics to no avail; am I wrong?" she asked chidingly.

She was right; begging had failed. Violence, as well as seduction, had failed. They would not be directed away from the course that they had set. Their honor was at stake They simply wouldn't see reason.

"What makes you think Jasper's plan will work?" she asked.

"Jasper and I used to be lovers. He is extremely intelligent. He has a way of looking forward and predicting the outcome of events with a large degree of accuracy," she told her.

"Are you saying he is some kind of psychic?" Alyssa asked, gaping.

"He denies it, but I think so. He says he just reads a situation and figures things out through simple deductions and calculations," Marjorie said.

It all sounded incredible to Alyssa. They were leaving way too much to chance. She debated whether or not to listen to Marjorie and let the outlandish plan be played out. She just didn't want to risk losing Gabriel to chance, deductions or anything else.

Gina Rose

Chapter Twenty-one

"Gentlemen, I believe we should take a moment to seek a peaceful end to this situation," Jasper said when he and Gabriel had reached the dueling destination.

"There is only one way to resolve this. That is for Windhaven to die so my honor will be restored, and I may reclaim what is rightfully mine," Alistair said, his voice firm with conviction.

"You would not accept an apology if one were to be offered?" Jasper clarified.

"I would not," he stated emphatically.

"Well, I suppose that settles it then," Jasper said with resignation.

Gabriel and Alistair stood facing one another with steel in their spines and fire in their eyes. Jasper could see that neither could be swayed with a simple apology, so with much regret he began to cite the rules of engagement.

"My lords, the terms of the duel are as follows. You will place yourselves back to back at the center mark and each man will then take ten forward paces. After having taken the appropriate amount of paces, you shall turn and stand with your sides facing each other."

"On the count of one, you shall take aim until the count of five when I will drop this handkerchief and you may commence to fire. If neither of you has scored a kill shot, then you will break and reload and repeat the process until one or both of you have been successful," he told them.

Neither man spoke to acknowledge their

understanding of the rules; instead they continued to glare hard at one another.

"I would like to add this. After careful consideration, I have decided, with the agreement of Lord Glenmont, that you should only have three chances to kill one another in this fashion. To prolong it would be cruel and barbaric and I, for one, should not like to be a party to it. If there has been no success and or honor restored to each man's satisfaction, you shall have to find another way to achieve your ends," he explained.

Alistair snapped his gaze to him, then. He could see he was dissatisfied with this addendum to the rules, but he said nothing one way or the other. Clearly, he didn't think it would be needed. He fully intended to kill Gabriel without having to go to any extra measures. Indeed, Alistair fully intended to kill Windhaven with one shot, so he wasn't too concerned beyond it, but he was angered that they would have made such an agreement without his approval. This further proved that the three men had conspired against him from the beginning as he had begun to suspect.

Alistair had thought long and hard throughout the night about all that had transpired. He had come to the conclusion that whether Alyssa wanted him or not, he had been wronged, and the only way to restore his honor was to kill Windhaven, then reclaim his intended bride. He had briefly considered just giving her up and going back to Jamaica, but he simply couldn't allow such a slight against him to go unchallenged. She and her fortune had been promised to him. Right was on his side.

Windhaven and his stepfather had conspired against him from the beginning. They had tried to swindle him out of his rightful possessions. No one could blame him for demanding satisfaction for the wrong he had been dealt. He fully intended to have justice. It mattered not that Alyssa didn't love him and that she had given herself to Windhaven. She belonged to him. He truly believed that even now, if he were to be kind enough to her, she would come to love him again or at the very least respect him, as a wife should. Once he had successfully placed a babe within her belly, she would see that he was her destiny, and she would no longer seek to escape him. He only wanted to love and possess her, and he would move mountains to that end.

One thing he truly regretted in all of this was Marjorie. He had grown very fond of her. He knew that his feelings were very close to love. Last night, he had considered just marrying her, Alyssa be damned. He had been surprised when he learned that Marjorie was in fact a countess, not just a whore as he had previously believed. She deserved an honorable marriage. But he was in too deep now with Alyssa and could not walk away from her. He would simply have to be content to keep Marjorie as a mistress.

It wasn't uncommon for men in marriages of convenience to love their mistresses and have a long- lasting relationship with them. Many had even fathered families with their mistresses and never departed until death. He could see himself with Marjorie in such a way. He didn't really want a marriage of convenience with Alyssa, but if she forced his hand, it would have to be so; either way, he would have her. There was nothing or no one that would stop him.

"Gentlemen take your places at the center mark," Lord Pembrook said, breaking into his thoughts.

It was time to put this matter to rest.

*****

Alyssa experienced a moment of panic when she saw the men take their positions back to back and begin counting out their paces. Without thinking, she began to run toward Alistair for what, she knew not. All she knew was that she had to stop this madness somehow; she simply couldn't allow Alistair to kill Gabriel. She would beg or plead or whatever she had to do to get him to listen to reason. Her heart seized. She realized she might not make it in time. Both men had reached their mark. They turned, leveling their weapons at one another. Then Jasper had begun to count. She increased her speed with all of the strength she had in her body without thought of anything else but reaching Alistair before it was too late.

Time seemed to have slowed as she reached him. It was as though she were locked inside a dream for which she could not wake. She vaguely heard Jasper as he shouted out the count of five or Marjorie, shouting out for Alistair. For a strange suspended second, her eyes locked onto Alistair's, and she saw horror in his eyes. She had been about to leap for him but felt a shove on her back from behind that sent her hurtling to the ground just the explosions of gunfire and the agonized cries of several people followed.

She had been too late; someone had been hit, but whom? She quickly rolled over and sat up, and her eyes frantically sought out Gabriel. He was running toward her, and he seemed unharmed. She had been momentarily elated but another agonized roar sounded. She looked up to see the source and was stunned by the sight before her.

Alistair was cradling Marjorie in his arms. He was wailing at the heavens in his grief. She jumped up and was going to go to him, but she was quickly intercepted by Gabriel.

"No!" he told her sternly and kept her closely to his side with a firm grasp upon her arm.

"I must go to her, Gabriel; she has been harmed," she told him.

She tugged away from him, and he let her go. She quickly dashed over to Alistair and Marjorie, kneeling down beside them. Alistair seemed unaware of her presence. He clutched Marjorie to his breast and continued to cry. She reached out, touching him upon his bleeding arm. He looked at her then, and she nearly lost her breath when she saw the pain in his eyes.

"Let me see her, Alistair," she softly commanded.

Alistair very gently laid Marjorie back onto the ground and allowed Alyssa to attend her. She had never had experience with such a thing before, but she didn't let that stand in her way.

"Marjorie?" she called to her, moving her hair

out of her face.

Marjorie's eyes fluttered, then opened slowly, and Alyssa breathed a sigh of relief.

"She lives!" Alyssa cried out.

"Where is the physician?" Alistair barked.

"We did not call for a physician as it was to be a duel unto death," Jasper calmly stated.

"Where are you hurt, Marjorie," Alyssa asked.

Marjorie was quiet for a moment, and she closed her eyes. Everyone held their breath as they thought she had expired. But she had only been taking a mental inventory of her body so it seemed as she opened them again and looked up at Alistair.

"My shoulder," she rasped out.

Alyssa quickly started searching for the wound, but the light was poor, and she could not see very well. Jasper must have realized this was a problem because he brought the lantern closer, providing the much needed light. Alyssa tore away the material where the blood seemed to be coming from, revealing a wound on the fleshy part of her upper arm just below the shoulder.

"Stand aside and allow me to look at the wound," Jasper commanded her.

She did as she was bid, watching as Jasper very tenderly probed the wound.

"Tis only a flesh wound. She was grazed," he told them.

Alistair shoved Jasper out of his way, grabbed Marjorie in his arms and once again cradled her like she was the most precious thing in the world to him.

"You too have been hit Lord Keith; your arm is bleeding," Jasper pointed out.

"Tis nothing," he stated, continuing to hold Marjorie.

Alyssa was relieved that everyone would live, but she was angry now. They could have killed one another. They very nearly killed Marjorie, and for what?

"I hope we have seen the last of this nonsense," she found herself saying.

Alistair looked at her with fire in his eyes. She suddenly realized that it wasn't over at all. He still wanted vengeance and had only been put off by Marjorie's injury.

"You listen to me, Alistair, and you listen well! I am another man's wife now. You must put this obsession for me out of your mind. I will never love you. Even if you did kill Gabriel, I would never have you. I would die before I submitted to your cruelty. Do you understand me?"

He didn't respond to her words but looked at Gabriel, who was standing behind her. The two men glared at one another for a moment, then he looked back at her briefly before he shifted his gaze to Marjorie and it softened with warmth.

"She is right Alistair," she heard Marjorie say.

"She belongs to me, Marjorie. I cannot let her go. Please try and understand that," he told her.

"Why can't you?" Marjorie and Alyssa both asked at the same time.

Marjorie pressed on when Alistair gave no answer to the question.

"Alistair, why can you not love me as I love you? Why can I not be your wife? If it is only her fortune that you covet, I can assure you that you will have no need of it. I have a fortune of my own. I would gladly give it to you to become your wife," Marjorie pleaded.

"It is not really her fortune that I covet; it is her. She was promised to me, and what is mine, I keep," he stated.

"I never promised her to you Alistair. You blackmailed me into consent," Glenmont put in from behind Alyssa.

"Blackmail?" Alyssa asked gasping.

"Aye, he was going to tell The Times how I mistreated you while I embezzled from your fortune if I did not give my consent to the match. At the time, I was scared of the ruin that would surely follow, so I cooperated, but I am no longer afraid. What I did to you was wrong, Alyssa. If I must suffer the consequences to keep you from him, so be it," he said with conviction.

This was the first time she had spoken to her uncle since before she had escaped his house. What Gabriel told her had been true; he had changed his heart toward her. She felt moved and tears began to flow silently from her eyes. She looked back at Alistair. He was gazing back at her. She saw a change in him then and wasn't sure what to make of it. His eyes were filled with something that looked like a cross between shame and utter defeat.

"Is this true Alistair?" she softly asked him.

He nodded that it was, then put his head down to avoid looking at her further. He truly seemed ashamed by his actions. Alyssa found that to be absolutely astounding. Maybe he wasn't the cold, heartless bastard she thought he was.

"I forgive you Alistair, but I will never have you. This ends here and now," she told him.

He looked up at her, then nodded his head that he understood. He stood then, lifted Marjorie into his arms and started walking away with her. Everyone stood in silence as they watched them go. She felt Gabriel touch her shoulder. She looked up at him, and he was smiling at her.

"I think he will trouble us no more," he said softly.

"I think you may be right," she agreed with a smile of her own.

"I need a drink," Jasper said.

"I think we could all use a drink," Glenmont put in.

Gabriel lifted her into his arms. Together they all headed back to the Gray Horse Inn and to what she hoped would be a peaceful future.

*****

Alistair realized he no longer had a legitimate claim on Alyssa. What his stepfather said had been true. When confronted with the ugly truth of it, he felt ashamed by it. He knew he had lost her forever. She was right; he had been obsessed with her. He was ashamed of that, too. He would never forgive himself for the cruelties that his obsession for Alyssa had brought about. He had hurt people; nearly committed murder to possess a woman who did not want him in return. He wished he could have come to his senses sooner before he had dishonored himself so completely. The sooner he could get out of England the better. As far as he was concerned, he could live the rest of his life without ever coming back.

There was nothing for him here. He held what was truly important to him in his arms, and he would dedicate himself to loving her with all of his being from this day forward. It was love, he was sure of that now. He had not fully accepted it until she lay bleeding from a wound she had received by his own weapon.

When he realized what had happened, his heart stopped beating. All he could think of was that he had lost her. His obsession for Alyssa had nearly cost him his dear Marjorie. He shuddered when he imagined how bad things could have turned out. He was grateful he had not killed Windhaven now. He was a good man who would be a good husband to Alyssa. He would protect her from his insidious family. She would never again be mistreated.

When he had learned who Alyssa was, and how she had been treated by his family, it became a mission to right those wrongs. In the doing, he had exacerbated those wrongs. The only way to right those wrongs now was to step aside and allow her to have the happiness she had found with Windhaven. He looked down at Marjorie, and she was smiling. He leaned forward, kissing her tenderly.

"What has you smiling so, my precious lass?" he asked.

"I am proud of you Alistair. I love you very much," she told him.

"I love you too Marjorie, and I'm going to make things right, by making an honest woman of you," he told her.

"I know you are my sweet; I never doubted it for a minute," she told him.

"You will love Jamaica. I have a grand home there that has a very large nursery to be filled," he told her.

"That sounds lovely Alistair," she told him.

After a moment, she asked, "What of Batiste?"

"You will love her too," he told her, then planted a passionate kiss upon her lips.

*****

"I felt a little sorry for Alistair there at the end," Gabriel told Alyssa as they were getting dressed.

"I know what you mean; he fairly broke my heart, as well. Do you think he will marry Marjorie?" she asked.

"I believe they are a match made in … somewhere," he said with a chuckle.

"Marjorie is a strange woman, Gabriel. I got the feeling that she has never known true kindness, but she herself is one of the kindest people I have ever met. I hope he will be good to her," she told him.

"Aye, she is good as gold. I am grateful to her for all that she did while you were ill. I couldn't have made it without her. She gave fully of herself, asking nothing in return," he told her.

"Remarkable," Alyssa returned.

"You are remarkable, Mrs. Hawkins; come here," he said, tugging her to his embrace.

Alyssa had just finished pulling her gown over

her head in preparation of their departure from the Gray Horse Inn. She barely had time to shift it into place before her husband was removing it.

"Aren't you in a hurry to leave this place?" she asked, a little breathlessly.

"Oh, I am in a hurry, but not for that. I have other priorities that need to be seen to," he said, kneading her breasts.

"And what would those priorities be?" she purred.

"I have to make things up to my wife. You see, I was quite rough in my handling of her this morning. I must show her that I am repentant and make love to her properly now," he said with a sexy smile.

"If the circumstances had been different, I think I might have quite enjoyed your rough handling," she told him with a flirty grin.

"Would you, now?" he asked. He moved in closer and nuzzled her neck.

"It was quite spontaneous," she allowed with a pant.

"And you like spontaneity?" he asked, removing her chemise.

"Mmmhmm," she answered with a shiver.

He had removed all of the offending garments now and quickly picked her up, wrapping her legs around his waist. He began walking to the closed door that connected the two rooms that she had occupied and pinned her between it and his body.

"Unbutton my breeches," he commanded.

He leaned back and held her up with his knee to provide her access to his breeches. She quickly reached down, and without so much as a fumble, did as he bid. He kept them positioned in this way, and she looked his eyes while she awaited further instructions. She realized he wanted to see what she would do so she boldly grabbed his shaft and guided it into position. His reaction was swift. He lunged upward and impaled her with a force that made her breathless. He had reached high into her womb, with a slow and determined thrust. When she moaned her approval, he leaned forward, took the tip of her breast between his lips and began to suckle.

She was quickly swept away on a tide of ecstasy. She closed her eyes, rested her head on the door and let it take her away. He groaned and increased the pace of his thrust, then reached between them to massage the sensitive flesh at her private center, and the feeling intensified tenfold. Her eyes flew open wide, and she cried out, grabbed his shoulders to gain leverage. Then, she began to grind against his hand as he worked his shaft in and out of her with a vengeance. He growled and lifted his head from her breasts and leaned in, breathing naughty nothings into her ear. She had never heard such language in her life, and instead of being offended, she found herself excited by it.

With every word he spoke, she heated up another degree and ground herself harder upon him. When he commanded her to come to him, she instantly obeyed. It was mind-bending. Her whole body tensed, pulsed. She cried out as her release took her to the stars. He started thrusting into her much faster and harder, then, with a shout, he reached his own release and nearly collapsed to the floor. He pressed himself against her to keep from dropping her. Together, they slowly slid to a heap on the floor.

When she found her breath, she laughed and said, "I'm not so sure that was at all proper."

"You liked it, though," he told her smugly.

"Yes, I rather think I did," she smiled.

"That's good because there is plenty more where that came from," he said waggling his eyebrows up and down.

"Naughty beast! We shall never get home at this rate," she admonished.

"Home is where you are, my sweet Alyssa."

Epilogue

A lot had happened in the year that had passed since they left the Gray Horse Inn. She and Uncle Morley had reconciled, and he became the uncle he should have always been. She had been surprised by her inheritance, never dreamed it would have been so massive. By comparison, the money he took from her was a mere pittance, hardly worth mentioning, therefore, she never would. She would have gladly given him that and more had he ever asked for it. He was the last living link she had to her father. She was pleased that they now had a positive relationship. He was unable to successfully divorce Esmeralda, disavow Diana as his offspring, so instead he had shipped her back to Scotland where she resided in one of his castles in the Outer Hebrides. Alyssa didn't miss her. She was glad she would never have to see the cursed woman ever again. Diana, however, resided at Bedlam and was considered a homicidal danger to herself as well as others. It was not known if or when she would ever recover.

Gabriel hired a team of solicitors to help Alyssa manage her inheritance. They had helped her with her plans to start a foundation for women suffering from domestic violence. The construction of the housing project had begun. It was hoped that by Christmas time they would be able to start housing and educating women who found themselves in difficult situations. Her activities had generated a lot of interests from other wealthy members of the ton, and they too were putting up funds for the project.

Alistair and Marjorie married. They were
expecting their first child together, sometime in the
spring. Together with their very close friend, a lady
by the name of Batiste, they lived quite happily on
Alistair's plantation and no longer harbored any ill
feelings toward her or Gabriel. Alyssa and Marjorie
had corresponded back and forth a couple of times,
deciding to treat one another as cousins, forever
putting the past behind them. She had forgiven
Alistair and she dearly admired Marjorie. She
wished them both every happiness in the world, but
she had a strange feeling about their relationship
with this Batiste. Marjorie spoke highly of her, but
there was just something there in the underlying
words that Alyssa couldn't quite put a finger on that
made her feel that the relationship with the woman
was unusual.

Dylan was still a very sad situation, and she
was quite concerned about him. He had become
very withdrawn from the group of friends. The
rumors were that he was drinking rather heavily.
Every attempt to bring him back into the fold had
been rejected, and she was becoming quite
convinced that they would lose him forever. She
learned from Gabriel that Dylan had decided to ask
Wishy to marry him, and that was why he had been
so affected by her death. She felt bad for him and
hoped he would find another woman he could love
someday. He was such a nice man who deserved to
find happiness.

Jasper and Luther became closer with the
defection of both Gabriel and Dylan from their
nightly carousing. Luther had practically taken up

residence with him at his home. Gabriel said it was to keep a close eye on Jasper because he had a tendency to lose himself to his inventions. He was currently working on some strange flying apparatus. Luther was staying close by to ensure that he continued to eat properly. Gabriel had gone over there many times to see about his friends because he felt like Luther being in charge of Jasper, was a bit like the child caring for the nanny.

And last, though not least, she and Gabriel had brought their first child into the world, just two months ago. They named her after Wishy, whose Christian name had been Violet Wisteria. It was a good name. It would suit their daughter well. She had been gifted with eyes the color of violet. Violet had been an easy birth. To Gabriel's elation she was born with a shock of auburn curls upon her sweet little head. Gabriel had hoped that his children would have her hair, and it seemed he was getting his wish.

Gabriel was a good father, doting on his daughter like a besotted man. She had been disappointed that she had not given him his heir, but he assured her that they still had plenty of time for that.

The End.

ABOUT THE AUTHOR

My father was a great storyteller and always said that one day, he would like to write a novel. My sister is a writer as well, so naturally I'm a dabbler. I thought I'd try my hand at writing romance novels because I love to read them. Romance novels have everything you want, mysteries, villains, wonderful characters, and I easily find myself living in the moment with the story. I hope that readers will find my stories as entertaining as I have found so many. I like to mix tragedy and comedy too, with a cast of colorful characters that I come from people that I have met in my life. I will visualize a person that I know as this or that character, and the rest is history.

I hope you enjoy my warped sense of humor and the stories that I tell. With that, I present you My Sweet Alyssa, the first of the Brother's In All series.

Gina Rose is the pseudonym for a very prolific author who spins tales in the Regency Romance genre.

Look for many more of her books to be available soon on Amazon and most other online bookstores.

Check her website, ginarose-author.com, often for more information and reviews.